CW00570989

Perfect
No More?

Adrianna Smith

Perfect No More?

Copyright © 2020 Adrianna Smith

All rights reserved.

No portion of this book may be reproduced
stored in a retrieval system, or transmitted in
any form or by any means – electronic,
mechanical, photocopy, recording, or any other
– except for brief quotation in printed review,
without the prior permission of the author.

All scripture quotations in this work are taken
from the Holy Bible, English Standard Version,
published by HarperCollins*Publishers*, © 2001
Crossway Bibles, a publishing ministry of Good
New Publishers. Used by permission. All rights
reserved.

ISBN: 9798680962749

Cover design by Adrianna Smith

This is a work of fiction. All the names,
characters, business, places, events and incidents
in this book are the product of author's
imagination. Any resemblance to actual persons,
living or dead, or actual events is purely
coincidental.

DEDICATED TO

My beloved husband
who accepts me as I am,
whose commitment is total and never swayed,
who gives me spacious room to make errors and mature,
and time and space to create.

My two darling children,
who are my God-sent inspiration,
who have taught and healed me much more than they know
through their unconditional love and generous encouragement;
and have filled me with both tears and laughter,
extending my life into a whole new dimension.

My parents,
who raised me out of hardship,
taught me honest living through their own examples,
and gave their children the best that they knew of.

Contents

*Deep in her heart was death which believed
that a life like hers could be perfect no more
with such a ruinous start.*

1 An Age-Old Regret

The sky was grey; relentless gale was churning the sea and made it roar tempestuously. Menacing waves were foaming on the edges and splashing the shoreline, displaying unashamedly their prowess. The sea echoed the wind, performing a symphony of nature so loud that it could deafen, so energised that it arrested our heartbeat, and so magnificently mighty that it reflected us as nothing but dust.

It was the festive season and in the twinkling of an eye, the year 2006 would be ushered in. The hype surrounding the turn of millennium was still like yesterday; how could we have marched through half a decade into 21st century already? It was bitterly cold. Going down to the seashore on a day like this would be the last thing that the majority of people would conjure up. But Yuetching (悅晴) never belonged to the majority; she had always existed on the fringe of society. She cut a lonely silhouette especially in this party season. When she was in a state of self-pity, she would even consider herself as flotsam and jetsam cast overboard of a ship, left to struggle for survival. It wasn't her choice to be thrown in at the deep end, but whether she sank or swam thereafter must partly depend on her will.

Wind was brushing through her hair and the chill biting into her bones. She did not mind it at all. The taste of life had always been bitter for her. She closed her eyes to feel the full impact of the bitter cold which, like a therapy, worked the magic of a temporary physical relief from the bitterness that she had fought hard to stamp in her heart. Who would understand how hard it had been for her? She would have liked to scream at the top of her voice or to cry her eyes out; and in the past, she would have done, but no longer. Who would have heard her feeble voice in the midst of the heavy sound of the weltering on the shores? When you scream or cry, subconsciously you expect someone to receive the distress call and come alongside you in response. But no one had ever come for her and therefore she believed no one ever would. This was why she no longer screamed or cried, lest she was hopeful, lest she looked pitiful.

What's the meaning and purpose of my pitiful existence? She had come back to this question over and over again, but found no answer. She opened her eyes and stared at the rough sea, which seemed to lure her forward. The sound was mesmerising; in it, she heard her parents' call – to go to them.

What if I die? No one in the whole world would even notice that I'm gone. Damn it... Oh no! Haven't I made a promise to myself that I mustn't curse my life, for it's disrespectful to the one who died to save me? I mustn't dishonour her. For her, I must walk till the end with dignity and honour, no matter how other people think of me. She thought my life was precious and I must believe it. No one can belittle me or make me feel otherwise. Besides, how can I know my life is cursed until the day it is concluded? Maybe, just maybe, there are blessings ahead of me...

She choked on her train of thoughts as doubt started to creep in and she could reason no more; not even she could convince herself that blessing awaited her. To carry on the line of thoughts was to transport herself to the territory of a fairyland, which she had rejected as a childish game. Deep in her heart was death which believed that life like hers could be perfect no more with such a ruinous start. This endless tug of war between hope and despair was emotionally exhausting. Tears blurred her visions. She blanked out her mind and let the nature symphony filled her senses once more.

She walked into a café-bar, shivering from the cold and looking like a mad woman with the most unkempt hair – not that she cared; no one ever noticed her, she thought. Festive season was in the air and no one was alone except her. Oblivious of the surroundings, she sat down at a table and ordered a hot chocolate to defrost.

"Mind if I sit down?" a voice made an unwelcome intrusion into her world. She looked up and saw a specimen of the opposite sex standing in front of her with a stupid grin on his face. She frowned and looked askance at him with suspicion.

"I mind very much actually," she replied curtly to deter his advance.

"Wow! A lady of ice, I see. Very fitting in fact with how you look; you look as if you'd just been to the North Pole and back."

"It's none of your business," Yuetching was not amused.

Her hot chocolate was served up.

The guy sat down on the other side of the table and pushed the hot chocolate towards her, "Drink up, this is what you need."

Yuetching snatched the hot chocolate from his hand, and said, "Don't patronise me! Have you no respect for other people's personal space?"

"Do you really need more personal space? In my opinion, you've had too much of it. Look, everyone has company here except you, so you shall too!" The guy sounded peculiarly confident as if he knew her.

Instinctively suspicious and guarded, Yuetching was alarmed by his familiarity and charted her flight without hesitation. Yuetching slammed her hot chocolate on the table, and spurted, "Don't pretend you know me, stranger. You can pay for this hot chocolate, as you've spoiled it for me."

"Wait, I –" shouted the guy after her, but she was already out of the door.

"– I do know you a little," the guy lowered his voice to a whisper only audible to himself, "I knew you from the past when we delivered pizza together."

What is life? We conjure up images of life in a newborn's first cry, toddlers running around in the playground full of giggles and joy, youths' appetite and growth spurt, and adults in their prime full of health, energy and ambition. We have life in us when we rise from our sleep, embracing the new day ahead, our bodies able to repair and regenerate itself overnight, our hearts beating, our breathing regular, our minds sharp and responsive, our thoughts articulate, our will desirous of life. Yet – DEATH – yes, death can spoil it all and strike when we least expect it.

Life and death are often poised as opposites in our minds that fool us to think there is a huge distance between them. Our current health can further lure us into a false sense of security that it will take a long time for us to be dead. This is irrational. Does death necessarily owe us a warning? Does it ever follow any rules? Does it even need a reason to claim a life? Death can snatch anyone away without any warning in many different ways and circumstances. Death is most poignant and tragic especially when we have a sense that it shouldn't be. We grieve, we feel angry, robbed and wronged. I suppose some deaths are easier to accept than others, but no matter how it happens, it does not diminish its dissonance and distaste with us.

Even though death is commonplace, we haven't gotten used to it at all.

Somehow we feel it shouldn't be the end.

Death is our enemy.

The truth is we are all dying; each day is counting down to death.

Decay is already set in us to march us indiscriminately to this same destiny.

Life and death are but a breath away.

Life is fragile even if it portrays an image of vitality before death invades.

It defies our concept of the natural order when the young should die before the old. There is something extra poignant when a father has to attend the funeral of his son. But the truth is that no one is ever ready for death even when it is threatening after a period of continual decline in health!

Death in the family leaves an aching void that cannot be filled.

The beauty and happiness in its completeness is no more and can't be restored.

There is soreness in this finality itself.

Waiting by the bedside of his granddad, Chisau (志修) was lost in a reverie of his own struggle to come to terms with his father's sudden death. It had been over two years, but it felt as raw as it was yesterday. Death lingered in the household and spread like a silent infectious disease. Granddad had lost his lustre; grief had robbed him of life. Bit by bit he was fading away, his eyes dim by sorrows, first of his son's death and then of his wife's death. *Death is a process, not a moment.* Chisau had witnessed that cruel process of wasting away in Grandma. Now it's Granddad's turn lying motionless in bed, suffering from a stroke. Even if the stroke did not kill him outright, would he have the will to live? Whatever the assessment of his physical condition was, Chisau knew the outlook of Granddad was not optimistic unless the sickness of his heart was somehow treated alongside. He had failed Grandma on this mission; would he be in time with Granddad? The pressure was on.

Time always seemed to pass most slowly when one was waiting eagerly.

Chisau's mother, Puiyin (佩然), was waiting anxiously with him.

Both kept their anxious thoughts to themselves.

When Granddad began to stir, the suspense was over.

"He's waking up; he's waking up!" Puiyin called out in excitement as if seeing the vitality of spring breaking through the ground after a long, harsh winter. Both rushed to his side. "*Loye* (老爺 meaning father-in-law), are you all right? How are you feeling?" The doctor had said that they could not fully assess the impact of his stroke until he woke up. Puiyin inquired with urgency, "*Loye*, do you recognise us? Can you hear me? Can you talk?"

All that he managed to bumble was *granddaughter* as if nothing else was on his mind. It didn't come as a surprise but the confirmation still weighed on Chisau's heart. Puiyin looked at Chisau, feeling sorry for the impossible burden that was laid on him.

Chisau and his mother made it back home, physically and emotionally shattered after a long day. They leant back in the sofa, immediately feeling the weight of their bodies once they relaxed from a day of high tension. It was Puiyin who broke the silence and lamented, "This is hopeless, isn't it? What is the chance of finding her after so many years? Had *loye* known how much he would regret it today, perhaps he wouldn't have done what he did all those years ago. Sadly we're only wiser in hindsight.

"Back then he was so ruthlessly uncompromising towards his own daughter, when she most needed the support and understanding of her family. What was his complaint about her? Being pregnant outside the wedlock shamed the family name. He cared about his reputation and was guarded about his fortune. From the beginning he was suspicious of the boy. He measured him up and judged that he did not deserve *muimui* (妹妹 little sister), or rather, her family and all that came with it. Love? He sneered. He told *muimui* she was naïve to believe he loved her and not her fortune. He would not approve of their marriage no matter how many times they tried to convince him. He accused the boy of purposefully getting her pregnant in order to force his hand on their marriage but he vowed not to be held hostage. He even threatened to call the police to arrest the boy for violating his daughter in retaliation. At that point, *muimui* stood up to defend her love that not only did she consent it, it was her idea! Whether *muimui* was telling the truth or saying what she had to say to protect the boy, only the two of them knew for sure. *Loye* slapped her on the face and called her *shameless*. With tears in her eyes, *muimui* yelled, 'We're getting married whether we have your blessing or not! We elope and you can't stop us! We have nothing but we have our independence – of YOU! We won't take a cent from you even if you beg us. You can huddle your damned fortune to the grave if you can!' At that heated moment, *loye* challenged them to stay true to their words about being financially independent, and never to come back for a handout. He even said that the further she went the better! A runaway tongue in a conflict situation only makes matter worse which quickly spins out of hand. Harsh words only pour petrol on the fire, cornering both sides and shutting down any room for manoeuvre. It's really damaging.

"*Muimui* stormed out with her boyfriend. *Loye* was happy to let her go so that she would 'learn her lesson', confident that when a child was hungry, she would find her way back to her provider. He genuinely believed he had the upper hand in the conflict which would eventually settle in his favour. What he hadn't foreseen was that youngsters could be as stubborn as he was in their pride.

"*Muimui* stayed with her boyfriend's family. At the beginning your dad and grandma kept in touch with her and wanted to give her some subsistence support. But she turned it down flat, saying that to earn respect from her dad, they must stand on their own feet. About ten weeks later she was suddenly uncontactable. Your grandma was sick with worry and became a shadow of herself, unable to tell day from night or when mealtimes were. I made every effort to try to locate her but to no avail. It was as if she didn't wish to be found. Could this be a gesture of protest? Time passed on, we didn't even know if she gave birth to a boy or a girl or if they had got married. When *loye* knew that she had cut off all contact and made herself vanish from us, he read it as a declaration of war and the final bridge was burnt. Rather than admitting wrong and facing his guilt, *loye* severed his emotional tie with his 'unfilial' daughter as if she had never been born. When both sides hardened their hearts like that, what's the chance for reconciliation; how could we even begin to patch up the crack? You were only three at the time, and probably don't remember much.

"Of course, we didn't give up searching for her. In that effort, your dad learnt that the boyfriend's parents emigrated to England to help a relative run a restaurant business. We guessed most likely they had followed them and made a new start. They should have known this plan for a while; if that's true, they had never told us. We thought at the time she disowned her family as much as *loye* did. *Muimui* had always been well-behaved and compliant, so her defiance and hardheartedness came as a total surprise. She told us her discontent decisively not by many words but by her action, didn't she?

"For all these years, we had been waiting for her to make contact, but she never did. When your dad passed away suddenly two years ago, *naainaai* (奶奶mother-in-law) was inconsolable. She blamed *loye* for the loss of her daughter and admitted that she had never forgiven him for that. To redeem himself, *naainaai* told him to bring her daughter back *home*. For the first time, *loye* did not defend himself. Was it a sign of remorse or his desperate attempt also to find solace for his loss by clinging on what he believed he still had? But finding his daughter after twenty-odd years was no easy task. If not for your search, we would have never known what had happened. Who would have guessed that what you uncovered didn't bring the elderly parents hope but struck them with another blow! Who would have guessed that both their daughter and son-in-law vanished on the same day 19 years ago, trying to save their five-year-old daughter? This piece of news probably has killed your grandma and shifted *loye's* obsession totally from his daughter to his granddaughter. How possible is it now to find this orphaned girl in this vast sea of people without any trace? She could've been anywhere; she may not even be in this country. It's harsh on you that the burden has fallen on your shoulders, and you've been working tirelessly on it."

"Actually it isn't harsh on me; it's something I'm willing to take on. When I learn that she has been all by herself, I wish to know how she lives and if she has been all right. I wish it very much to see her living well; only then could I be set free from this regret, just like Granddad, I suppose. I do regret that it's too late for Grandma now but I very much wish it won't be for Granddad."

"These past two years have struck a big blow on *loye*. To him, it was as if he lost both of his children in quick succession and he had to suffer twice the intense pain of separating from his own flesh. For most part of the past 24 years, *muimui* has been dead, so she couldn't have contacted us. Our memory of her has been wrong. The missing members in a family are sorely missed especially when they passed away in such tragic circumstances. Irreparable incompleteness of a family leaves deep wounds in our hearts which are here to stay. Whenever we think of them, it was as if our heartstrings had been plucked and we feel the pain afresh. On top of that adds the disappointment of not having a chance to say sorry and right some of our wrongs which just makes it even more unbearable. I'm really worried if *loye* will recover from this. Now that he's paralysed on his left side, will he have the determination and fighting spirit to endure the long rehabilitation? Doctor has said that encouragement from family is key to his recovery. But who in the family can give him the motivation that he needs right now?" Puiyin heaved a heavy sigh. Chisau looked downcast as he felt the pressure from the urgency of finding his cousin.

"Chisau, be honest with me, is there any realistic chance of finding your cousin?" Puiyin asked earnestly.

"I don't know, but at least I have a name."

A ray of hope lifted Puiyin's spirit. "Really? That's a real progress, isn't it? What's her name?"

"Cheung Yuetching (張悅晴), her name is Cheung Yuetching. To aid Granddad's recovery, I now have to work even harder in finding her," Chisau tried to spur himself on with determination, "I only wish she hasn't changed her name because of adoption, or –" Chisau paused; right now, he wasn't ready to contemplate the "or-else" possibility because it would be crushing.

2 A Carefully Orchestrated Coincidence

After three days of absence, Chisau went back to the office and faced a heap of work to be cleared. He spent most of the day meeting with staff from various departments to catch up on the routine business. Back-to-back appointments had meant that he did not even pause for lunch. At long last, he returned to his office and took a break. But these days, whenever there was some space in his mind, his thoughts would habitually wander to the business of finding his cousin.

Just when Chisau was completely absorbed in his own thoughts, Samyin (深研) leisurely walked into his office and sat down in front of him, pulling Chisau back to reality from his reverie.

"How is Uncle Lee? Is he any better?" Samyin inquired.

Chisau shook his head and replied, "Little changed."

"I'll go and visit him often."

"Many thanks."

"If there's anything I can be of help, just ask."

"You've helped out a lot already. If not for you, I wouldn't have been able to be away from my desk for three days without any phone calls or worries."

"This isn't just helping you out; my family fortune is at stake here in this business too, you know," Samyin jested and earned a smile from Chisau.

"Even so, I can't be your deputy on everything,' continued Samyin. "Some decisions are reserved for you and require your *undivided* attention," Samyin exaggerated with comical animation in his tone in order to brighten up a mundane task. He continued, "Here are the applications for the vacancy in the Strategy Department. To make your task easier, I've gone through them and eliminated all who obviously don't meet the criteria. All you need to do now is to shortlist from the remaining candidates for assessment and interview." Samyin passed the pile of applications to Chisau.

Sipping his coffee, Chisau put the files on his lap, and had a quick flip through the one on top with one hand, casually asking, "How's the quality of applicants?"

"Not bad at all. A handful of them have left me with strong impressions. For example, Cheung Yuetching –"

THAT NAME! That same name! Upon hearing the name, Chisau choked on his coffee, and exclaimed, "What?" His heart nearly arrested. He could not conceal his surprise, and pressed on, "Where's her folder? Find it for me, QUICK!"

He dumped his coffee on the table so that he could fumble through the pile. His clumsy attempt landed all the files on the floor. Samyin was taken aback by Chisau's unexpected reaction. He knelt down and picked up all the files.

"Are you all right?" Samyin asked with concern, seeing his face all flushed as if with hyperventilation! He sensed that this must be ultra-important for Chisau to lose his signature calm. Samyin quickly sorted through the files and pulled out Cheung's application.

"Here it is; this is she." Samyin passed her file to Chisau. "What's the matter?" He was dying to know.

Chisau grabbed the file, frantically devouring all the details about her and finding it incredulous that Cheung Yuetching's personal details could be dropped into his hand just like that. He checked her date of birth, which did not match totally but still within the margin of plausibility. The shock that this pleasant surprise had brought to him was inexplicable. Even though this could be someone with the same name, Chisau simply could not let this lead slip through his fingers without following it up. He had a quick glance at his watch – it was nearly the end of office hours. Totally absorbed in his mission, his mind was churning on the best course of action to take from here. He decided to go straight to her office and waited for her – he would not delay in confirming her identity. He thrust her file into his briefcase and dashed out of the office in an instant, as if Samyin was not even there.

"Where're you going in such a hurry?" Samyin called out after him but he was already out of the door. Bewildered, Samyin was left to ponder on the questions: "Who is this Cheung Yuetching? Why does Chisau have such a reaction?"

Following the information provided on the application form, Chisau arrived at the office block where Yuetching worked. In anticipation of the imminent encounter, Chisau was so nervous that he found himself panting for breath. He reasoned with himself on his next move: *Should I go up to her office to find her? But for matter as personal as this, perhaps it's best to be away from her colleagues. What if I fail to spot her as she comes out after work? Then I'll simply try her home address ...* As he carefully mapped out his plan, he could not contain his excitement. He grabbed her file tightly in his hands, anchoring his gaze upon Yuetching's picture so as to secure a photographic memory of her face before the crowd started gushing out of the building. The last he wanted was to identify the wrong person or to completely miss her by.

Office hours finally closed and the army of workers started flooding out of the building. Chisau was busy scanning through the crowd but the voluminous flow simply overwhelmed his processing capacity! After searching for an hour without any luck, Chisau was disappointed. The flow started to peter out, and his mind quickly moved onto the next possibility: *Should I go to her home address directly or should I give her a call first?* Until three hours ago, he would not have believed that he would have the luxury of having Plans B, C, D ... to find Yuetching.

With a shivering hand, Chisau fumbled around his pocket and got his phone out. With clumsy fingers, he dialled the unfamiliar number as listed in her application. While waiting for connection, he looked up and took a deep breath to calm his nerves. *She is within reach!* Chisau leapt for joy in his heart. Just at that moment, his sight caught the glimpse of a girl about five paces away, whose journey back home was halted by her phone ringing. Chisau froze: *it's her – the one in the photo!* The girl got her phone out and answered, "Hello." Chisau hung up and went up to approach Yuetching, who looked perplexed and suspicious.

It was such a relief to have found her that Chisau smiled childishly with satisfaction, and took time to study her: rustic in her dress sense, she was neat and tidy but was guarded in her body language; her straight hair straggled to her shoulders, a no-nonsense simple style; her eyes were bright, showing intelligence; she could have been a comely face even without the enhancement of makeup, if only she was a little friendlier. Although slender in her frame, determination and a strong will were written on her mien, clearly signalling that she was not someone to be trifled with. Chisau took pleasure in the moment that he had been eagerly awaiting but he had not gone as far as working out what to say once he had found her! She gave him an unfriendly and impatient stare.

"I – wonder – if – we may – er – sit down somewhere and talk for a while please?" Chisau approached awkwardly.

Looking immaculate in his tailored suit, Chisau looked like a smashing, handsome salesperson ready to woo anyone with his smooth talking. She acted on her presumption to decidedly ward off any marketing tricks. Her reply left no ambiguity, "Sorry, I don't think I have much to talk about with a stranger." She turned and resumed her journey home. Chisau moved in front of her to block her way. He thought: *There's no possible way to smooth out the awkwardness of this encounter. Rather than beating around the bush, it may be better to be direct.*

Chisau opened his briefcase, took out an old photo and went straight to the point, "This was your mother – Lee Oiyee (李藹誼) – and that was your father – Cheung Saiyuk (張世旭)." He swapped the photo over to present a newspaper cutting, and continued, "Nineteen years ago, you went on a family seaside holiday in England. You were suddenly engulfed by high tide, and your mother jumped into the sea to save you without second thought. You were passed to your father who brought you to safety but your mother was struggling against the strong tide herself. Your father went back to the sea for her but both vanished and never returned, and you became an orphan. You were five years old then. If this is you, then I'm your cousin. If this isn't you, then I'm terribly sorry to have taken up your time and to have disturbed you unnecessarily. For that I apologise, but I must verify your identity."

Stunned, Yuetching lost the grip on her phone which slid through her hand. Chisau's every word was like bullet aiming at her heart. She had no preparation for such a ruthless assault on her. The pain was not just about the grief of losing her parents but also its harsh implications and reality of being an orphan.

How she had lived for the past 19 years! Everyday since then she had been living in the aftermath of the incident that Chisau had just outlined so clinically and to the point. She could not speak for a long time. *Who on earth is this person, barging in unannounced and digging up my pain like that? Who gives him the right to cause such havoc in me?* Despite being in turmoil inside, outwardly she gave little away in her countenance; she had been well trained at keeping her thoughts to herself. Yet, this pain was too deep and personal this time even for her to keep her composure after a while. Tears started to trickle down her cheeks in defiance, and how much she hated showing her tears in front of others, let alone a stranger.

Chisau bent down to pick up her phone, as this seemed to be the last thing on her mind right now. While he was happy to have found her at last, her restrained sadness touched him. He returned the handset to her, and said sympathetically, "I've gathered that this is you, right? Sorry that your phone is damaged. I shall replace it."

"There's no need," Yuetching was brusque in her manners, especially to someone who came to disturb her peace. She snatched her phone from him and walked away to steady herself on a nearby bench. Chisau followed and sat down next to her. She did not object. For a long time, they sat in silence. Chisau could tell that she was still struggling with her thoughts and emotions.

"After your parents had passed away, who took care of you?" Chisau tried to break the long silence.

Now what? Want to intrude into my private life as well? This was the instant thought that came to Yuetching's mind, but instead she answered curtly, "*Guje* (姑姐 meaning father's younger sister)." This surprised her: had she been desperate in having someone to talk to about her past? If so, she did not even know it herself.

"I see. I thought you could have stayed in England to live with your grandparents after the accident. And now –"

"I know nothing about my mother's family, nothing at all," Yuetching interjected for she was not interested in what she knew but what she did not know. "Based on what *guje* told me, she had been disowned and kicked out by her father before she gave birth to me. Was that true?" She looked at Chisau intensely.

Chisau nodded with reluctance as well as shame.

Having that confirmed, Yuetching turned her gaze back to her feet as she organised her thoughts. "It was because of me, wasn't it? Before I was even born, he already disliked me and discarded me."

"This –" Chisau tried to search for words that would make a grave mistake more palatable to the ears, "It wasn't exactly because he disliked you personally. But as a conservative elderly, he couldn't accept the *timing* of your conception at the time."

"I see," Yuetching nodded and fell back into silence.

"Why now?" Yuetching resumed, "What's so special about now? For 24 years, he hasn't seen or treated us as family. Why all of a sudden is he searching for me? Why? Or – is he dead?" Yuetching was relentless in pressing for the truth, which was awkward for the messenger to deliver. Why were all her questions searching? But at the same time, Chisau felt that she had every right to ask those questions.

Chisau tried his best to smooth out the rough corners of the truth and make it slightly more presentable, "No, he isn't dead, and yes, he is searching for you all of a sudden in great earnestness and urgency. In life, we could have stayed unchanged for decades or even for our whole lifetime. But equally, unexpected adversities can hit us unannounced and from nowhere, enlightening us with a new perspective on the one hand and prompting us to reflect on our past on the other. Suddenly we see our past mistakes clearly and regret them terribly. When that happens, it's only natural that we wish to try our very best to right some of the wrongs that we've made, hoping that it won't be too late. Regarding your mother, it's already too late. But through you, we wish you would give us a chance to make up for our mistakes. We know we can't turn back the clock, and understand profoundly that this wrongdoing has left you with an indelible scar. We don't seek to elide it or to disregard your pain. Our only wish is that our wrong isn't perpetuated through our neglect and continues to wound you endlessly. If at all possible, we would like to mitigate some of the damage done."

Yuetching lifted her head to look at Chisau. In place of the facileness of a salesperson that she first saw in him was some compelling gravitas. *He is someone of standing,* thought Yuetching. There was so much truth and sincerity in what he had just said that an array of mixed feelings was stirred up in her. Tears welled up again and she did not know how to respond. Those words were like salve working wonders on her aching heart that she had never known. She began to sob. Chisau would like to comfort her but did not know how. After a long while, her tears started to dry up; she took a deep breath while wiping her tears, and asked, "What powerful adversity has hit this person to wake up his conscience after a quarter of a century?"

"Two years ago, his elder son, that's my father, passed away very suddenly. A year later, his wife followed."

"Oh no!" With mouth agape, Yuetching was shocked, but strangely this common experience connected them. "Fortunately, you still have your mother; you do still have your mother, don't you?" Yuetching asked compassionately.

Chisau smiled to thank her kindness. "Yes, my mother is still alive. But I don't think I have fully accepted Dad's passing yet because, I suppose, it was too sudden. Sometimes it feels like he had gone on an extended business trip … So I can't even begin to imagine what it was like for you when you lost both of your parents suddenly, at the same time and at such a young age. I'm really sorry."

If Chisau was trying to con her, he was flawlessly skilled indeed! He had said all the right things with convincing sincerity on her most gullible points. This had never happened to her before; effortlessly he had taken down all her usual defences. Why did she so want to trust him, why did she so want him to be true? Yuetching could not explain it but she found an understanding in him that she had never found in anyone. Even though they had never met before, he seemed to have known her forever. In a flash her longing became more concrete for her to see – to be known personally and no hiding of secrets. But there was no basis why anything he said about himself was true.

Sensing she was vulnerable to his charm, she knew instinctively she should flee to protect herself. Hastily she got up and drew their conversation to an abrupt close. "Thank you for coming to find me today. You've filled in some gaps I have about my parents. If you would excuse me, I've go to now."

Surprised by this abrupt end to their encounter, Chisau jumped to his feet and grabbed her wrist to stop her from going. "What? Just like that? No, no, no. You have to come with me. Granddad is sick. Will you pay him a visit?" Chisau blabbed out his motive without thinking it through. Meanwhile Yuetching got rather alarmed as he tried to detain her! As she struggled to break free, she suddenly felt a bit light-headed and wobbled on her feet. Chisau quickly lent her some support. "Are you all right?" inquired Chisau.

"Chocolate," Yuetching replied weakly.

"What?" Chisau did not understand. Yuetching opened her bag and frantically searched for something. At long last she took out a bar of chocolate. She unwrapped it with a sense of urgency and gobbled it up in no time. Then she seemed to feel and look much better.

"Sorry. I've got to find something to eat." Yuetching turned and ran in a hurry. Chisau could not let her leave like that, so he chased after her.

Yuetching disappeared into a nearby fast food restaurant, sat down and ordered a set meal. Chisau followed her and ordered the same, since he had not eaten properly for the whole day himself.

Food was fast! Yuetching focused on gobbling it up. Chisau watched her and found her funny, "You're really starving!" Yuetching ignored him and continued to down her food until all was gone, and she was satisfied! Only then did she have the strength to explain, "You shouldn't have seen me in such a state. I have been so good that I haven't needed my chocolate for a long while. I apologise for my bad manners in front of you, but because of you, my mealtime was too much delayed. I'm under no obligation to explain to you my eating habits, but –"

"You can't be over hungry or your blood sugar level will drop, causing nausea," Chisau completed her explanation for her.

Yuetching had never been more surprised in her life, "How – how do you know?"

"I can work things out, you know. Today it's indeed I who has caused you embarrassment in front of a stranger. Let me treat you." But Yuetching did not accept people's favour as a rule. This was no exception according to her book. Hence she declined, "Please enjoy your dinner, and I must go. I'll settle my bill on my way out."

Chisau grabbed her hand as a reflex. Yuetching protested, "What do you want from me? My department has a very important conference tomorrow and I can't make any mistake. I didn't work late tonight so that I can go home early and be in my tiptop form tomorrow. I need to go home now; it's already very late now, you know."

"Would you come with me to the hospital and see Granddad before you go home, please?" Chisau pleaded.

"I haven't decided if I should love or hate that person yet. But right now, I don't want to see him. When I'm ready to see him, I'll contact you. Goodbye."

Chisau still would not let go of her hand, "How long would I have to wait, one day, two days or one week?"

"I don't know, alright? It could be very soon or it could be never. In fact, does it even occur to you that you've bombarded me with so much information tonight that I haven't the chance or energy to digest it all? Right now, I'm too tired mentally and emotionally to think straight, so I don't know how I would decide. Don't ask me for answers that I don't have!"

"It's possible that when you decide to see him, it'll be too late," warned Chisau.

"Is he so ill?" Yuetching softened.

"At his age, his health condition is not separated from his frame of mind. If you don't go to see him, he's depressed and loses all hope to live. His condition will deteriorate – even rapidly. Right now, you're the only one who can lighten him up – you are the knot in his heart."

"You're exaggerating." Yuetching was sceptical.

"No, I am not; I've seen it happen with Grandma not that long ago. This is why there's such urgency for me to find you." While Yuetching was considering her response, Chisau continued to persuade her, "You don't lose anything by paying him a visit. On the contrary, you can let out all your displeasure by giving him a good telling off, as you two have no existing relationship to ruin anyway. But for Granddad, even if you go there to tell him off, I believe it will still have a positive impact on him; at least it helps lessen his guilt."

"Do you understand what you're asking me to do is beyond reasonable? I'm not obliged to fulfil that."

"I understand. But I can see that you aren't a heartless person. Under normal circumstances, if there were any gravely ill, bed-ridden elderly whose dying wish was to see you, I believe you would've gone to visit him without hesitation. Am I wrong in my judgement?"

Yuetching was stumped. Chisau's filial affection towards his granddad was admirable, and his perspicacity was shocking, at least about her. He was also impressively eloquent in prose and irritatingly persuasive. How could she ever win an argument against him? Why did she feel so exposed in front of him? While Yuetching was deep in her thoughts, Chisau was eager to confirm, "You aren't leaving, right?"

"You make me into a subhuman if I am! How can I leave? Now finish up quickly; I'm pressed for time as you know!" Chisau was pleased to have secured Yuetching's visit to Granddad. He quickly finished up his food as he was told.

On leaving the restaurant, Chisau naturally led the way towards his car. Yuetching shouted from behind, "Where are we heading?"

"My car is over this way," Chisau continued to lead the way.

"I'm not getting into your car." Yuetching was not following him.

Chisau stopped and turned around. "Why?" he was surprised.

"Think about it. I don't know you really. I don't even know your name. How do I know all that you've said is true? Your only proof so far that you're not a fraud is the consistency of your story; that's all! How can I be sure that you are not kidnapping me by getting me into your car?"

Chisau was stunned by her opinion of him! "Are you naturally that suspicious?"

"When you're on your own, you can't be too careful."

She does have a point, Chisau thought.

"You want to know how an orphan lives?" Yuetching suddenly blurted out. "Always insecure, always paranoid!" *Oh, Cheung Yuetching, why do you offer more than you need to? This is unlike you. Where is your guard? I don't know. Maybe I also want to be known, and my voice to be heard just like everyone else.* Yuetching debated with her inner self.

Unnerved by her unusual forwardness, Yuetching felt unsure with regret.

Chisau approached her, and introduced himself, "Lee Chisau."

"What?"

"Let me start again by formally introducing myself. My name is Lee Chisau," he extended his hand to greet her, "I'm your cousin. Let's be acquainted from today."

18

Yuetching found his gesture quite warm. *Is this how a family should make one feel?* She pondered in her heart. In response, she slid her hand into his which instantly formed into a firm grip. "I'm Cheung Yuetching. I'm happy to make your acquaintance."

"Let's take a taxi to the hospital, shall we?" Chisau offered with a friendly smile.

Chisau and Yuetching arrived at the hospital and went into Granddad's room. *A private hospital,* Yuetching made a mental note. She felt the gulf between their worlds already.

"Granddad, how are you today?" Chisau inquired tenderly.

Granddad did not move or open his eyes, but mumbled almost unintelligibly in broken sentences, as if in his dream, "Oiyee, I've really wronged you… Where's your daughter? … Would I see her? Oiyee, I'm so sorry … Have we lost her forever? … I'm so sorry …" As he was murmuring, his tears were rolling down his cheeks.

Yuetching did not know what to think. On the one hand, didn't it served him right to be tormented by his guilt? Was his pain even comparable to hers? No one would blame her if she had no sympathy towards him. On the other hand, it moved her somewhat to be so much on someone's mind. In her life, except for her parents, she had always existed on the edge in everyone else's heart, always come last in other people's priority list. Wasn't life ironic that she now took the central place in the heart of the very person who to a large extent had single-handedly precipitated the series of tragedies in her life? Suddenly she wasn't the *nobody* that she believed she was. Rather, she was *somebody* at the very heart of someone. Had she not witnessed it herself, she would not have believed it. She did not know whether to laugh or to cry, to be thankful or to be angry. Shouldn't she feel gloated just a little over his suffering from his own action? But now bed-ridden and paralysed, he was like a tiger without its teeth. They could not even have a proper fight over it. *So far, Chisau has not been lying. Perhaps this is really happening – I'm meeting my family.* She gasped at the significance of the moment. How had this happened – this momentous day was thrust on her without any prelude? It's true that she was not prepared for it but one can't say she wasn't ready for it either because it had been a dream never far from her mind-game. Yuetching couldn't help being slightly fluttered with nervousness, excitement as well as curiosity.

"Granddad, I've found your granddaughter. I've brought her here to see you. She's called Cheung Yuetching. She's standing right next to you now."

On hearing the news, Granddad struggled to open his eyes; he must see her with his own eyes. He turned to look at Chisau, stammering with excitement, "Real – ly? F– found her? N – no l – lie?"

"No, I haven't lied to you. She's right here. Take a look yourself." Chisau pushed Yuetching next to Granddad.

Granddad saw Yuetching, and he was elated, "G – good. F – found – her. I – am – re – lieved." Granddad tried to raise his right arm. This was the first time in three days Chisau saw Granddad attempt to move at all.

Granddad tried to wave his arm, as if gesturing, "Come closer for me to take a good look of you."

Chisau held his breath and watched how Yuetching would respond.

Yuetching stared at this invitation for a while, then decided to move forward; slowly she grabbed his hand. Granddad was so moved that he started to sob. In between sobs, he managed to mutter, "Real – ly sor – ry to – you. Let – you – you – suf – fer. Wi – Will you – for – give – your heart – heart – less Granddad?"

The word "Granddad" came to the edge of her lips, but she just could not utter it. She swallowed it back. In its place, she said, "Lobaak (老伯, an address for a senior male of no relation), you better not to think too much right now. Instead, you should focus on getting better and we can talk later."

"Chi – Chisau, r – raise – me," Granddad ordered.

"Yes, Granddad."

Chisau raised his bed and Yuetching sat down by his bed.

"Yue – Yuetching" he started to well up in tears. "I – I've a – lot to say – say to you, but – do – don't –know – where – where to – start. H – heart is – sad. If – If possi – sible, I – would like – to t – turn back the clock, when – when I did – didn't ask – your – your mother – to leave, and you – could – have – grown – up – up by – by my side.

"Now – now, I'm pun – punished. Both children – gone. Tor – tormented. G – Guilt. To – day, I can – say sor – sorry to you, a – a relief – for me. That – we – we've found you is – is a bless – blessing." Granddad got agitated again.

"Granddad, don't overexert yourself. Please rest," Chisau interrupted. Granddad nodded.

Chisau rolled the bed down again, and helped Granddad to lie down properly. Before closing his eyes, Granddad looked at Yuetching, full of hope when he confirmed, "You – you'll c – come again, right?"

Looking at those watery eyes of an elderly man, Yuetching could not find the heart to say no and dash his hope. She nodded, and confirmed, "Yes, I'll come again to visit you. But for now, you must rest, and you must get better soon. Understand?" Yuetching patted on Granddad's shoulder, gesturing that he should now sleep. Granddad nodded. He closed his eyes, feeling that he could finally sleep well. Even as he fell asleep, he did not let go of Yuetching's hand.

Yuetching sat beside Granddad patiently till he fell fast asleep and released his grip. Yuetching withdrew her hand and tucked Granddad's hand neatly under the blanket. Yuetching stood up and had a good stretch. As she turned round, she nearly ran into Chisau's embrace. She had forgotten he was standing right beside her! She was a little embarrassed.

"Thank you very much for today," Chisau showed his gratitude.

Yuetching nodded; his gratitude was accepted. She walked towards the sofa to sit down while still stretching her arms, and said, "Exhausted. I bet I can fall asleep in no time!"

Chisau went to sit next to her, and thanked her sincerely one more time, "Have troubled you today."

"Enough, enough! Please don't keep repeating your thanks," retorted Yuetching; she was not used to overly sentimental words.

"You didn't tell Granddad off. Have you forgiven him?" Chisau was curious.

"Interestingly I was not looking for revenge…" she muttered to herself on reflection; she has learnt a lot about herself in just one day.

"Sorry, what did you just say?" Before Yuetching could reply, she had already fallen asleep on Chisau's shoulder.

Chisau was surprised, "How could someone fall asleep so quickly? Maybe you're really exhausted." Chisau studied her face for a little while: how peaceful she looked when she slept; how trusting. He decided that it might be best to let her sleep through the night rather than to disturb her. He got up and rested Yuetching's head on the sofa. He went to find a blanket and a pillow, tucked her in cosily on the sofa before dozing off himself in the chair next to Granddad's bed.

The morning light streamed through the blinds, softened by the filtering effect and gently brushing Yuetching's eyelids, as if to urge her to wake. Yuetching opened her eyes, and for a moment she wondered where she was. Only when she saw Granddad sleeping peacefully in front of her did she start to remember the surprise encounter from the day before.

Suddenly, the door was thrust open, and in came a group of people, busily exchanging greetings with each other. Yuetching got on her feet quickly. Surprised to find someone in the room even before them, everyone stopped abruptly. Yuetching thought that maybe she could just take her leave without explaining anything.

"Excuse me. Who are you?" asked Puiyin.

Samyin thought she looked familiar. When he remembered her photo from her application, he screamed the answer, "Cheung Yuetching – you're Cheung Yuetching. Chisau has really found you!" To have another stranger call out her name like that, Yuetching was shocked, feeling extremely exposed and insecure in an unfamiliar environment and company!

Meanwhile, Granddad was woken up by the commotion and held out his hand, calling, "My grand – granddaughter?"

"Granddaughter?" Everyone called out.

"Yuetching…" Granddad called out again.

"You're Uncle's granddaughter? Does Uncle even have a granddaughter?" Samyin tried to work out what was going on.

Yuetching did not know what response would be the best. She walked to the bedside and held Granddad's hand. At this moment, Chisau came in with breakfast in his hand. Seeing so many people crowding in the room, he immediately walked to stand by Yuetching's side.

"Chisau, your arrival is timely. Is this lady here really your cousin? Is this true?" Puiyin asked on behalf of everyone who was curious to know.

While Chisau was about to answer, Yuetching checked her watch and screamed, "Oh dear! I'm dead! *Lobaak*, sorry I've got to go. I'm so late for work that I must go right now in this minute. I'll visit you again after work."

Only then did Chisau remember that Yuetching had mentioned an important function at work today. He immediately said, "I'll go with you. I need to pick up my car from near your office anyway." Having no time to chit-chat, Yuetching quickly dodged everyone in the room and was already out of the room in a panic. Chisau chased after her, but was stopped by his mother on his way. Before his mother could say anything, he said, "Later, all right? We're in a hurry." Chisau went past his mother, leaving everyone in the room puzzled about what had just happened. Only Samyin's brain was churning. By putting together Chisau's reaction to Cheung Yuetching's application the day before and this morning's incident, he quickly drew the connection and looked rather smug with himself.

Yuetching called a taxi and Chisau squeezed in too.

"Why are you following me? Where've you been at the crack of dawn anyway, leaving me to be besieged by your family like that? Guilty or what? I'm also so late for work; I've already told you I've an important conference today –"

"Sorry," Chisau interjected, "I didn't know that they'd turn up so early to visit Granddad. As to where I've been this morning –" Chisau handed over the bag in his hand to Yuetching, and explained, "You've said that you've set mealtimes and can't skip meals. I therefore went out to buy you breakfast. This will save you a bit of time and count this as my apology for this morning."

Yuetching was caught off guard by this unusual attention from a stranger. Chisau watched and said, "No need to be so moved. Eat quickly. Aren't you in a hurry?" Chisau fished out Yuetching's breakfast from the bag and offered it to her. Yuetching took it, and said, "Thank you." Chisau smiled and started eating his as well.

Accompanied by Chisau, Yuetching went back to the office directly without a change of clothes! Her colleagues had already started loading their company car with conference materials. Yuetching walked up to them and apologised. Her colleagues just screamed at her: "Look at you! Are you even presentable? Did you go home at all?" "How can you be so late when you know we need manpower?" "Go and freshen up! Quick! Now!"

"Why are you still standing? Go upstairs!"

"I'm really sorry," Yuetching apologised and took off. Chisau watched everything and felt really bad. He therefore lingered around and saw how he might help. When Yuetching emerged again, she was carrying the last boxes down from the office.

"It's full, can't take you. Find your own way to the venue," she was ordered.

"Of course, I'll follow straightaway." Yuetching saw the company van go off.

Chisau approached her, "They are quite mad at you. I'm sorry."

She was surprised, "How come you're still here? No need to go to work?"

"Granddad's sick, so I've arranged flexible working hours. Can I help you? My car is over there. I can give you a lift to the venue, if you wouldn't mind?"

Before she could answer, Yuetching's phone rang. "Hello … Got it."

She turned and ran back inside the office.

"Where are you going?" asked Chisau.

"They have left three boxes in the office; I have to bring them," she called back.

Chisau followed her and said, "Let me help you; it's my fault."

Yuetching had no time to object. Given the circumstances, having a spare pair of hands was actually handy. When they were at the entrance, Chisau left the boxes with her and said, "Wait here. I go and get the car."

Yuetching looked hesitant and Chisau read it. "You still think I'm going to kidnap you?" It sounded so absurd from Chisau's mouth that she had to agree, "Then I must trouble you this once. Many thanks." Chisau was pleased that Yuetching began to trust him.

Once arrived at the venue, Chisau helped carry the boxes up; he was also very curious. He would like to observe what Yuetching did and how she worked, so he hanged around. Yuetching was in charge of everything at the reception. When she had a moment, he approached her and requested, "Can I sign up for the conference?"

Yuetching looked askance, asking, "Why?"

"Do attendees need to justify their interest?"

"No," Yuetching had to admit. "I'll register you now and you can settle the payment later. Details are inside the folder." She handed to him the delegate pack and his name tag.

"Thank you. See you later."

The conference ran smoothly. The most memorable part for Chisau was of course Yuetching's item. She took to the stage and wasn't nervous. The presentation was very clear in its organisation and structure. The concepts were complicated but the flow of reasoning was well thought out and in turn made them comprehensible as well as convincing for the audience. At the end of it, the conclusions were necessary, almost indisputable! It was unusual for someone so young to command such an authority in a presentation. What a performance! It was impressive! Chisau could see all the hard work that had gone into preparing the materials.

The conference closed successfully and the department head was very happy with everything from organisation to the delivery of the conference. It was an impressive showcase of their work. He invited everyone out for a drink to celebrate but Yuetching excused herself, explaining that she needed to get ready for her two-week break. Having said goodbye to her colleagues, she walked up to Chisau who had been waiting for her.

"Are you waiting for me to say goodbye? Have you enjoyed the conference?"

Chisau nodded.

"You probably are in a hurry to leave, aren't you?"

"Yes, I'll go to see Granddad first."

"Then, please let him know that I'll visit him later today."

"You're going?" Chisau did not expect that.

"I promised him this morning, didn't I? Promises are made for keeping, not for breaking, to the best of my capability."

"But don't you have to pack for your holiday tomorrow?"

Yuetching laughed, "So you're eavesdropping? Yes, I'm taking two weeks off but I'm not going away."

"You've turned down going out for a drink in order that you can keep your promise with Granddad?"

"Yes, you can say that."

"In that case, why don't we go together?" Chisau suggested.

"But I'd like to go home, freshen up and have something to eat first."

"Then if you don't mind taking a ride in my car, I can drive you?" Chisau offered. Yuetching laughed, "Mind? I think it should be me who asked if you would mind giving me a lift. Let's go."

The door to Yuetching's world had been firmly locked against all visitors until then. *You don't normally bring people home. I know, but this is not normal – he is family.* Yuetching reasoned with herself, although her understanding of *family* was only academic. *You trust him too much too soon.* She paused at turning her front door key on hearing this warning issued by her inner voice. *But there is much more to know,* Yuetching continued to reason with herself. Sensing her hesitation, Chisau said, "Sorry, I'm imposing on you. I shouldn't have assumed. I shall go and wait for you in the car." He turned to leave. *Goodness me, he reads me like a book – and he just accepts it without judging me.* This was shocking to her.

Sometimes life needs to take the plunge in faith; take courage!

She turned the key and opened the door.

"Please come in," she called him back.

Chisau stopped and turned round to face Yuetching, "Are you sure?"

"Well, please – do – come in," she reiterated awkwardly.

Chisau walked back to her and stopped by the door. "A step at a time, you don't have to go faster than you're comfortable. Trust takes time to build, I totally understand, and we have done nothing to deserve your trust."

"This door is shut on those from whom I want to shield my secrets. This does not apply to you as you already know them. Symbolically, you've already smashed down this door and I'm only acknowledging it!"

"Well, if you put it this way, then I would infringe upon your hospitality." Reassured, Chisau crossed the threshold and entered into Yuetching's world.

"Welcome," was Yuetching's simple greeting.

While she went away to freshen up, Chisau had a good look around Yuetching's living space. It was small and compact, but neat, simple and comfortable. It did not have any fussy decorations or ornaments; everything was plain and to the point. The beauty was in its simplicity, which was very inviting. "Just like her," Chisau thought. Suddenly, Chisau noticed something was missing in this place though – there were no photos displayed, not even one. In fact, there were not any personal traits in this place at all. The whole space did not give away any hints of her life, past or present. It was totally faceless and impersonal. Anyone could have lived here. "This is odd," Chisau wondered.

It didn't take long for Yuetching to return in her casual wear, and she offered, "Please feel free to use the bathroom. I've put out some fresh towels if you need them. In the meantime I will make something quick to eat. After eating, we'll set off for the hospital." Yuetching struck him as a methodical person, and he understood her. He accepted her offer.

Yuetching served up two big bowls of soup noodles, and Chisau joined her at the dining table. "Hope you wouldn't mind some fast food. This is the kind of food that a singleton cooks."

"Don't mind at all. Thank you very much."

While eating, Yuetching asked, "Actually, how did you find me?" Despite a busy day, she had not stopped replaying and thinking about what had just happened in her life. There was still so much she would like to know.

Chisau answered with a mysterious smile, "You won't believe it, but it was in fact you yourself who put your personal information into my hand, and in the greatest detail I could have ever hoped for."

Yuetching nearly choked, "How could that be?"

Chisau reached over for his briefcase and took out her application folder. Sliding it across the table, he invited, "Take a look yourself." He was enjoying how stunned she looked.

Yuetching opened the folder and saw her application. She was really puzzled, "How did that get into your hands?"

"I'm on the screening and interviewing panel."

Wide-eyed in astonishment, Yuetching cried out, "What's your position at Arlando Hotel?"

"Well that? Arlando Hotel belongs to the family. Ever since Dad passed away and Granddad was not well enough to run it, I've been taking over gradually with the son of the other partner. It's been two years."

"What a coincidence!"

"Precisely, you think so too. What a coincidence! I think this is a divine setup that we must meet. Otherwise what hope did we have in finding you? If your details didn't just land on me like that, I really didn't know where to find you. Do you know how difficult it's been? We should marvel at how this encounter has come about, indeed."

"What was your interest in today's conference?" It didn't make sense to her.

"I did have a business interest in that."

"What do you mean by that?"

Chisau only smiled and did not reply.

"Okay, I get it; you don't want to spill. I wouldn't force you."

"Thank you. Now may I ask you a question?" Chisau grabbed the opportunity.

"That depends on what the question is."

"Why aren't there any photos in your home?"

Unwittingly he had just asked the most searching question, which wiped out the smile on Yuetching's face! No one had ever asked her such a question and she had never intended to tell anyone because she was always guarded. *But,* thought Yuetching, *Chisau is different; he is not just anyone; he already knows, so what's the need to hide?* Suddenly she felt a relief – for the first time she could talk about herself without any worries of backlash.

She plucked up the courage and replied dolefully, "I'm someone without a family." With the sudden descent of melancholy in the air, Chisau felt a little uneasy. He began to regret asking the question.

Yuetching stared at her soup noodles, with her thought travelling to far far away. After a long pause, she lamented, "Many years ago, when I was in high school, I trusted a friend and one day I'd like to share with her what was deep in my heart. Even before I could finish, she stopped me and said, 'Sorry, Yuetching, this is heavy stuff; I don't think I can handle it.' In one act, she has shut me up forever. I felt so betrayed and embarrassed at that point that I couldn't hide my thoughts and feelings fast enough. My feelings were hurt – a lot in fact. My personal matters were sealed up and not for disclosure from then on. I was naïve to have trusted anyone and to believe that someone would be interested enough to know about me. I swore I would never assume myself more important than I really was in people's hearts, lest I be slighted and embarrassed. Call it pride. I'm aware of the consequence: the world deep inside my heart has only one person, and that person is me, only me. Besides me, it's empty – there's nothing and no one.

"In this world, nothing really belongs to me. Something that is secure in my possession today can be snatched away

28

tomorrow unannounced and mercilessly. This is why I don't want to hold on to anything or anyone either because parting is painful. The fact that there are no photos in display perhaps subconsciously reflects my inner world: there's no one and no thing. On top of that, I'm not self-obsessed. Actually I can't bear any image of myself. I therefore have nothing to display."

Chisau's heart was stirred and he really felt for her. How much he wished he could give her some warmth! So he suggested, "Someone is really watching over you, and has arranged us to find you and in so doing, gives you a family."

"When your granddad gets better, and his treatment is on track, I'll retreat from your world. I've no expectations from you or anyone. I stay for now because it seems like I'm the only one who can give him the encouragement and motivation that he needs for recovery right now. This responsibility therefore I can't offload just yet."

Yuetching could be brusque and harsh at times, inevitable, Chisau thought, *with all those years exposed to the bitter cold in her world.*

"You wouldn't give us a chance to make up for it? Is there really no room for us to repay a little of our debt to you?" entreated Chisau.

"There's nothing to repay. Knowing is already enough. Besides, now I realise we live in two different worlds. For your granddad to formally recognise me as a full family member, doesn't it mean that he has to make a public announcement on what he did and be known for his heartlessness? Wouldn't that damage his public image? Can you imagine him doing that? His pride will forbid it.

"I also don't want that to happen. I don't want people to gossip behind my back, calling me a gold-digger or a climber who climbs on rich people or whatever to the same effect. I don't want to be the subject of other people's gossips, or to have to justify myself to everyone. Do you know how tiring this will be for me? Any intrusion into my private life will seriously disturb my peace and how I'll loathe it. Why would I go out of my way to find myself troubles? When your granddad's condition improves and stabilises, just let me retreat back to my world as an invisible member of the crowd. That suits me just fine."

"Yuetching –"

"Let's drop the subject," Yuetching interrupted Chisau, and

did not let him continue. "Eat up, so that we can go. We don't want your granddad to wait for too long, do we?" She turned her head, so that Chisau would not see the sparkles in her eyes.

On the way to the hospital, Yuetching was silent. Chisau therefore started a new topic, "Are you a natural extempore speaker? You were so natural and engaging today that you didn't seem to be reciting notes from memory."

"I've no talent in thinking on my feet. What you saw today was through weeks of planning and rehearsing. Of course, directly reciting notes from memory will sound mechanical and detached. The purpose of rehearsing the speech therefore is to remember it so well that you don't need to consciously think about it. Then on the day, it can be as natural as you were thinking on the feet. It's no difference from rehearsing for a performance. Behind any dazzling performance is simply hard work; there is no shortcut and no other way."

That reminded Chisau of *the* violinist whom he knew very well and how she prepared for her performance every time... He carried on, "How long had you rehearsed for today's presentation?"

"Excluding researching for the talk and writing up the presentation, about one week of rehearsing the speech countless times."

"I see," and Chisau changed the subject, "What's your plan for your two-week leave since you aren't going away?"

"Plan? I've no plan. I'll do whatever I like doing when I wake up."

Surprised by it, Chisau observed, "It doesn't sound like you. You strike me as someone very organised and everything is well-planned."

"Precisely because my normal life is so well-planned and organised, when I'm on holiday I do something opposite. Planning in fact is very hard work. Why would I like to plan even for holiday?"

"You have a point there," Chisau was impressed with her unique reasoning.

Yuetching went quiet again. She was debating within herself if she should ask for a favour. In the end, she decided to ask, "Can I ask for a little favour?"

Sensing the sudden change in the tone, Chisau paid his full attention, "How may I help?"

"You know, the picture you have of my parents? Can I have it please?" Yuetching paused a little and then resumed, "After they were lost in the sea, I never had a chance to go home and pack anything for keep sake. Therefore I don't have any memories. I've always thought if I had a chance to return home, I could have picked up something to keep. But in reality, what would a five-year-old girl know what to do? Even if I stood there in the flat, I probably would not have understood the gravity of the situation. The only thing I've managed to keep was my luggage I packed for that trip. That's all."

What Yuetching had said brought a lump to Chisau's throat. He was angry – angry at the adults around her at the time. *How could they be so insensitive to the emotional and psychological needs of this little girl that they could have overlooked such basic comforts for her grief?*

"Of course. Get my briefcase from the back seat," replied Chisau, determined to right something for Yuetching. She turned and fetched the briefcase. She opened it and found her folder with all the information that Chisau had collected. She had a quick look through, and was astonished, "You probably know my background better than I know myself!"

Chisau put on a smile and said, "I've expended a lot of effort and time on gathering this information about you. Apart from your application and CV, everything in the folder is now yours to keep."

"Really?" Yuetching could not believe it; she was overjoyed. "Thank you so much. Really thanks a lot. You don't know how much this means to me." That was from the bottom of her heart.

"Trust me, I know."

Chisau took a glance of Yuetching's face full of joy. That he finally could do something for her gave him enormous pleasure.

3 Courage for a Fresh Attempt

Yuetching was a serious person, who put in her best effort in all that she did. She seldom considered her preference as choice was a luxury in her life. To her, a promise was no trifle and she would like her "yes" be yes and "no" be no, at least on her part. Keeping her words was a resolute lesson taught to her by the influential negative examples in her life; she did not wish to be one who hurt others by her broken promises, knowing first-hand how soul-destroying it was to be at the receiving end of it. A promise could cost a great deal to keep, so naturally she was not generous with them and it shouldn't go against her conscience. Pledging to assist Chisau's granddad on his recovery journey was not driven by charity or impulse of the moment, but by her love for her late mother who, she believed, would not have left her father to die. This was to honour her. If she held grudges and was interested in settling the score between them, this wasn't the time to do it until at least Granddad was better.

Yuetching did not know how to fulfil a promise half-heartedly. Helping Chisau's Granddad regain his health was no exception. No one told her what to do; it was her own initiative and interpretation of what that task was, which surpassed all expectations. Perhaps lucky for Granddad, she was there in the hospital by his bedside from dawn to dusk. She was there largely to boost his morale while she also learnt quickly by observing how his carers did their job. If you did not like her, you would say that she was intense. But to Granddad, she was like sunshine, casting away the dark cloud that had been overhanging his heart. She was as if Granddad's best possible internal medicine. The speedy progress that Granddad had made in a short space of time surprised the medical staff but delighted his family. Chisau was relieved and could shift his attention back to the business, while his mother was grateful to have someone as devoted and competent as Yuetching to share the care duties.

After a busy morning of physiotherapy, Granddad was settled back in his room.

"Oh what's that?" Yuetching found a bag next to Granddad's bed. She took out the contents and had a look. "They are company reports and proposals. Chisau must have left them in a hurry this morning."

Seeing that Yuetching was putting them back, Granddad tested, "Why don't you read them? Aren't you curious? Haven't you applied to our position in the Strategy Department?"

"They are all marked CONFIDENTIAL, so I can't read them."

"But you would have liked to?"

"Well..." she shrugged, "it will help pass the time."

"Then go on and read them; if you are not reading them, you will be reading something else."

"That's true."

"I give you the permission to read the files. When I wake up, give me a debrief."

"A debrief? Am I working for you now?"

"I'm sorry; this is just how I talk. I'm not giving you an order but you see, Yuetching, this was my professional life. I want to stimulate my rigorous thinking. Would you help me?"

While Granddad was taking a nap, Yuetching settled down in the sofa with the files and began to skimp through them, one after another. At times, she would frown as if bothered by some less than robust arguments; at other times, she would pause and ponder on the points being made. As her mind was vigorously occupied, time flew by quickly.

Granddad woke up, when Yuetching was immersed in her thoughts. Granddad invited, "What are your opinions? I'd like to hear them."

Yuetching looked up and asked, "Are you sure?"

"Yes, I'm sure."

Yuetching thought: *this isn't bad as a subject of discussion to kill some time.* She got up and walked towards the bedside, ready to entertain Granddad with her faithful analysis of the proposals. In particular she identified the tenuous arguments, and put forward ways to improve them as well as some new ideas. In this informal setting with no pressure, she let her creativity run wild without any restraints, and had a great time coming up with spontaneous ideas. Granddad listened attentively and realised that Yuetching had an exceptionally good brain.

With her back facing the door, Yuetching did not notice Chisau standing by the door and listening closely. Somehow she had managed to put into words what had been perturbing him about these proposals. He was somewhat bewildered.

"Chisau, have you heard everything? Not bad, is it? You better follow up thoroughly with Yuetching. Understand?" instructed Granddad.

Granddad's call pulled Chisau from his own thoughts back to reality. "Yes, Granddad," he replied, walking into the room.

Yuetching turned round and saw Chisau coming through to the room. She was totally embarrassed, and asked, "How long have you been standing there for?"

Seeing Yuetching blushing like a beetroot, Chisau teased her further, "Long enough to catch most of the great presentation."

"Really? Sorry…"

"No, it's stimulating to hear a fresh perspective. You can be stuck in something for too long and become blind." Chisau then turned to Granddad, "Granddad, how have you been today? How were the test results?"

"Not so soon. But the doctor has said if the test results come out normal, I can go home."

"Really? That's such good news." Chisau raised his eyebrows in elation.

"Now, please take Yuetching home for me. She has been up and down with me for the whole day. Poor child, she must be tired. Bless her."

"Granddad, now that you've your granddaughter, you don't need your grandson. I haven't even sat down, and you're kicking me out already."

"You should go and pick her brain."

"What?"

"You have work to do, haven't you, with those proposals?"

"Yes, that's true."

"Then go."

"All right, we'll go now. Please rest well."

"Then I'll say goodbye too. See you tomorrow." Yuetching picked up her belongings and followed Chisau out.

Inside the car, Chisau asked, "Where are we going?"

Yuetching was puzzled by the question. "Aren't you taking me home?"

"Would you help me with these reports? The presentation is tomorrow."

"Don't kid me." She laughed it off as a joke. "Just now you were playing along with your granddad to keep him happy. I have no complaint about that but you don't need to keep it up with me."

"No, I'm serious. Would you help me?"

"Seriously?" Yuetching did not believe him.

"Let's go back to my office?"

She frowned at him, questioning what it would achieve.

"Please?" Chisau entreated.

"What can you do in a night? Your presentation is tomorrow!"

"That means I'm desperate! Can't you see?"

"Why have you left it till the last minute?"

"Quite the contrary! I've worked hard on it, but I didn't have your ideas until now!" His desperate plea evoked a smile on Yuetching.

"All right, if you think I can help. But I don't promise a miracle. Let's be clear I'm not in any way responsible for the outcome of your presentation tomorrow."

On that note, Chisau immediately started up his car. "You don't need to promise; I know a miracle is already at hand!"

Wide-eyed, Yuetching exclaimed, "You have no shame in your flattery!"

"It's not flattery!" The car zoomed off.

Having secured Yuetching's help, Chisau breathed a sigh of relief.

"You know, I thought I had lost all my reports today."

"Perhaps you're exhausted these days, and didn't realise where you had left them. Why did you bring them up with you to the room in the first place?"

"I don't know. Perhaps subconsciously I wanted to pick

Granddad's brain, but then I dropped the idea, thinking that it might be too onerous for his current state. I don't know. Did you read through all of them in half a day?"

"Not in great detail, but yes, I skimped through most of them. Why?"

"Do you know you're very efficient? I've always felt that something isn't quite right in those proposals, but couldn't quite pinpoint them. You seem to have nailed them for me."

"The reports are well written as the key points are easy to pick up. But don't take what I said too seriously. I was only blabbing out whatever came to mind, as it seemed to entertain your granddad. What do I know about the catering business?"

"No, seriously. Take me through your reasoning step by step."

Yuetching found it a little incredulous that first Granddad and then Chisau valued her opinions so much; she had never been asked to speak her mind like that before, not even at work. Encouraged, Yuetching had sparkles in her eyes and became energised. She started to take Chisau through her thinking process. In an instant, it turned into a dialogue and they rigorously bounced ideas off each other. They had such a great time with brainstorming that in no time they were back at the office.

"Oh, Director Lee! I didn't expect you to return," greeted his secretary, Miss Wei, who was about to leave for the day.

"Neither did I! Please order two dinners delivered to the office before you leave. We'll be working. Thank you."

"Yes, Sir."

Chisau walked into his office followed by Yuetching, who greeted Miss Wei with a nod. He dumped his stuff on the meeting table and announced, "Let the work begin!"

"Okay…" Yuetching replied sceptically.

They settled at the table sitting side by side with one another.

"Oh! I've nearly forgotten…" He took out a bag from his briefcase, and continued, "This is to replace what has been damaged."

"What is it?"

"Open it and you'll know."

Inside the bag was a new mobile phone.

"What's this for?"

"I'm partly responsible for you dropping your phone on the

first day we met. I've meant to replace it but haven't had the time to shop until today."

"This is the latest model. I don't usually go for the latest model – what a rip off! Besides, if I'm that bothered, I could have asked for an upgrade. Why spend that sort of money? Take it back." Yuetching passed it back onto Chisau, who refused to take it back.

"I'm not going to return it and have no use of it. What are you going to do? It's just a mobile phone; it's no big deal. Your handset is taped up, so it's time to change."

"Why does it matter that it's taped up when it's still functioning fine?"

"See it as a gift. Can't you accept a gift with gratitude?"

Yuetching saw all gifts as indebtedness which necessarily incurred repayment of some sort in the future. She was unconvinced, and Chisau was exasperated, "You can be irritatingly stubborn sometimes! All right, I'm not going to fight with you over this. I've got more urgent thing to attend to."

Chisau loaded his presentation to show Yuetching. Then they worked on the new structure together. "The key point is the vision, not so much on the details at this stage," Chisau clarified. After they had mapped out the flow of the presentation, Yuetching asked, "Have you got another computer I can use? I can help you plot some charts."

"Of course. Use mine. I can use my desk top."

Dinners were delivered. They ate while working at their separate stations.

Gradually, a tighter proposal was beginning to take shape.

Yuetching finished her last chart, and called out to Chisau, "I'm sending the charts over and you can merge them into your file."

"Thank you!"

As she pressed the *send* button, she considered her job done. She got up and had a big stretch. She yawned, "What's the time? Oh, my goodness! Is it that late already?"

She went out to have a comfort break, thinking she should make her way home. When she came back to the office to gather up her belongings, she found Chisau fallen asleep on his desk. "Have I been away for that long?" she mumbled to herself. She walked up to him and observed him. *Well, what should I do now? He looks pretty sound asleep... Even if I wake him up, he probably is not much use.* Yuetching went to get his mac and put it round his shoulders. *Lucky you, your screen saver has not locked your computer yet! I can still do something.* She copied his file on a USB stick, so that she could finish the presentation for him on the laptop at the meeting table.

Chisau woke up with a start. He didn't know where he was or he had fallen asleep. He checked his watch, which said 7.14am and he screamed! "What! I have slept for all this time!" He got into a panic. "Where was I with the presentation?" He unlocked his computer. As he moved, he noticed his mac on him. He looked up and saw Yuetching passed out on his sofa! "Oh!"

He went over and woke her.

"So sorry, I did not drop you home last night."

Yuetching sat up, and answered, "Drop me home? If you were that tired, I did not want to be in your car! What's the time now?"

"Coming up to half-past seven. I'm not sure if I still have enough time to complete the presentation before the meeting." Chisau shook his head, and added, "But I will try. Sorry, I can't take you home now but I can send for a company car to take you home. Let me do that."

"Surely, I can take care of myself. Your presentation is all done – it's on your laptop."

"What?" Chisau was pleasantly surprised.

"I finished your presentation for you last night. That's why I had not gone home or I would have. Do you suppose that I just walked off, knowing that you might miss your deadline?"

Chisau did not know what to say. That he felt relieved was an understatement.

"Go and check on your presentation. You still have time to do some last minute tinkering. You're the one who has to present it, not me, so you have to be comfortable with it."

Chisau went over to the meeting table and checked the presentation, while Yuetching was rubbing her face and eyes, trying to wake up fully.

He walked back to her, and said, "It looks pretty good. I can't thank you enough."

Yuetching shrugged, "It's no big deal. It's your lucky day that I'm on holiday!"

"*No big deal?* This presentation practically is all yours, from ideas to the final composition! And you call it *no big deal?*"

"Not true. Your original version provides the backbone to it, so that we can turn it round so speedily."

"But still, to be fair, it should also be accredited to you, but then you have no position at the Hotel…"

"Don't worry about that. I don't mind not to be mentioned," Yuetching jumped at it quickly to dismiss it as an issue.

"Don't you worry about people stealing your ideas and getting credit for them?"

"I don't worry about that. You are not someone who is in direct competition with me. Besides, my ideas are nothing out of the ordinary."

"*Nothing out of the ordinary?* Are you kidding me? Do you know how smart your brain is?"

"Really? No one has ever told me that before. If this is true, then I'm in an even better position not to worry about people stealing my ideas."

"Why?"

"Ideas that are already out are old, so they are not worth as much. What's really valuable is still in here," Yuetching pointed at her head, "that is, the continuous flow of all the future ideas! Since they haven't even taken shape, no one can know and no one can steal; I'm the sole owner of them, so they are very safe with me!" Yuetching looked so mischievous that it was almost funny, and once again, she had her own perfect logic.

"Seriously, yesterday was fun for me. I think a lot of things but they are usually stupid and crazy. Whether a wacky idea is brilliant or stupid is a fine line and I can never quite tell. If my ideas are of any use to you, I'm glad. So use them and don't worry about accreditation."

"Have you always been like that at work? You aren't doing yourself justice if you don't ensure proper accreditation of your work."

"I know. But so far, I haven't encountered any gross injustice. Like at the conference, they let me present, didn't they? Also, I'm still young, and I feel what's more important at this stage of my working life is to strive for opportunities to learn than making myself known."

"*Strive for opportunities to learn?* Then would you like to come to the meeting this morning when the proposal is discussed?" Chisau suggested.

"I'd have loved to but I am not presentable, neither are you!" They looked at each other and laughed.

"Don't worry. This is a hotel. Surely we can freshen up here!"

"Yes, but what am I going to wear?"

Quick-witted, Chisau suggested, "We have uniforms. You can wear our uniform."

"Okay. That sounds like a workable plan. How about your granddad?"

"Don't worry. I'll give the hospital a call and leave him a message."

Chisau sprang to his feet and started enacting on the plan.

Washed and changed in hotel uniform, Yuetching returned to the office ready to go. While waiting for Chisau to return, she noticed a magazine on the coffee table. She picked it up and started reading the page on which it was opened. It offered a very flattering profile of Chisau and worked to confirm what she had known all along – this family was famous in certain circles. Chisau walked in, also looking refreshed.

"All's set?" Chisau sought confirmation.

Yuetching nodded and rose from the sofa.

Chisau went to his desk and picked up the phone to offer it to Yuetching again.

"Please accept this –"

"We have been through this last night, haven't we?" Yuetching interjected.

"Let me finish. Please accept this, not as a gift but as my gratitude for your help last night. I have to thank you one way or other. It's fair, isn't it? You have to let me find a way to repay my indebtedness to you, don't you?" Chisau began to speak Yuetching's language, applying her own logic to convince her. It had to work or she would be contradicting her own principle. All that was left for her to say was, "Then thank you very much. I accept it."

"Good. I'm glad." Chisau was quite smug of himself. "Let's go then."

"Wait! You've forgotten the bag of reports." She turned back to fetch them.

"Since we have the new proposal, why do we still need the old materials?"

"You never know when these will come to be useful. It's

better to be over-prepared than under-prepared. Does that make sense?"

When they arrived at the conference room, everything was already set in place. Attendees began to trickle in. As Yuetching was in uniform, one of them mistook her as from the Hotel catering team and ordered, "Coffee please."

It was a bit unexpected, but Yuetching responded, "How would you like it, Sir?"

"Milk and two sugar please."

Right at that moment, Samyin entered the room, and made the same mistake about Yuetching. He added his order, "A black coffee for me please."

"Yes, Sir."

The meeting started at 9am sharp. Chisau presented the proposal they drafted together last night with confidence and authority. Everyone was pleasantly surprised by its freshness – the structure, the approach and some of the concepts were all brand new. When he sat down in the chair again, Chisau found the experience gratifying – he felt that it went well but above all, he presented a vision that he truly believed in. That was why he was persuasive.

After the presentation, discussion started and Yuetching was busy taking notes. Instantaneously, she was already making connections between points, identifying gaps or things that had been overlooked.

"Doesn't the overall proposal sound a bit far-fetched? How realistic is it? Can you take us through the supporting figures again?" one challenged.

Chisau was tongue-tied as he had not really looked at the figures. There was silence in the meeting room. Everyone was staring at Chisau and saw how he would respond. Sensing a sticky situation here, Yuetching quickly looked through the reports she brought with her and turned to the pages where the supporting figures were. She walked up to Chisau and put the reports in front of him. Seeing a sea of figures, he did not know how to look or what to look for. Hence he said, "Let's have Miss Cheung take us through the supporting evidence."

"What?" Yuetching was caught by surprise.

"Please introduce Miss Cheung to us." Everyone was baffled. All thought that she was a catering staff, but Chisau's gesture suggested that in fact they worked closely together.

Chisau and Yuetching looked at each other, trying to find an answer.

"She – She is my temporary assistant for this work," Chisau used his quick wit in response to the situation, "Now let's hear from her on the statistics."

Yuetching thought: *If I retreat, Chisau will be roasted. I have to go along with it.* In fact she did know the figures better than Chisau. It was important that she performed well for it was Chisau's reputation, not her own, that she was saving. She therefore stood up tall, cleared her throat and guided the attendees, "The thinking behind the proposals is based on the statistics from last year's Annual Report page 118, and from Hotel Guest Analysis and Projections page 25…"

Yuetching confidently took the management board through the figures and explained articulately the ways they supported Chisau's proposals. The board was satisfied with her answers. As soon as Yuetching stood up, Samyin immediately recognised her. After her brilliant performance, he was enormously chuffed about being proven right in his judgement! He had picked her out from among all the applicants even before he met her in person!

The meeting finally closed. Most of the board went up to Chisau, saying how pleased they were with the new proposals and that they were worth considering.

"Miss Cheung is very capable. How come she is only a temporary staff? Perhaps you should make her permanent? Talents are not easy to come by. Once you have met one, you should try your best to retain. Understand?" advised a senior.

"Yes, I'll look into that," answered Chisau politely, while Samyin could not stop laughing.

Meanwhile, Yuetching habitually started clearing the room after the meeting.

"I can take over from here," said Miss Wei.

"Yes, of course." Yuetching had forgotten that she was not employed here, so she stood aside.

Samyin went up to her and greeted her properly for the first time, "Miss Cheung, how do you do?"

"How do you do?" Yuetching responded.

"Do you recognise me? We met each other briefly in the hospital a while ago. Then I did not have the chance to introduce myself. I'm Chiu Samyin (趙深研)."

Yuetching shook his hand and replied, "I'm Cheung Yuetching."

"Sorry that I asked you to make coffee for me."

"I don't mind. In my own office, all of us have to take turn to make coffee or tea for everyone, so I have experience in taking orders and making coffee for others!"

Samyin thought: *she seemed easy enough to get along with.*

Chisau came over, and thanked her, "Really have to thank you today for saving my skin. If not for you, I don't know what I'd have done and how the meeting would have turned."

"I've said that we need to bring along the supporting materials; you never know when they'll become useful," Yuetching did not miss the opportunity to tease Chisau, now that she had been proven wise!

"Yes, you were right. Ah, this is Samyin, our business partner. Have you introduced yourselves to each other yet?"

"We just have," Samyin replied.

"Let's go for lunch now. Three meals must be regular," Chisau winked at Yuetching, who returned with a smile.

Samyin saw the peculiar exchange, and asked, "What's the signal?"

"Nothing at all. I'm only saying that we need look after ourselves," Chisau replied casually.

"Let me go and change out of the uniform first." Yuetching took her leave.

"Have you really hired her?" asked Samyin.

"No. Today's work was all voluntary. Today's proposal was mostly based on her ideas too. We raced through the presentation together last night, so I invited her to join the meeting, initially for her experience. Who would have guessed she became so useful at the meeting?"

"*Voluntary*? She worked overtime with you last night on the report, and you didn't even pay her? This is called exploitation! Do you have a conscience? As your business partner, I'm ashamed of you." Samyin was half-serious, half-joking.

Chisau continued, "Well, I did pay her in lieu, sort of, well, long story. Back to the story, yesterday, she was in the hospital with Granddad. In the morning, I forgot my bag of reports and left it in the hospital. When Granddad was having an afternoon nap, she picked them up and started reading them to pass time. Then ideas just flew out facilely. And out came today's proposal!

In fact, she had no new information; what's new was her perspective. With the same set of statistics and analyses, she can see relationships and draw inferences that no one else can. That is why she will tell you, all that she has done is information organisation, *nothing out of the ordinary!*"

"Wow! This sounds extraordinary! The report our staff spent several months to write is bettered by Yuetching's one day effort! Would you really consider hiring her? If you don't, I would, and then I don't need to ever work again!"

Chisau shook his head, "You only concern how to slack as always!" He then became serious, half talking to himself and half talking to Samyin, "I'm not sure if Yuetching's willing to join the Hotel now. Besides, with her new identity, hiring her will set off a series of tricky chained effects which make the decision of hiring her a lot more complicated. We can proceed only after some careful consideration about how to deal with the related issues."

"How complicated can it be?" Samyin could not comprehend the situation.

"For the time being, you won't be able to understand it. Let's go and have lunch. We shouldn't keep Yuetching waiting for us."

After lunch, Chisau told Yuetching, "I have a meeting in 15 minutes, so I can't drop you off at the hospital."

"Don't worry. I can make my own way there," Yuetching assured him.

"Chisau isn't free but I am. I can take you. I'm going to see Granddad," offered Samyin eagerly.

"There's no need; I can make my own way there, honestly," Yuetching insisted.

Remembering how Yuetching refused to get into his car the first time they met, Chisau leaned forward and reassured her, "It's safe to take his lift."

Yuetching gave Chisau an unwelcome stare.

"What? Who does she think I am?" protested Samyin.

"Just let him give you a lift. It is unkind to treat a gentleman as a bandit. It's also silly not to accept it when both of you are heading to the same place."

In this way Yuetching was arm-twisted to leave with Samyin or she would look paranoid and mean! Back to her normal guarded self against a stranger, she got into the back of the car and took up the seat diagonal to Samyin. He turned round and inquired, "This is astonishing! I don't know what to make of it! I have never had that done to me before."

"What are you talking about?"

"Where you are sitting."

"This is where I normally sit in a car," she replied.

That was true with the exception of Chisau's car.

"So you're treating me no different from a taxi driver? Why am I so offended?"

"That's your interpretation, not my meaning."

Failed to find words to say, Samyin grudgingly drove off – as a chauffeur.

Staring out of the window was Yuetching's way of shutting the world out. The rocking of the car soon hypnotised her to forget the here and now, and transported her to a world of her own. Her vision was blurred as the street scenes rushed past the window. Her thoughts were many but they were equally vague and fuzzy.

Catching her in his rear mirror, Samyin saw a melancholic face with sorrow in her eyes. He was baffled by her exceedingly. Her mood was more changeable than the weather!

"Are you all right? You are not car-sick, are you?" inquired Samyin.

"…." Yuetching made no reply. Being left on her own in this new world made her uneasy. It was an unfamiliar world to her. She had no idea how she was supposed to conduct herself or what she was supposed to talk about. She felt exposed and vulnerable, out of place and self-conscious.

"You must be tired as you didn't sleep much last night. If you feel like dozing off, don't mind me."

She was offered an easy way out of an awkward conversation, so she took it.

As they parked up at the hospital, Samyin announced, "We're here." Seeing that Yuetching was awake, he turned round and asked, "Did you have a good sleep?"

"The ride was not that long; I was just resting."

As Yuetching seemed to have softened, he grabbed this opportunity to find out something he had been dying to know, "You know, you're somewhat a mysterious figure to me. You're Chisau's cousin, but I've never heard that he has a cousin. Are

45

you a distant cousin or even a lost cousin since he seemed to have to search for you? Basically where did you come from?"

"Is it even your place to ask such a private question of me?"

"Of course! If you are his cousin, you're part of the family!"

"Well, then, it may be your place to ask, but it is not my place to answer. I'm not in a position to divulge to you anything regarding this matter. If you wish to know, you should ask Chisau or his Granddad, and see how much they'd like to tell you. It's their matter, not mine."

"Are you suggesting that who you are is a hidden secret? Oh how I love a mystery!" Samyin looked at Yuetching and bantered in a dramatic tone, "Imagine you're an enigma to crack!" Unfortunately Yuetching did not fall for his playful charisma. Instead, being joked about her background touched on a raw nerve. Yuetching opened the door and got off the car to end the conversation. Sensing that he had upset her, Samyin got off immediately to chase after her.

"So sorry," he called out.

Samyin caught up with her and reiterated, "I'm sorry."

She hated people getting close because they demanded to know things about her and it hurt. Between the pain of having no one close and the pain of exposing her past and being ridiculed, she had always chosen the former. This uncomfortable ride convinced her of what she had known all along, and she told Samyin to shut him up once and for all, "Sorry? What do you know? But don't worry, I won't be around in this circle for too long. In fact, I reckon I'll return to my own world fairly soon. Where I came from doesn't matter to you. How much you find out about me in the end doesn't matter to me either as it's unlikely that we'll ever meet again. Go and crack your enigma or not as your intellectual pastime, I can't care less!" Yuetching stormed off.

Samyin was shocked by this revelation, "What are you saying? But you've just arrived on the scene!" He kept up with her pace. "You mean there'll be no contact, no news in the future as if you didn't exist?"

"I wish you all leave me alone and never to bother me again."

"How can you say or do such a thing? No matter where you are, family is family and this tie cannot be severed. Do you know how hard Chisau has worked to find you? Shouldn't you be grateful? How can you run off and let him down!"

This was preposterous, so Yuetching retorted, "Perhaps there are certain questions you should never have asked, and opinions that you should never have uttered, for you know not what you are talking about!"

"Have I said something wrong?" Samyin held his line.

"You are not guilty because you know not. But it's advisable for you to stop pursuing the subject in order that you don't continue to offend unknowingly!" Red with rage, Yuetching told him off in no unmistakable terms. She ran off as far ahead of him as possible to get away, while he had taken the hint that it's best not to pursue.

The sight of Samyin and Yuetching lifted up Granddad's spirit. The first thing he asked was, "How did the meeting go?" Sensing the awkwardness between the two youngsters, Granddad asked, "What's wrong with you two? Why does Yuetching look downcast?"

"Nothing. Just tired. Rushing the presentation with Chisau last night, so did not get much sleep," answered Yuetching.

"How did the meeting go?"

Samyin moved to his side, eager to recap the highlights of this morning's meeting vivaciously, "Granddad, do you know how superbly great your granddaughter was? She saved Chisau from being roasted by standing in for him on expounding the supporting evidence, based on which the proposal was formulated. Your granddaughter did such a great job that the board was satisfied and most have said that it's worth considering. Who Yuetching was however stirred up some curiosity. On the spot, Chisau just blabbed out that she was his temporary assistant drafted in for this work."

On hearing this, Granddad looked concerned, "Was that true? It's not yet time to make her known. Samyin, can you promise me to keep her background under wraps for the time being?"

Sensing the seriousness in Granddad's tone, Samyin was now convinced that Yuetching's background was a delicate matter. He could only oblige, "Of course, Granddad. But in fact, I know nothing about Yuetching, so there isn't much I can let leak."

"Even the fact that she's my granddaughter people need not know."

Samyin was surprised, "Why?"

"Unnecessary public opinions always spell troubles. The wish of Yuetching is also not to attract attention. We must wait till the time is ripe before we make her identity and background public. Is that clear?"

"Yes, Granddad. I'll be careful," Samyin promised although he did not understand. He was truly intrigued by Yuetching's story.

Yuetching awoke after dozing off in the chair and it was already far gone into the evening. Granddad was asleep peacefully. She packed her stuff and left hospital for the day. There was no direct bus service between the hospital and home, so it was a long journey home on the bus. That night, the road shone like a river and the temperature had dropped abruptly. Yuetching felt the chill while she was waiting for the bus. She kept moving on the spot with hands tight in the pockets to keep herself warm; she wished she had worn something warmer.

Chisau was delayed by some emerging business. When he arrived at the hospital, Granddad was asleep and Yuetching was nowhere to be seen. The nurse on duty told him that she left about 90 minutes ago. Chisau was a little worried, and wondered if she would take a taxi home and if she had eaten yet. He decided to give her a ring to find out.

"Yuetching, why didn't you wait for me?" Chisau asked.

"Have you asked me to?" It's true that it was never a formal arrangement but more of an understanding and expectation of what turned out to be a routine.

"Have you taken a taxi home?"

"Why does it matter?"

"It's cold, windy and raining. Taxi will bring you home faster."

"I see."

"Have you arrived home yet?"

"I'm nearly there, don't worry."

"You're on a bus?" guessed Chisau.

"Yes."

"Have you eaten yet?"

"I'll eat when I get home."

"But it's late. What if you faint again? Why don't you look after yourself?"

"I always have chocolate with me," reminded Yuetching.

"Yuetching –" Somehow Chisau felt he had failed her.

"It's late. You should go home too. Don't worry; I can take care of myself."

Yes, she has always been taking care of herself for all these years before now. Where were we then? Chisau sighed and was ashamed. *We really have failed her.*

"See you tomorrow then."

"See you tomorrow." Yuetching hung up.

Yuetching held the phone tightly. The call warmed her heart like nothing had before. As far as she could remember, that was the first time in her life that someone cared enough to inquire after her whereabouts like that. Perhaps this was the feeling that a family brought – a glow of warmth that emitted from deep within the heart.

"Chisau, I've heard from Samyin that Yuetching performed well at the meeting," said Granddad.

"Yes."

"Should we invite her to join the Hotel?"

"Everyone was very supportive of the restructured proposal. The chance that they will pass it is high. To secure a competent helper to assist in the next steps would have been rational and marvellous for me. But in what identity is she going to join the Hotel and in what capacity?"

"This is tricky. Based on her age and experience, she shouldn't be placed in a senior role but her strength is in strategic planning and will be of great assistance to you. Why not hire her as your Project Assistant, just as you have led everyone to believe at the meeting? Under your protection, she'll have the room to develop her potential while avoid unwanted attention. Do you think this will work?"

"The post of a Project Assistant does not exist at the moment and will be created especially for her. It is nonetheless an important post with influence. I don't believe placing her in such a position will dampen any unwanted attention unless we make her identity publicly known."

"But if we make her identity publicly known, it'll lead to another set of issues relating to her special status. Her title will go before her and she'll be treated differently. Then she will never have the opportunity to learn the job from the ground level. It will also bring along another kind of public pressure and expectation that she is inapt to handle right now. Before she has built up her self-confidence, it's best not to make her identity known. Otherwise we risk frightening her away from working at the Hotel or even from this family."

"I know. That's a very realistic risk."

"Yuetching left home at 16, supporting herself while finishing off her schooling. She then got herself into university on a full scholarship. What she has achieved is astounding; her determination and perseverance is admirable. It's high time we chipped in, lessened her hardship in life, and helped her develop her full potential. It's entirely my fault that she has endured beyond her fair share of hardship but she has self-respect and doesn't give up on herself. She has worked so hard to come to where she is today. I like this girl very much. I regret that I haven't nurtured her up to this point, and now it's my wish to provide the best possible environment for her to flourish into a young and confident lady, who doesn't keep underestimating herself." Granddad could not hold back his tears. Chisau could sympathise; it was almost frustrating to see Yuetching have so little self-belief.

"This is the only way I can think of to repay your grandma… and Oiyee," Granddad sobbed. "Chisau, your grandma died a miserable person; how can I ever forgive myself? I've hurt her much. I've broken up her family. I thought I had time so I kept waiting for tomorrow and had never acted. But suddenly time's up! What am I to do? Guilt is a terrible thing to live with; it gnaws at you on the inside. There's no time to lose; I must recompense my wrongs NOW when I still have a chance…"

At this moment, Yuetching entered the room and greeted them with her usual infectious brightness, "Good morning. How are you *lobaak*? Did you sleep well or have you been worrying about the test results which are due out today?"

Granddad quickly wiped away his tears, but Yuetching caught it, so she inquired, "What's wrong? Why are you crying?"

"He's missing Grandma," answered Chisau.

"Yuetching, when will you call me 'Granddad'? I'm not some random *lobaak* from the street!" Granddad expressed his heart's longing.

Yuetching did not expect such a question and did not know how to answer it. During this time, she had been reminding herself to keep her distance. Otherwise the day when this family did not need her and she had to return to her own world, she would be very sad. Yuetching dropped her head and did not answer.

"Yuetching, you live so far away and on your own. Why don't you move in with us? What do you think?" Granddad proposed. Chisau was shocked too by Granddad's sudden proposal. But since this question was out in the open, he eagerly awaited Yuetching's reaction.

"No, I can't. If I move in with you, how am I going to work?" Yuetching found a convenient impersonal excuse.

"Quit that job and help out at the Hotel, like you have already done. What do you think?"

Chisau widened his eyes – *no time to lose*, Granddad meant what he said! But since Granddad had laid their wishes bare, he could only reinforce to test the waters, "Yes, are you still interested in working for us? After all, you've applied to us and we are seriously considering your application." Chisau made it formal.

"That was before, now is after. Right now I have no intention to work in the Hotel, or move into your home. It's better for us to keep the distance as it is," Yuetching said it in the end without betraying that she had been reconsidering her situation.

"But..." Granddad tried to persuade.

"Please drop the subject, or I'm going to leave and never to return again," Yuetching made the threat sound as light-hearted as possible. Chisau laughed: in this world, she probably was the only one who could put a restraint on Granddad! But how serious was her standpoint regarding this matter?

"All right. You win. We'll talk about this some other day," Granddad gave in.

Granddad's report came out and the patient was discharged as he had anticipated. Puiyin, Housekeeper Choi, the newly-hired carer, and family chauffeur came to take Granddad home, whereas Chisau was tied down at work. The outcome was gratifying for Yuetching; it was like another job well done and she had achieved something meaningful with her annual leave.

"Today's a happy day. Why don't you come home with us to celebrate?" invited Granddad.

"That's true. The fact that *loye* can be discharged today is all down to your hard work, Yuetching," Puiyin concurred.

Yuetching used her smile to hide away her sorrow. She had told herself that the day when Granddad left hospital was the day when she would retreat from this family. Besides, she felt rather under the weather. Perhaps she was exhausted with the commuting and long days at the hospital. As the day wore on, she felt increasingly unwell. She was full of coughs, so she declined the invitation so that she could go home and rest.

"In that case, please rest well. When you feel better, come and visit us. We'll follow up on *loye*; you don't need to worry. Thank you for all that you've done for us," Puiyin said.

"I will. Enjoy your homecoming party and please take care of yourself. Till we meet again," Yuetching said her goodbye and left with a sense of mission accomplished.

After work, Samyin followed Chisau home for the celebration dinner. They naturally assumed that Yuetching would be there, but she was not.

"Where's Yuetching? Why isn't she here to celebrate?" asked Chisau, when he noticed she was missing from the gathering.

"I agree; why isn't she here? The fact that Granddad has recovered so well and speedily to a large extent has been down to her devotion and hard work," Samyin echoed.

"We did invite her to come, but she said she was a little tired and would rather go home to rest. She did look a little pale today and was coughing a lot when we saw her. Perhaps she was exhausted. Come over and join us for dinner; you must be hungry now," Puiyin invited. They all sat down at the dining table.

Chisau felt uneasy for reasons that he did not know. His mind kept replaying something that Yuetching had said before: the day when Granddad was well enough and his treatment programme was put in place would be the day when she retreated from the family. He also remembered her concluding remarks to this morning's discussion. Chisau thought to himself, *would she really believe that once Granddad's better, there's no place for her in the family because she's no longer needed? Would she think that the reason I went to find her was purely because Granddad was sick? Would she really return to her world like before as if she had never known us? Even though these might have been what she believes, we must not let her down this time. I must go and make clear to her that if she's willing, this is her family independent of Granddad's condition.*

Chisau stood up abruptly, and interrupted everyone's conversations. All eyes stared at him as if he had an important announcement to make. Feeling a little awkward, he apologised to everyone, "Sorry, I suddenly remember something urgent that I must attend to." As soon as he finished, he dashed for the door without giving anyone a chance to ask what the matter was!

Chisau arrived at Yuetching's home. He rang the doorbell but there was no answer. He rang it again and again and again. The longer he had to wait, the more panicky he became. He would have broken down the door if he could. At that point, the handle was turned. Chisau was relieved. But the door was only pulled ajar; Chisau caught it just in time before it slammed shut again. As he pushed open the door, he found Yuetching behind the door. But before he could say anything, she collapsed into his arms. She was burning with a high fever and appeared to have difficulty in breathing. Affrighted, Chisau immediately carried her to his car and took her to the hospital.

After receiving Chisau's call, everyone rushed to the hospital. "How's Yuetching?" Granddad was the first to ask.

"Pneumonia, but she should be fine," answered Chisau.

Everyone breathed a sigh of relief.

But seeing Yuetching on a drip and an oxygen mask, Granddad blamed himself, "It's my fault. I've tired her down and made her sick. I was too demanding."

"The weather in the past two days has been changeable. It's easy to catch a chill," Puiyin tried to console.

"How can I let her live on her own after a situation like this? Chisau, arrange the termination of her tenancy and move all her stuff over with immediate effect," commanded Granddad.

Chisau was put in a difficult position with this command, "Granddad, this surely goes against her wishes. Have you forgotten how firmly she declined our offer this morning?"

"In time of crisis, the elderly of the family makes decisions. Are you going to send her home when she leaves the hospital? You go and implement my instructions without delay. I'll be held responsible for all the consequences," Granddad would not budge this time.

Although Chisau shared Granddad's concern, imposing a decision against her wish could force her into open defiance.

"When Yuetching's discharged, we *will* take her home to rest until she fully recovers. However, I insist that we must gain her approval before we move her belongings," Chisau proposed a practical solution.

"What if she doesn't approve? If I don't impose my decision, she'll never come to live with us," Granddad continued his line of reasoning. Chisau had to admit that this was the most likely scenario.

"If you can't find a better way to make this happen, then follow my way. Understand? I won't have Yuetching living by herself; I won't allow it. Is that clear?"

Chisau nodded reluctantly, even though he did not believe that they should force Yuetching into anything against her will.

"Good that we understand each other. I'm going home first with Puiyin. You stay by Yuetching's bedside and call us if there's any change in her condition."

"Yes, Granddad."

"Thank you," softened Granddad, "Thank you for sensing something's wrong with her in the first place and acting on it."

Chisau nodded to acknowledge, "We were lucky."

When the room was clear, Chisau sat down and felt he could finally have some breathing space! It had been such a tense evening. Samyin lingered. Chisau addressed him, "Sorry for ruining your evening. You don't need to stay with me, you know. Feel free to go."

Instead of leaving as told, Samyin pulled up a chair next to Chisau and sat down, offering, "Let me keep you company. It's a long night."

"I'm fine. Just tired. We don't need both of us to lose sleep here. You still have to cover for me at work tomorrow."

Samyin was not going anywhere.

"You want something else?"

"Well, you must admit that this all looks rather perplexing and emotionally charged from an outsider's point of view. Your position seems particularly hazardous, standing in the crossfire between Yuetching and Granddad. I can be your sounding board on the situation. Two brains to work out a way forward are better than one. I may even help persuade Granddad for you. What do you say?" Samyin tried his best to coax Chisau into telling him the full story about Yuetching, "One minute she's friendly and humorous, and the next minute she's icy and curt. It was as if she deliberately tried to shut people out of her life! Who is she? Why does she behave like that? And why is Granddad so touchy about her?"

Chisau smiled; nothing seemed to have escaped Samyin's watchful eyes.

"It's such a mess. Are you serious in getting involved?" warned Chisau. "This is first and foremost a family matter, so I am not inclined to tell others. Besides, it isn't really our business either as it concerns more about Yuetching. To respect her privacy, it's really not up to me to disclose it to others."

"Funny how you say the same thing about each other! Neither side is willing to spill in order to protect the other side! She thinks you need to be protected while you think the same about her. It looks to me perhaps both sides need to be protected? Just tell me, what's going on?"

"You have asked her?"

"Yes."

"What exactly did you ask her?"

"Who is she? Where did she come from?"

"As direct as that! What did she say?"

"As you can imagine, nothing. She asks me to ask you if I wish to know. I have been waiting for my opportunity to ask you. Are you going to tell me or not?"

"If it had not been for one thing, no, I would not have told you. But both Granddad and I would like to find a way for her to work with us. Under normal circumstances, with her competence, there is no problem in hiring her. But for you to understand the intricacies of the matter, then you must know her story."

"It sounds very solemn."

Chisau took a deep breath, and reflected, "Life itself is a solemn endeavour. Some sufferings are inflicted by man, while others are led by fate. These events interact and weave our life. What's really in our control is how we face up to life situations. Sometimes we make grave mistakes, which not only cause direct hardship on others but also to set things off on a chain reaction aggravating the initial impact. When we come to realise what we've done, we regret terribly. But then, isn't it already too late?" Chisau turned to Yuetching as he thought about her story.

"Are you going to tell me or not?" entreated Samyin, who was dying to know.

Chisau nodded, "Yes, I will. But knowing the secrets of another person is a privilege as well as a responsibility. I'll tell you on one condition, that you won't use what you learn to harm anyone, but to protect, especially Yuetching. If you can solemnly promise me that, then I'll tell you."

"You have my word."

"Deal." Chisau shook his hand. "Here is how it began…." Chisau narrated what he knew of Yuetching's story, which was skeletal; there was still much they did not know about her. Samyin could not believe what he was hearing. Suddenly Yuetching became all awe-inspiring. She looked so fragile and delicate outwardly that who could have guessed she had such extreme inner strength and resilience to sail through the worst adversities in life?

"Why did she leave home at 16? Didn't her *guje* treat her well?" asked Samyin.

"I don't know; she hasn't said anything about that. We'll find out when we need to know or when she's ready to tell."

On reflection, Samyin pulled a wry face, realising what a grave error of judgement he had made. "No wonder she was so mad at me the other day. She said she would return to her own world soon, and wouldn't linger in our world for too long. At the time, I even lectured her on family values: 'No matter where you are, family is family, and this tie cannot be severed.' I ask how she could let you down by running off like that, considering how hard you had searched for her, and if she should be more grateful instead!"

"You said what?" Chisau was shocked and judged, "It's about the most insensitive thing you could have said to her!"

"I'm not proud of myself. I'm totally embarrassed here. She said, 'Perhaps there are certain questions you should never have asked, and opinions that you should never have uttered, for you know not what you are talking about!' Her stare was terrifying."

Chisau covered his eyes with his hand and shook his head.

"What I said was most unforgiveable and insensitive considering the truth, I can see it now," Samyin regretted. "In the context, her response was very generous and restrained. What am I going to do? I haven't made a good impression, have I?"

"We look to a better time; it can't be worse than this!" Chisau patted his shoulder.

"But time is not on our side! Isn't she determined to return to her own world?"

"Granddad would like her to work at the Hotel, but the setup won't be simple."

"Shouldn't be too complicated, should it? She's his granddaughter; how complicated can it be?"

"On the one hand, we don't wish to disclose her identity, so that she gains experience and builds up her confidence in as natural and unpressurised environment as possible. We worry that she isn't ready for handling the expectations and pressure that the status brings. On the other hand, based on her experience and merits alone without disclosing her identity, we can't get her in a position which will develop her strength in strategic planning. Granddad came up with the idea of her being my Project Assistant. But to carve out a high profile position especially for her does not, in my opinion, bypass the issue."

"If she can't be the Project Assistant to the Director, how about being my secretary? I've always been acting like your deputy and helping you out largely behind the scene. While you're the face of the Hotel, I don't attract as much public attention. Besides, people have always thought it strange that I never have a secretary. Hiring a secretary now will just be doing something that everyone has expected me to do for a long time. No one will raise an eyebrow over it. With that position as cover, Yuetching can have as much involvement in the Hotel's strategic planning as she likes. Do you think this will work?"

Chisau stroked his chin as he considered the idea with interest. "This is by far the most constructive proposal we have. I think it's going to work just fine. I'll discuss it with Granddad. But then, doesn't this proposal incur a great personal sacrifice on your part? You must have your reasons why you are reluctant to have a secretary."

"I have turned it down on the pretext that I don't want anyone to tell me what to do. Deep down, the real reason is that I don't wish to settle down in this job. Hiring a secretary makes me feel I'm here to stay, which I don't want to admit, as you know."

"What has changed now?"

"Well, just say this is what a friend is for! Besides I don't expect her to function as my secretary, right? It's all but a disguise."

"We have to wait and see about that!"

Yuetching was eating her porridge when Chisau walked in.

"It's so good to see your appetite return," greeted Chisau. "You also look less pallid. How could you be so careless? You gave us all a scare," nagged Chisau.

Yuetching pulled a face, and provided a self-assessment, "Life is about learning our limits. While people have others to guide them or warn them about theirs along the way, I don't. I reckon that I have to learn my limits through mistakes more than others. This episode is just another one of them. Don't worry. I'm a keen learner and I won't waste my mistake. I'll be wiser next time." Yuetching tried to downplay it as a normal aspect of her life but Chisau only heard the sorrow underneath the gloss.

"I should thank you for rescuing me," she continued. "That night, why did you turn up at my place? Was there something urgent?" she was curious.

They hadn't had a chance to talk properly yet, so here was Chisau's opportunity to give her the proper account of the event, "I went to see you because I was afraid that you were upset, because you might have mistakenly thought that this family had no place for you once Granddad was discharged from the hospital. I intended to say that we had never seen you as Granddad's nurse; even if Granddad fully recovered one day, this family still welcomed you. I wished to tell you that independent of your views, you were already a member of this family; in our hearts, there was no more distinction between your world and ours," Chisau spoke of his tender thoughts, and continued, "But I didn't get to deliver what I intended to say. I hadn't anticipated you collapse into my arms, feverish and semi-unconscious, but looking back, it was fortunate that I was there to catch you."

Yuetching's feeding hand was suspended in mid-air. She fixed her searching gaze at Chisau with disbelief in how much he knew her thoughts and how comforting his words were to her! If not for her exceptional self-control, she would have cried.

"Now, I do have a matter for which I wish to have your approval," raised Chisau. Diverting the subject was good, Yuetching thought.

"You sound serious all of a sudden. What is it?" asked

Yuetching, unfreezing her feeding hand.

"This mishap has made us increasingly uneasy about you living on your own. Granddad is adamant that you come to live with us. Would you agree to it?"

"And find a new job at the same time?" Yuetching spelt out the implication of the proposal straightaway.

"Do you like your current job?" tested Chisau.

"Well, it's not bad; there is no urgency to move on. But it's my first job and I've done it for three years. It's getting a little stale, that was why –"

"That was why you started looking for a new challenge and in the process, you applied for our vacancy?"

Yuetching nodded.

"If you were given the opportunity to work on refining the details of the proposal for the Hotel, and later even to implement it, would that be a tempting challenge for you?" Chisau lured.

"You mean?"

"We would like to formally hire you."

"Position?"

"As Samyin's secretary, but this is only a disguise to enable you to work closely with the two of us. In this way, you will be open to opportunities to learn about the business and to get involved in the process of making challenging decisions. In so doing, you will be given ample room to develop your strengths without needing to handle the pressure that comes with high positions. After you have gained more confidence and are comfortable with the running of the Hotel, we will then consider making your true identity publicly known and offer you a proper position to go with it. What do you think?"

"Does Samyin know about me?"

Chisau nodded, "Hope you don't mind, but yes, I've told him. I can assure you that he can be trusted. Hope you see it as necessary. Would you accept the offer?" Chisau was hopeful.

"Are you sure I can manage?"

"You'll never know until you try."

Yuetching recalled the thrill she felt when working with Chisau on the proposal. Having had the foretaste, she found the current offer almost irresistible to the adventurous side of her.

She returned to her porridge. Chisau waited patiently while she considered the prospect. When he saw sparkles in her eyes, he knew he had hope in persuading her.

"If – I – were to hold a position, I'd like to earn it and not to be given it. It puts my mind at ease that room has been made for me to explore the business freely without the pressure from public expectations and to find my footing in relative privacy. I – I would love to give it a try. Thank you for the offer, which is very kind. I'll try my utmost. Thank you," she told her decision with timidity and gratitude.

"Then why not move in with us too? We could look out for each other as a family. What do you say?"

"This is another step… I'm not sure if I'm suited to live with others. Family tension I don't know if I can handle. I've had very little training with family dynamics. I'm used to my own space, which is my sanctuary."

"This is all part and parcel of family life. Would you not like to try it out?"

"Less than a month ago, you were all but strangers to me. How are we family all of a sudden?"

"I think this is very easy to explain on our side. Although we do not know you very well as a person yet, our love and care for you is projected from our love and care for your mother whom we did know."

"Family love is positional and transferrable?"

"You can say that."

She thought she understood it as it was similar to how she decided to take care of Granddad in order to honour her mother. Then she asked, "What do you think my mother would do? Do you think she would reconcile and play happy family? Is it that simple?"

This was a tough question for Chisau to answer directly one way or another, so he suggested a different angle. "If you are not ready to play happy family yet, how about treating us as you housemates? Have you shared accommodation before?"

"Yes, at uni."

"Is the prospect less daunting then?"

"But I had nothing to do with them except sharing the facilities. Would that be rude if I were to treat *family* as housemates?"

"Don't worry too much. We play it by ear. We would like you to move in not to restrict your personal freedom or have any expectations but simply to look out for you. I hope you don't think we are worse than your housemates who must have been strangers to you also?" Chisau had checkmated Yuetching! *Can I ever win an argument against him?*

"Would that be imposing on your family?"

"Of course not," assured Granddad as he entered the room with Puiyin; they had been listening in for a while outside the room. "We're a family and a family doesn't think like that."

"Granddad; Mum," greeted Chisau.

"Yuetching, I've heard you're discharged today. So we've come to collect you. Perhaps it's best for you to come to stay with us even only for a little while till you've fully recovered," said Puiyin.

"Yuetching, I don't know where to start," pleaded Granddad, "but I can't even begin to express how much I regret my decision and inaction back then. The pain I've caused you in the past can't be changed, but now that we've found you, I won't let you continue a solitary life like you've been. It's just dangerous for you to live by yourself. I dare not hope you would forgive me; I only wish an opportunity to make amends. Would you grant me that wish?"

"Granddad, you don't need to feel guilty about the past," said Yuetching.

"You – you just called 'Granddad'!" Granddad was overjoyed and moved to tears. Yuetching was a little embarrassed.

"I've already forgiven you," revealed Yuetching, "because I can see your remorse is genuine. I don't intend to torment you any longer with your guilt, and neither should you. Whatever debt you think you've owed me is cancelled!" Chisau could not believe what he was hearing! Granddad was lost for word; he just sobbed.

"If – if you really have forgiven me – then there is no more excuse – not to come home with us. Please don't decline it," entreated Granddad.

"We've agreed that Yuetching moves in as our housemates at first," Chisau tried to make clear her commitment to Granddad.

"What do you mean by *as housemates*?"

"It's no difference from how I've been living at home, that you don't bother me!"

"Ah?" Granddad was slightly confounded.

"This is to give time for Yuetching to adjust." Puiyin had got it.

In this way, Yuetching got committed to their plan!

Yuetching consented by not objecting; Chisau breathed a sigh of relief as he was no longer trapped between the two opposing positions on this matter. He moved straight onto organising the move, "In this case, mum, please take Granddad home first. After we are done here, I'll take Yuetching back to her home and help her pack."

Right at this moment, Samyin stepped into the room and greeted everyone with his usual glee, "Hi, everyone. I've come to send Yuetching home as she's discharged today. You look so much better."

"You've come at the right moment. Go with Chisau and help Yuetching move. Make sure you don't tire her out; she still needs a lot of rest," ordered Granddad.

"Yes, Granddad, I won't let her lift a finger," promised Chisau.

"Then Puiyin and I will go home first. We'll wait for you at home," Granddad went away happily.

"Wow! You really have managed the feat of persuading her to move in with you guys?" Samyin expressed his amazement.

"Must he come along with us?" annoyed, Yuetching asked Chisau.

"I dare not disobey Granddad's order," Samyin joked.

Yuetching shook her head; here in front of her stood the first challenge of her future position. She wondered if she would regret it.

"So this is where you live. I'm intrigued," Samyin announced.

Felt intruded upon, Yuetching summarised it for him, "It's small, bland and empty, just like its owner. There's nothing intriguing, I promise!"

Yuetching went into her bedroom and started sorting.

"I've told you that she doesn't like me," Samyin whispered to Chisau.

"Talk less and work more," advised Chisau.

Yuetching packed up her personal items, and left the rest to the boys under her instructions. They were not trying to complete the move in one go but to pack up what were needed for the temporary stay. Within no time, they were ready to go.

"Your books must account for most of your possessions,"

observed Chisau.

"Books are the best companion in solitude."

"It'll take a while to pack them all when we come to complete the move."

"No, it won't because they stay put."

"What do you mean?" asked Chisau.

"I'm keeping this place as my refuge in case living with you doesn't work out, so these books can stay and here serves as my library."

Only then did Chisau realise that Yuetching had not completely committed to the new arrangements; she was keeping an easy exit clear. He was not too upset by this revelation though. They had gained a lot of headway with her already today; there was no need to push her further. Given time, Chisau was confident that they would gain Yuetching's trust. For now, it was more important to respect her wishes and let her take things at a pace that she was comfortable with. As for Samyin, he was following Chisau's advice to "talk less and work more", so he kept his comments to himself.

"Let's all sit down, and have some refreshments before we go. I have nothing fancy but tea and a few biscuits I do have. Please make yourselves comfortable."

"Let me help you," Chisau offered.

"It's all right. Let me. I can manage."

Chisau pulled up a chair to sit opposite Samyin.

"She's fiercely independent. Will she get used to living with you guys?" whispered Samyin to Chisau.

"Sh —" Chisau stopped him from making comments like that. "You don't always have to think out loud, you know."

Having served her guests tea, Yuetching sat down so that the three of them formed a triangle. Chisau raised a subject, "Actually I'm curious."

"About what?" asked Yuetching.

"What made you suddenly change your heart to forgive Granddad?" Chisau asked. "You must admit this is a sudden dramatic change of position.' Samyin nodded in agreement that this was a very curious question indeed.

"Oh, that," Yuetching paused as if to articulate her thoughts before explaining, "It may have appeared as sudden to you but I have been constantly pondering upon the matter since the day you found me and I also have been working hard all my life to stamp the curse of this nightmare. Suddenly I realise the two converge. The subject was thrust upon me since I have been in constant contact with the family. At the practical level, I had to ask myself with what attitude I should go to look after Granddad everyday. Can you imagine what a challenge it was for me to do that?

"This is how I see it. I have two choices: one is to let hatred and anger to nibble away my heart, and to continue my separation from the family and a life on my own. In so doing, I'm only extending the past, a state that I'm used to and very familiar with. This prospect doesn't excite me, although it's my safest bet. The other choice is to forgive Granddad, and kick away that guilty feeling between us so that we can have a fresh start at mending the relationship and see where our effort will take us. What is offered in front of me is an opportunity to possess something I have never had; that is, being part of a family. I thought it would irk me but it doesn't really. Instead it has given me warmth that I've never experienced before. I want to find out more and understand it more.

"My choice is then very clear: I would have been stupid to condemn myself to living in the impact of a regrettable mistake and the subsequent tragic events in my life. But if I can let it go, and don't ask who was wrong and who was right, who owed whom by how much, everyone can be liberated from this guilt and the pain of being wronged. By forgiving, I can give everyone a fresh start, including myself, and free us all from living in the shadow of our past. Isn't this the best way to overcome our mistakes and break the curse that they have brought to our life? All those years ago, Granddad refused to forgive my mother's mistake and look, what regret it has brought. In hindsight we lament what mistake was so grave that he could not forgive at the time and went on to cause so much pain. Would I want to repeat his mistake back then?

"Given that both parties would rather the mistake have never been made, why should we perpetuate it? I realise reconciliation is impossible on a one-sided effort. Granddad has reached out to seek forgiveness, how about me? Why would I insist on not forgiving if it were not to punish him by his sense of guilt? What would be my gain in seeing him suffer? Nothing. It won't turn back the clock or change anything of my past. I don't want to feel bitter all my life. By putting this chapter behind me, my heart is lifted; it's for my own benefit as much as for Granddad's. Hatred is a destructive emotion, and I don't want to harbour it. I don't know what the future holds. But I'm very curious about this new format of life that is on offer to me, and would like to experience it and find out more. Having tried it, I may decide that family life doesn't suit me. But the point is, I should not have denied myself the prospect of it.

"In simple terms, therefore, I've decided to forgive Granddad, so that we can all move forward and don't keep looking backward. Granddad has said sorry, hasn't he, something he could not bring himself to say 24 years ago? This is a goad for reconciliation. It's not just a head decision; it's the heart's desire too."

Samyin could not help but exclaim, "Wow! You thought all that!"

"What's your problem?" Yuetching had little patience for him, "Would you mind? We're having a family conversation here!" These private thoughts were never directed to Samyin.

"Sorry," apologised Samyin immediately to pacify, "But this is sincere. Far from being facile, I can tell that you have given this a lot of thoughts. You kept challenging your views from different angles before you decided on the best way forward. From this, I can see that you are a genuine, serious and cautious person. Still is forgiveness a rational decision that can be instructed by the head? It is not easy to forgive when it hurts so deep and in most personal way as in your case."

When Samyin was not jesting, Yuetching engaged with him, "Forgiveness is hard as usually it involves something that cuts deep. But contrition on the part of the offender goes a long way to make this possible. I didn't do it on my own. Granddad and everyone else are sincere to move forward. This may be the treatment needed for the wound to heal. Should I not take it when everyone involved is ready to give it a try but to insist on denying myself the only chance to be healed?"

The position was so poignant that neither Chisau nor Samyin could respond. Chisau just wished they would make this treatment work wonders and would not squander her goodwill. Her heart was fragile but she was still willing to trust. This showed amazing courage. Not all sick people would automatically agree to treatment. Some, drown in self-pity, clang onto their misfortune in life as part of their identity and spent a lifetime imprecating people. Yuetching was different; she wanted to be well. He admired her for her positive outlook in life despite the hardship. There was a huge difference in outlook of life thinking the best or the worst of people.

"You two seem to have made up too,' observed Chisau.

Since Chisau had given him his opening, Samyin took the opportunity to apologise formally, "I know we've got off on the wrong foot. I'm a little rash, don't always think before I speak and may have offended you with what I've said. I'm sorry. Could you forgive me?" You have just said, '…so that we can all move forward and don't keep looking backward.' Could you let that apply to us also?"

Could she argue against herself? Yuetching laughed.

"Then let me be your witness. Chiu Samyin and Cheung Yuetching also have a new start today; all that has gone on before between you two is wiped clean," declared Chisau.

Besieged by the two of them, Yuetching had nowhere to retreat but to agree to the proposition. Although these two were of different characters, they were like brothers. Having someone like that in life was very special, and Yuetching envied them! She came to realise that perhaps to accept this family, one had to accept Samyin too.

4 The Return of a Graceful Shadow

For the first time, her heart fluttered with excitement, rather than anxiety, about a new beginning in life. Perhaps it was because for the first time she entered a new phase in life by choice and not by a sudden change in the circumstances out of her control. After recuperating from her spell of pneumonia, Yuetching went back to her old life to serve out her notice period before leaving her job. Chisau insisted on her taking a week off to settle in her new home before she officially started at the Hotel.

This evening she retired to her room and leisurely occupied herself with a book.

"Come in," Yuetching answered to a knock on the door.

Chisau walked into her room with a pile of clothes in his arms.

"What are these?" asked Yuetching, looking surprised.

"Your work clothes," answered Chisau matter-of-factly.

Yuetching put down her book and went over to have a look.

Having checked the labels, she exclaimed, "Wow! How am I supposed to wear them?"

"What do you mean? You don't like the style? Mum and I have given it a lot of thought."

Perhaps he had no idea how grassroots actually lived. Yuetching set to enlighten him, "Haven't you said that you'd like to keep my identity under wraps? Now you're asking me to wear these expensive clothes to work. Isn't it a giveaway?"

"Is that a problem?" Chisau could not see the linkage so far.

67

"The way you dress shows your status," explained Yuetching. "It needs to match your income. A suit here costs most of my monthly salary. What do I eat and where do I live then?"

"But I think somehow girls would find the money to spend on their clothes. Perhaps I'm wrong in assuming that. Even if what you said is right, your salary now is several times what it used to be. Surely you can now afford more expensive clothes, proportionate to your new salary. I've actually taken that into account for you," Chisau countered her argument.

"Hmm –" Yuetching failed to find anything to say, and came up with, "but these are not clothes that I wear."

"Since you're in the spirit of attempting new things in life, why not widen your wardrobe in order to find out what your personal style really is?"

Seeing that Yuetching was struggling with her thoughts, Chisau gave her a pat on the shoulder, and said, "Don't think too much; just accept them and enjoy." He then left her room.

Yuetching looked at herself in the mirror, and wondered: *Is there anything wrong with my dress sense?* Enjoyed them, she was told. *How do you enjoy clothes?* She looked at the heap of clothes on her bed, and thought that she had never had the chance to play dressing up before. In the spirit of attempting new things in life, she started trying on the clothes to see what they would do for her. To her pleasant surprise, she began to understand the unspoken message that was embodied in their choice of clothes for her, what they wanted her to see and experience, from design to the craft of tailoring and the choice of materials, and how her posture was straightened up in order to carry the clothes. Instantly she looked more confident. *There was in fact much to discover and enjoy about clothes*, she came to agree. She was surprised by how much they knew her before she knew it herself! Without her realising, this was only the preamble to what would turn out to be a journey of her remarkable makeover, not only outwardly but also inwardly.

Chisau and Yuetching were setting off for work and Granddad came to see them off at the door, "First day at work, no need to be nervous. Just try your best and enjoy."

Yuetching leaned forward and replied, "Thank you, Granddad. You too have to try your best to get out of this wheelchair. Don't slack on your exercise."

"Of course I'll try my best while you try your best! We work hard together. Yuetching, you look great today."

"Thank you." Yuetching was a little embarrassed.

They waved goodbye and were off.

Chisau remembered Yuetching once said that she could not bear any image of herself, so she did not display her own photos at home. So when they were in the car, Chisau made a point in praising her, "As Granddad has said, you look great today." Yuetching was wearing the new clothes he bought for her, which did smarten her up!

"Why do you look doubtful? I just want you to know that you're by no means an ugly duckling. Since you don't have parents to tell you that, I thought I'd make a point to let you know."

What a nice thought! Yuetching was grateful.

"Stop here!" Yuetching instructed out of the blue. As a reflex to hearing the instruction, Chisau braked the car to a halt!

"What's wrong? Have I offended you somehow?" asked Chisau.

"No, I'm grateful for your kind thought. But if we were to pretend we did not know each other, I should probably get off here and walk the rest of the way. When I arrive at the Hotel, I'll report to Samyin's office. Have a good day, Director Lee."

"What did you just call me?"

Yuetching smiled.

"It's still about 20 minutes' walk away."

But Yuetching was already off the car, and waved goodbye to him, leaving him with no chance to negotiate. "This girl surely has a mind of her own," muttered Chisau to himself before driving off. "She is headstrong for sure."

Escorted to Samyin's office by a Receptionist, Yuetching found him reading newspaper on the sofa. Upon her arrival, he quickly got up from his seat and greeted her, "Good morning."

Yuetching gave him a broad smile and greeted, "Good morning. Today it's my first day. I shall trouble you to take care of me." Yuetching gave Samyin a little bow.

Samyin was surprised by her formality, so he said, "No trouble at all."

Samyin's dress sense was playful, expressive and edgy. His

style carried a spirit of non-conformity. He had an artistic flair that was unmissable. He came across as someone with taste. With the eye of an epicurean, Samyin registered what Yuetching was wearing straightaway. "Very nice indeed," he remarked.

"What is?" Yuetching was clueless about what he was referring to.

"Well, nothing." Something was better left unsaid, but Samyin could see Chisau had already begun his nurturing work on her.

"Where's my desk?" Yuetching asked.

"Oh yes, come this way," said Samyin.

Samyin showed Yuetching to her desk, on which there was only a desktop with her login details written on a post-it stuck on her screen. "Oh, and here is your staff pass," Samyin took it out of his pocket.

"Thank you very much. Is there anything you would like me to do today?"

"What?" While Samyin did prepare her login details, he had not prepared his instructions for her.

Yuetching walked round her desk and habitually switched on the computer.

"Should I answer your calls? How would you like me to screen your callers? What's your schedule today?" suggested Yuetching.

"What?"

"Am I not your secretary?"

"I thought it's only a disguise."

"To make the disguise believable, don't you think I need to perform some minimal secretarial duties for you? I believe I can manage that much for you, unless you're super busy or you want me to keep out of your business completely. It's up to you; I don't mind either way."

"Ah, right. You see, I'm a bit like you – an independent agent and a free spirit. Besides my mum, you are my first PA and I have done many years without one in between. And my mum never needed instructions from me; she just knew what to do and did it before I even knew what I needed done? Does that make sense to you?"

"You want me to model on your mother?" Yuetching made it sound dubious.

"Oh no, of course not. I'm just saying that I too need to

adjust to this arrangement." Samyin cleared his throat and started giving instructions, "My schedule is indeed on the Hotel intranet but at the moment, only Chisau and I have access to it. So far, I manage my own schedule, albeit not very competently, but from today, I'll enable you to have access to my calendar. In addition, you'll have editing right as well."

"What's the use of your schedule if it is not public? Does it mean that I would receive a lot of calls to check your availability?"

"Well, we shall see how it goes....You see, I've kept it private because I'm a very private person and I have trouble with the idea of having my life being laid out in front of the whole workforce!" Yuetching raised her eyebrows while Samyin found it awkward that the briefing got so personal and exposed his quirks. He cleared his throat and continued, "During office hours, I'll take only business calls. For all other calls, just ask them to leave a message."

"Why would personal calls come through your office number?"

Samyin looked a bit embarrassed and forced an answer, "Inevitably in our business we do get to know a lot of people."

"Then how can I tell if a call is personal or business?"

"I'm sure you will develop your acumen in the role after a while. Do you have any further questions?" asked Samyin.

"What's your schedule today?"

"Clear."

"Clear?" Yuetching repeated in disbelief.

Samyin was embarrassed again, so he rounded up, "If you have no further questions, I'll go back to my office."

Samyin turned and walked away, leaving Yuetching to ponder: he really was an idle person, wasn't he? What could he be *possibly* doing all day?

Having settled down in front of the computer, Yuetching began searching through the internal database. When she found reports or documents that might help her understand the business, she would copy down the titles for future reference. After a couple of hours, Yuetching got up and went into Samyin's office.

"Manager Chiu, here are the messages left by your private callers this morning so far. Here is a list of documents and reports. May I request copies for them on your behalf?" asked

Yuetching, passing both lists to Samyin, who was reading lifestyle magazines with intense focus. The television was on mute in the background.

What an idle person! Yuetching thought. *He came into the office to play?*

Samyin lifted his head, while feeling awkward about how Yuetching addressed him, "Manager Chiu?"

"Yes, in the office, it's better that we keep it formal."

Samyin frowned on Yuetching's expectation, but he did not dispute. He ignored the messages but looked at the second list and asked, "Can't you download them from the intranet?"

"These are confidential, so I need your authorisation to request them individually from the relevant departments as required by the internal procedure."

"I see. I believe that you would like these documents to help you understand the operation of the Hotel?" Samyin tried to confirm his understanding of her intention. *He is no pushover; he does inquire and check the details*, noted Yuetching with interest.

"Of course, what else can it be?"

"Don't be too curt with me; I thought you said you would like to keep it formal in the office. Is that how you speak with your superior?" Samyin turned the table round, and Yuetching was silenced.

"All right, I give you authorisation to request these reports," agreed Samyin. As he passed the list back to Yuetching, he caught the news on the television, reporting the conspicuous home-coming of a rising violinist Yan Sinyin (甄倩妍) who was surrounded by a throng of fans at the airport, after she had just won a prestigious international competition. Samyin turned up the volume and walked up to the television to listen to the clip. Yuetching noticed the disdain on his face during the report. Normally she was not nosy to avoid being noticed, but a new start called for a new approach; she wanted to get to know people when she had no worry about them probing into her past in return.

"Why? Do you know her?" she stepped out of her usual self and asked.

Samyin was a little startled; he was not used to having his every move and every look observed either!

"Who would want to know her?" Samyin behaved as if nothing had bothered him and walked back to his desk.

"Why do you dislike her?" Emboldened, she continued. "She's very popular with fans. Be careful that you don't offend millions of people."

"As if I care! I think what I like. This is my right," Samyin did not care to be political.

"She's a role model for youngsters. Why don't you like her? Her story is an inspirational one – left her home country on her own after gaining a scholarship to Vienna to study music, worked hard towards her goal with intense focus, finally achieved her dream and came home victorious. Isn't she the pride of the nation? I think she deserves the attention and some respect too."

Samyin switched off the television, and said, "Now who is having an opinion on things that she doesn't know? This is what the media lead you to believe. When you know the whole truth, your viewpoint may well be different."

"So you *do* know her and know her very well, by the sound of it?" Yuetching deduced.

"Why would I want to know her? I was only an onlooker but felt wronged on behalf of someone else," replied Samyin, "Why are you prying into other people's business? Keep to your high ground of aloofness; I like that too. Now go back to work." Samyin sent her away and she could only comply.

Approaching lunchtime, Yuetching stopped by Samyin's door on her way out and explain, "There is something I don't understand in the reports. I'm going to ask Chi – no, it's Director Lee."

"Wait," called Samyin, "I'm coming along." He followed her out.

Yuetching knocked on the door. Chisau looked up and was pleased to see her. He welcomed her warmly, "You've come. Are you inviting me to lunch with you? How has your first day been so far? Samyin, you've come too." Seeing the pile of reports in Yuetching's arms, Chisau asked, "What are these for?"

"Well, my intention is to come here to ask you questions about these reports to clarify my understanding."

"You spent the whole morning reading reports?"

"No, I spent most of my morning locating them. Now I'm reading them."

"Is that so?" Chisau glanced at Samyin and smiled; Samyin shrugged.

"If you have questions, why don't you ask Samyin directly?" Chisau suggested, but that possibility had never crossed her mind.

"Does he have any interest in the business at all?" Yuetching queried.

Chisau turned to Samyin and laughed out even more. "Don't be deceived by appearance. Samyin has much to do. In fact, he's quite busy. But he has cancelled every appointment and meeting today to make himself available for your first day," disclosed Chisau. "This is to say, he does know stuff about the business. You can ask him and discuss with him. He is not my deputy in name only; he is my great helper. He covers for me often."

"It's enough! Don't embarrass me!" interrupted Samyin.

Yuetching was confounded exceedingly; it was hard to believe what Chisau had just said. She now did not know what to believe: her instinct or Chisau's words.

"Let's have something to eat first," suggested Chisau and they all went together.

In a secluded private corner of a Hotel restaurant, the three of them were enjoying their lunch with friendly chats largely between Chisau and Samyin. Being a newcomer, Yuetching was a willing listener to find out more about them. Suddenly coming into their view was a stylish lady looking much like a movie star who glided into the room towards them. She knew how to make an entrance; everything about her was to be noticed. Yuetching was the first one to catch sight of her and was transfixed. Seeing the stunned look on her face, both men turned to look what had caused it, and saw Sinyin walking towards their table.

"How're you, Chisau?" greeted Yan Sinyin, elegantly taking off her sunglasses and brushing her hair away from her face. The sudden appearance of Sinyin gave Chisau a fright, not delight. She bent down trying to kiss his cheek, but Chisau stood up to avoid it. Insulted, Sinyin straightened up and put her sunglasses back on.

"Is that how you greet someone whom you've longed to see?"

"You can't be serious," replied Chisau.

"As soon as I touched down, and managed to get away from the crowd, I came here to find you, even before I go home to see my parents. Do you know why?"

"I'm not interested."

"You're the person whom I most want to see. Can't you tell?" She took a deep breath and continued to charm, "I have butterflies just thinking about our reunion!"

"You can say whatever you like."

Seeing that she was not getting anywhere with Chisau, Sinyin turned to the rest of the party. "I see you're having a cosy lunch here. Hi Samyin, you're still here. I'm pleased to see you again too, of course. And who is this young lady beside you? Shouldn't I be surprised? I've known you as someone inseparable from female company. Is it even worth introducing her to me since it's changed so very often back in those days?"

"You've mistaken, Miss Yan," Yuetching could not clear the misunderstanding fast enough. "I'm his secretary."

"Then may I ask how a secretary comes to enjoy such a privilege to dine with the top two chiefs-in-charge of the Hotel in such a cosy and friendly setting?" quizzed Sinyin.

"This is Miss Cheung's first day, so I've arranged this opportunity to introduce her to Chisau," Samyin churned fast to come up with a believable reason, "Why do I even need to explain to you?" Samyin hit back, deliberately showing his annoyance.

"I see. Then may I sit down and join your friendly and cosy lunch?"

Chisau cut in to say, "We're just leaving. By all means, enjoy your lunch, but please excuse us." To show their solidarity as a team, Samyin and Yuetching got up and prepared to leave.

Sinyin grabbed hold of Chisau's wrist and would not let go, begging, "I've just arrived. Is this the way you're to welcome me?"

"Your coming and going has nothing to do with me. If you have business matters, please make an appointment with Miss Wei," said Chisau coldly, withdrawing his wrist from her grip but Sinyin grabbed hold of it again, she was persistent.

"May I have a private moment with you?"

Chisau was not granting it.

"Are you still angry with me?"

Chisau didn't answer.

"I haven't heard from you at all, not once. Do you know how painful it was for me to endure your silence?"

His silence continued.

"Do you not appreciate my difficulty? I left without saying goodbye to you because I couldn't do it. Because of my cowardice, I couldn't face you. It was because I loved you too much that I didn't know if I came face to face with you, I would still have the determination to go. Do you understand my struggle? How many times do I have to tell you this?"

Sinyin's revelation left Yuetching agape. Samyin on the contrary was repelled by what she said. *How could she have done the most heartless thing in the world only to turn it round and call it love?* Samyin thought. *That's ridiculous and infuriating, presenting herself as the victim in the matter!*

"The more pain I felt in my heart, the harder I drove myself," continued Sinyin, "These two years I've worked hard to ensure that I'll succeed so that our painful separation wouldn't have been in vain. Today I come back with the hope that you'll share the fruit of our effort together. I won this title for us. We've waited long for this moment, our reunion at last after our triumph, haven't we?" She was all smiles, looking sweet!

She's truly deluded! thought Samyin.

Chisau took her hand off his wrist and said indifferently, "Thank you for your kind words but really I can't take credit for things that I did not do. Your achievements have nothing to do with me. It was your decision alone, so they're *your* achievements. I have no part in it." He turned and left the restaurant, quickly followed by Samyin and Yuetching.

They followed Chisau back to his office.

"Don't say anything; just go," ordered Chisau.

"Actually –" Samyin wanted to comfort but was interrupted.

"Just go. We'll talk about business later," requested Chisau.

On that prompt, Yuetching picked up all her folders and left with Samyin.

When they were back in Samyin's office, Yuetching deduced, "Chisau must have liked Miss Yan a lot. It's the first time I see him so distraught."

"It was precisely because they were so good together that you can tell how cruel and ruthless she's in nature. She's merciless; she may even be cold-blooded!" Samyin could not help giving his judgement, sizzling with indignation seeing the pain his best friend endure.

"Two years ago? Wasn't it roughly the time when Chisau's dad passed away?" observed Yuetching.

"You miss nothing, Yuetching. Yes, she left three months after uncle's death. His death was very sudden. But in its immediate aftermath, Chisau was so preoccupied with so much to do that he moved back home. I reckon three months after uncle's death might well be the critical time when Chisau first had the time and space to properly mourn. I imagine it was the time when grief would have really hit him and he could do with all his loved ones standing by his side, and Sinyin was one of them at that time. What did she do? Rather than standing by his side, she was scheming to leave the country behind his back all along! From the beginning to the end, she hid it all from him. All that Chisau got was a letter in the post, telling him that she had left for Vienna on a scholarship. Not only had she not discussed her plan with him, she didn't even say goodbye in person. Can you imagine the shock he was in when he got the letter? To me it was a betrayal – an unforgiveable betrayal! You don't need to be very smart to imagine how Chisau must have felt. Two closest people vanished from his life in a puff without any forewarning and both times he had no say! Absolutely awful!"

Samyin folded his arms in disgust and Yuetching was moved by his loyalty to his friend. "She said he was too preoccupied with family matters that she did not wish to bother him and add to his burden. But when you can't come clean about a decision, what does it mean? It means deep down you know it's wrong but you don't want to be conscious about it. So she just ran away, forcing Chisau not only to accept her decision but even to bless it! That's what she's expecting, isn't it? Ludicrous!"

"How did Chisau react?" inquired Yuetching caringly.

"Chisau is someone with a lot of self-control, and is not easily overcome by emotions. It's been said that one should be very scared if he ever raises his voice. Besides, at that time, his family needed him to be strong, especially when both grandparents were stricken with grief and their health was going downhill. Apart from having to make decisions concerning family matters, Chisau began to take over the management of the Hotel. He did what a man needs to do in a crisis situation, that is, to put aside self and focus on the tasks in hand for the good of all. Or perhaps he was in so much shock that he just carried on with what he was doing, so that he did not need to think? This might be the only way he coped? Who knows? The fact was he did not react at all, never talked about it; somehow he just buried it.

"Now it has also transpired that he was putting in a lot of effort into tracing your family. Even I didn't know about this until you turned up on the scene. In hindsight, searching for you probably provided an all-consuming distraction for him. That is to say, it's highly probable that Chisau has never worked out his feelings about Sinyin properly."

"That means Chisau could be a time bomb and the sudden appearance of Sinyin could be a trigger for it to go off?" Yuetching now realised what a rough time Chisau had had, even though he looked serene and in control all the time.

"I won't be surprised, so we have to watch him. Now do you still think Yan Sinyin's is an inspirational story?" Samyin asked seriously.

Yuetching was a little startled by this question. She sighed and admitted defeat on this one, "Love and career, how do you choose between them? Her story is not an inspirational story, but a lamentation of the high price one has to pay for success. Striving to fulfil your potential and making a bid for your dream is not necessarily evil; in fact it's a laudable goal in life. But she made the grave mistake in resorting to deception to get her way. Once you have done that, what wouldn't you do on the road to success? Had she been more open with Chisau, the outcome might have been very different. Now her success is tainted."

"It's not something we would do to people we love, so we'll never understand or accept her reasoning, even if she has any."

"Perhaps success is reserved for certain kind of people – ruthless and self-centred?" reflected Yuetching.

"As to the reports, what don't you understand? Shall we take a look together?" invited Samyin. Yuetching frowned at his offer.

"I'm not as useless or clueless as you think. Can you give me a chance to prove to you?" requested Samyin.

Chisau sat in his office. The tidal waves of high emotions, which he had successfully buried up till then, had made a comeback, rending his heart so forcefully that he almost could not breathe. He could not tell if he was happy or angry to see Sinyin again. Her leaving had once caused him so much pain that he should have been happy to see her again. But he was angry at her for inflicting him with so much pain in the first place that he did not want to see her ever again! He was also angry at himself that Sinyin still possessed such power to cause havoc in him. He thought by now he would have had no feelings towards this person, but it hadn't been the case.

When he was deep in his own thoughts, Miss Wei knocked on the door and relayed, "Director Lee, sorry to disturb you. Miss Yan is waiting in the office reception and requests to see you now. Would you spare her a few minutes?"

"No. If anything, I should be preparing for my next meeting in half an hour."

Miss Wei came back with another message, "She asks for ten minutes, for old time's sake." Like a spell, *for old time's sake* seemed to unlock the door that had barred his past with Sinyin. He had not visited that chamber in his heart for so long that he did not know what was still in there. *For old time's sake* seemed to awaken something he had carefully put to sleep, even buried. Chisau breathed out a heavy sigh. *Perhaps this day must come and I can't keep running away from it.* He therefore agreed to give her ten minutes.

Miss Wei went to pick her up from the reception and showed her in.

"If you have something to say, say it quickly. You have ten minutes as you have requested." Chisau tried to deal with her in a business-like manner.

"I understand that you're still angry at me. I can only sincerely apologise. At the time, I was immature. Perhaps I didn't handle the matter in the best possible way. I didn't tell you when I was attempting it because I didn't expect I would succeed, so there was no need to mention it to you. Do you think it was easy for me to make the decision on the offer? Do you know how confused I was and how many times I swung between 'go' and 'not go'? I couldn't bear to leave you but neither could I bear to stay. It was torturous. In the end, I thought, it might be just this one chance before I was too old; if I let it pass, there might never be another one. Then I would be left to wonder 'what if' all my life. At the time, I was sure that you would understand."

"But you deceived me till the very end; you just couldn't come clean with me!"

"How could I tell you? You were dealing with the death of your father and your family was falling apart. There wasn't the time to tell you."

"Then perhaps it wasn't the right time to go? Did it even cross your mind?"

The pungent truth caused the time to freeze momentarily in silence...

Unable to answer that, Sinyin pleaded on the same line again and again, "How could I let a once-in-a-lifetime opportunity go? It wasn't as if it was an easy decision for me. Do you know how heart-broken I was? I didn't have the courage to face you. I was afraid that seeing you face-to-face would sway my determination to go. At the airport, and on the plane, I cried buckets of tears. I kept asking myself if I had made the wrong decision. But I spurred myself on. I told myself that if I achieved nothing after two years, then the decision was wrong. But if I managed to turn this opportunity into a success, at least the pain we felt would not have been in vain. For you and for myself, therefore, I couldn't fail. That's why I worked hard and was totally focused. I have never given up loving you and this love has been my inspiration. When I won the competition, the first thing came to my mind was to share this moment of glory with you. This trophy is yours," Sinyin took out the trophy from her bag and gave it to Chisau, "Without you to motivate me, I wouldn't have been able to endure the torturous practice regime, and to continuously demand myself to make breakthroughs in my play. I won this for you."

Sinyin wiped away her tears and put on her sweetest smile, offering, "Would you accept this trophy? This is for you."

Miss Wei knocked on the door to give a reminder, "Meeting is in five minutes." Chisau acknowledged and began to sort the documents to take with him.

"Chisau," called Sinyin, "please accept this; I won it for you." She presented her trophy once more.

Documents in his hand, Chisau was ready to go. Before he left for the meeting, he replied, "Ultimately we can find justification for *any*thing our hearts most desire. That love you talk about is phantom existing only in your head. This trophy is the fruit of your hard work *alone*; it's your glory *alone*. You can keep it and enjoy it for the many years to come. Miss Wei will see you out."

Watching Chisau walk out of his office, Sinyin felt that it was as if he was walking out of her life. Together with the humiliation of being turned down, Sinyin's world was imploding, stifling her. She broke down into a sob. She stared at the trophy in her hand. In a flash, it was not treasured anymore; it had completely lost its meaning and become hollow. As she seemed quite settled in the office, Miss Wei intervened, "Miss Yan, this way please."

"I'm not to be hurried! Do you even know who I am to your boss?" She would like to claim the special status she no longer enjoyed. "Just leave me alone."

"Sorry, I can't."

She was infuriated that she was not preferentially treated. She was not allowed to linger, so she quickly jotted him a note before she was escorted out.

After the meeting, Chisau returned to his office. He found her note weighted down by her trophy on his desk, saying, "I won this trophy FOR YOU. It's meaningless to me. It's up to you what you want to do with it. I can't care less even if you throw it away!" Chisau sat in his office chair and did not know what to do with it. His head started to ache and did not want to think more about it. He randomly put it away in a cupboard so that it was at least out of sight even if it was not out of mind.

Chisau drove home, and was surprised to see Yuetching pacing up and down by the front porch. He wound down the window and asked, "What are you doing?"

Yuetching lit up when she saw him, answering, "Waiting for a ride with you."

"Ah? Where to?"

Yuetching already jumped into the car, and answered, "Anywhere will do."

Chisau went along with the suggestion, and drove off.

"How was your first day at work?" Chisau first opened a subject.

"It's all right. After lunch, we went back to Samyin's office. He asked me to give him a chance to prove that he wasn't as clueless or useless as I thought. Hence, I fired all kinds of questions about the reports at him. Only then did I realise he was actually not that shallow, quite the contrary in fact. He's knowledgeable; his brain turns really fast, so are his reactions. He's rather interesting after all. But his personal life seems rather chaotic."

"What do you mean?"

"He has a lot of calls that he does not want to answer. Who are all these girls?"

"Really?"

"And why do they call his office number and not his mobile?"

"Maybe they aren't given his personal number, so they can't call him on that."

"If they aren't personal friends, then why do they keep calling him?"

Chisau smiled.

"It's kind of consistent with what Sinyin said about him this lunchtime," observed Yuetching.

"Don't jump to conclusion. It's true that when younger, he went through a period of being a little wild. He was searching for his identity. For a time he thought his worthiness was measured by having girls hanging out with him. But he has gone over that phase and is now more secure in himself."

"You mean personality can change just like that?"

"No, what I'm saying is that he now knows what his personality is *not*."

"Then where are all these girls from?"

"Well, you may not think so but looking at it objectively, he's a very eligible bachelor. He enjoys life and has various club memberships of his interests. He does meet people when he goes to those functions, and many do join the clubs to look for dates, even if he isn't. Sophistication in taste and aesthetics are not something you were born with but something you cultivate on an intense knowledge base with much detail to learn. He wants to be not a man of pomp but a man of substance albeit with great taste. He can be a lifestyle guru anytime. Actually in this respect he is a valuable adviser to the Hotel. Look, I'm guessing here that many would be dying to be in your shoes, being his secretary. He declines to have one for all this time partly because, I believe, he doesn't want the complication of office romance. He wants to be able to come into work to work and not to be distracted. That gives him peace."

Yuetching was stunned by this account.

"Do you mean that he reading lifestyle magazines is actually work?"

"Well, it's work as well as a hobby. He's in a dream job!"

Chisau chuckled.

"Why does he take me on as his secretary when he doesn't want one?"

"He's doing us a favour, and not the other way round. He gets out of his way to make this work for you and for us. He's a private person. He even made a secluded corner into his office in order to be away from the staff!"

"First impression can be so deceptive."

"Quite right."

"Why isn't he looking for love?"

"I think he's giving himself time to look for himself first. I think he was tired of chasing fad or girls for the sake of it. In recent years, he believes that lifestyle should not be about how you want to live but an expression of who you really are underneath, or you are just a fake. He believes that how you live should be connected with the inner person of who you are. I think he's investing in knowing himself better."

"This sounds very soulful."

"This is called growing up."

Chisau stopped at a public square; they got off the car and sat on the bench by the fountain. Yuetching took out some beers from her big bag.

"What are they for?" Chisau did not understand.

"Samyin said that you drank beers when you're unhappy," explained Yuetching.

"I've guessed that you two would be talking about me behind my back. I am not wrong, am I? Am I unhappy now?"

"I guess so."

"If I drink, who's going to drive?"

"Don't worry. I have driving licence. I can drive home."

"Drinking on my own is no fun. Why don't you drink with me and we take a taxi home?"

"Sorry, I don't drink."

"Why?"

"Wine is a mocker; it's a great cheat, deceiving many that they are the masters when they are really the slaves. It ruins life." She spoke with conviction.

"This isn't a general observation, is it?" Chisau raised his eyebrow at her.

"Let's just say I've seen it ruin lives."

"In that case, I'm not going to drink either. Today, I'm not that dejected."

"Then when was the last time you drank beers?"

"When I discovered Sinyin had left the country on her own and I knew nothing about it until she kindly notified me." There was sarcasm in his tone.

"That means you have had a good run of over two years free from dejection. This is a pretty impressive record," praised Yuetching.

Chisau pulled a wry smile; it was hardly something to boast about! "When the heart is dead, it can't be hurt anymore. What can you do when two of the closest people in your life abandon you one after the other but to put your heart away and conceal it in order to protect it? Rather than saying I haven't felt dejected, it is more accurate to say I've been unfeeling."

"Is that how you feel – being abandoned by your dad?"

"No, he couldn't have helped leaving us, I suppose." Chisau heaved a sigh as he lamented. "He died of a viral infection causing fatal complications in him. No one saw it coming, and he deteriorated very fast. Before we could comprehend the severity of his condition, he was already gone. All of us were stunned by the shock; we stared at the reality and kept asking what had just happened. The brevity and fragility of life struck home. Like any grieving family, we had asked why, but we were none wiser except that we had little control over our life. The whole thing was just inexplicable and incomprehensible, leaving us with a bitter aftertaste. Grandma never got over it. Granddad found a way to understand it as a divine punishment on him, a grief that weighed on him heavily. As for me, I don't pretend I understand it all, but I've coped with it. At the time, I felt sad, but I wasn't angry. That was a blessing, and now I'm more at peace with it."

"And Sinyin – do you feel being abandoned by her?"

"Absolutely," Chisau answered categorically, "I don't know how else I could see it! My dad left us involuntarily but she left me as her active choice. It was an emotional assault! She treated me like the biggest fool in the world. What hurt most, I realise, was not that she walked out on me but that she concealed it from me. It's hard to believe she harboured any love for me."

"These are very strong words."

"Naked thoughts don't know correctness; we have to know them first before we can deal with them. If you hadn't asked, I wouldn't have told anyone."

"How did you feel after seeing her again?"

Chisau heaved a sigh and tried to articulate something that he didn't quite know in words yet. "Perhaps it was like when you met Granddad for the first time."

"Ah? How come?"

"The one whom I should love is the same person who has hurt me rather badly. Like you, I struggle with a feeling of ambivalence. Seeing her again was as if the thorn in my heart were being toyed with once more. It hurts and I don't like that feeling. My anger towards her is like a wall separating us now. I don't want to be angry at her or anybody for the rest of my life! I would like to learn from you the lesson of forgiveness. You've said that only through forgiveness can everyone be released from living in our unhappy past and look forward. You've said it well. If those were unhappy days, it'll be foolish of us to want to linger in them, right?"

Chisau paused and was wrapped in his own thoughts. At length, he sighed, "It's easy to understand the theory, but try putting it into practice? I'm not as magnanimous as you both in heart and nature, but in my defence, she isn't sorry. We're doomed, aren't we? We people are contradictory! We're a hopeless race. I fear that the sight of blood can't be spared when we are pulling out a thorn in the heart. I don't know how much blood is yet to spill because I don't know how deep this thorn goes."

Yuetching didn't know what to say, except, "Whatever happens, remember you are not alone; I will be here for you, and I'm sure Samyin too. I believe the day will come when your heart will be free," encouraged Yuetching.

"Thank you," Chisau smiled.

"When you can finally forgive, will you get back with Sinyin?"

"Trust once shattered is never the same anymore. Right now, it seems impossible. I only wish that no turbulence would ever be stirred up in my peaceful existence because of her. I wish one day I would have no feeling for her, positive or negative. Then I know I'm truly over her."

"These are all angry words."

"Are they? She turned up at the office and left her trophy."

"She would like to make up and get back to where you were

before?"

Chisau gave a wry smile, "To 'make up' may still be possible; 'to get back to where we were before' as if nothing had happened is out of the question."

"What's your decision then?"

"Feelings for someone are not something one can force. As you've said, perhaps I'm still angry at her," Chisau paused for thoughts, and continued, "It isn't the act itself but the revealed person behind the act – there is something unnerving about her. Can I ever trust her again? If there is no trust, there can't be a future about us."

Yuetching listened attentively.

Chisau turned to look at her, and said, "Now I know what it's like to have a sister. I've never talked to anyone like this before." He was grateful.

"Really? How about Samyin?" Yuetching was a little surprised.

"Samyin? He only knows how to drink beers!" he laughed.

"This isn't true, is it? I observe that he's quite attentive."

"Am I hearing a change of opinion here?" teased Chisau.

"I'm just being objective and fair here," protested Yuetching.

"How about you? When you're unhappy, whom do you talk to?"

"Me? I utter not a sound."

"Really?" Chisau was surprised. "Are you really that lonely?"

"There's only me and any dialogues I have take place in my mind, so there's no need to use my speech at all. But there was one place that I used to go when I was unhappy."

"Where?" Chisau was curious.

Yuetching smiled and disclosed her childhood secret, "I owned a castle on the clouds, where there were no tears, no sorrow, no distress, and no worries; there was only peace and joy. When I was unhappy, I escaped to the castle, where no one could find me. Even to this day, whenever I see the Disney logo, I will be reminded of my precious castle on the clouds that I once owned!

"Translated into action, it meant I went hiding in my sleep. When I was little, a lot of us lived in a crowded place. There was no private space that I could claim my own, so I created some. This was what I did. I went to my bed, and pretended I was sleeping. I turned my face to the wall, so close that I could feel the chill of the wall. There, between the wall and me, was a little private space where I wept in silence. I developed a technique of crying that I just let the tears roll down in complete stillness. Sometimes I did fall asleep though. That was why my cousins called me lazy pig. When I grew older, it was as if tears had dried up and I could cry no more."

"And you don't go to your castle anymore..." It was so poignant that Chisau found it hard to respond rationally. *How did this little girl grow up?* He could not even begin to imagine; he was grieved.

Yuetching caught the sad face of Chisau, and admonished him, "This is why I don't like talking about these things to anyone. I know this will be the reaction because I sound pitiful, but I don't want people's pity and I don't invite it. You better not give me any. This is meant to be a sharing to say that yes, sometimes we are in tears and our hearts hurt but tears will dry and we will *always* find a way forward – always."

"Always?"

"Yes, always!" affirmed Yuetching.

Chisau nodded and said, "Got your message and it's right here," he rested his right hand on his heart. He was reminded that Yuetching was a veteran in coping with heartaches and hardships. Her words were to be believed, and her sunniness must not be taken for granted but as inspirational. She was the best and most convincing person to help people see hope in hardship, just as the wonders she had done with Granddad. Chisau acknowledged that she was truly an amazing person. She had so much to give, if only she and other people would give her a chance.

"By the way, you remind me of little Cosette in *Les Misérables*; she went to her castle on a cloud in her sleep too."

Yuetching looked puzzled.

"One day I'll take you to see it." Chisau wrapped up a night of open-heartedness.

It was the weekend, and Yuetching was pushing Granddad around the park for a stroll.

"The weather is nice today. It's refreshing to come out for a stroll, isn't it?" commented Yuetching.

"Well-said. But what's rarer to come by these days is a young person who is willing to spend time with a useless elderly."

"Don't say that. Are you trying to make me feel guilty? I don't spend enough time with you as I've to go to work. How's your progress with physiotherapy?"

"Not bad at all, but still need a bit more time."

"Granddad, you should focus on convalescing and don't worry about anything. Work hard on the exercises everyday and you'll gradually see progress," encouraged Yuetching.

"Since you're working hard at the Hotel, your Granddad won't lose to you in effort!" Both laughed.

"Yuetching, tell me about your work. How is it lately and have you got used to the new environment yet?" inquired Granddad.

"I'm attempting a new way of working. In order that I get to understand the operation of the Hotel, I've requested to have work experience in all the departments in turn. Chisau has approved, so every week I get to work in a different department. I could be a waitress in the restaurant one day and a receptionist the next. Apart from gaining work experience, I have some windfall as well. Because everyone thinks that I'm a temporary worker to help out in the departments where they're short, colleagues are treating me like one of their own. Therefore I get to see how it's really like on the ground, and not a demonstration; I get to see their spontaneous reactions to situations arising, and not some considered responses. Above all, I get to hear what they really think, and not all the 'correct' answers. What is their job satisfaction if any? Are their working conditions reasonable? Sometimes their comments about the guests are quite funny. At other times, they moan about the management. All these are important for us to listen carefully. The inevitable distance between management and staff isn't naturally conducive to honest opinions coming forward. The management is then detached from the people they are managing. What I'm gathering from the ground could be informative for the management on, for example, how to raise the morale of the staff and how to improve on their welfare and in turn loyalty to the Hotel."

Granddad was surprised to hear that but he felt Yuetching was already making contributions with her unconventional approach. He encouraged her, "Then you must gather all that you can see from the ground and present them systematically to the management for careful consideration."

"I will. After a day of work, I usually stop by my desk in Samyin's office to make notes. It was as if I were gathering up the pieces of a jigsaw puzzle; the more I gathered, the clearer the big picture became. It's probable that in the end, all is distilled to a handful of policy points to be passed upwards for consideration."

"Good. Which department are you going to help out next week?"

"Housekeeping."

"Would that be a bit strenuous?"

"Don't worry; I'm used to physically strenuous work."

"Granddad," Yuetching turned cheeky and tested, "do you know popular actor Huo Anze and actress Miao Xiuhui are having their wedding banquet at the Hotel?"

"Of course I know. How could anyone miss that?"

"There's such a buzz at all levels in the Hotel because of this big event. Even though the big day is still a year away, the preparation has already started. Organisers at the Hotel have moaned about how fussy the rich and famous sometimes can be, and one needs the whole world of patience to get every detail precisely right for them. Furthermore –"

"There are still some more?"

"Yan Sinyin has signed a contract with a label. She'll have a celebratory banquet and a small recital at the Hotel, on the condition that Chisau is the person-in-charge of this function."

"Really? What's her real intention to have such a condition?"

"Her intention is very obvious; just that it's hard on Chisau. You see, to do business with the Hotel is a way to gain access to him."

"Ask him to decline it."

"That would be discrimination, wouldn't it? When comes to business, we can't always act on our hearts but on our heads. Sometimes what's good for the business is not necessarily what you like to do personally. Then how do you choose? However, Chisau has derived his own defence, which is to bring along Miss Wei and Samyin to every single meeting with Sinyin."

Granddad could not help but laugh out loud. "Really? Good. Good. Good. I take comfort in that you youngsters united. Seeing how you support and look out for each other in face of a difficult situation, I have nothing to worry about."

"Life at the Hotel isn't dull. But now, we should head home

as it's getting a little chilly," suggested Yuetching.

"Yes, let's return." Granddad was content.

Yan Sinyin held a press conference at the Hotel, making public the details of her contract with a label and the ensuing celebratory banquet. While Chisau and Samyin were present to make sure everything ran smoothly without a glitch, Yuetching was watching the live coverage in the staff room during break time.

After the record company had finished its announcement, reporters started firing their questions at Sinyin. "Miss Yan, have you returned to your home country for good, or is it just a short stay?"

"Let's put it this way, I have no plan to leave any time soon. This is my home. If possible, I would love to stay. But no one can say for sure what the future holds and music is a very international business, so I won't rule out the possibility of working abroad at some point in the future either."

"It's rumoured that you've been offered a priceless antique violin. Can you tell us more about it?"

"I have a couple of violins that I use. But it's true that after winning the competition, we've been approached with regards to an antique violin dated back to 18th century. We are excited about the prospect but at this stage, it would be premature to disclose more. Please watch this space."

"Miss Yan, what's the secret of your success? Is it 10 per cent talent and 90 per cent perspiration, or 90 per cent talent and 10 per cent perspiration?"

"I would say it's 10 per cent talent, 80 per cent perspiration, and the remaining 10 per cent is down to the opportunities that are open to you and if you take advantage of them."

"Your success story has always been inspirational to young people. What is the motivation behind your determination?"

Sinyin looked up and naturally fixed her gaze on Chisau. Following her gaze, Samyin turned to look at Chisau too, while Yuetching in the staff room also held her breath in suspense. What would Sinyin's answer be?

"It's a person," she replied.

"Is it a family member or a mentor?"

Sinyin could not stop stroking the ring on her right hand's ring finger. At that moment, she wished to shout to the world,

"The person she loves is Lee Chisau." But she did not; she had not lost her mind yet.

"Neither," Sinyin answered, fixing her gaze on Chisau. She was prepared to tell the world half of the truth, if not the whole truth. This unexpected revelation created quite a commotion among the reporters.

"Then it must be someone special on your heart. We weren't aware that Miss Yan was romantically linked to anyone. Would you disclose who this person is? I think everyone is very interested in knowing his identity."

"This is a private matter, and I request the media to leave some space for my private life," declined Sinyin politely.

"The person who has won Miss Yan's heart must be someone very special and really lucky too." Sinyin only smiled to acknowledge, while Chisau rubbed his forehead in disbelief.

At long last, the press conference was over. Sinyin and her manager, Miss Lau, met Chisau and Samyin back at the office to firm up the details of the celebratory dinner. Miss Wei had already completed the preparation for the meeting. From invitation card designs to menu choices, all were ready for Sinyin's decisions.

Having gone through numerous decisions, Sinyin asked impatiently, "Is there anything else?"

"How about the programme of the night? Are you going to have an MC? Will there be any speeches? Is your recital programme ready for printing?" Chisau listed.

"I haven't thought that far. Can we leave them till another day and call it a day for now?" demanded Sinyin petulantly.

"Decisions need to be made or there will be delay in the preparation," reminded Samyin in his professional tone.

Miss Lau took out her electronic diary and tried to find another time slot to continue this meeting. Sinyin stopped her and made an offer on how to proceed, "All right then, let's continue the meeting in my room. I work with physical address book for business. Business cards of relevant people are all in my room. Looking through them will jog my memory and help me make decisions faster."

Yuetching happened to be cleaning Sinyin's room. When she was clearing the rubbish, she found Sinyin's crystal trophy in the bin. She picked it up and found her name engraved on it. Only then did she realise whose room she was cleaning. The trophy was badly chipped, exposing a sharp edge. At that point, the door was thrust open, and in came Sinyin, with Chisau, Samyin and Miss Lau. Yuetching was surprised to see them stream into the room.

Seeing Yuetching holding her trophy in her hand, Sinyin dashed forward and snatched it back, asking brusquely, "What are you looking at?"

Chisau and Samyin would like to do something to protect her, but Yuetching gestured that they stayed put as Sinyin did not seem to remember having met her before out of context.

"Good day, Director Lee and Manager Chiu. Sorry, Miss Yan. While cleaning your room, I found this trophy in the bin and wasn't sure if it fell into it by accident or not. I was just wondering if I should treat it like rubbish or return it to the desk, when you stepped in. It's timely that you return. Perhaps you may advise me what to do with it: bin it or keep it?" Yuetching explained.

When Chisau returned the trophy to her, she was so angry that she hit it on the table a few times to break it and then threw what's left into the bin. But when she saw it in the hands of a stranger, she seemed unable to let go.

When Sinyin was still deciding, Yuetching said, "I'll leave you to decide what to do with it. But please be careful with the sharp edge. I've noted the serious damage on the table. I'll report it to Housekeeping and see what could be done about it. You are having a meeting here. Would you like me to return later?" asked Yuetching.

"No," Sinyin hissed. "You stay and finish your cleaning. Go to scrub the bathroom especially. If I find your work substandard, I'll surely report you to the management." By highlighting the damage on the table, she felt Yuetching had publicly insulted her, so she revenged, even though Yuetching had never allocated blame to her.

Who is this woman? Chisau was shocked in witnessing how Sinyin treated other people – he must have been blind when he was in love with her that he did not see it before; he could hardly recognise her!

"Of course, Miss Yan." Yuetching went straight to the bathroom through the bedroom. Samyin went over to inspect the damage on the table. "You're quite violent, weren't you, Miss Yan, no doubt in a fit of temper with your trophy?" He spelt out the obvious in retaliation for Yuetching's sake.

"Make me pay for it, as if I care!" Sinyin snarled.

Samyin was not in the slightest threatened, and replied, "At least you're honest. Thank you, I may indeed."

Sinyin darted at him with a sharp stare and moved on with the agenda; one could not fault her for her work ethic. She put down the trophy and picked up the business card holder on the desk. Efficiently she jotted down names of her choice while flipping through the business cards. When she was done, she passed the list to Miss Lau and asked, "What do you think of the list?"

Miss Lau had a quick glance through, and said, "This is very good; all the choices are apt. I have no comments."

Sinyin turned to Samyin and Chisau, and began, "The programme of the night runs roughly like this: the MC welcomes the guests and briefly states the aim of the banquet. Dinner is followed by two short addresses by people representing the record company. Afterwards the small recital starts. When we are eating, please arrange some classical music to run in the background. Please arrange a grand piano in the banquet hall for my recital. I'll let you have the titles of my pieces and the guest list later. Any further questions?"

"What kind of background classical music do you mean?" asked Samyin.

"A string quartet would do."

"Would you recommend any to us to convey the standard you're expecting?" asked Chisau. She scribbled a few down on a notepaper and handed it over to him.

"In no specific order?" Chisau clarified.

"In no specific order."

"Then we will check their availability."

"Any further questions?"

"No."

"In that case," said Miss Lau, "I'll go and contact the people on my list and confirm their availability."

"Many thanks in advance," said Chisau, and Miss Lau left the room.

Chisau concluded, "Today's meeting is very productive. The format of the evening is shaping up nicely. We'll firm up the fine details. You have worked hard today. We'll leave you to take some rest." Chisau and Samyin stood up, and were ready to go also.

"Wait!" she called out, her heart still stirred after today's press conference.

"Is there anything else?"

"Must you be so cold and formal with me? Besides business, is there nothing else we can talk about? Are you still angry at me? Is that why you want to torture me?"

"I'm not angry at you. Nor do I intend to torture you. Both you and I have changed. The earlier you accept this reality, the less you'll suffer."

In her fury, Sinyin stood up and challenged him. She raised her right hand and showed her ring. "This couple ring I have been wearing everyday. Where's the other half in this pair?" Sinyin took hold of Chisau's empty hand and demanded an answer.

"I took it off the day when you left me for Vienna. It's somewhere in a drawer. I haven't thrown it away yet. Would you like it to keep yours in pair?" Chisau gave a straight answer without even a stir in his heart.

Yuetching had finished cleaning the bathroom and bedroom, and was standing by the bedroom door, unsure if it was convenient to leave the room.

"How could you speak so heartlessly about our memory? Is it a toy to be passed around? Doesn't it mean anything to you? Who is breaking the promise here and who has changed? It is you not me! I have never stopped loving you!"

"The choice one makes at a crossroad changes the direction of one's life forever. There is no turning back. Now you're on the road of a rising star, and you must continue on that path. You mustn't try to reclaim the things that you've given up while making that choice at the crossroad – they are not yours to have because you have no right to them anymore."

"I have never given you up!"

"I don't understand you. You're a talented person. Your future in music is bright. I'm only someone from your past. You've reached another milestone in your life, so why would you want to cling onto your past? Let your past go and you will feel a lot freer. Only then will new people be able to enter your life. You have to put yourself together and don't make it difficult for me or for yourself. For your benefit, I've to be resolute about us. Do you understand?"

"What do you mean by *being resolute about us*?"

"There are differences in our expectations and in our life goals now."

"We can start all over again," pressed Sinyin.

"What you want in life is no longer what I want."

"Have you had another person in your life? Who's she?" screamed Sinyin.

Yuetching came to his mind instantly – as a project he had been engaged in and not in the way that Sinyin meant. "No," he answered.

Reassured, Sinyin softened, "Doesn't our past mean anything to you at all? Don't we deserve another chance?"

Chisau did not relent from his position, "From today, find another driving force behind your music. Perhaps someone more suitable and better than I is just waiting round the corner for you. Please give him, and yourself, a chance."

Sinyin could not believe what she was hearing. She was so shocked that she got unsteady on her feet and fell into the armchair behind her. She muttered in distress, "Have I committed a mistake so grave that you must punish me so severely?"

"This isn't a punishment," Chisau tried to reason with her.

Sinyin could not accept it; she was not ready to pay the price for what she had gained in her career. Meanwhile, Yuetching looked at her watch. Oh dear! She was very behind her schedule. But how could she make an exit?

"Why can't I have both?" argued Sinyin.

"Because you've made a choice, which means to take one and let go the other."

Samyin caught the sight of Yuetching trapped in Sinyin's bedroom, so he interrupted, "Chisau, we still have work to do. Let's go."

Sinyin stood up from the armchair and bellowed at Samyin, "If you're in a hurry, you can leave first. No one has asked you to stay!"

Samyin could not hold his tongue anymore, "The world doesn't revolve around you, nor does it stop because of you. Besides, you have nothing new to say anyway."

Seeing the conversation was not going anywhere, Chisau turned and headed towards the door with Samyin. As they were leaving, Yuetching quickly stepped out of the bedroom to excuse herself too, "Sorry, I've to go as well. Your room and bathroom have been serviced, Madam. Have a good day."

Sinyin was cross and embarrassed at the same time.

"You stop right there. How much have you heard?"

Yuetching did not know how to answer.

"You must be thinking, what a good story to sell to the tabloid!"

Yuetching instantly refuted it, "We can't; we will get fired if we do." She thought this was a sticky situation and it was wise to get out of it as quickly as possible, so she said, "Please excuse me; I still have work to do." She quickly caught up with Samyin and Chisau who had turned to leave the room.

"What's it now? Even you a lowly cleaner are telling me I'm a waste of space and time!" In a tantrum, Sinyin grabbed her crystal trophy, which was the nearest thing, and threw it in their direction, screaming, "You can all get out of my room!"

Seeing the trophy flying through the air and directly at the back of Chisau, Yuetching caught it in a reflex, before Samyin and Chisau turned round and realised what had just happened. Instantly, blood gushed out from Yuetching's hand. Yuetching was frozen as if in shock. Samyin walked up to her, opened up her hands and threw the trophy on the floor.

"The cut is deep. We need to go to the emergency room," said Samyin. He opened the door and got a towel from the trolley to stop the blood from dripping all over the place. Chisau looked up and gave Sinyin an accusing stare that terrified her.

"What have I done?" she pleaded innocence because her pride forbade her from admitting wrong. A rage rose within him and he retorted, "Who are you?" He turned and escorted Yuetching to the hospital with Samyin, leaving Sinyin all alone in her own distorted world.

Chisau and Samyin were waiting in Accident & Emergency, while Yuetching got treatment. "She has gone ballistic today. Only you can let her get away with a crime like this," complained Samyin.

"Let's be clear; I do *not* condone what she did, all right? Don't make me one of her kind. I can hardly recognise her. Has she always been like that? If yes, then I must have been blind that I didn't see it before. Or has the attention that comes with fame and success changed her beyond recognition? How can two years change a person to that extent? She's insolent and beyond reasons. I don't ever remember her being as obnoxious as today."

"This was because you were the one whom she would like to please. You got to see all her good sides, lucky you! On my judgement, these obnoxious traits have always been in her but were tamed in the past, thanks to a certain nice guy in her life. The difference now lies in her inflated ego from fame and success which has magnified them to a monstrous scale for everyone to see. This monster is particularly ferocious in a situation which doesn't go her way!" Samyin gave his analysis.

"If this has been your truthful opinion of her all along, why didn't you say something to me earlier? Shouldn't a true friend counsel?" protested Chisau.

"People in love are usually blind and irrational! Also I was in America back then, remember? I only saw you occasionally during that time. Strictly speaking, I was *not* in your circle," defended Samyin. "What's her intention at today's press conference anyway? For a moment, I genuinely thought she was to blast out her relationship with you on the front page tomorrow."

"Nay, she still has her pride and hasn't completely lost her mind. She isn't going to blow all that she's been working for on an impulse."

"Is there really no return for you two? You've loved her, right? Love like that isn't easy to erase. Are you as resolute as you have wanted her to believe?"

"Who knows? On this matter, I haven't found a way to reason with my head yet, so I follow my heart. Right now, my heart asks me to stay away. I don't even want to do business with her, let alone be a friend," Chisau sighed.

Yuetching came out from the treatment room, with her hand all dressed up.

Chisau and Samyin walked up to greet her.

"How're you? Is it painful?" inquired Chisau tenderly.

"Six stitches! Other than that, I'm fine," smiled Yuetching.

"I'm really sorry that you're injured at work and to a large extent because of me," apologised Chisau.

Yuetching shook her head, "You are not to blame. If you are to blame, blame the fact that I was in the wrong place at the wrong time!"

"Why did you stretch out your arm to catch it though? For

most people, they would have tried to dodge it as quickly as possible," asked Chisau.

"Well then it would have flown straight at you! I couldn't do that. Call it a reflex ... to protect things from breaking or people from getting hurt. Enough brokenness has scared me and I don't wish to see any more. Silly as it may sound, but when I saw the trophy flying towards us, my reflex was to stop it on its track before it caused damage – to you, to the hotel property and even the much battered trophy."

"You keep everything and everyone safe but yourself?" Chisau pointed it out.

"Silly as it may sound, but you're right – I didn't think of myself!" Yuetching was thoughtful about what the situation had transpired about her reasoning.

"Yours is a faulty equation of situation assessment," Samyin made the observation clear, "with one important, essential parameter missing!"

Yuetching nodded, "Yeah, you're right ..." She looked at her hand.

"Yuetching –" Chisau was saddened by how little she valued herself in general.

"No need to thank me anymore. Thanking me once is enough. You two please go back to work. I don't deserve the simultaneous attention of both chiefs-in-charge of the Hotel over such a non-issue. I'll take a taxi home," urged Yuetching.

"You will certainly not. Chisau is busy but I'll take you home and *then* I'll go back to work." Samyin would not take no for an answer.

"It's decided then. Thank you Samyin." Chisau entrusted Yuetching in his care.

Firth thing in the morning, the family gathered round the breakfast table.

"Good morning, Granddad and Auntie," Yuetching greeted.

"Good morning. How's your hand? Does it hurt?" inquired Granddad.

"It's a little sore but as long as I look after the wound properly, it should heal fine. I can still go to work back in Samyin's office, but will have a break from housekeeping."

"Sinyin has gone too far this time. How could she attack people like that? If it were not for Yuetching, it would have been

Chisau who got hurt," Puiyin expressed her gratitude.

Granddad was displeased at the mention of Sinyin, "Totally unacceptable! Take a look. What's this?" Granddad opened the morning paper to let everyone see the headline, which said, "Who could be the mysterious love in Yan Sinyin's life?"

Chisau couldn't say he didn't see it coming.

"Chisau, you must stay low-key, and try your best not to attract the media's attention. We don't want this family to be the focus of the media for the wrong reason."

"I understand, Granddad."

Yuetching worked hard for the whole day at her desk, organising her notes and information. Samyin came back to the office after the last meeting of the day. He was surprised that Yuetching was still working.

Samyin stopped by her desk and started prattling to her, "You really love working, don't you? Many people would have used the injury to take leave from work, and the company won't and can't dispute the ground. I don't know if I should say you're conscientious or just stupid. Is your hand sore at all?"

Yuetching smiled, "Of course, *very* sore."

"Then why came in to work?"

"It hasn't crossed my mind. Look, I've been in a worse state than this before and I still struggled to get into work because not going to work wasn't an option."

"You work like an ox?"

"You can say that. It wasn't my choice then and it's a habit now."

"Are you not angry?"

"Angry at what?"

"Of course, at Yan Sinyin! Who else?"

"No. Is my injury her fault or my *faulty equation in situation assessment*, as you say? I can't tell, can you?"

Samyin found her incredulous. "You're one very special person. Most people can't see faults in themselves and are quick to blame others but you seem to be the opposite."

"It's a survival skill, I suppose. Nothing changes and nothing happens when you blame others. But if I learn from my mistakes, often I can improve my lots."

"Precisely, most people are prideful and lazy; we like to blame everything and everyone else but ourselves so that we don't have to change. It is our nature that we are partial to ourselves in our judgement that we are always in the right."

"Well, if I am partial to others but myself, this is still a bias, isn't it? Our vision is always distorted; it's very difficult to be totally objective. I don't have the luxury to blame others. I don't trust others and I don't believe that anyone would bend for my sake either."

"It's the first time I meet a girl with such a rational mind and a forgiving heart," exclaimed Samyin.

"Are most girls you've met mean-spirited and irrational?"

"Don't be harsh, but the fact that you don't realise you're special and unique makes you even cuter."

Yuetching rolled her eyes and dismissed the praise, "Save your adulation for your girlfriends. It has no effect on me."

A whim came over Samyin, and he suggested, "Let's have dinner together, shall we? Is Chisau giving you a lift home again?"

"Where do you get that idea from? I make my way home most days," corrected Yuetching. "But I think he has a business dinner tonight. How come you are not attending?"

"Precisely because Chisau is hard-working, I can enjoy my leisure! What do you say? Let's go out and have some fresh air," invited Samyin.

"The places that you would go are most likely those that I would not want to go or can't afford to go. I know my place. Against your sophisticated taste, I'm like a savage. We have little in common."

"Then where would you like to go?"

Entertainment was never a part of Yuetching's life, so she had no idea where she would like to go. She rebounded the question to Samyin, "Let me hear your suggestions; then I may consider it."

Samyin walked round Yuetching's desk, shut down her computer, and pulled her away from her desk. Yuetching protested in vain.

"OK, let me go. I can walk by myself."

"And tonight, we can't talk anything related to work," Samyin laid down the rule for the evening.

"If we don't talk about work, what can we talk about?" Yuetching protested.

"If you have nothing to talk about outside work, you have a

choice to be the listener the whole night. Alternatively, you can think of how to answer my questions."

Yuetching put her coat on and left the office with Samyin, wondering what kind of night would be ahead of her.

Samyin wanted Yuetching to relax so he brought her to places where she would feel comfortable. Their first stop was dinner at a Korean BBQ and he was delighted that Yuetching relished the food. Although Yuetching was never particular about what she ate, she would still appreciate tasty food.

"Do you really intend not to say a word the whole night?" asked Samyin.

"Didn't you ask me to be a listener?"

"Then what would you like to know?"

That was an unchartered territory for Yuetching. As far as personal relationships were concerned, Yuetching had always been passive. She never sought to know someone proactively, so she did not have much practice to phrase personal questions without context.

"If you forfeit your right to ask questions, then it's my turn to ask you questions!" threatened Samyin to turn the table round.

Thinking on her feet, Yuetching jumped in and asked, "What's your dream? What is the one thing you have to achieve before you would think your life is not in vain?"

Samyin nearly choked. He had never had such a searching question asked of him before! "How am I supposed to answer such a question? Why can't you ask the standard questions like what my likes and dislikes are or what my hobbies are? To get acquainted, we normally start with the subjects on family, hobbies, interests, and so on. What kind of person would ask such a testing question that requires so much thinking?"

"That's why it's interesting; it reflects your thinking and your heart's longing! Simple and direct questions won't require answers because they are obvious. I ask the question because I want to know if the position you hold at the Hotel is your *active* or *passive* choice."

Samyin paused from his food, and stared at Yuetching in despondence! *What kind of girl is she? What does she hold in that mysterious brain of hers? She is refreshingly different as well as difficult at the same time!* He was challenged!

"Talking to you requires a lot of effort," Samyin remarked.

"Really?"

"I reckon most people won't want to talk with you."

"I don't talk with people, I don't have friends." Then Yuetching became thoughtful and noted, "But.... this seems changing…"

"That's good," Samyin nodded in approval.

He then paused to think of his answer to Yuetching's question.

Yuetching glanced at him, gesturing that she was eagerly awaiting his answer.

"I got it. Don't hurry me; I need to think," said Samyin.

Once he started to compose his answer, he realised how penetrating Yuetching's question really was. Not even he was used to revealing that much of himself, but any less would be insincere. He took a deep breath and decided to take the risk with Yuetching, so he began, "Ever since I was little, I've always been interested in buildings. When I went to different places with my parents on holiday, the things that most attracted me were buildings. Sydney Opera House, the unfinished Sagrada Familia in Barcelona, and the 'ruler' building in Melbourne were among those that captured the imagination of a young mind, but the urban landscape of Tokyo had a special charm on me. It was dense without being disorderly; it was orderly without being boring. Its insipient skyline was etched by a few ostentatious landmark buildings which cried out about their personalities and characteristics without being awkward or out of place in its surroundings. The city, reflecting the society, spoke of a tacit understanding of all the parts which came together in a peaceful and harmonious co-existence. I was totally captivated by its charm. Japanese also introduced me to the art of space creation. I was fascinated by their skills in making a tight space look spacious, and in turn inviting and comfortable. Nothing in the layout was an accident; instead, every detail was written with much care and thought, celebrating their appreciation of nature and life. I began to read the minds of the anonymous architects who spoke to me so passionately that I could not possibly miss the calling. Marching towards my dream then, I went to America for training. As you know, it's a long process to qualify as an architect."

Yuetching was totally captivated by Samyin's beautiful words, which opened a window to his soul! Here he spoke with passion. Those words were from deep within, and she felt his sincerity in his honesty.

"Five years ago," Samyin continued, "my dad was diagnosed with cancer. He spent one year battling it and thankfully he has been in remission ever since. But after a life-threatening illness, inevitably his perspective was changed. He came to the decision to retire from managing the Hotel. He joined my mum in the UK to be with my younger sister who was studying there, while I resumed my training in America. Then Chisau's father passed away, and Granddad's health started going downhill as a result. Without a head, the Hotel was thrown into a state of disarray. Chisau had no choice but to take over as Director, partly to give some comfort to Granddad in an otherwise extremely distressing situation.

"In the meantime, I came back originally for a little break after having qualified! With a distressing situation unfolding right under my nose, I could not walk away and leave Chisau shouldering everything; I simply couldn't do it. Perhaps I was a little bit older then. I saw that beyond my personal dream, there were family responsibilities and loyalty to a lifelong friend, or even comradeship, which were also important to me. Seeing him cutting such a lonely silhouette, I couldn't walk away from my responsibilities and my friend at that time to chase after my personal dream. Therefore I put my dream on hold, and stepped into the Hotel in order to assist Chisau. My motive was purely to share his burden and boost his morale; after all it was our family business too and it was unfair if Chisau had to shoulder it on his own. If we were to learn how to manage a hotel, we learnt it together. We work like our dads did.

"So back to your questions: is my position at the Hotel my passive or active choice? It was my active decision, but it was *not* because I was interested in hotel management. And what would I have to achieve before I would think my life is not in vain? Under the oversight of my conscience, try my best in everything I do and take care of all the people in my life to the best of my ability. If I can have no regrets, then I'm a happy person. I realise recognised success to me is secondary to that. Am I not ambitious enough? I do have a dream though, which is to make visible the space that people cannot see, and in turn, to continuously discover for them new angles to appreciate the beauty of this world."

Samyin was a total surprise to Yuetching, from his depth and eloquence to who he was. There was so much to mull over that she did not even notice she had stopped eating altogether! In contrast to his own choice, she began to understand more why Samyin found Sinyin's decision to leave Chisau for Vienna at that critical time such an unforgiveable and odious offence! In fact both were faced with the same dilemma but each had made a different choice: a brother had chosen to stay, while his love had chosen to leave.

"Don't tell me that my answer is so impressive that has rendered you speechless!" Samyin joked and broke her thought.

"You and Chisau are like brothers."

"We grew up together. He's the quiet one and I'm the flamboyant one. He's the good boy and I'm the bad one. I talk, and he works. This same pattern carries on to this day." Samyin laughed at his own self-parody, but Yuetching knew it wasn't true.

"Who is older?"

"I am."

"So you are his big brother."

"Yes, you can say that."

"I'm thinking it wasn't a simple choice for you to stay at the Hotel, and you are changing my impression of you."

"Really? How?" Samyin was lit up.

"I used to think that it had always been plain sailing for you, that you didn't care about anything in the world, and that you were here only to enjoy a good life. There was no need to try hard on anything and life would still be fine for you. But now I realise that you have a passion, that you've worked hard from the bottom to gain your qualification, that you have had moments of sadness and that you have had the courage to make some difficult choices in life too."

Feeling closer to Yuetching, Samyin was secretly overjoyed.

"Boys grow up when they take up rather than run away from their responsibility."

"How about five years later? Would you leave the Hotel and resume the pursuit of your dream?" asked Yuetching.

"Five years later, do I want to re-enter the profession, start from the bottom and compete with the new blood who are much younger? I'm not sure. When you're young, you don't mind anything, while everything is an experience. But when you are older, your expectations are different. You move on to another stage in life and accordingly the focus of life shifts. Perhaps dreams are reserved for the youths. Once it has slipped away, it's difficult to chase it back."

"Is this not a regret? Do you like the work you are doing?"

"I believe every job has its appeals under an inquisitive mind," stated Samyin, and Yuetching could not agree more.

"But," continued Samyin, "no matter how I think about it, I can't escape the fact that the core aim of the business is to cater for the haves. At times we even go to the extent of creating a bubble world for them, within which everything goes according to their wishes, and everything is gratifying and pleasing to the eyes. It was as if a deception to gloss over the reality. I used to live like that but I don't want to anymore. I must admit I'm not convicted of this business aim and can never bring myself to commit my all."

Yuetching remembered what Chisau once said about Samyin: *he doesn't want to be a man of pomp but a man of substance albeit with great taste.*

"It's not totally like that," Yuetching tried to lift his spirit. "Our business is to facilitate communication and contact. We assist people to come together, bring them face-to-face to mark special occasions, exchange ideas, discuss issues of the day or share their experience together. Whether it's at a personal or corporate level, these occasions are needed to foster relationships and make memories. If in the process, consensus can be found, progress can be made, and breakthroughs are precipitated, one cannot say this is not a valuable service that has something to contribute.

"Besides, if you're eager to give something back to the society, initiatives are abound. For examples, we can throw a memorable birthday party at the Hotel to brighten up the life of a gravely-ill child, deliver Christmas dinners to an elderly home, invite children from an orphanage to come for Christmas dinner at the Hotel, allow staff to spend one working day a year helping out on some Hotel-designated charity projects, and so on. If you're willing to think creatively, what the Hotel can do may surprise you. Sometimes we don't necessarily need a grand plan to shake the world. Rather, the totality of numerous small initiatives may just be enough to make a difference."

"Wow! Whenever you open your mouth, out comes another

business proposal! What do you store in that mysterious brain of yours really?" teased Samyin.

"A belief," answered Yuetching.

"What is it?" Samyin got curious.

"Even on my own, and with my negligible ability and influence, I can still make this world a better place to be," said Yuetching with conviction.

"Is this a dream?"

"You could say that – a very naïve dream, which could only be owned by an equally naïve person!" Yuetching laughed at herself.

"No, not naïve at all. On the contrary, it's a laudable dream, which everyone should share."

"Yours is too - to make visible the space that people cannot see, and in turn, to continuously discover for them new angles to appreciate the beauty of this world. I wish to see that very much one day." Yuetching changed the subject, and asked, "Did Chisau need to give up his dream just like you when he took over the Hotel?"

"About this, perhaps you should ask him yourself one day. Didn't we agree not to talk about work? Perhaps we should stop the subject and focus on eating. When we're done here, we've to hit our next stop."

Yuetching was surprised, "I haven't agreed to be out all night with you. Where are we going anyway?"

"You only think about work, so tonight I'm taking you out to play." Yuetching gave Samyin her usual suspicious look!

After dinner, Samyin took Yuetching to an arcade. Just hearing the noise from inside, Yuetching did not want to go in, but Samyin pulled her in regardless. In there, they competed in car racing, skiing, tennis, dancing, hitting objects and so on. Given that Yuetching was novice in everything, she lost in every single game but this did not stop her from having a surprisingly fun time! Her clumsy attempts gave both of them a good laugh, and it was the first time Samyin saw her guffaw wholeheartedly. No matter what she did, she always gave her 100 per cent. This was Yuetching's characteristic charm, admired Samyin.

When they had a break, Yuetching looked at her injured hand. Samyin caught a glimpse of red. He grabbed hold of her hand and screamed, "Oh dear! Blood is oozing out from your wound, isn't it? Are you all right? Does it hurt?"

Yuetching pulled back her hand, and said, "Don't worry. I just got too excited in playing."

"It's my fault. If Chisau finds out, he'll surely lambast me without any mercy!"

"You're exaggerating again."

"I'm not. Honestly I've never seen Chisau so concerned about anyone before."

"Now you've gone over the top! He must have treated Sinyin very well."

"He might have, but I didn't see it because I was abroad, so I haven't lied! Come, let me fish you a big soft toy as a way to say sorry," Samyin pulled Yuetching away.

"There's no need, honestly."

Yuetching waited by the machine for a long time. There were countless failed attempts, but Samyin would not give up until he accomplished his goal of grabbing the biggest soft toy for Yuetching with the robotic arm. He presented the gift to Yuetching, declaring, "This is for you."

Accepting the huge snow-white bear from Samyin, Yuetching teased him, "Now I understand how arcades make money. But I still thank you for your hard work in winning this for me – my first cuddly soft toy." Yuetching cuddled the bear tight; tears welled up and made her eyes sparkle.

"What's wrong? Why are you upset all of a sudden?" Samyin was genuinely concerned.

"It's not sadness; it's happiness. This was one of my many wishes when I was little – I mean – to own a huge sized cuddly soft toy. This has remained an unfulfilled wish until today, thanks to your effort. I'm moved."

Yuetching's tears melted away Samyin's heart. Suddenly he had the desire to wrap her into his arms to give her warmth, to make her happy and to protect her, but he restrained himself from acting on his impulse.

"Your wish is so small, and you are so easily pleased. How can you be moved to tears with such a small wish?" Samyin said tenderly.

"To a little girl back then, it definitely wasn't something small or easily accomplished. Otherwise it wouldn't have remained unfulfilled for all these years!" Yuetching wiped away her tears and smiled happily, "Today my wish has come true, and I've overcome a defect in life. Today's a happy day." Suddenly she was like a kid!

"Not having a big cuddly toy is a defect in life?" Samyin found it incredulous.

"Yes, when you saw everyone had at least one special cuddly toy, not having one was a huge defect in life. I was left to wonder what's like to own one and if there was anything magical."

Looking at Yuetching's happy face, Samyin had a wish himself, which was to stay beside her and try his best to help accomplish her wishes, no matter what they were.

"Let's go," said Samyin.

"Where to?" puzzled Yuetching.

Samyin took her to a high-end bar for a drink to wind down for the day.

"What would you like to drink?" asked Samyin.

"Juice is fine."

"No wine or cocktail?"

Yuetching shook her head.

"Any particular reason?"

"You don't need to know."

Yuetching sat the bear on her lap and had her arm around it.

"You're very attached to the bear, aren't you?" commented Samyin.

"Yes, indeed, very attached," she grinned, not ashamed of behaving like a little girl. *Is she making up for the childhood that she didn't have?* Samyin looked on. *She is attached not to the bear but the emotional significance that it represents. What is the emotional significance?* Samyin had not fully grasped it.

Drinks were brought to them, and they had a good time chatting. Just when Samyin was thinking what a nice way it was to wrap up a magical evening, a girl tottered up to him and was over the moon in seeing him, "Chiu Samyin? Is that really you? It's been such a long time. Why haven't you called me? Why haven't you been coming? Finally tonight you show up. Do you have any idea of how many nights I have been waiting here for you, hoping to catch you?"

"You're drunk." Samyin grabbed Yuetching's arm to leave.

"Not so fast! We haven't even had a chance to catch up yet. I don't mind you bringing a new friend, just let me join the party, please?" she pleaded. She then cast her eyes on Yuetching and wondered, "But really since when have you gone for the childish type? How old are you to still bring a soft toy out to play?" She laughed out loud.

Offended by how Yuetching had just been insulted, Samyin tried more assertively to push through but this lady would not let him go. Yuetching on the other hand was free to go, so she took her leave. "Please excuse me. I'll get going first." Then she rushed for the exit. By the time Samyin broke free and went after her, Yuetching was already gone. He was utterly disappointed beyond words – a beautiful evening spoilt by a grave misunderstanding. He knew how it must have looked. How was he going to clear his name?

Chisau heard the door and rushed out of his room to see if it was Yuetching.

"How can you be later than I back from a business function? Where've you been?"

"Are you interrogating me?" Yuetching was a little surprised.

"No, sorry, I don't mean to come across like that. I'm only worried and I couldn't get through to you on the phone either. You haven't said you would be late, so…"

"Have you called me?" Yuetching got her phone out and checked, "Oh! Sorry, it's out of battery."

"Where've you been all night?"

"Samyin took me out to play on the spur of the moment."

"Can't miss the bear, can we?" Chisau eyed the big cuddly toy in her arms.

"Samyin won this in the arcade and gave it to me as a gift."

"Then why didn't he bring you home?" a logical question from Chisau.

"He ran into an old acquaintance in the bar and I left them to catch up. My golden rule is to avoid being caught up in the crossfire of any emotionally charged situations. So I retreated before I got dragged in."

"Then why did you proactively come to ask me about my affair with Sinyin?"

"That was because I am concerned about you. But if you two are to confront each other face to face, I also don't want to be on the scene. Like yesterday in her room, I was trapped without an easy escape. And look, what was the outcome? I was injured leaving the scene," Yuetching expounded on the soundness of her theory. "How people behave in that kind of situation is often beyond reason, man and woman alike. My injury proves the wisdom of my simple rule." Yuetching waved her injured hand to reinforce her point.

When Chisau saw the blood-stained bandage, he was alarmed, "Your hand? What's happened to it? Why is it oozing blood? It looks wet."

Yuetching quickly put her hand away, "Nothing."

"Let me see in this instant," Chisau went to find her hand. "You can't hide it from me. Tell me now, how did you aggravate your wound?"

"We went to an arcade and competed in a lot of games. I got a little carried away and my hand, I suppose, got a little distressed," confessed Yuetching. "Samyin said that if you find out my wound is reopened, you will lambast him without any mercy."

"He's absolutely right. I'll go and 'lambast him without any mercy' tomorrow. Now, you first have to sit down and let me dress your wound."

Yuetching had no choice but to let him take care of her wound. It looked raw and swollen, truly distressed. Chisau cleaned it with great care and dressed it up neatly. Chisau had always been the youngest in the family and never had the chance to take care of anyone; Yuetching had brought out his tender side which he did not know exist. But how much he loved taking care of her!

5 A Decision Made

Sinyin stared at her own reflection in the mirror, but even the most glamorous look could not mask her haggardness. Chisau had pained her; she was angry that she could not have her way with him. Why? She kept asking. Losing was not her game. In everything she did, she was in for the win. But with Chisau, it was not totally a game; she adored him, even loved him. Why wouldn't anyone love him? His devotion to her was so total that it would touch anyone's heart. His love was so tender that it let you be while bringing out the best in you at the same time; so loyal that you could not but feel secure in it; so honest that you could not but trust. It was loathsome that she could not have him; otherwise her life would have been perfect! Why must he elude her and become the missing piece of her otherwise perfect life? Why couldn't he cooperate in completing her masterpiece of her life for everyone to admire and envy?

Since their last confrontation, she let herself indulge in melancholy and could not bring herself to do anything for a while. But one day, she snapped herself out of the spell of sluggishness, and went over to the other extreme of putting every ounce of her energy into work and practice as a way to vent her frustration. Music gave her a feeling that she was in control; it was also an outlet for her turbulent emotions. For the past month, she had been practising long hours. She neglected her meals and did not rest. She played until she was exhausted and could think no more. Her manager had tried to talk some sense into her and requested her repeatedly to look after herself

111

but to no avail. How could she rest? Music was like a drug that she hooked on in order to numb her feelings.

"Today is my day," she told her own reflection in the mirror, "and I must pull myself together! I must let everyone see my flair, and made Chisau feel his loss. This night is to be a revenge!" She spurred herself on with a reason why this performance *must* be the best of her best! The moments just before one took the stage were always the loneliest when she was supposed to compose herself. "If only – if only Chisau were here to keep me company," she thought with a sense of loss.

This was the night of Sinyin's celebratory banquet. In the banquet hall, hotel staff was busy with the final preparation. Chisau and Samyin were present on behalf of the Hotel, whereas Yuetching was busy as a waitress!

Samyin pulled Yuetching to a corner, and asked, "What're you doing here?"

"The catering department chief called me in the last minute, saying that they're short of staff this evening, and asked if I could help out. What am I supposed to do?" Yuetching explained.

"Then you'd better be careful."

"Don't worry. When you attend an evening like this, how often would you remember the waitress who serves you?" Yuetching's question met with no answer from Samyin, so she continued, "The dim light is my best cover; I should be safe – no one will remember me. I'm going back to work now."

Guests started to trickle in. While Samyin and Chisau were busy at greeting the guests and networking, Yuetching was busy at shuffling among them, serving cocktails, soft drinks and canapé. After the informal drinks, guests were seated in the banquet hall. The MC welcomed the guests on behalf of the organisers, and restated the cause of this joyous occasion. He introduced Sinyin, who made her entrance in a rapture of applause. Admirers were dazzled by her grace and elegance. She wore her usual infatuating smile and bowed to acknowledge the warm welcome, before moving to the seat for the guest of honours. The background music from the string quartet filled the hall, and the first course of the dinner was served to each guest with the grace as well as efficiency of the well-trained staff. It so happened that Yuetching was assigned to serve Samyin and Chisau's table, and Samyin found himself watching every move of his waitress.

"Why do you keep staring at Yuetching? Do you want to draw attention to her," whispered Chisau.

"Sorry," Samyin lowered his head.

"Are you worrying about something?"

"I feel uneasy because she's physically too close to Sinyin. I just wish that she has no time to take notice of the waiters and waitresses this evening. We've an army of reporters present here. I hope that this evening will pass without any incident."

After a delightful meal and while the guests were having their coffee and tea, the MC introduced the two representatives of the record company, who welcomed Sinyin as one of their artists. Afterwards Sinyin was brought back onto the stage.

"After our delightful meal, Miss Yan has prepared for us a small recital to round up the evening. Miss Yan, could you please tell us why you've chosen the particular pieces to recite for us this evening?"

"Of course. The three pieces I've chosen were landmarks in my music career. The first piece was the one which won me the scholarship to go to Vienna. The second piece was for my graduation exam, and the third was a movement in the concerto I performed at the international competition which I won."

"In other words, this is a highly personal programme charting your music journey, isn't it?

Sinyin concurred with a bright smile, "Yes, you may say that."

"This evening we are in for a real treat, aren't we? Without further ado, Ladies and Gentlemen, let me present to you Miss Yan!" The MC retreated and Sinyin took the stage. Spotlights were on her and guests became shadowy outlines in the dark. Yuetching and the team lined up on one side, standing by to heed to any requests that the guests might have.

Sinyin composed herself and began her first piece. The beautiful melody glided off from her violin like silk, and began to convey a captivating story. The lush and warm sounds were inviting and drew the audience into the world of imagination. Her narrative was mesmerising. In synch with the melody, her magical fingers were dancing seductively and rhythmically on the fingerboard, with lightning steps that teased the eyes. Working in perfect harmony with the bow strokes on the strings, they had the power to build up from the gentle humming of the sea to tidal waves that splashed with conviction, or to change the mood from cheekiness to melancholy with seamless transition. The dynamics and contrasts brought such sumptuous colours to the performance that Yuetching was transfixed with awe and amazement. Whatever kind of person she was, she was undoubtedly talented; her sparkling virtuosity deserved recognition.

To Chisau, this was a personal story in which he had a part. He was there when Sinyin first worked on this piece. He had heard her practise it countless times, to the extent that he knew how each phrase was supposed to be played; the only thing he didn't know about this piece perhaps was her intention to make a bid for the scholarship with it. What an irony! A piece of music that was full of their happy memories together was at the same time the very means through which they were eventually separated. On hearing Sinyin perform it again, Chisau wasn't sure if it brought him joy or sorrow. The familiar tune carried him down the memory lane to the time and space he once shared with her, and flooded his mind with their memories. He was reminded of that loving feeling towards her, and why he had once liked her. It was true that she was capricious and unruly, but she was also disciplined and demanded herself as a true professional. He enjoyed her wicked sense of humour (which, he sighed, somehow seemed to have disappeared from her completely). He admired her artistic flair, which was everything that he was not, and how she always boldly loved or hated. Violin had always been her first love. Whenever she picked up her violin, she was transformed into a different person. First she had to be a tamer, taming her violin into listening to her commands on how to play each new piece. Then she was turned into a fairy who had the music tamed at her fingertips and subsequently could do whatever magic she wanted with the wand in her hand! Chisau knew behind each successful performance was hours and hours of practice. He admired her unwavering determination to strive for goals she set and how she always pushed for her very best. The violin was inseparable from her; like a child to his mother, it was always on her back! When she felt like it, she would stop in the street, open the case and start busking. Her music never failed to act like a magnet to pull coins from the pockets of the passers-by. She happily said that it was their entertainment fund! Looking back, Chisau realised that the violin had always been the "third person" between them. When she had to choose between her violin and him, she had chosen the former. The live performance of the piece was drawing to a close now. This ending was much better than the ending he had had with Sinyin; at least one knew it was coming and could prepare for it. With Sinyin, it was abrupt and sudden, in the same manner as how his father was snatched from his life. There was not even a chance to say goodbye. He was abandoned and he didn't even have a say! No, his wishes had no place in the decisions of either of them leaving him. He was hurt.

These were all in the past now, sighed Chisau in his thought.

Sinyin began her second piece, which was no longer familiar to Chisau. Suddenly Sinyin became like a stranger to him. She was no difference from any other successful violinist standing on the stage playing commandingly. He was not there when she tamed this piece. In a flash, she was distant. He took a look around, and all were spellbound by her, so powerful was her stage presence.

The second piece came to a close as well, and a thundering applause erupted. But Chisau noticed something wrong with her; she looked pale and unsteady. Chisau stood up from his seat, which was close to the back of the hall, and attracted the attention of Samyin who sat next to him.

"What's wrong?" Samyin stood up and asked.

"She doesn't look right," murmured Chisau.

Chisau instinctively moved towards the stage and caught Yuetching's attention. When he arrived on the stage, he was just in time to catch Sinyin who collapsed into his arms. This sent shockwaves through the hall and a commotion ensued. Reporters sprang to their feet and moved forward to get pictures. Meanwhile, Yuetching instantly called the chauffeur to get the car ready. Both Samyin and Yuetching walked towards the stage at the same time. Chisau pried her fingers off her violin and passed it on to whoever was on the stage and then picked her up to leave. Samyin kept the crowd back for Chisau to pass through, while Yuetching rushed to his side and whispered the message that the Hotel car and chauffeur were waiting by the entrance.

Miss Lau stayed behind to handle the reporters while Chisau rushed Sinyin to the hospital. Samyin shut the car door for them and saw them off. He turned round, and found Yuetching standing behind him. He asked, "Would you like to come?"

Yuetching nodded.

"Then come with me in my car."

Samyin and Yuetching arrived at the hospital, and found Chisau sitting in the corridor on his own.

"How's she? What's wrong?" asked Samyin.

"Not sure. Doctor is inside with her."

Sinyin's manager, Miss Lau, arrived also.

"How's she?" inquired Miss Lau nervously.

"We don't know yet. The doctor's still examining her," answered Samyin.

At that moment, the doctor came out of the room, and reported, "She seems fine. Preliminary examination suggests that she most likely suffers from exhaustion. We'll keep her in for observation overnight to confirm."

"Thank you very much," said Miss Lau and the doctor left.

"I've asked her repeatedly to take care of herself. She just wouldn't listen," complained Miss Lau. Then she turned to Chisau, and said, "Tonight, thank you very much. Fortunately, you were observant and reacted in time to catch her and her priceless violin! I can't thank you enough."

"You're welcome. Looking after our guests is our responsibility. Let's go in and see her," answered Chisau. Yuetching did not follow the rest into the room.

As soon as they were in the room, Miss Lau started scolding Sinyin for neglecting her health.

"You don't have to repeat yourself. I've heard you," Sinyin was annoyed.

"Do you know how much trouble you've brought me? What's going to be in tomorrow's paper?"

"Miss Lau, it may be best to let Miss Yan rest. Tomorrow's problem can wait till tomorrow," advised Samyin.

Miss Lau softened, and offered, "Would you like me to stay with you tonight?"

"Of course not! If you stay, I won't have any rest." Sinyin was still cross.

"All right, I'll do as you say but will you promise me that you'll rest properly?"

"I will," Sinyin assured her to stop her from nagging.

"Well, since you so wish me to leave, I will. Please keep your promise and rest well. See you tomorrow." Miss Lau turned to

Chisau and Samyin, thanking them once more, before she took her leave.

"We should get going too. You should rest," said Chisau.

Chisau turned to leave; Sinyin grabbed his wrist, and requested, "Stay. Would you stay?" Chisau looked torn. "You still care for me, right?" asked Sinyin.

"You're our guest at the Hotel. This makes your welfare our responsibility. Don't read too much into it," Chisau loosened Sinyin's grip and walked out of the room without even turning. Samyin followed behind.

Looking at the sad face of Chisau, Yuetching was puzzled, and asked, "Is everything all right?"

"You've been waiting? Everything's all right. Don't worry," answered Chisau, but he seemed preoccupied. Yuetching wasn't sure that everything was fine with him. "Sorry, please excuse me." Chisau left without saying another word as if he would like to be alone. Yuetching had no choice but to leave the hospital with Samyin.

In the car, Samyin asked, "Go home?"

"Go home? I still haven't properly signed out yet! Could you drop me back to the Hotel?"

Samyin glanced at Yuetching's waitress uniform and smiled.

Yuetching was quiet on the way.

"You're exhausted, aren't you?" asked Samyin.

Yuetching's thoughts were pulled back to here and now from afar. She was not paying attention, "Sorry, what did you say?"

"What've you been thinking?"

"Nothing. Perhaps I'm tired."

"It's understandable. You haven't had a moment to sit down the whole night," sympathised Samyin.

Yuetching was a little touched, and replied, "In my student days, I waited table and didn't go home till the small hours in the morning. Exhaustion was felt in every part of my body, even deep in my bones! I was out the moment my head hit the pillow. No one had ever asked if I was exhausted. There was no one. So thank you so much for asking tonight; it means a lot to me." "But it was well worth it tonight," Yuetching added, content.

"Why?" Samyin did not understand.

"What a concert it was? Whatever kind of person Sinyin is, you can't deny that she's impressive as a violinist. Her stage presence, her techniques, and the way how she makes her music

117

sing were just amazing. She must have worked really hard to be where she's today."

"She grabbed Chisau's hand and asked him to stay," Samyin told Yuetching.

"Then why didn't he stay? He still cares for her a lot, doesn't he?"

"He said he didn't want her to read too much into his action."

"But he noticed that she wasn't right before anyone else in the hall tonight."

"Yes, I know."

Yuetching gave out a heavy sigh, "This business about love is so vexing and tormenting, isn't it? It's been said, love is like the threads of lotus rootlets – it can't be severed, and the more you want to sort, the messier it becomes."

"Wow! You talk like someone who has had much experience," exclaimed Samyin.

"Me? Of course not. On this matter, who can compare with your experience?"

"What has it got to do with me?"

"I witnessed it."

"You mean that day at the bar. Actually –"

"You don't need to explain to me," interrupted Yuetching.

"No, it's all right. Is it all right that I want you to know?" he insisted. "I had met that girl at that bar a few times. The first time I met her, she drank a lot because she was unhappy in her relationship. She was on her own and I was sitting close by. She came up to me and blurted out everything. Like you, I didn't actually want to know; it was none of my business, so I got up to leave. Before I left, I went to use the washroom. When I got out of the bar, she was sitting by the entrance. She was so drunk that she couldn't even get onto her feet. I couldn't leave a girl drunk on the street on her own, could I? It was dangerous. With a great deal of effort, I got her to unlock her phone and tell me whom to call. I stayed till two of her girlfriends turned up to take care of her. Since then, every time I went to that bar, we would exchange greetings if she was there. That was all. She gave me her number which I didn't keep. She doesn't know anything about me, and doesn't have my number. She isn't my old flame or anything like that. Perhaps I should stop going to that bar altogether, because nearly every time I go there, I see her."

Yuetching recalled: *Perhaps what Chisau said is right; he is a very eligible bachelor and many would like to date him. They call the office number because they are not given his mobile number.*

"Why don't you have any response? Are you still cross with me?" Samyin was keen to clear the misunderstanding.

Yuetching found this funny, and said, "Who am I to be cross with you over this matter? It's none of my business and you aren't obliged to explain anything to me."

"I don't want you to misunderstand. As a matter of fact, that girl told me she had left her boyfriend and had been waiting for me at the bar every night since then. I hadn't been there for a long time and the night when we were there was the first night she saw me after their breakup. I really had no idea that she was waiting for me. Really I should avoid that bar, and the neighbourhood altogether!"

Yuetching laughed and could not help but feel a bit sorry for Samyin.

"You're no doubt popular with girls. Why do girls like you so much?"

"I respect them; I don't belittle them and I don't take advantage of them."

Having changed out of her uniform and packed her belongings, Yuetching went to Chisau's office to find him, and discovered he was in a daze in his office chair.

"I've come to take you home. Let's go," Yuetching interrupted his thoughts.

"Ah?" responded Chisau, coming back to reality.

"Today let me drive." Yuetching opened her hand for Chisau's car key.

Chisau hesitated but Yuetching insisted, "Haven't you said that I can drive your car? Do you need to see my licence?" Yuetching opened her bag to look for her licence.

Chisau held her hand and stopped her, "No need." He handed over his car key.

All the way, Chisau was quiet. He did not know what he was thinking and did not pay attention where Yuetching was driving him, until the car turned into the hospital car park. When Chisau realised where they were, he questioned Yuetching, "What do you bring me here for?"

"Isn't this the place you want to be? I see that you're worried about her, so why don't you just go and see her? Do you want to sleep at all tonight?"

Chisau dropped his head, and said, "No, I can't go."

"Why? Isn't it what your heart tells you to do right now?"

"Yes, but not everything your heart asks you to do is wise," said Chisau thoughtfully.

"Why are you so adamant in refusing to heed and in torturing yourself over it? Why can't you give yourself a chance to get back with Sinyin if that's what you want? Why not, if you two still love each other that much?" Yuetching could not understand why it must be so torturous.

Chisau stared ahead into nothingness. It was hard for him to explain and he was not sure if he was ready yet to thrash it out with anyone. It had been an inkling until tonight when he was clear in his head for the first time how this relationship should go. But emotionally he still needed time to accept this decision. Was it premature to tell? No, it wasn't because it was Yuetching. Chisau felt he could tell her anything, even his premature thoughts.

"The deeper one loves, the deeper one hurts," Chisau began to articulate himself slowly. "Sinyin's first love is never going to be me; it's her violin. When she had to choose between me and her violin, she chose her violin. When she focuses on her violin, look what she has achieved. In that sense, she was right to get rid of me. Tonight, on that stage, she and her violin made the perfect pair. If we get back together, and she has to choose between us again, I know she will choose her violin every single time. How many times can I live through the same trauma? Even if she chooses me instead of her violin, would I want that to happen? It was as if to ask Yan Sinyin not to be Yan Sinyin anymore. I can't ask that of her either. Yan Sinyin and her violin have been melted into one; they can't be separated. And if what I'm seeking in love contradicts her undivided attention to pursue her dream in music, then this relationship is doomed. Yes, I'm sad but the decision is right: a doomed relationship is not worth restarting, is it? She thought I could make her happy, but in fact, I can't and she hasn't realised it yet. How can a soaring eagle willingly become a bird with clipped wings to stay with me?

"The role that I'm left to play in her life is to admire her elegant flight high up in the sky from the ground, an onlooker who has no demand on her and will not restrain her. While I can't be up there with her, it would be equally wrong for her to stay down on the ground with me. Up there is where she should be, not by my side," concluded Chisau with some visible pain.

This was – sad. Yuetching could not fault Chisau's reasoning and he seemed clear now what should be the way forward. There was only one thing left for her to do for him tonight.

"Since it's inconvenient for you to visit her, I'll do it in your place, so that you won't need to worry." Yuetching got off the car and rushed inside the hospital before Chisau could respond. Having made sure that Sinyin was sleeping peacefully like a baby, Yuetching returned to the car.

When she approached the car, she realised that Chisau had gone back in the driver's seat. She got in on the passenger side, and joked, "You don't trust my driving after all?"

"It's not your driving that I don't trust; it's *you*! I don't want to be driven to places I don't want to go!" Chisau started the car and set off for home.

"You haven't asked?" Yuetching had waited for Chisau to inquire about Sinyin but he did not.

"If you have nothing to report, then I know everything is normal. Why do I need to ask?" Yuetching was enlightened! The fact that he did not ask was not because he did not care but because he already learnt his answer from the silence, so he needn't ask! How interesting!

"Oh, I see, this is *Managing* Director Lee's unique approach of management," responded Yuetching.

"Meaning?"

"If the ears don't hear, it means things are managing fine as they are, and can be ignored," Yuetching spelt out her meaning.

"Of course. I haven't enough time to manage everything that is reported. Why would I go out of my way to inquire about a 'normal status'?" Both laughed; this did sound like a reasonable survival strategy.

"Sometimes," Yuetching was keen to point out the weakness in this management approach, "things that are not reported do not necessarily imply 'normal status', you know. It could be a deliberate effort of people who want to hide something from you. Your unique, meaning lax, management approach only works with a loyal supporting staff to be your eyes and ears, which competently filter and organise information before it reaches you. Or you're set up to be easily deceived. You put a lot of trust in your people."

"This is correct, and lately I've acquired another pair of competent hands to join my loyal team."

"Who's it?"

"It's you, of course," Chisau smiled.

That was a surprise, but a nice one. Being praised by the boss was always an encouragement to a conscientious worker. Yuetching was chuffed to bits.

Chisau returned to his room, feeling both physically and emotionally drained. He lay down on his bed, and as soon as he shut his eyes, the night's events quickly replayed in his mind's eye. His thoughts were only interrupted by a knock on the door. He sat up and replied, "Come in."

It was his mother. Surprised to see her up at this hour, Chisau asked, "You still haven't slept yet. Is something wrong?"

"No, don't always just worry about others. How about yourself?" Puiyin pulled up a seat and sat down in front of him.

"What do you mean?"

"Tonight was Sinyin's banquet at the Hotel. Did it go well? How do you feel? Are you angry or sad?" Puiyin inquired with motherly love and care.

"She collapsed in the middle of the performance and we had to send her to the hospital. That's why we came in so late."

"Oh dear! Is she all right?" Puiyin was alarmed.

"She's fine, just suffers from exhaustion."

"Are you worried about her?"

"She seems fine, so there's no need to worry."

"How do you feel about her? Actually we've been selfish. While we keep piling our demands on you, we've neglected your feelings on a lot of the things. When she sneaked out of your life without even telling you, you must have felt awful. But we so focused on our own grief at the time that we completely overlooked your pain and did nothing to comfort your broken heart. I'm sorry for our insensitivity. How do you feel seeing her again, joy or sorrow?"

"I can't say I'm overjoyed. The feelings are complicated and mixed. Now I realise I've never sorted out this mess. Perhaps now is the time to do so. Sinyin is right in one thing – we've never officially broken up. To her, she has just gone on a vacation for two years. Now that she's back, she expects to pick up everything from where she left off. This has put me in an awkward situation."

"What does your heart say? Do you still love her?"

"I don't know. I find her irritating, and wish she has never turned up in my life again. But Yuetching has said that these are all angry words."

Puiyin was surprised, "I didn't know that you and Yuetching get along so well?"

Chisau admitted, "Perhaps because she has been through a lot in life, I find her easy to talk to on everything from work to personal matters. She's able to empathise and with a sound mind, she often comes up with something noteworthy to say. Together with Samyin, the three of us has formed a strong partnership in all matters."

"It's true that she has been through more than her fair share in life. What's special about her is how pure her heart has stayed despite all the hardships. She's independent and yet easy to get along. We're very fond of her too. Do you know if she's happy here?"

"I haven't heard her say otherwise."

"What a relief! It's a bonus that you've an extra person to shoulder your burden at work. When you were trying to find her, we had no idea what kind of girl we were going to find. Yuetching is an unexpected blessing to this family. Just look at how she has taken care of *loye*. No one could have expected that of her."

"How's Granddad doing lately?"

"His progress is good. Yuetching has given him a lot of motivation. The fact that *loye* can recover so speedily is all down to her, who has plucked the thorn from his heart and healed his wound."

Chisau nodded and could not agree more.

"It's getting late now. We shall go to bed now. Sleep tight. Look how exhausted you are. Please take care of yourself or you will be the next one to collapse after Sinyin," Puiyin ordered.

"I promise; don't worry. Goodnight."

After Puiyin had left the room, Chisau got up and went to ransack the drawers of his desk. At long last, he found it – the couple ring that he bought to seal a promise. He remembered how resolute he was in that promise and how excited he was in presenting the rings to Sinyin over a romantic dinner that he had planned. That day was their second anniversary of being together. With the rings, he promised to take care of her if she would let him. But within a year, she was gone without a word. She signalled that she could take of herself, thank you very much; he was not an indispensable but a redundant part of her life. His heart wrenched as if it was trampled on; she had taken him for a fool. She had never needed his love or care. He still remembered the moment he took off his ring on the day she left him. How could he fulfil the promise when she was not even there? She effectively dissolved the promise, making it hollow, void of any substance. But this night, when Sinyin collapsed, why was he the first one to run to her rescue? Why did he still know her? Why did he care? Was it a reflex? Was it a habit? Was it because of this promise? Had he forgotten that this promise had been dissolved by her for more than two years? Had he forgotten that he had no role in her life anymore?

Staring at the empty circle bound by the ring, he told himself, "We can't muddle along anymore. This ambiguity must be cleared; I must give this relationship an official and unmistaken closure."

The family gathered for breakfast at the start of the day as usual. Glancing at Granddad's face, Chisau was wondering what could have upset him the first thing in the morning! Without a word, Granddad handed him the morning's newspaper, gesturing that the answer was in there. Chisau opened it up, and to his surprise, he saw a half-page picture of him carrying Sinyin out of the banquet hall with the accompanying headline on the front page of the entertainment news, which read, "The mysterious man in Yan Sinyin's life: could it be…?"

Granddad spelt out his concerns in full, "My biggest worry is that reporters may start probing into this family because of this. If they keep investigating, their reports may not be confined to the relationship between Chisau and Sinyin. It's possible that everything in relation to Chisau's family background could be splashed on papers to fuel public curiosity, and *all* family members may receive some unwelcome attention as a result. Chisau, we must nip the butt out before it's fuelled into a frenzied flame. In handling this matter, the focus is on putting out the curiosity before it even has a chance to grow. We must paint the incident as an uninteresting, normal reaction to the situation arising, dispelling any ground for further speculation. If we fail to achieve this, then we must focus on damage control by narrowing the media attention on you and Sinyin alone. Do you understand?"

Chisau nodded, "Yes, Granddad, we'll try our best to normalise it, but still we have to be prepared that people know us from the past may have read this and come forward with what the reporters wish to find. In that case, the story may spin for a while."

"What is the current status of you two? Are you or are you not an item?"

No one had expected Granddad to come out so blunt to the point! Chisau was embarrassed, while he reckoned that it was a perfectly legitimate question to raise given the circumstances.

"No, we are not an item," answered Chisau definitively. Both Yuetching and Puiyin fixed their gaze on him in surprise as this adamance was not there the night before.

"Very well then. Yuetching, during this sensitive period, it's better that you keep away from Chisau. Understand?"

"Understood, Granddad," answered Yuetching.

Sinyin woke up in the hospital bed after a good night of sleep. She felt rested and more refreshed. Miss Lau came in to see her and inquired after her.

"I'm feeling much better now," answered Sinyin.

"That's good. Have you eaten breakfast yet? Has your appetite returned? Do you experience any discomfort in any part of your body?"

"Appetite is good. Don't worry, I'm fine," reassured Sinyin.

"Good," Miss Lau was pleased to hear it.

Seeing that Sinyin was in good form, Miss Lau sat down by her bedside and pulled out the morning paper. "This is the coverage of last night's dinner and your performance."

Sinyin opened the paper, and was shocked to see herself not as a commanding violinist, as she would expect, but as a wimp collapsed in someone else's arms!

"How did that happen?" Sinyin frantically skimped through the text.

"The coverage is actually quite fair and honest. Apart from introducing who you are, and what the occasion was, it's also complimentary about your performance. But all these are not as

125

attractive as the gossip about Mr Lee and you, and hence they've chosen this as the headline to draw public attention. Although this may only be a bit of harmless speculation at the moment, it may just get people curious enough to spur the reporters' interest on the subject. We must be clear of our stance and be consistent with it. It's best to have some sort of understanding with Mr Lee so that we won't be contradicting each other. In the meantime, you should get more active in your professional engagements in order to divert attention back to your music. Of course, our course of action will be different if the media have got it right about Mr Lee and you. Have they?"

Sinyin put down the newspaper and lamented, "They are not totally wrong. It's true that Chisau has been my motivation, but this is no longer. He has made it very clear to me that today there is nothing else between us except business and asked me to find another driving force in my life to replace him! I've no wish to make our past public. Above all, it has no relevance to here and now. If he really cares for me, he would have come to visit, but no one had come for the whole night."

Coincidentally, a nurse walked into her room to check on her. She corrected her, "Who said you had no visitors the whole night? Last night, a lady came to check on you, but you were asleep. I asked who she was. She said she was a staff from the Hotel to make sure everything was fine with their guest. I checked her ID before I allowed her in." The nurse walked up to Sinyin and caught a glimpse of the newspaper opened on her lap. She said casually, "This is she in the photo."

Sinyin was surprised. In that photo, she could only see Chisau and no one else. Pointing at Chisau, Sinyin tried to clarify, "You mean *he* came to visit me? Then why did you say it was a lady?"

"It's not *him*; it's her!" the nurse pointed out Yuetching who was next to Chisau in the picture.

Sinyin picked up the newspaper and looked closer. She found her familiar but could not remember where they had met at first. After searching hard through her memory, she suddenly clicked – she was the cleaner who caught her crystal trophy and hurt her hand!

"It's her?" muttered Sinyin to herself. "Wasn't she a cleaner? How come she was a waitress last night? And why did she come to check on me?" Sinyin had a lot of questions for Chisau.

As Chisau approached the Hotel, he could see reporters gathering at the entrance for comments. Luckily he was not spotted and managed to sneak into the car park without being swamped. He took the staff lift which went directly to the office floors. This level of interest was totally unexpected, and made the situation more urgent than he originally thought.

When he arrived at his office, Miss Wei passed on the message, "Good morning, Director Lee. A few newspapers have contacted the office and would like your response to this morning's report on Miss Yan and you."

"Please call PR's Mr Pang and Miss Lam for an emergency meeting in relation to this matter," instructed Chisau.

"Yes, Director."

Soon after, Mr Pang and Miss Lam from Public Relations gathered in Chisau's office to discuss the best way to handle the current media interest.

"Granddad's wish on this matter is to calm the interest as effectively and efficiently as possible, so that the privacy of the family will not suffer from any unwelcome intrusion. Mr Pang and Miss Lam, how do you think is the best way to achieve this outcome?"

"If we were to keep our silence, and the curiosity of the media was not satisfied, this might backfire on us and encourage them to probe into the matter somewhere else. This is why I advise to issue a public statement about last night's incident. But it's better to obtain a consensus with Miss Yan before we release our statement for consistency," analysed Mr Peng.

"Miss Lam, could you please contact Miss Yan and see if you can get their response to this matter?" requested Chisau.

"Yes, Director Lee." Miss Lam then left the office to make the call.

"Regarding last night's incident," Chisau continued, "our stance is very simple: we always seek to do our best to serve our guests in all circumstances, and last night was no exception – our reaction last night was driven by what was best for our guest in the situation arising. What Miss Yan needed last night was to be sent to the hospital as quickly as possible; this was what we did, and I so happened to be on the scene to help out," Chisau laid out the direction of the public statement, while Mr Pang made notes.

"Please forgive me for asking, do you know Miss Yan personally?"

"Yes, I do."

"What is your personal relationship with her?"

"It's true we had a history together but that was before she was famous."

"So there is some truth in the speculation?"

"Yes, you can say that."

"Then denial can make it more suspicious and spark more vigour in their pursuit of the story."

"There is a difference between denying and not admitting. We shouldn't freely offer up what the reporters do not know but will respond to what they do know or find out subsequently. Should we need to divulge more in our future response, we have to make sure what we may say then would not need to go back on our words now. This is our position now. So, no, denial is not our strategy."

Miss Lam returned to report, "Miss Yan has been discharged from the hospital and they'll be coming over here for a meeting straight away when they're ready to leave."

"That's good. Mr Pang, could you make a draft of the statement based on our discussion ready for the meeting with Miss Yan please? Remember no comments to the media until we've met with Miss Yan. Is that clear?"

"Yes, Director. We'll go and write up the draft now."

"Thank you."

Samyin bumped into Yuetching as she came out of the lift; she was panting.

"You're so late this morning?" asked Samyin.

Yuetching did not stop but walked in a hurry to her desk. Samyin followed.

"Have you – not – seen the – newspaper – this morning?" panted Yuetching.

"Of course I have and spotted your three-second fame!" joked Samyin.

Yuetching gave him an unfriendly stare, and said, "You too – enjoy your – three-second fame! You were right behind Chisau – busy controlling the crowd, were you not?" Yuetching arrived at her desk, took a deep breath and continued, "This is serious and no joking matter. Granddad ordered this morning that I should keep away from Chisau until the media's interest has ebbed. The bus was late – very late – this morning! So I'm late. But it won't happen again."

Right at that moment, Samyin's phone rang. "Hello," answered Samyin.

"Do you have time? Please could you come to my office for an emergency meeting with Sinyin later?" requested Chisau on the other side of the phone.

"Of course, I'll be right there."

"I'll give you a call when they arrive," said Chisau and then he changed the subject, "Have you seen Yuetching today yet?" asked Chisau.

"Yuetching?" repeated Samyin. He turned and looked at Yuetching, who gestured that she had no time but to leave straight away.

"She's just arrived and now she's off," answered Samyin on her behalf.

"Really? I couldn't give her a lift today. Was she in a state this morning?"

"She's as bright as normal. Apart from being a little late, I didn't see she was in any other way affected. She has vowed it won't happen again."

"That means she'll set off much earlier to accommodate."

"I guess so."

Chisau was working in his office when Miss Wei announced the arrival of Miss Yan and Miss Lau. "Please send them in and call Mr Pang and Manager Chiu to come over," replied Chisau.

"Yes."

Sinyin and Miss Lau sat down in Chisau's office.

"I see that a night of sleep has done you much good. You look well. How are you feeling this morning?" inquired Chisau caringly.

"I feel much better. Thank you. Thank you also for taking care of me last night," replied Sinyin with butterfly in her stomach.

"Don't mention it; it was what we should do. What would you like to drink?"

"Fruit tea please."

"English tea for me please with milk and no sugar," said Miss Lau. Miss Wei left the room to make the drinks.

"The press this morning must have inconvenienced you. I'm sorry," apologised Sinyin.

"Inconvenience is not a problem. What's important is to find a way to resolve it," replied Chisau.

At that point, Mr Pang and Samyin entered the office.

"Samyin requires no introduction, while this is chief of PR, Mr Pang," Chisau introduced.

"Miss Yan, nice to meet you. We've drafted a public statement in response to this morning's press coverage. Please take a look and comment," invited Mr Pang.

"Impressive efficiency!" Sinyin exclaimed. Having glanced through the draft, she said, "It's fine by me. Miss Lau, could you please cast your eyes on it too?"

Sinyin continued, "In fact, our stance is the same as the Hotel's. I would like the media attention to be focused on my music, not on my private life. We'll publish a statement to say that I fainted due to exhaustion and have since recovered. We'll also say that we're grateful for the Hotel's professional response to the emergency situation and how well you've served the best interest of your guests.

"Later on, I'll start the promotion activities of my charity concert and recording for my album. Hopefully this will redirect the media attention back to my music, which was the intended focus of the function last night.

"With regards to the 'secret driving force' in my life, I'll openly confirm it's my mother and apologise for the misunderstanding."

Mr Pang nodded with approval of all the suggestions made.

"Hopefully these will be enough to guide the focus of their attention back to where we want it to be," concluded Sinyin.

"Mr Pang, do you have any suggestions or questions?" asked Chisau.

"What Miss Yan has proposed is very comprehensive, and should work well towards the outcome we're striving for here. Just one question, however: you have said previously your driving force is not a family member. If asked about it, how would you reply?"

That was true. It was this statement that got the speculation going in the first place. It's important that Sinyin had a believable answer.

"My relationship with my mother has not always been easy

to say the least. What child would love the one who drives her to work hard all the time with a rod of discipline? I hope you would understand my love-hate relationship with my mother. It was against my rebellious nature and my pride to acknowledge her role in my career in private, let alone in public. It was childish of me not to tell the truth in the first place and have subsequently caused the misunderstanding. The fact is my mother has been the driving force behind my music career, since I was little. Without her discipline, drive and planning, I would not have put in all the hours of practice necessary to get where I am today. She has always been the one who drives me to aim high and never to be satisfied but to demand a bit extra of myself in each performance. She's distilled in me professionalism and pride. I should right the record now and give her the credit that she deserves. Mr. Pang, does that answer it?"

"Oh, yes. There is no right or wrong answer in these things. As long as you're prepared with an answer so that you won't be caught off guard, this should be good enough."

"That's good. Let's hope together we can bring this matter to a close," said Miss Lau.

"Director, if there's no further business, let me go and handle this matter accordingly. The quicker we release a statement the better," suggested Mr Pang.

"Many thanks," Chisau answered.

After Mr Pang had taken his leave, Sinyin took the newspaper out of her bag and said, "Chisau, I have something to ask you."

"Ah?"

"It's about this person," Sinyin pointed Yuetching out from the picture. "Who's she?" Samyin sat up and was alarmed!

"She's one of our staff. Why?" Chisau was testing the waters, unsure where Sinyin's questions were going to head.

"She was a cleaner, wasn't she? She was the one who was injured in my room, right? How come she was a waitress at the banquet last night?"

"She's a floating employee, who works to fill in departments' short-term staff shortage. We are testing it as a new employment scheme," explained Chisau.

"Then why did she come to check on me last night at the hospital?" interrogated Sinyin. Samyin was surprised; he did not know Yuetching returned to the hospital after they had left.

"Why is she so interested in my business that I don't seem able to get rid of her? Who's she?" pushed Sinyin. Chisau did not know how to answer but Yuetching's identity could not be disclosed yet.

"The nurse at the hospital told us that she came to visit Sinyin," added Miss Lau. "If she's some kind of crazy fan who stalks, we have to heighten our security around Sinyin."

Samyin found this accusation ridiculous, and said, "You're implying that our hotel staff means harm to Sinyin?"

"She's a floating employee. That means she hasn't a stable job. How much do you know about her? Can you rule out this possibility? Can you establish the motive of her visit last night?" insisted Miss Lau.

Just when Chisau wanted to tell what happened last night in order to clear Yuetching's name, Samyin jumped in first, "I sent her to check on you. You can see here in the picture that I was pushing the crowd back for you to pass. I mentioned to her in passing, as she was standing close to me, that Miss Yan was our VIP, and we must ensure that she was well taken care of. That must have been why she went to check on you after work. Knowing that you were fine and in turn the Hotel had nothing to follow up on, she went home relieved. This is a very conscientious employee, who takes customer service personal. Not only are you not grateful, you even take her as a dangerous stalker!" protested Samyin.

Miss Lau and Sinyin were embarrassed.

"I'm really sorry," apologised Miss Lau.

"If this is the case, perhaps I should thank her myself for last night and apologise to her for injuring her hand earlier. What's her name?" suggested Sinyin.

Samyin and Chisau exchanged a look. Samyin tried to come up with something quick, "We'll pass on your sincere gratitude and apology to her. She's a mobile worker around the Hotel, so it'll take a while to locate her. Please be assured that we'll pass your message to her." The offer was music to Sinyin's ears as she had no interest in dealing with a worker of insignificance anyway.

"Then we entrust this matter in your capable hands," Sinyin happily accepted the offer, "and we shall go now."

"Please take good care and don't overwork," said Chisau, relieved.

"In the short term, I'll continue to stay in the Hotel suite. I've considered moving out but the service is so good here that I feel very at home. As I've been and will be busy, I have great inertia to move to something more permanent. Additionally, living in the midst of so many guests, I don't feel lonely. I also like the fact that you and Samyin come here to work everyday. I feel living very close to you – two friendly faces." For some reasons, Samyin found all the mentions of his name redundant to what she really wished to say; her interest was only in Chisau.

Unexpectedly, Chisau took this opportunity and turned the table round, "We of course welcome your stay. But the Hotel is a public place, with people coming in and out. As your fame soars, living in the Hotel may not be convenient for you and we will also struggle to provide the level of security that you may need. Although I am confident that the threat is not from our staff, Miss Lau's concern about your safety is not totally unfounded. If you cannot find time, perhaps you can delegate to your team to find a more suitable long-term accommodation for you. Please consider carefully how you may weigh up the pros and cons of your living arrangements. The Hotel would not wish any unhappy incident to materialise."

Irritated with Chisau who stealthily turned her notes of gratitude into a polite expulsion order, Sinyin snapped at him, "All right, I'll consider it." Then she walked out of his office abruptly to show her displeasure; Miss Lau followed.

When they were left alone, Samyin looked at Chisau with new found admiration of his skills. "How did you just turn defence into offence in a stroke? That was some brilliant manoeuvre!" he exclaimed.

Chisau was not amused; he was more concerned about Yuetching, "Which department is Yuetching working today? Please warn her to avoid Sinyin at all costs."

"I'll ask her to be careful. But why did she visit Sinyin last night?" Samyin wanted to find out the missing link.

"She saw that I was worried but it was inconvenient for me to visit her, so she rushed in to check on her for me. That was so that I could sleep, she said. Who would have thought that she would be recognised, and even seen as a dangerous stalker? Who would have foreseen development such as this?" Chisau exclaimed in disbelief.

"I see. Now I can see Granddad's wisdom in his advice."

"What advice?"

"That Yuetching should stay away from you! Look what trouble you've brought her!" exclaimed Samyin and Chisau protested to no avail.

Samyin said, "Yuetching has just finished her role with catering. Today she mans the Hotel booking line. You can ring her up, and instruct her yourself." Then he teased, "Yes, go ahead and explain to her how she has been mistaken as a crazy fan and a dangerous stalker!"

Samyin got up and walked towards the door, while Chisau prepared to call Yuetching. "However," continued Samyin while on his way out, "Sinyin lives here and Yuetching works here. Just how you are going to eliminate the chance of them bumping into each other, I don't know." Samyin stated a reality that Chisau did not want to confront.

6 A Life Almost Perfect

In keeping with her promise, Sinyin had been busy with frequent promotion activities and the preparation for her charity concert. The strategy seemed to have worked well to complement the public statements issued by the Hotel and her agent respectively. To everyone's relief, the media interest had been successfully switched from the romantic relationship to the mother-daughter relationship instead. Sinyin introduced her mother to the media who was overjoyed on hearing her public expression of gratitude towards her! The two made a great duo and captured the public imagination for a while. Her mother was open to interviews to recount how she nurtured her daughter into a rising star and quick to share parenting tips. She totally embraced the limelight!

During this period, Chisau hardly saw Yuetching as their life seemed to have gone completely out of synch. She set off for work earlier than he; when he came home from work, she was either asleep or was still working. Sometimes she even had to do night shifts and work on weekends; after all the catering industry is one that works round the clock. Yuetching helped him see first-hand how physically exhausting the ground work of the Hotel could be. The days when she was not working, she either kept Granddad company or went out on her own without telling anyone where. As she was used to living on her own, the need to communicate with others on her whereabouts did not come naturally to her. Chisau dared not ask too much in case she felt infringed. She agreed to move in with the family on the basis that they would be like housemates. After a while, however, he did begin to miss her presence. Life seemed a lot duller without the sunshine that she brought.

One day, Chisau was thinking about her while leaving the Hotel in his car. Not far from the Hotel, he saw Yuetching walking along the pavement as he drove past. Catching a rare glimpse of Yuetching made him feel excited, and he refused to let the moment pass. He braked harsh on the car and the screeching caught Yuetching's attention. She walked up to the car, and was greeted by Chisau, "Stranger, long time no see. Where are you heading?" Chisau could not stop smiling smugly.

"I've just finished a shift, and have no particular plan. Perhaps I'll go and watch a movie. Where are you going?"

Chisau was supposed to go out and deal with some Hotel business, but it was not urgent. He decided to delay the business and spend time with Yuetching instead.

"I'm going to see a movie too. Let's go together," suggested Chisau.

Yuetching looked doubtful, and hesitated, "You are not shirking, are you?"

"I can find time. I'm flexible," Chisau grinned.

"But Granddad has said that I should not –"

"If you don't get in quickly, then more people will see us! Jump in quickly."

Yuetching had no choice but to get into the car to cut short the public view. Just at that moment, Sinyin's car was passing, and she saw everything but not who the girl was! *Is he dating again?* Sinyin surmised that much. *Who is that girl?* She suspected that Chisau might not have been truthful with her. A rage rose up within her.

"What are we going to see?" Chisau asked excitedly like a little kid.

"What would you like to see?" Yuetching bounced the question back at Chisau, and added, "You may not like what I like to see."

"I don't mind. Today we follow what you want to do."

"What's so special about today? I intend to see a romantic comedy –"

"Then romantic comedy we're going to see," Chisau echoed.

"Ah?" Yuetching found him strange. "What's up with you

today?"

"Nothing." As Chisau was not himself today, Yuetching saw no points in arguing with him about the movie choice. She stared out of the window and her thought seemed to be miles away.

"Have you been very busy? Haven't seen you much lately," asked Chisau.

"Ah?" Yuetching was still thinking about something, so she answered simply, "Yes, a bit busy."

"What exactly are you thinking?"

"Some interesting questions."

"You don't intend to tell me?"

"I don't intend to tell you *now*, but you'll know soon enough."

"You're thinking about work again," Chisau deduced.

Yuetching smiled to confirm.

"Have you completed your work experience around the Hotel yet?"

"Nearly. As a matter of fact, I can start organising the materials and information gathered, and thinking about the structure of the proposal. When I have drafted the outline, I'll present it to you. Then you can identify what are worth further investigation and what not. But then you must ask the departments to cooperate, or any further work will be impossible. A better way actually is to put Samyin in charge of the report; then I can go round departments to collect information as his secretary."

Chisau laughed at her, "You've already worked it all out. There is no need to run past me!"

"You're teasing me; I'm not going to talk to you," said Yuetching sulkily.

Chisau sat through the romantic comedy, but he never quite understood the charms of this kind of movies on girls. He could not help but wonder what Yuetching was thinking when she was watching it. He was truly puzzled when Yuetching looked as if she were completely engrossed. When they walked out of the cinema, Yuetching looked relaxed and satisfied. Chisau was even more intrigued.

"Do you like watching romantic comedy very much?" Chisau could no longer hold back his curiosity.

"I can't say I like it *very much*, but I do enjoy watching one every now and again."

"If this is the genre you like most, you must be full of longings for love."

"Me?"

"Yes, you. Don't you have longings for love?"

"I haven't thought of that. I'm preparing for a life as a spinster. If I expect nothing, I won't be disappointed! It's precisely because I don't think I can find true love in real life that I try to experience it through romantic movies."

Suddenly Yuetching turned serious, and said, "There's no perfect love in real life. Perfect love only exists in fictions, so fictions you turn to if you want to know what perfect love is."

"That is your standard of *perfect love*?"

"I don't know but at least it's happy."

"Have you been hurt before? Why are you so pessimistic about love?"

Yuetching struggled to articulate; words could not form and ideas could not take shape but were swallowed back down. In the end she just sighed.

"If it's that painful, then don't talk," Chisau spoke tenderly.

"A lot of people," Yuetching lamented, "after seeing perfect love or a perfect life in movies, try to imitate in their real life. Perhaps life for some people is really perfect, but I don't know what perfect is because I feel I have never experienced it in my life; it's like chasing after the wind.

"Originally I also had a happy family, and parents who loved me. But in a flash, this scene of a perfect family vanished. Thereafter *guje* took me in. Her family should have been my extended family, but my cousins shut me out and ganged up on me. Even though we had a full house of people, I grew up in loneliness. At that time, I wished I had someone to show me a bit of love. Among all the people, *guje* treated me most kindly. But with four children of her own, she couldn't openly favour me or I'd have attracted the jealousy of my cousins. She could only be kind to me behind the scene.

"Even so, there was stability in our life, until when I was 12 years old, and *gujeung*'s (姑丈 meaning *guje*'s husband) business hit a crisis. Unable to turn it round, they were bankrupt and the family was wrecked to pieces. *Gujeung* never got over it. He turned to the bottle and was drunk all day long and everyday.

After his perfect life had been shattered, he failed to stand up again. Seeing this, *guje* went out to work to support the family. But it was very hard work for her to be the bread-winner as well as the parent at home. Inevitably we had to downsize. The family was gradually disintegrating. What is perfect if it never lasts? A sequence of shattered perfectness seems to be the pattern of life, always ugly, always heart-breaking.

"To stand up after you've been battered requires a lot of effort. After a few times, one couldn't help but feel a little tired. You don't dare hope, and begin to tell yourself that life can be perfect no more. When you're exhausted with the effort to get up after each time you've fallen, you don't want to hope for perfectness anymore in case it gets shattered again. Rather you compromise to stay low in an imperfect state; and if you're going to fall, it won't be as painful. In so doing, life is ironically cursed, as this attitude shuts out all good things that could've happened but were not given a chance to happen in one's life. Is it fair to self? I've lived through episodes of shattered perfectness not out of choice. But if as a response, I stop looking out for something better in life by choice, because I'm too afraid of the unknown, then it's cowardice, a negative attitude towards life. My mother died to bless me, not to curse me; I could not let her die in vain and turn away the blessing that I could have, could I? After struggling with my own thoughts, I've decided to be a tumbler, who would always spring back upright after being pushed down. Then at least my life will sing the song of human fortitude and be a bit fuller.

"In that spirit, I stepped out of my comfort zone and made a bid for a new life with my third family. Do you realise how much courage it took me in making that decision? It's always much easier to cling onto the known than taking on the unknown. I'm glad that it has paid off so far. I feel the warmth of a family, and enjoy a challenging job. Everyday there're new things to learn and to ponder over. I also have a boss who appreciates my effort, a friend who takes me out to play and an aunt who treats me like her own daughter. My life at the moment is almost perfect. But at the same time, at the back of my mind, I always ask – when will this shatter and under what circumstances? Now I don't fear this possibility anymore. I know what it'll be like when this happens, and I know from experience I've got what it takes to get up again. I tell myself, the perfect life now is like a bubble, and I should cherish every moment of it before it bursts for whatever reasons. Anything perfect is but momentary.

"My attitude towards love is the same. The only difference is that I have yet to go past the state when I shut out all possibilities. So right now, I have no longings for love." Yuetching was surprised how liberating it was to be able to pour out her heart contents freely!

Chisau's heart was stirred by sadness as he listened attentively to Yuetching. He halted his steps and stood in front of Yuetching. Trying to reassure her, he stated as firmly as he possibly could, "Your relationship with this family is *not* a bubble; under *no* circumstances will your perfect life now be no more. Once a family, always a family. No matter what happens in the future, I'll *always* be here as your big brother, who will listen to whatever you want to share, to cheer you on, and to give you my blessings – always. You are *not* alone anymore. Do you understand?"

Yuetching smiled, "What you say means a lot to me." She resumed her steps and Chisau followed by her side. "But, Chisau, life is unpredictable; not everything is within our control. For a lot of people, the goal of life is to tirelessly chase after and meticulously sustain a perfect life; but the focus of my life has always been on how to stand up after life-shattering events, how not to let myself be knocked down, and how not to let my inner soul rot. If we have the choice, we won't choose to have our perfect life shattered, will we? When that happens, we are often helpless; like my parents being snatched away and your father being snatched away, did we have a say? Only our response is within our control; some people can stand up again while others, like *gujeung*, fail to do so. But you can be sure that *I* will try my best to stand up if I fall again. This is why you don't need to mind too much what is or is not going to happen in the future, or to worry about me. Neither do you need to promise me anything. Let's just cherish the time we have together while it lasts; who knows what tomorrow will bring for us? You shouldn't overburden yourself."

Chisau had the desire to protect her for the rest of his life but would that also be a hollow promise one day? What could he guarantee? He was only human; he was limited. The death of his dad had made the frailty of life plain. *She was right: what could a mere mortal promise her?* He could respond only with a long silence.

To lighten up the atmosphere, Yuetching pulled Chisau away, suggesting, "Let's eat. I'm hungry now."

After they had settled down for dinner, Chisau observed, "Given your background, a positive attitude like yours can't be taken for granted. Where do your courage and enthusiasm come from?"

Yuetching paused from her food, and spoke solemnly, "From my mother, who died so that I may live. I'm not a saint; I too have my moments of despair! But as long as I remember my mother, I feel loved and my life precious. Does it sound strange to you if I say that my life is not my own? This is why I have self-respect, and try to live a life with my best effort. Even though my mother isn't beside me, I still want her to be proud of me. Even though she has left me since I was little, she has given me the greatest thing possible – my self-worth, which has kept me buoyant in life, urges me never to give up, and guides me at every crossroad. She'll forever point to the light; that's what she means to me. Deep in my heart, I'm not an orphan as in there I too harbour the undying love of my mother for me."

"Life is ironic sometimes. Even though you had little time with your mother, her influence on you goes deeper than many and is long-lasting. If she could hear you, I'm sure she would have been very proud and pleased."

"The least I can do for her is to cherish what she has saved," smiled Yuetching.

Chisau suddenly remembered something that he had been dying to ask, "Lately you've been out on you own a lot on your days off. Where do you go and what do you do?"

"Live sketching."

"Live sketching?"

Yuetching put down her chopsticks and bowl. From her bag, she took out her sketchbook and showed it to Chisau.

"Sketching is my hobby," explained Yuetching. "It's cheap and helps me observe people and the surroundings. It also calms me down when I have problems to solve. When I've nothing to do, or when I'm troubled, I'll go out to sketch."

"Then lately are you idle or troubled?" asked Chisau while flipping through the sketchbook.

"Lately it's because I'm curious," answered Yuetching.

"Curious about what?" Chisau looked up from her sketch book and asked.

"Samyin's passion."

"Samyin's passion?" Chisau was surprised.

"He talked to me passionately about buildings once as if they had characters. I'm curious about what he can see from buildings, so I've been going out to observe." Yuetching turned the pages in the sketchbook to where she started to sketch buildings. "From here," she said.

Chisau found Yuetching's perspective of the world in her sketches – solitary, quiet, humble, full of details and care.

"You only have this one sketchbook?" asked Chisau.

"Of course not. While other people keep a diary, I sketch. This is my chosen form of expression. Over the years, I've collected quite a few of them."

"Have you ever learnt how to draw?"

"Only in the art lessons at school."

"Why don't you draw people?"

"People move! They don't sit still for me to sketch! But when I sketch the scene, I watch people too. Like this one," Yuetching turned the page to explain, "this was a bench in a park. I remembered a little boy eating ice-cream with his mum, and how his face was all covered in chocolate! I also saw a wrinkly elderly resting from his walk around the park, with worries written all over his face. At another time the bench was occupied by a group of teenagers, eating their sandwiches with an unbelievable level of noise! While you see a static scene, I see a motion picture!"

Chisau was impressed; Yuetching never failed to give him pleasant surprises. He returned the sketchbook to her, who then put it away.

"You don't do anything with other people?"

"What do you mean?"

"I mean, do you ever ask your friends out to do things together?"

Yuetching shook her head.

"And no one ask you out to play either?"

"Do work socials count?"

"That means you seldom hang out with a friend like we do now?"

"Err…. Correct. What do you try to get at?"

"That means, if I'd like to do anything with you, I have to initiate while you won't?"

Yuetching looked away to ponder her answer, replying, "I suppose you're right; this is my default position."

Chisau nodded, "I see. If you have a companion, what would you like to do?"

Yuetching did not know an answer.

"How about – tennis?" Chisau suggested at random, "Can you play?"

"Not really. It was my favourite sport at school but I never knew my potential."

"Would you like to find out – I mean your potential in tennis?"

"I wouldn't mind having a go."

"This isn't difficult," muttered Chisau to himself.

"What?"

"Nothing. Let's eat up."

After dinner, they had a little stroll along the street.

"If you were not working at the Hotel, what would you be doing now?" probed Yuetching.

"By training I'm a material engineer."

"Do you like your profession?"

"Different compounds have different properties, and new compounds have new properties. From here, there are endless possibilities in improving our products, or even to invent new ones. Finding new solutions to the old problems is creative, so is finding solutions to new problems! I like that it moves the society forward."

"Like Samyin, you too have big dream!"

Chisau laughed, "Everyone can talk big a dream that has been given up! If I were really a material engineer, you might only get to hear my moans about the difficulties at work, cuts in research funding, the importance of commercial relevance in what we do, and so on. There are always discrepancies between ideals and reality. What's important is to do our best in whatever positions we find ourselves in. Now Samyin, you and I are all working at the Hotel. This makes us share a common goal, agree?"

"Do you like the work at the Hotel?"

"Actually I haven't asked myself this question. What I liked was irrelevant relative to the needs of the family at the time when I took it on. My main concern was not to do what I liked, but to do what I had to do to protect this family, to give them a bit of stability in the midst of their sorrow. My role out there in the workplace is not unique in that they can replace me in no time. But no one can replace my role in the family. When that role calls upon me, I don't think I have a choice. This may be the difference between Sinyin and me; and because of this difference, I can't have her level of success."

"To you, is responsibility very important?"

"This is not totally because of responsibility. This is a way to love people. If you love someone, you don't want to do something that will hurt them; if love has never inconvenienced you, you have never loved."

"Is loving people a burden then?"

For emphasis, Chisau paused in his footsteps, and Yuetching stopped too. "Yuetching, the opportunity to love and to be loved is a blessing, not a burden. Understand?" He resumed his steps and Yuetching kept pace with him. "In fact, working at Hotel gave me a surprise gain, which I had not anticipated. Getting into my dad's old shoes, and taking over what he had worked hard to build up with Granddad, has helped me see another side of my dad which I didn't see before as his son. Walking his footsteps has helped me know him and has unexpectedly helped me mourn. I may have given up my interest, but I've gained something quite precious. How're you going to weigh up the gains and losses? This is why I say we need to be flexible in facing the changes in life, and we should never lose that sense of wonders when we stumble upon some precious find. It's great to have big dreams, but it's equally important that we're patient."

These were meaningful words to Yuetching.

"Then will you stay at the Hotel forever?"

"Never say ever, right? Who knows what tomorrow will bring? That's why we need to be flexible! When Granddad passes away, his estate may be divided up. Then the management structure of the Hotel may be subject to drastic changes, and I might even be kicked out!" Chisau joked, but Yuetching took this possibility seriously. "Then I may go back to material engineering. Is this a blessing or an adversity?"

While Yuetching was still thinking, Chisau laughed at her, and said, "Stop thinking; let's go. It's late."

To Sinyin, this was a special day because she was going to have dinner with Chisau. That prospect put her in high spirits. She cancelled all her work schedule to rest so that she could look glowing; she must look her best in front of him.

She spent a lot of time getting ready. From her choice of outfit to her hairdo and makeup, everything was meticulously put together to perfection. She walked into the restaurant where Chisau was already waiting. He got up and pulled her chair for her. Her glamorous look was a little too dazzling for him, and her makeup was like a mask which he found fake. He would have much preferred her turning up in more day-to-day attire and make up.

"Thank you," said Sinyin courteously.

Sinyin presented her most charming smile, but Chisau was not besotted.

"What would you like to eat?" Chisau asked mechanically as a formality.

"Don't you know best what I like to eat?" Sinyin tried her best to reignite the sparks they used to share.

"That was in the past. People change, so does their taste."

"The favourite deep down in the heart will never change," affirmed Sinyin.

Chisau did not reply, but focused on the menu. When he was ready, he called the waiter over. Having taken Chisau's order, the waiter turned to Sinyin, and asked, "Miss Yan, what would you like?"

Sinyin thought that Chisau would take care of her order too. His icy attitude was disappointing. She stared at Chisau, who refused to respond. Waiter then suggested, "If Miss Yan cannot decide, would you like some recommendations?"

"There is no need. I'll have what he's having."

Waiter noted and left.

"In the past, you always rushed in to order for me. Guessing what I'd like was our game. Why aren't you participating in that game today?" Sinyin was feeling hurt.

"Sadly, I no longer possess that tacit understanding with you anymore."

"Is it because you *deliberately* try to forget?"

"You're a stranger to me."

"We can get it back; just give us a bit of time."

"I feel I hardly know who you are. I've never understood why you try so hard to restore a relationship that you've given

145

up."

"I've never given up this relationship. This ring," Sinyin raised her ring-bearing hand, and continued, "I wear everyday. The one who has given up on this relationship is you, not me."

"It may not be to you but to me, you left me without a word."

"Why couldn't you wait for me?"

Their waiter served up their soups.

There was silence as they drank their soups.

"What do you hope to get from me?" Chisau sighed, looking down at his soup.

"Our happy days in the past. I hope you'll continue to support me, share my success with me, and love me, just like before."

"In your world, it's all about *you*, isn't it?" Chisau expressed mournfully. "You could drop everything and left but you expect the life of others to pause and wait for you. We aren't even supposed to have any reaction!"

"I'm only asking for another chance. Is this request so repulsively unduly? If we've never tried, how do we know we can't get back to where we were? Do our happy days in the past mean nothing to you? Why are you so prepared to call it a day?"

Their waiter came to collect the empty dishes.

"There are certain things in life we can't walk backward to retrieve. In any personal relationship, we need to move forward together. If what's left between us is only our past, and there's no present and no future, doesn't it mean that this relationship belongs to the past?"

"Chisau, all right then, let's start from the beginning again, shall we?" Sinyin reached out to hold his hand across the table, but he withdrew it from her touch.

The waiter served up the main course.

"How did you spend your two years away? Did you meet any interesting people?" Chisau tried to talk to her normally as a friend.

"Those two years were dominated by practice, of course. What else could it be? Two years were actually a very short time and the programme was very intensive. It was tough to continuously challenge myself and make breakthroughs. But the effort has not been wasted. I've something to show for it at the end. That was about it. Everyday I thought of you, wished you were by my side, to encourage me and to comfort me. The people around me were all in the same boat, fighting for the same thing. That made us competitors. Those were lonely days. Even so, I asked myself never to give up, or I would have nothing and all the sacrifice would be in vain."

"Then you really have iron determination, very impressive," Chisau was genuine in his praise.

"Those days have passed, and I don't need to practise as intensively as I did. I can live a more normal life now. You can come back to me and share my life again. That will complete my life and make it perfect for me."

"I'm sincerely happy for your success. But there's distance between us now."

"Why? Is it because I have eclipsed you in fame and success?"

"Apart from yourself, can you see anyone or anything else?"

"What do you mean?"

"You've been back for so long, have you ever asked how I passed those two years? Have you asked what my dreams are for the future? Have you ever cared about my family and people who are part of my life? Have you ever considered what worries I may have? Has it ever occurred to you that your dream is not *our* dream? If the kind of life we're striving for is different, is there any foundation for us to get back together?" Chisau tried to lead Sinyin to arrive at his decision herself.

"But you supported me in my pursuit of music in the past. How can you say that my dream is not *our* dream? The difference between now and then is one thing – my fame and success, and you can't take it. Is that it?"

"It's true that from the beginning, I knew that violin was an important part of your life. What I didn't know, however, was that violin was your first love. When you dropped everything, and concealed your decision from me in fear that I might hinder you from pursuing your music career, you treated me as your *enemy* and not your love.

"How am I supposed to bounce back from that?

"I felt I was hated, but you call that love, ironically.

"At that time, you gave me up, no matter what you said or say.

"You have betrayed me, and how can I trust you again?

"You've assumed I'll wait for you; but have you ever asked

me?

"Have I agreed to it?

"It's not that I can't live with your success and fame.

"What I can't stand is how you're obsessed with your success and fame.

"It's not that I have *not* considered picking up from where we left off. But when I contemplated this possibility, my heart didn't leap with joy. Instead, it was filled with a sense of exhaustion; the truth is that I can't muster the strength to love you anymore."

Sinyin's heart rent and tears started to roll; those words could not have been plainer. She put down her cutlery, muttered tearfully, "You've asked me out today to list my wrongdoings?"

Chisau put down his knife and fork. He fetched his ring out from his pocket and presented it on the table. He announced to Sinyin, "I've asked you out to confirm a reality that has been for almost three years: our relationship has officially ended."

Heartbroken, she broke into a sob.

"You can't really say that you don't see it coming. This ring and yours are a pair. I don't mind if you would like to keep them as memento because I have no use of it," offered Chisau.

"These couple rings symbolise a promise," Sinyin snivelled.

"You have trampled on that promise as dirt."

"You're cruel."

"To give you a clean break is for your own good, so that you can move on."

"Have you got someone else in your life?"

"No, this isn't because of a third person. You haven't lost to anyone."

"I don't know you've learnt to lie. I – saw – you!"

"What did you see?" Chisau was baffled.

"A girl climbing into your car. Can you deny it?"

"It doesn't mean anything. I should know whether I'm in a relationship or not."

"You think this would be easier for me to take? Then you're wrong," roared Sinyin. "At least I still treasure what we had between us, unlike you." She grabbed Chisau's ring and stormed out.

Chisau felt terrible, so he left soon after without finishing his dinner either.

When he got home, he found Yuetching watching the news

in the lounge. She was surprised, asking, "Aren't you eating out? Why are you home so early?"

Chisau sat down beside her, and said, "We were only half way through the dinner and then I couldn't eat anymore."

Yuetching was even more puzzled, "Why? Have you got a tummy ache?"

Chisau laughed, and replied, "No. Tonight I asked Sinyin out for dinner to officially break up with her."

Wide-eyed in surprise, Yuetching speculated, "How did it go: angry or upset?"

"A bit of both, and additionally, I suppose wounded pride too."

"She left half way through?"

Chisau nodded, "She said I called her out to list her wrongdoings."

"You really did that? How dare you!" Yuetching could not imagine how this could go down with Sinyin without a storm.

"What could I do? I did try to explain my decision and hoped she arrived at it too," protested Chisau. Then he sighed, "Perhaps breaking up with someone is always ugly; no matter what you do, its unpleasant nature can't be glossed over."

"How're you feeling?"

"Terrible, of course. It's never fun to break someone's heart, no matter who this person is. I don't know if I could've been less blunt to dampen the blow. But no matter how I said it, it must be said! At least I've achieved a proper closure of this matter. I'm relieved."

"Hungry? Want something to eat?"

"What can we eat?"

"I don't know. I haven't cooked since I moved here. Let's go and see what we can find in the kitchen," invited Yuetching.

It was Yuetching's last day and last task of her work experience across the Hotel. Swimming pool was about to close and she was getting ready to clean it. When she walked into the pool area, it was all quiet. For a moment she thought there was no one there, and perhaps she could start cleaning. When she got closer, alas, to her horror, there was someone in the water, submerged. Without thinking, she jumped in and pulled the person above water. She was lifeless. She rushed her to the pool side, and, summoning all her strength, pulled her out of the water. She was unconscious. In a frenzy, Yuetching started CPR on her, while yelling, "HELP, SOMEBODY, call the ambulance NOW!"

She kept yelling until someone came and called the ambulance, while Yuetching never stopped performing CPR on the person she was trying to save. She yelled at her, "Don't die on me! Don't! Wake up! Please don't die. Come on." Tears were streaming down, as she started making association with how her parents drowned. She felt the fear of that little girl, her helplessness, her sadness and the tremendous sense of loss in the aftermath. Fear gripped her. She wasn't to witness another death in the same way; she wasn't to go through that terrible experience again. Back then she could do nothing to help; but now she could and she wasn't going to let her die.

Just when the ambulance was pulling up at the Hotel, Samyin and Chisau returned after a business function. They exchanged a look at each other and followed the paramedics in. They all rushed to the pool side, and the paramedics took over from Yuetching. Chisau and Samyin pushed through the crowd to see what had happened. They made their way to stand by Yuetching, who was shaking all over.

"You can't die! Please don't die! No, you mustn't die. Don't you know you mustn't die! Please don't do that to me AGAIN…" screamed Yuetching; she was hysterical.

At long last, Sinyin was revived, and Yuetching breathed a sigh of relief but then started to convulse herself. Chisau moved up to grab her and then she passed out.

In a Hotel suite, Yuetching was resting. Chisau called his mother, "Mum, I've sent the Hotel car to pick you up. I need you to come to the Hotel. It's an emergency. Please bring along a set of comfy clothes for Yuetching to change into."

Yuetching looked tense and anxious, even in her sleep. The paramedics said that she was in shock and needed rest; the symptoms should pass on their own accord. Chisau had dried her as much as possible before laying her down on the bed.

What's it? How could we ease your pain? Chisau asked himself.

There was a knock on the door. Chisau went to open the door for his mother.

"What's happened?" asked Puiyin with concern.

"Sinyin drowned in our pool tonight and Yuetching saved her. Then she passed out herself," briefed Chisau. He brought her to the bedroom where Yuetching was, and requested,

"Could you change her out of her wet clothes and dry her please?"

Mum nodded. Chisau went out of the room and closed the door behind him.

Having taken care of Yuetching, Puiyin came out and sat down beside Chisau.

"What's wrong with her?" inquired Puiyin.

"The paramedics checked her over and said that there wasn't anything wrong with her. She's most likely in shock; they asked if she had had some traumatic experience related to drowning. Her symptoms should pass on their own accord."

Silence ensued and sadness was astir in their hearts. They did not know what to say. It was the first time that they saw a violent physical manifestation of Yuetching's emotional scar from her childhood trauma. It was not something that they could help erase. She had been so strong and positive mentally that they felt guilty of forgetting how traumatised she must have been emotionally. This night, however, shattered this cosy view of her. Instead they caught a shocking glimpse of the monster that had been tormenting her for all these years, and were in turn awe-struck by how much she had to struggle with for all her life and how well she had overcome.

There was a knock on the door.

"Who could it be?" asked Puiyin.

"It's Samyin. He was with us tonight. I sent him to the hospital with Sinyin." Chisau got up and opened the door.

"Oh, Auntie, didn't expect you're here!" Samyin looked surprised.

"I called mum to come to change Yuetching out of the wet clothes."

"I see."

"How's Sinyin?"

"She's fine. She drank before she got into the pool. She was a whisker away from death tonight. Yuetching saved her, literally," reported Samyin.

"Reckless!" Chisau could not conceal his irritation.

"She was really lucky tonight," reiterated Samyin.

"Lucky?" scorned Chisau. "While she doesn't give a damn of what happens to her, others are trying hard to save her. This is crazy. What kind of a dumb person would drink and then get into a pool with no one around? Has she got an IQ of a three-year-old? Why is she doing this to herself when life seems going so well for her? Hasn't she got all she has ever wanted? Does that make any sense at all?"

"Wow! Calm down. Yes, she has everything except you, Chisau. You've just dumped her, remember? I know it's ridiculous, but I don't think she intended to kill herself. It was an accident and she wasn't thinking straight."

Chisau sank into the sofa, sulking, "At this rate, I won't be surprised she does get herself killed by *accident*."

"How's Yuetching? Can I go in to see her?" asked Samyin.

"She's resting. Yes, you can go in," answered Chisau. Then he turned to his mum and said, "Why don't you go home? I'll stay. Hotel chauffeur will drive you."

"Should I stay?"

"No, go home now and come back tomorrow."

"All right. Call me if you need me to bring anything."

Chisau slept on the couch overnight while Samyin turned up bright and early! He came into the room and woke Chisau up.

"What time is it?"

"7.30," answered Samyin.

Chisau sat up and stretched. He looked a bit stiff.

"Why didn't you call Housekeeping to make up an extra bed?" asked Samyin.

"Try to limit the exposure to protect Yuetching."

"Of course, I've overlooked that."

"The couch is a very decent bed, I have to say so myself."

"I should hope so, given that this is a suite to take up to four guests!" They laughed. "Let's check on her," suggested Samyin.

They pushed the bedroom door open and walked up to Yuetching, who was just beginning to wake up. She opened her eyes, and saw Samyin and Chisau staring at her. She had trouble recollecting where she was and why they were here. She tried to sit up, and felt her body aching all over.

Samyin helped her sit up, and she was beginning to remember the night before, hazily at first but getting clearer. Fear began to grip her again, as the scenes were replaying in her mind. Her heart was wrenched and pulsating. She curled up for comfort like a baby. It was like living in her worst nightmare. She screamed and she wailed, shaking her head hoping that she could shake it out of her head. It was a delayed reaction to her parents' drowning. When it happened, she was too young to understand, so she had never reacted to it. Sinyin's drowning was the trigger that brought it all to the surface.

She was overcome by hysteria. Fear engulfed her and the sadness was inconsolable. She sobbed uncontrollably. Her whole body was convulsing with tension. In between sobs, she called out, "Mum" and "Dad" in the most heart-rending way. Then Chisau and Samyin realised that she was mourning too, for she never had their graves as the focal point for her grief. They tried to calm her and comfort her the best they could. In the end, they decided that it might be best for her to let all the emotions out. But it was painful for them to watch, while they could do nothing. They had tears in their eyes, just by watching her. It was like tidal waves that had just burst through the embankment. How many years of suppressed emotions were they witnessing in one go? The relentless intensity and velocity was enough to wash anyone off his feet! Even though Puiyin arrived in the mid-morning, Chisau and Samyin were too concerned to leave.

Hours later, having exhausted Yuetching, the tidal waves ebbed. Her tears ran dry. She was not hysterical anymore. Instead, she felt unspeakable sadness weighing her down. She looked dazed and mournful. The happy, cheerful and sunny Yuetching whom they had known had vanished behind a grief-stricken face. That worried them.

Chisau went to the bathroom and wet a towel. He brought it to mum who sat on the bedside with her and gave her a good face wash to dry her tears and her nose, but she was not responding.

"Would you like something to eat?" suggested Chisau softly.

The thought of food made her nauseous. She rushed to the bathroom and vomited. Then she passed out again into Chisau's arms. After giving her some water and tucking her into bed to rest, they breathed a sigh of relief. They looked at each other and were still in shock how ill Yuetching had got.

Samyin turned to Chisau, and asked, "When your dad passed away, did you mourn and grieve properly?"

"What are you suggesting?"

"Just checking. This is scary," admitted Samyin.

"I wasn't five years old at the time! Let's eat something to keep our strength up," suggested Chisau.

"You two go; I'll stay with her," said Puiyin.

"Thank you. I'll bring you something to eat."

Between the three of them, they made sure that she was never left alone. Puiyin covered their office hours, while the boys took charge of the nightshift. On the third day they gathered again in Yuetching's room after work. When they walked in, Samyin and Chisau found Yuetching sitting up in bed and Puiyin was sitting on one side of the bed talking to her. Chisau sat down on the other side of the bed and inquired, "How're you feeling?"

"Better."

"Has this happened to you before?"

Yuetching shook her head.

"So you're as shocked as we are?"

Yuetching nodded.

"Do you understand what happened?"

"No, not scientifically, but by my first person account, I was reliving those moments, and felt all the emotions for real; everything came at once, if that makes sense to you. Flashbacks were like a machine gun firing non-stop and the power of those emotions they released in me was scary," Yuetching was trying her best to put her experience into words. "I never knew I was so sad and so frightened. I never realised how deep it had pierced and how painful it had been. What had been suppressed for years suddenly all erupted. To feel them all at once is overwhelming. My chest was tight as if I couldn't breathe. Perhaps subconsciously I was protecting myself that they had never surfaced until now. At least now I'm stronger to cope with them than when I was little."

"Have they all come out or are there more to come?"

Yuetching looked down and sighed, "I wish I know. I wish I could say it's over and done with and it won't happen again. But I realise I don't know myself what are there in my heart; I guess healing is a long process and calls for patience."

"Take your time, Yuetching. There is no need to rush," comforted Puiyin.

"Now, are you well enough to eat? You haven't eaten for 48 hours. Would you like us to take you somewhere nice to eat?" asked Chisau.

"No, a quiet meal at home is the best. Sorry to have troubled you all. It's embarrassing for you to see me in such a state. I'm sorry to have scared you."

"Don't be silly," said Puiyin. "We regret terribly that we were not there in the first place to pick you up when it actually happened, but we are glad that we are here this time to take care of you. It should be us to say sorry that you have suffered so much. Poor child," Puiyin held her hands, "Please don't suffer on your own but come to us." This got Yuetching all tearful again. In between sobs, she muttered, "Thank you; thank you so much." The thought that she was not alone anymore in this world was simply too overwhelming and comforting for her current fragile state of mind.

Samyin passed her a face towel, and said, "You can come to me too, you know. You're not alone anymore." He spoke her thought right there. She was choked by her own emotions that she could not speak anymore.

Chisau leant forward and wiped away her tears, and said, "Back then, you had no family; now you have a family and a friend. Remember that. Please don't feel embarrassed about it because home is where you convalesce and grow strong; it's your refuge. Are you ready to go home? Granddad will be happy to see you."

"Yes! I'd love to go – home!" Her heart was glad that there was somewhere she could truly call *home* and it sounded so sweet that it was like a dream.

Sinyin barged into Chisau's office in a rage. Miss Wei followed her, and apologised, "Sorry, Director, she was making a lot of noise and there is a conference going on, so I let her through –"

"It's all right, Miss Wei. I understand," said Chisau. Miss Wei left them alone.

Sinyin stood in front of Chisau and threw a newspaper in front of him. Chisau was familiar with the story, so he did not need to read it. Rather he gave her an inquisitive look, questioning the purpose of her visit.

"What am I going to do? Now they're speculating that I'm emotionally unstable and it was a failed suicide attempt."

"Can you say they're wrong?" asked Chisau sarcastically.

"What do you mean by that? Of course, I'm not emotionally unstable, and it was an accident. I did NOT attempt to kill myself."

"You call dipping into the pool after drinking heavily an accident? Anyway, call it what you want. What has it got to do with me?"

"Whoever called the ambulance is out to ruin me! Fire her!" Sinyin wanted a scapegoat.

"What?" Chisau was utterly astounded by her request. "Are you crazy?"

"Look what mess that stupid staff of yours has got me into! Do you know that they're probing into why I tried to drown myself? As a consequence of her reckless decision, she has ruined the reputation of your guest. This is gross misconduct. I say FIRE HER!" screamed Sinyin.

Chisau stood up and confronted her, "Are you out of your mind? You very nearly died. Do you realise that? Not only do you not thank her, you're now blaming her! Are you deluded?"

"Thanks to her, I've to face the backlash of her inept action regarding my personal life. Does she have any idea of who I am? She should have called a private doctor to the Hotel or something. She didn't need to send me to the hospital. Do you know how embarrassing it's for me?"

In disbelief, Chisau defended Yuetching with conviction, "Have you any idea how close to death you were? You haven't, have you? We had no idea why you drowned – you were unconscious! It could have been a hidden serious medical condition rather than just 'a little bit of alcohol'. And do you know how traumatised the person was after saving you from the brink of death? You don't, do you? Now you call her action that has saved your life 'inept'. This is however not an opinion shared by the paramedics. They said that thanks to her action, you're alive! In return, you're filing a complaint against her and want to get her fired? How absurd is that?! This is gross injustice!" Sinyin had never seen Chisau so cross before!

"Tell me once and for all," continued Chisau, "what's more important to you, your life or the public opinion? If you value your life, then you should go away and reflect upon your action. If you carry on with your reckless ways, blaming others for everything but yourself, it's a matter of time that you WILL kill yourself, I can assure you. Do you realise that you're on the course of self-destruction? Pull yourself together before IT'S TOO LATE! No one is responsible for your silly actions except YOURSELF," shouted Chisau back at her before storming out of his office.

Chisau signed Yuetching off for the rest of the week on sick leave. She returned to work in the following week for a fresh start at Samyin's office once more. As she approached her desk, she found Samyin was sitting in her chair. As soon as he saw her, he stood up and greeted her with excitement, "Welcome back."

Yuetching asked doubtfully, "Welcome? Why? It isn't my first day. Why are you so early this morning? Do you have some special schedule?"

Samyin stood aside and let Yuetching have her seat. He responded to Yuetching's questions one by one, "I welcome you back from your work experience. I'm glad that you resume being my secretary 'full-time'. Today I don't have any special schedule. I've come in early especially to welcome you, just like your first day here."

"Is this a bit over the top?" Yuetching was a bit overwhelmed by the attention.

"No, I miss you."

"You've been round nearly everyday to visit during my sick leave. How can you say you miss me?"

"I miss you at work," Samyin gave her a cheeky smile.

Yuetching frowned, "Please save this kind of wordings for other girls. No wonder why girls always misunderstand you."

"Can't you take what I say as sincere?"

Obediently Yuetching spent a few seconds contemplating this possibility, but she returned the same answer, "No."

"Don't you have any work to do? Why don't you go back to work? Let me take a look at your diary, and then I'll know if you've been slacking." Yuetching logged on and found Samyin's calendar. "What? It's blank everyday! Where's your schedule?" Yuetching demanded.

Samyin pointed at his head.

"That's hardly of any use to me."

"Well, they all come through as emails to me copied to you anyway. You should find them all there."

"Are you worse than what you used to? There are too many to sort through in this instance. You'd better spill out what you have stored in your head for me, so that I have a rough idea what's going on. Let's go into your office and work out your schedule for this week from your memory. I'll take notes." Yuetching grabbed her notebook and led him into his office.

Samyin started spelling out his schedule, while Yuetching

listened carefully and took notes. Everyday was packed. When he finished, Yuetching asked, "How come all of a sudden you're so exceptionally busy?"

"It's the peak season. That's why I don't even have time to keep my calendar up-to-date," Samyin tried to find an excuse to cover himself.

"Manager Chiu, according to your memory, you're about to have a meeting at nine. Are you prepared for it?"

"What do I need to prepare?"

"Do you ever prepare for meetings?"

"I just turn up normally."

"Where are the agenda and accompanying documents for the meeting? Have you read them?"

"They normally come through as emails. Sometimes they are backed up in paper copies too; it depends on the department and the size of files." He pointed to the pile of internal mails which were stacked up in one corner like a skyscraper. "The papers for this morning's papers may or may not be in that pile?" Samyin shrugged.

Yuetching was stunned, and did not know how to respond. She walked up to the pile and started searching for the needed documents, while asking, "Are they in any order like chronological order?"

"Err… they should be stacked up in the order of when they came in, yes!"

While she was busy searching through the pile, she was curious, "I begin to wonder how you could've gone without a secretary for so long. How *did* you cope without a secretary actually?"

"I coped in some form of orderly chaos," Samyin tried to find the best way to describe his way of working.

"What does *orderly chaos* even mean? I can't even imagine it," responded Yuetching. "It's an oxymoron."

"Putting documents in order is too tedious for me; I don't have the patience for that kind of mundane tasks," admitted Samyin.

"Found it," Yuetching was pleased with herself. "It's a miracle!" She put the envelope in Samyin's hand and instructed, "Here're the documents for the meeting in 45 minutes. Manager Chiu, please use the next 30 minutes to skimp through them before you go into the meeting. I'm going back to my desk and start logging your appointments in your calendar. Is that clear?" Yuetching left him to work.

Samyin turned up for the meeting and sat down next to Chisau. When Chisau saw the folder in his hand, he could not help but laugh. Samyin waved the folder in front of him, and stated simply, "Yuetching."

"Impressive," exclaimed Chisau.

"That's not all. She even forced me to read the documents for 30 minutes before I was allowed to come to the meeting!" whispered Samyin embarrassingly.

"Wow! She has found a way to tame a wild horse," teased Chisau. "It looks like she *really is* your secretary from now on, and not just pretends to be one."

"You see, she does get copied in nowadays."

Yuetching's wit made Chisau laugh.

Meanwhile back in Samyin's office, Yuetching spent the whole morning going through his emails, filling in his calendar and organising his documents. She derived a filing system which was clear and self-explanatory. Samyin had no more excuse for not knowing where things were. Suddenly, reception gave her a buzz, saying that Samyin had a visitor waiting in the office reception.

"But he isn't expecting any visitor," answered Yuetching. "Could you put her on the line please?"

"Sure, wait a minute." The receptionist called the visitor over to speak with Yuetching directly.

"Manager Chiu is in a meeting at the moment. He hasn't said that he's expecting a visitor. Would you mind telling me who you are?"

"Who are you?" the girl bounced the question back at Yuetching.

"I'm his secretary."

"No way, he does *not* hire secretary."

Hmmm…This person does know Samyin a bit, thought Yuetching. As Yuetching could not comment on this, she changed the subject, "Could I take a message?"

"What time does the meeting finish? Can I wait for him in his office?"

"Would you mind telling me your name and what business you have with Manager Chiu please?" Yuetching tried again to get some information out of her.

"It's personal matter and you don't have to know."

"If you don't tell me your name and why you're here, you won't be allowed in."

"Come on, I'm here to give him a surprise, that's all."

"Then tell me your name; what are you afraid of, unless you know he doesn't wish to see you? In that case, I'm calling Security."

"Okay, you win. Do Szeman (杜思曼)."

"Miss Do, Manager Chiu should be back in about 15 minutes. I'll let him know you're waiting for him at the Reception."

"You are not letting me in?"

"Not until Manager Chiu authorises your entry. I'm sorry."

After they had hung up, Yuetching texted Samyin: *Do Szeman is waiting for you at Reception.* Samyin saw the text after the meeting, and exclaimed, "Oh no!"

"What's the matter?" asked Chisau.

"Trouble ahead," said Samyin.

"What trouble?"

Samyin showed him the text.

"Let's get back to sort this out."

"I'm coming along," said Chisau.

"Where's she?" Samyin asked Yuetching back at the office.

"At office reception still."

"You've left her there waiting?"

"You haven't authorised her entry and you were not here."

"Please go and fetch her."

"Of course."

Yuetching brought Szeman to Samyin's office where he was waiting. As soon as Samyin was in sight, Szeman ran up and greeted him enthusiastically. "Samyin *gohgoh* (哥哥 an address for a male friend older than self)!"

"Hi. When did you return?"

"Yesterday. I'm eager to see you," she said. Then she pointed at Yuetching and asked, "What's happened here? Everything has become so formal! It's so difficult to see you! I thought I had to pass a security test before I could be admitted! Who's she?"

"She? She's my secretary. Why?"

"You said you didn't need one. What makes her so different from others including me? Why would you let her be your secretary and not anyone else?"

I'm out of here! Yuetching turned and headed back to her desk.

"Look, she's rude. What kind of attitude is that? How can she be your secretary? Fire her and hire me instead." Samyin buried his head in his palm!

Chisau followed Yuetching, who returned to her desk and collected her things.

"Where're you going?" Chisau was surprised.

"I've asked Granddad to come to the Hotel pool at this hour so that I can work his water exercise with him. The pool is least used in this hour. In this way, I can make some mundane exercise more fun for him."

"I was thinking of having lunch with you."

"If you have time, why don't you come along? Granddad will be happy to see you too. He's doing really well. He has regained 80 per cent of his mobility. You can encourage him too. After the exercise session, we may have 15 minutes to eat a sandwich. Are you interested?" Chisau agreed to tag along.

On her way out, Yuetching informed Samyin, "I'm off for lunch now; back in an hour." Samyin would rather go with them but he was detained!

When they arrived at the pool, Granddad was already waiting. Puiyin was sitting on the side watching. Yuetching quickly went to get changed while Chisau sat down next to his mum.

"You have free time today?" Puiyin was surprised to see Chisau.

"It's lunchtime. Arrangements made by Yuetching won't affect work," Chisau stated the obvious.

Yuetching came out in her swimsuit and got into the water with Granddad. She started assisting him in the exercise routine, while Chisau and Puiyin watched on.

"It's difficult to find a girl like her nowadays. She is so –" Puiyin paused to find the word, "so magnanimous in her soul, isn't she? She has a big heart to forgive, which is not easy. In her interaction with others, she's genuine without pretence; everything comes from her heart too. She always thinks of others before herself, and never minds inconveniencing herself for others. Today's arrangement was also her initiative, and got *loye* so excited that he behaved like a little kid waiting eagerly for his outing. Yuetching has this wonderful gift of seeing through

161

people and calming people. A mundane and tedious task in her hands will magically transform into something interesting, even exciting, driving out all the initial reluctance to face the task. I don't know what it is but it was as if she had magical hands which could iron out all the roughness of a surface, or like a moisturiser, she could soften out all the harshness of life. She brings a sense of peace and harmony into people's life. This is her beauty."

"Mum, you see through her too," commented Chisau. Yuetching's care for other people was second to none and had a sharp perception about others that nothing could escape her attention. Perhaps it reflected the years she had spent in observing people. Often she would pick up details that had been overlooked by him. She would apply her usual careful consideration for others over those details, and then a scheme would effortlessly spring to mind on how it could be made easier for others. If it was within her ability, she would proactively implement it to improve other people's life. She never needed to be asked. Watching how she patiently worked with Granddad in the water, Chisau knew he could not have done it. Perhaps this was the soft touch of a female.

After the session was completed, Yuetching helped Granddad out of the water. Puiyin took over and walked him to the changing room.

"Are we ready to go now?" asked Chisau.

Yuetching gave him a mischievous smile, and replied, "No, not yet." Then she returned to the water and did ten laps at thundering speed with all four styles. Wide-eyed in astonishment, Chisau never knew Yuetching swam like a champion!

Yuetching leapt out of water, panting, "I'll be very quick!"

After changing, they went to the rooftop garden reserved for staff use to have their sandwiches.

"You know, this is a very nice space you have given your staff. During my work experience, when I was a little tired and would like a break from people, I came here to be alone. Often I was not disturbed."

"Does it mean that it's grossly underused if no one comes?"

"Well, if you ask me, it's a very nice goodwill gesture that the Management is willing to plough back resources for their welfare. It's an investment. Whose idea was this?"

"Samyin's. It's among the first things he did when he took

up the post. He saw the whole project through from concept to finish."

"He designed this!" Yuetching was impressed.

"Yes. It was truly a wasted space of concrete before he turned it into a secluded charming recreational area. It's his little pet project that he could put his architectural skills to use."

"Wow! He sees potential of a space that we can't see."

"Yes, that's his gift."

Yuetching was reminded of Samyin's dream, which was *to make visible the space that people cannot see, and to continuously discover for them new angles to appreciate the beauty of this world.* "He surely has done it with this space," she muttered to herself.

Chisau was most impressed by Yuetching's swimming skills, so he suggested innocently, "I only know today that you swim like a professional. You must have been in the school team and won a lot of trophies!"

Stunned by how far off this was from reality, Yuetching sighed, "Sorry, but is the world of the affluent really that perfect all the time? At school, was everything really that rosy and fair? Were you never boycotted, rejected, excluded, discriminated, insulted, ridiculed, scoffed at or made fun of? This is unreal." Yuetching then told him the truth, "When I was at school, I could not swim at all. I was afraid of water. Don't you remember my parents were drowned?"

Chisau suddenly realised how naïve he was to assume. "This makes it even more incredible! How come you could swim so well now?"

"Swimming was something I used to train myself for overcoming my psychological hindrances in life," Yuetching stated matter-of-factly.

Chisau was intrigued, and wanted to know more, "Please continue."

Yuetching then expounded for him, "I left home at the age of 16. Where did the courage come from? Did you seriously think that I was fearless? I was very afraid; I lived in a state of fear. I preached to myself: I could decide to live a life like this, in fear, in cowardice, in timidity; or I must find a way to stand up, and overcome the fear that was debilitating me. I decided what I had to do was to train my courage. Then I asked myself, what was the one thing that I feared most, and couldn't imagine I would ever do in my life? The answer was swimming. I feared water and I did not swim. Then I confronted my fear head on. I went to the swimming pool, getting in and out of the water at first. When I was comfortable with that, I progressed to putting my head under the water. When I stopped panicking in water, I enrolled myself on a swimming course. In between classes, I practised on my own three times a week. After three years, I told myself I had passed the test I set myself; I had achieved my goal. I kept swimming until I graduated from uni. I don't swim as much now, but every time I swim, there's still a thrill rising within me. That I can swim freely reminds me of the courage I had to overcome my worst fear! That taste of victory is always sweet!" Yuetching was excited just by recalling the experience. It was as if she had been to the fiercest battlefield and came back triumphant.

Chisau was in awe and could not find words to say. Nothing in life was simple with Yuetching. Everything had a moving story behind. Compared with what she had been through, his worries were like storms in a teacup.

"While at uni, I even took a lifeguard course; I thought I couldn't save my parents, but I hoped I could save others," added Yuetching melancholily.

"And you saved Sinyin," stated Chisau solemnly.

"I would have saved anybody; life's precious. If you have to die, die fighting, not over a silly mistake like that. This is what I think."

"Had you saved anyone before Sinyin?"

"No, I had been on lifeguard duty before but she was the first person I saved from water."

"And that triggered your reaction."

Thinking that Sinyin worried about the backlash in public opinion more than her life, Chisau marvelled at the polar extremes that the cares of these two girls represented. He was silenced by the solemnity as well as the irony of life.

"What's the matter? Are you upset because I called you 'the affluent'?"

"No, not at all. All that you've said is true. I admire your fortitude and perseverance. In this respect, I can't compare with you and feel a little ashamed of myself."

"No need to be ashamed. You haven't met those circumstances in life that test your fortitude and perseverance; you have no need to pluck up *my* kind of courage yet. One day if you meet with circumstances that call forth your fortitude, which you fail to summon, *then and only then* are you entitled to be ashamed of yourself."

Chisau smiled, "Your ability to lift people's spirits is simply amazing."

Noting the time, Yuetching hurried, "We've talked too much! We better hurry!"

Feeling threatened, Szeman turned protective towards Samyin against Yuetching. Under the pretext of an internship, she gained a temporary pass to the office. Her aim was to shadow Samyin. Instinctively Szeman treated her as an enemy with distrust and there was no room for civility. She sought to prove her ability as Samyin's secretary, and interfered with the running of the office without an official position. Her intention was to make Yuetching redundant and for Samyin to offer her the post instead! Yuetching never had a peaceful day when she was around. She welcomed the little openings when Samyin was out of the office and Szeman took a break from coming into the office. She enjoyed the peace when she was alone in the office and worked efficiently to make up for the lost time. The permanent presence of Szeman had successfully changed the dynamics between Samyin and Yuetching. Yuetching tried to avoid them as much as possible and spoke to Samyin only when she absolutely had to on business matters. There was no more joking around or small talks. It did not take long before Samyin felt that Yuetching was miles away even though she was working side by side with him. He felt trapped.

Samyin had to act proactively to get away. He came out of the office, and suggested, "Let's go and find Chisau for lunch together."

Yuetching doubted, "Can you really?"

At this moment, Szeman came back from the restroom. Witnessing that Samyin was chatting with Yuetching, she came quickly between them, asking, "Where are we lunching today?"

Yuetching did not need to see a display of affection, so she turned back to face her computer screen.

"We're having a regular lunchtime meeting; it's confidential and you can't follow me."

"But it isn't on your schedule for today," Szeman had studied Samyin's calendar and remembered everything on it even better than Samyin himself! "Are you lying to me?" protested Szeman.

"There's no need to make note of something that is *regular*, is there?" Samyin turned to Yuetching, and commanded, "Let's go."

"Why can she go then?" Szeman was still protesting.

"She's my secretary, and a Hotel staff, while you are *not*," Samyin turned to Yuetching, and called, "Let's go."

Chisau, Samyin and Yuetching met up for lunch but no one spoke.

"What's happened between the two of you?" asked Chisau, sensing the awkward atmosphere.

"I'm enjoying some peace and quiet over my lunch hour," said Yuetching.

"She's angry at me," complained Samyin.

"Who has got time to be angry at you?" Yuetching denied.

"How can you say you are not when you're either not talking to me or trying to avoid me?"

"I'm not avoiding you but Miss Do. At the moment, you two are like Siamese twins; what am I supposed to do?"

"Please don't be angry at me," begged Samyin.

Decided to take this opportunity to speak up, Yuetching put down her cutlery and began, "As a matter of fact, I shouldn't have had an opinion on my boss's business. But if you must, then yes I'm angry at you. You're my boss; how could you let some random, idle person, who has nothing better to do than stalk you, come to the office all day long? If she really is an intern of the Hotel, then assign her to some proper work to do and don't waste her time. But if she is not, she shouldn't be around. What's she even doing here? We can't even talk about work without interruptions. She's distracting, making me unable to focus. This is exceedingly annoying. You're my boss, so you're responsible for handling this matter and finding a solution to ensure your subordinate can work to the best of her capability! Furthermore, private matters should stay between the two of you. Do you think you have contravened the common decorum of a workplace?" It was the first time that Chisau was made aware of Yuetching's grievances.

"On this matter, I'm passive. I've asked her not to come but she wouldn't listen. What am I to do?"

"This is just feeble. I'd like to see my boss exercising his authority to foster professionalism in the workplace. If you can't ask her nicely, then you have to take a tougher line. This is a workplace, not a playground. When would you let her grow up? If her parents don't discipline her, you, as a friend older than she, should teach her. Who's Do Szeman to you anyway? How come she has you wrapped around her finger?"

"She's the only daughter of an uncle, who has been a long-term friend of my dad. The request for the internship came to me through her dad, so it was difficult not to grant it. You can say that Szeman and I have known each other since the day she was born! One day I found her crying, and didn't know what to do. In the end, I bought her an ice-cream cone to make her smile again. Since that day, she has been following me around and kept saying that she's to marry me when she grows up. I've heard this for years and never taken it seriously. I thought it was just a harmless game that girls played in their imagination, and they would soon grow out of it. I've never thought she meant it, until lately when she does seem to behave as if we had a relationship."

"I've told you not to be so attentive to every girl. See that you've caused some confusion and brought on trouble," commented Chisau.

"This is hardly helpful, Chisau. I was only a child at the time when I bought her an ice-cream!" Samyin defended himself.

Yuetching had a different view, "I don't think this is where the problem lies. The problem is in your readiness to please everyone or in your unwillingness to confront. Correct me if I'm wrong, I say deep down you enjoy your popularity among girls and the attention that you get from them. You're flattered, aren't you? You don't want it to end but perpetuate it consciously or subconsciously. This is your vanity. But you can't try to please others in every single matter, not only for your own sake but for others' as well, especially when it comes to relationship. Look how many years you've wasted Miss Do in cultivating her love for you! How old was she when you bought her that fateful ice-cream cone?"

"Seven."

Yuetching shook her head to show her disapproval, "If you don't like her in this way, don't you think it's time you made it crystal clear to her? From a certain angle, she's the victim of this situation. You're older than she, so you should know better and the blame is on you for stringing her along. If she can't think rationally for herself, you should have guided her to protect herself and you should have been more decisive in ending her false hope."

Samyin felt exposed.

"Samyin, Yuetching has a point. Both as a boss and as an older friend to Szeman, you have the responsibility to make clear to Szeman that she can't keep coming to the office for no reason. You'd sort it out or I'd have to intervene. On the matter of your relationship with her, you're also obliged to make your stance clear to her so that she can move on," Chisau instructed.

"Yes, what can I say? I have no defence."

"Then I'll leave the matter with you and trust that you'll handle it properly. Let's change subject. Yuetching, are you free after work today? Shall we go and play tennis together?"

Yuetching was baffled at this sudden invitation. "Why?"

"Haven't you said that you wouldn't mind finding out your potential in tennis?"

"Yes, I've said that before, but I'm not prepared today."

"Don't worry. All gears are available from the Hotel."

"Are you kidding me? Do you know how expensive those shops are?!"

"I – no – it's Miss Wei has already prepared your tennis gears. Come to my office before you leave to pick them up."

"I'm coming along too," Samyin invited himself.

"You certainly are *not* coming along. If you come along, it means that Miss Do is coming too. Until you sort this out, you are not coming along to anything I do after work!"

"Look how fierce she is!"

Chisau agreed, "We better be careful in choosing our girlfriends or she would avoid us!"

"I don't mind whoever you go out with as long as you keep me out of the murky waters of love!"

"Looks like you couldn't delay this urgent business of having a proper talk with Szeman," concluded Chisau.

After work, Yuetching went to Chisau's office.

"Hi, I'm here. Where are we going?"

"The tennis club. The address is being sent to your phone right this instant." Chisau was tapping away on his phone as he was talking. When he's done, he handed her the bag that Miss

Wei had prepared. "Here is everything you need."

"Thank you. I'll meet you there."

"Wait. I've something else to give to you."

Yuetching was surprised, "What's the occasion?"

"Gifts are not reserved for special occasions! I think that this present really suits you, so I've bought it for you. Open it and see if you like it."

Yuetching unwrapped the present and out came a palm-sized camera. She was puzzled, "Is there any special meaning behind this?"

"My wish is that from this day onwards, you'll start collecting happy memories of your life, adding colours and people to your once lonely, monocoloured world as captured in the pages of your sketchbooks."

Yuetching understood what he meant.

"Genetically, girls are able to see more nuances of colours than boys. Use that gift to explore your world and tell its story or your story. It's all set up and ready to use," added Chisau.

Yuetching did not own a camera because she did not wish to hold on to anything or anyone. She fumbled this new toy in her hand and quickly snapped a shot of Chisau before he could respond. "Then my first coloured image of a person in my memory should be you," responded Yuetching with her usual cheekiness. "Thank you very much for the present. I like it very much – or rather the meaning of it."

Chisau beamed with pleasure.

"I should get going now." Yuetching set off on her own.

Meanwhile, Sinyin was meeting the reporters at the Hotel. Across the foyer, she caught sight of Yuetching walking past, all smartened up. *Who's that girl?* Sinyin was suspicious. *Why do I keep seeing her around? I must find out somehow.*

On the sound of her pulling her chair, Samyin came out of his office and greeted her, "Good morning." Yuetching jumped at his greeting, and said, "You scare me!"

"Sorry, I don't mean to. How was tennis yesterday?"

Yuetching laughed at herself, "I was terrible, and missed most of the balls. I was worried that Chisau would be bored but he said it was very entertaining for him. He suggests making this a weekly event and he can train me. I've heard that you're very good at tennis and that you represented the school and were even a prize-winner. I dare not play against you!" Yet Samyin's attention was elsewhere, which Yuetching did not miss. She asked, "What's wrong?"

"Last night, I made it clear to Szeman as you told me to."

"You mean the end of her puppy love? How did it go?"

"She cried. I hope she's all right. I've told her she can't keep coming here."

"Does she have anybody to console her?"

"She must have. I had to drive her home last night and met the parents. I had to explain to them one more time what had happened, why their daughter was distraught."

"Can they accept it?"

"Better than Szeman can, although they quite like us being an item. Thinking about it, it's unfair on me. I've never gone out with her but have to go through the unpleasant experience of breaking up with her, and being treated as if I were the villain. I believe she's not going to come today."

"Who says so?" Szeman approached the office, and asked, "Who's she anyway that you have to report to her of our business? Is she really *just* a secretary?"

"Szeman?" both Yuetching and Samyin were surprised to see her.

"Yesterday only you talked; today it's my turn to do the talking. Follow me to your office." Szeman pulled Samyin inside – she was assertive!

Yuetching reminded, "Manager Chiu, your first meeting at 9 o'clock."

"Thank you," acknowledged Samyin. Yuetching sighed and thought to herself: this business of love was really complicated!

Szeman closed the door, and began in a serious tone, "Yesterday you basically said that we had never started, that you had always seen me as your younger sister, and that I had mistaken. You also said that you had to be clear with me so that you would not waste my time. This morning I come to tell you that although we have never started, we can start from today."

That was an unexpected turn of events and Samyin had not prepared what to say! Szeman continued, "Given our age gap, I accept that you have never looked at me as a potential girlfriend. But I've grown up, and I'm not that little girl in your memory anymore. If you would look at me in the new light, how can you say that there's no possibility between us? Yes, you're right, I

170

was childish for coming into your office – I shouldn't have and I won't do it again. We should meet each other as adults now, rather than living in our puppy love, and I'll behave more maturely."

"Szeman, please don't."

"Not even a few dates?"

"Nothing will happen between us," Samyin affirmed calmly.

"I won't give up until you give me a reason why we're impossible,' declared Szeman. Raising her voice, she demanded, "I'm confessing to you. What's your reply?"

Yuetching could vaguely hear her through the door now.

"Szeman, please don't. I don't deserve your love."

"This is my decision, not yours, to make," Szeman was determined.

"It's impossible for us," said Samyin truthfully.

"Why? Why? Why –"

"– Because I'm already in love with someone else," slipped Samyin. Yuetching was surprised to hear that confession.

Szeman demanded, "Who's she?" Yuetching was asking the same question too. "At least you've to let me know whom I've lost to!"

Suddenly, the door was thrust open. Szeman rushed out and pointed at Yuetching, "It's she, isn't it? It's she!"

Yuetching stood up and was in total shock. Szeman walked round and pulled her out from behind her desk. Samyin went over to loosen Szeman's grip on Yuetching's wrist. Szeman asked again, "It's she, isn't it? Yes or no; why can't you give me a direct answer?" Samyin found himself unable to answer; Yuetching stood motionless, wide-eyed in bewilderment and terror.

"So it's a yes by consent. Right from the beginning, I've known that she isn't just a secretary. What's so good about her? TELL ME. How can she compare with our history together? We grew up together! For all my life, I've been dreaming about our wedding day…"

Tears rolled down in her rage.

"Please calm down."

"You ask me to calm down? I ask you to wake up! Are you a fool?" Szeman raised Yuetching's wrist in her grip. "At least, you have known me and I won't scheme against you. It wouldn't have hurt so much if I lose you to someone more respectable than her – sneaky, dubious and suspicious. She never talks about her family or friends as if she were an island. She is uptight, gloomy and unfriendly. She has no past, no background as if she came from nowhere. She is secretive. She has much to hide. No matter how she dresses up, she is coarse and has no taste. She is not the person she pretends to be. She is awkward in every way as if she were learning to be someone else whom she was not. Standing next to you, you just show her up! She doesn't fit in here, even as your secretary! How can you not be suspicious of her or are you too much in love to notice? How can you be sure she is not a gold-digger? Call it a female instinct. Seeing that you are bewitched by her, I hang around here to protect you from her. I'm collecting evidence that she is bad news, so that you would believe me and fire her. Then I would leave you in peace or you may hire me instead. But it doesn't matter, what matters is that I don't want to see you walk into a snare and get hurt. Whether you like me or not, I don't regret protecting you because you've been like a big brother to me and have been looking out for me. For that, I would do for you this much. Is that how you are to thank me: turn me out and trust her instead? Is this not an insult or what?"

Samyin separated them and shouted at Szeman, "ENOUGH! You have said QUITE ENOUGH! Now leave!"

"What?" Szeman, looking hurt, could not believe what she heard. "You still ask me to leave, when it should be her to pack up? You would rather believe her than me? Okay, okay. If you are such a fool, then perhaps you really don't deserve my love for you. Don't say that I haven't warned you!" Szeman pulled her pass off her neck and slammed it on Yuetching's desk. In her rage, she swept everything on the desk to the floor before storming out. At that precise moment, Chisau walked into the warzone, startled by the scene.

Samyin turned to Yuetching, who was stunned and confused by the reflection Szeman painted of her. *This is how people perceive me?* She looked at Chisau and Samyin before her, utterly embarrassed that she would like the ground to open up and swallow her. *I can never be someone whom I am not! What am I doing here? Whom am I kidding?* She too stormed off. Samyin went after her, and Chisau followed behind, asking, "What's just happened?"

Yuetching went to the rooftop garden for a bit of fresh air to cool her head and the boys followed. Samyin went up to her, and begged for forgiveness, but Yuetching was quite shaken by the revelation and the seed of self-doubt in this new environment took root.

"What am I doing here? Whom am I kidding? WHO AM I?" muttered Yuetching.

Chisau was in the dark, "What has just happened? What has been said?"

Samyin had no time to fill him in. "I'm sorry. Please don't take what she said seriously. She has no idea of the arrangements or your background. It doesn't matter that to others you seem secretive, as we know all your secrets. One day they will know your true identity. We just need to be patient."

"I'm a gold-digger..." muttered Yuetching, "Is that what people think of me? Why wouldn't they? Can I blame them?"

"What have you done to her?" Chisau asked Samyin, getting more concerned.

Samyin didn't know how to explain. His focus was still on Yuetching.

"I have no idea what she was doing, you have to trust me. I'm truly sorry."

"And why did you lie?"

"I didn't."

She turned to face him. "There isn't you-and-me."

"It's her assumption, not my lie."

"But you did *not* deny it! You lied by consenting to her assumption."

Samyin had no reply.

"Don't talk to me this week," Yuetching walked away upset and distraught.

"You let Szeman conveniently mistake you and Yuetching as an item in order to get rid of her, and she vented her anger on her and insulted her? Is that what's just happened?" Chisau tried to piece things together.

"I can't vindicate myself."

"What exactly did she say about Yuetching? She's quite shaken by it."

"I'm sorry; what she said was unforgiveable."

"I don't want to see you either; don't come to my birthday celebration." Chisau walked off in fury.

Samyin was left standing alone, his heart beating fast. Szeman had accidentally exposed his feelings for Yuetching to himself, and he did not know what to do or say. Instead of being a lie, it was actually an emerging truth. When confronted, he realised that he did not wish to distance himself from Yuetching for anyone. This feeling took him by surprise. His heart fluttered with excitement, and his head could not stay cool. He did not understand what this feeling was! What was he to do now? At the same time, it grieved him that he got Yuetching hurt. He saw that she was fragile in their world and made him want to protect her all the more. What a mess he was in with both of them! How he was going to mend the relationships he did not know yet. What he knew was that this love for Yuetching was totally unfamiliar to him.

After dinner, Yuetching got herself busy in the kitchen. Chisau was curious, and inquired, "What're you doing? Haven't you had enough for dinner?"

Yuetching laughed, "How could that be possible? Of course I've had enough for dinner. Tomorrow's your birthday and I'm making you a cake."

Chisau was pleasantly surprised.

"But don't expect too much," added Yuetching, "I made this cake base last night and I'm decorating it now. If it goes wrong, I'll buy you one tomorrow."

Chisau made himself comfortable in the kitchen.

"What are you doing?" asked Yuetching.

"To keep you company."

"All right. It's up to you."

Chisau watched Yuetching focus on the task in hand, wondering how she could put 100 per cent enthusiasm into everything she did.

"Are you really going to ban Samyin from your gathering tomorrow? Is it necessary to punish him like that? Please don't ban him for my sake," said Yuetching while whipping the frosting in the mixing bowl.

"Has your relationship with him returned to normal yet? If you're still angry at him, then he's not allowed to come. On this matter, I'm on your side."

"Chisau, he's your best friend, and it's your birthday. Please don't mind me."

"I don't like how he treats you. If you don't want to see him, then he can't come." Yuetching felt cosily warm under his wings. Feeling protected and sheltered from the storm outside, she was moved by how he stood in front of her and fought for her best interest without her even lifting a finger or uttering a word herself. Until now, there had been no one on her side and she had never believed that anyone would be willing to take up that position of being her advocate in life. *Is this what being a family mean?* She pondered.

"Seeing his gloomy face, I feel sorry for him," she noted.

"Has he managed not to talk to you?" Chisau was curious.

"In the past three days, he didn't even approach me, let alone talk with me! He behaves as though he was ashamed of himself, looking very guilty."

"He must be feeling pretty rotten; serve him right! In fact, what did Szeman say actually?" Seeing her pensive look, he surmised, "It's still affecting you, isn't it?"

She resumed whipping her frosting. Slowly she recollected, "She said: I'm awkward in every way as if I were learning to be someone else whom I was not. She's right, isn't she? This is what I'm doing, learning to be someone else?" She muttered as if to herself thoughtfully. "She also said: I have no taste and standing against Samyin just shows me up that I don't fit in here. Right again, isn't she? I'm coarse and have no taste, so why am I hanging out with all these stylish people? She calls me a gold-digger, up to no good. It's only natural she's come to this conclusion; can I blame her?"

"Has it been playing on your mind?"

"A little. She said all her action was to safeguard Samyin from falling into my trap. Whether he liked her or not, she would do that much as his little sister. It's really quite laudable of her! She has her logic and her affection for Samyin is purer than we've assumed."

"So Szeman has vindicated herself in your sight?"

"You can say that."

"Are you upset?"

"Well, it does make me self-conscious, but I still manage at work. From where you have put me, I have the flexibility to have as much or as little interaction with others as I want to. Samyin is pretty understanding."

"Why aren't you running back to your old life?"

Yuetching looked up and simply stated, "I'm finding myself and I want to find her. If I run back at my first hurdle, I'll never know whom I could be, will I? This is a pretty good reason to stay, for now at least."

"How about the lie that Samyin told about you and him as an easy way out of the sticky situation? Do you feel wronged?"

"At the time when he did not deny it, I felt I was used. Now looking at how different our worlds are, the impossibility between us makes the whole notion farcical. A joke is to make us laugh, not angry!"

"You're ready to forgive him?"

"So should you be."

"All right! I'm glad."

Working with the cake on its rotating stand, Yuetching looked like a true professional to Chisau. After she had finished frosting the cake, she said, "I've prepared a present for you, but I don't want you to open it in front of others. Should I give it to you now so that you can open it in private?"

"What's the present that you can't let others know? I'm intrigued!"

"Other people may not see the meaning behind it. My present's nothing expensive; its value is in what it represents. I hope you would like it. I'll go and fetch it for you now."

Yuetching returned to the kitchen with the present in her hands.

"Here it is. Happy Birthday! Hope you like it."

Chisau gladly received it, and asked, "Can I open it in front of you then?"

"It's your birthday present, so it's your decision."

Yuetching went back to her cake, and started cutting up some fruits.

"Then I'm going to open it now." Chisau unwrapped the present and revealed a portrait of him. It was unexpected! When did Yuetching draw him?

"This?"

"You were the first person I sketched. My technique isn't good; hope you won't mind. I don't want people to see it in case they'll laugh at me."

"You said that this present had a meaning behind it. What's it?"

Yuetching straightened up and solemnly declared,

"Remember the first photo I took with your camera? This portrait is a copy of that photo. You gave me a camera, and I've started drawing people. Through this gift, I would like to say to you, the blessings you wish me to have I'm willing to step out of my comfort zone to try and experience, even with things that I haven't done before. This attitude towards life is my promise to you."

Chisau was touched as well as elated. "You're a really teachable little sister."

"Yeah, I guess you're right." Yuetching returned to her cake decoration. "A lot of people spend time rebelling against what their parents tell them to do. But for me who grew up with no mentor in life, I treasure it if someone cares enough to spend time to guide and advise me."

"Then I wish you an abundant life with many colourful encounters!"

"Thank you. This portrait isn't very good, is it? I hope you don't mind."

"Don't be silly. I love it. It's not just a portrait, but weighted with a solemn promise, which makes it priceless. Thank you… Wow! The cake looks delicious!" praised Chisau.

"It's not done yet."

Having lined the top with colourful fruits, Yuetching finished it off with artistic drawing and the writing of "Happy Birthday"!

"Now that's done! It looks acceptable, doesn't it?" Yuetching approved also.

"It looks just like what we buy at shops, and better." Chisau clapped.

"You're exaggerating. I don't trust you."

"I haven't! Whether you believe it or not, I thank you for your effort and thought in making me a cake. You're creative, aren't you?"

"I never have a lot of money. When a present is due, I think not what I can *give* but what I can *do* for the person. This is me, not creative but resourceful."

"Is that so? I understand."

"Right. Bedtime. Let me clear up. Tomorrow, remember to *re*-invite your best friend," reminded Yuetching.

"I've got it!"

Because of Yuetching, Chisau did not invite anyone to his birthday gathering except those who knew about her. That meant only his family and Samyin. It was a low key affair, with a meal at home and time for unwrapping presents. After the meal, their helper brought out the cake that Yuetching baked. Candles were lit, and Happy Birthday was sung. Chisau was content. This was the first year when he felt he had a real *happy* birthday since his father died.

Yuetching took out her camera and started snapping random pictures around the table. Samyin walked over and offered, "Perhaps I should take pictures of you with the family. You are one of them now, so you should be in the pictures too."

Granddad couldn't agree more, "Yes, come over. Let's take a photo of all of us."

Yuetching felt a little awkward, but she was excited too – finally she had a family! She was included in a family portrait. What a privilege! What an honour! What a blessing! What a status!

After the photos, Samyin handed back the camera to Yuetching, and said, "Thank you for pleading with Chisau on my behalf. Otherwise I wouldn't have been allowed to come tonight."

"Don't mention it. It's my pleasure."

"I'm sorry about that day. I didn't anticipate how it would have turned out."

"I know."

"I'm sorry for what she said."

"No worry. You can't apologise for her and what she said was her honest opinion of me, and you can't really say it was untrue either."

"Come, it's present time!" Granddad announced excitedly, and interrupted the conversation between Yuetching and Samyin. Chisau went through the presents one by one, and everyone was excited to see what they were! They were either things that were nice and delicate or the latest models of some electronic gadgets.

When Chisau finished, Granddad asked, "Where's Yuetching's present? Have we missed it out somehow?"

Chisau exchanged a look with Yuetching, and said, "We've all shared her present."

"What do you mean?" asked Granddad, looking puzzled.

"My birthday cake was made by her. You couldn't tell, could you? It was as good as from the shop!"

"Really? Did Yuetching make that? It was good," praised Granddad.

"Of course, it was of professional standard," reinforced Chisau.

Yuetching shut her eyes, thinking, "How embarrassing!"

Early in the morning of one Saturday, Yuetching left home before the family was up. Chisau heard the door and wondered, "It's so early. Where's she going? Could she be out sketching again in somewhere far?"

Yuetching did not come home until evening. Hearing the rustles outside the front door, Chisau quickly came out to have a look. He found Yuetching busy unloading boxes from the boot of a taxi. He hurried forward to lend a hand.

"What are these?" asked Chisau.

"Largely my books," answered Yuetching.

After Yuetching had offloaded the last box, the taxi drove away.

"Now, they have to go into my room," Yuetching said to herself.

"Where do all these books come from?" Chisau was puzzled.

"Have you forgotten? I've left most of my books in my apartment."

"Yes —" Chisau began to remember.

"Now they've been made homeless, so they have to come and live here. Are you going to help me take them in?"

"What do you mean — why are they homeless?" Chisau still did not click.

"Where is your wit today? Today I went to clean and tidy up my apartment. I've terminated my tenancy."

"What?" Chisau's jaw dropped — that was big news!

Yuetching took pleasure in the impact she had caused on Chisau, and continued, "So the books have to come *home* with me."

"But what has convinced you to stay with us? Your time with us is far from plain sailing."

"My promise to you, remember? The blessings you wish me to have I will try to experience, even if stepping out of my comfort zone. This is my commitment to it. If I leave an easy exit, my resolve will be weakened."

"This decision is to strengthen your resolve?"

Yuetching nodded.

"Has it been so hard for you?"

"It's a little daunting at times, yes."

"Thank you for trusting us." Chisau did not know what else to say; here Yuetching demonstrated her courage and determination. Her action had made it tangible for Chisau how hard she had been trying to make this work. He suddenly came to realise that she must have had a tough day of cleaning and sorting out. "Why didn't you ask me to help? Was it hard work to do it all by yourself?" he asked attentively.

"No, it's nothing. I've been through even tougher tasks than this. It's the same that you're helping now," dismissed Yuetching. "Besides, didn't you go out today?"

"I could have cancelled it, you know?"

"Well, it's no need; I can manage," she shrugged.

Chisau was actually pained by her no-fuss-no-nonsense approach; everything to her was no big deal! Sometimes he wished she was not so weathered by hardships that she would at least moan a little. If she was tough, her life must have been even tougher! This reckoning was a stab on his heart. An account of what she had been through was like river flow, which would never run dry or come to an end. Even if he spent his whole life learning, he probably would never fully comprehend what life had been like for her. Like now, she worked hard in transporting the boxes inside; she would never wait for help or have any expectations of others. Had all the people around her really showed her so little concern that she had *no* expectations of people whatsoever and must rely on herself for everything? *Have we all failed her that badly? Haven't we all disappointed her? Her extreme self-reliance is her silent charge against all who are related to her and have encountered her.*

Thinking about this, Chisau got angry at all the people in Yuetching's life, including themselves, as all seemed to have failed her so badly. He walked up to her, snatched from her the box she was carrying, and said, "Let me do it." He took the box inside. When he came out, Yuetching already lifted another box. Chisau went up to her, snatched the box from her again, and said, "I've told you to let me do it!"

"Why're you so grouchy with me all of a sudden? I don't

need an unwilling helper, drop it." Yuetching snatched back the box from Chisau and walked towards the house. Chisau grabbed her arm, and stopped her right on her track.

"Could you unlearn some of your independence?" pleaded Chisau.

"What?" Yuetching was baffled; she did not understand.

"I'm not angry at you," Chisau confessed. "I'm angry with all that has happened in your life or what has not happened to you but should have; I'm angry at all the people in your life, including ourselves, who are so undependable that you can never trust anyone to help. If you're willing, from this day on, I'll share the burden of all the matters concerning your life, big or small. Can you be just a little less self-reliant and tough? Can you let people help?"

Yuetching was stunned, her grip loosened and the box dropped out from her hands. How could his words be so piercing as if he were there with her from the beginning? How did he know her hardships and bitterness as if he saw everything? She remembered how helpless she was when she was little. No matter how much she cried for help, there was no one to help. She had to teach herself to grit her teeth and overcome all difficulties. She had to toughen herself up so that she would not need to ask for help anymore. She told herself life was exhausting, and she was not allowed to complain about being tired. She did not let herself say "impossible", nor did she let herself feel fear. But every night when she lay down in bed, and when she let down her guard, what travelled with her into her sleep was always one fantasy – that tomorrow would be a little kinder. And in her dream she would see a mighty and strong arm waving at her and calling her. She did not have any longings, except for someone who would understand her toil, and such an understanding would be enough to rest her soul. She stared at Chisau with tears welling up. He debated in his head if he should or should not to give her a hug. In the end, he did, reaffirming unwaveringly, "From today onwards, this is your family. Your concerns are our concerns. There's no difference now. Understand?"

On hearing this, Yuetching broke down and cried. She felt she had finally come home. And in Chisau's arms, she felt the warmth and reassurance that made her never want to leave.

7 Battles with the Shadows of the Past

Sinyin bowed out of the stage in the thunders of applause. Judging by the reaction from the audience and the money raised, this charity concert was a success. Sinyin's galvanising power was impressive: there were no empty seats in the concert hall and her popularity was rising. Following the drowning incident, Sinyin adopted a strategy to dispel the bad press by her action. She threw herself into work, and was active at many events and functions. Her exposure was high. She talked eloquently and articulately at interviews to prove that she was not psychologically imbalanced! She also made a selection of guest appearances to foster her image as a talented musician, who deserved to be admired and be taken seriously with her dazzling virtuosity. There was however a price to pay for her celebrity. The public demand for her images and everything about her was growing stronger. Having to feed that constant insatiable desire was exhausting both physically and emotionally.

At last she managed to get away from the crowd and return to her room. Away from the gazing eyes of the public, she could relax and be herself for a little while. She removed her makeup and changed into something comfortable. Now that the concert was over, she could finally take a break. During the period of intense preparation for the concert, she spent so many of her waking hours in her public persona to satisfy demands from all sides that she no longer knew what she wanted for herself. Everyday she was surrounded by different work crews; there were also numerous people who would like to get to know her.

But the ridiculous thing was that it was impossible for her to get to know any one of them personally. Sinyin felt that she was living in a contradiction. The public attention was like a wall, marking out the boundary of her personal life and freedom in making friends. She had to laugh at her own situation; she was caged in by her own success. Behind popularity felt like absolute loneliness to her.

Following the climax of a successful performance, this loneliness was almost unbearable. She felt so lonely that her heart wrenched. Her thoughts wandered back to Chisau. "How did we come to this?" Sinyin sighed. The happy days with Chisau in the past made her feel acutely what she had lost. Her heart twitched, and tears started tumbling down. Sinyin opened the drawer and found Chisau's ring. That night at the restaurant when he formally ended their relationship was replayed in her mind. This ring now symbolised a lost promise.

"Why did I let this beautiful promise slip away from between my fingers like that?" Sinyin asked herself. "How could I be so mindless? Was it worth it? Did I really have the right to demand him to wait? Perhaps I was too naïve, believing that everything would stay put and waited for my return. When I came back, I realised time did not pause because of my absence. In contrast, all people and things have moved forward. The only difference is that they have gone ahead without me."

Sinyin took off her ring and stared at it. This ring she had been wearing for so long that she had gotten used to it. She reunited it with Chisau's ring in her palm. She thought, "When the pair was separated, the bearers were together; when the pair comes together like now, the bearers are separated. Isn't it ironic and regrettable?" She put the couple rings together on a chain. She recalled how decisive Chisau was in abandoning his ring. Her heart twitched again and the flood of tears resumed.

She was not ready to let it go yet. She put the chain with the couple rings round her neck as a memento for her loss. She comforted herself, "One day perhaps I'll be able to put this chain down."

Sinyin could not sleep, so she got up and changed into casual wear. She went out and wandered aimlessly along the Hotel corridors. She did not want to go to places where there were people. She found her steps bringing her towards Chisau's office. She was not trying to bump into him; she just wanted to be in a place full of his presence, so that she could feel close to him once more. Even Sinyin laughed at her own pathetic state of mind!

When Sinyin approached Chisau's office, she saw the lights were still on. *Could he still be!* Her heart fluttered with the possibility that he was there. She could have chosen to turn back, but her wish to see him was stronger than her rationality. Thus, she plucked up her courage and buzzed the bell. There was no answer. She buzzed again, reasoning with herself that if there was no one, it didn't matter how long she buzzed and how desperate that she might sound but at least her persistence bought hope. She knew she was deemed to be disappointed but she just couldn't give up. Yes, she was this pitiful and tears started rolling down her cheeks.

Suddenly the door was thrust open and the moment froze.

Neither expected to see each other but here they were, coming face to face.

Seeing her face awash in tears, Chisau tenderly inquired, "What's the matter?"

Flooded with happiness in seeing him, she was rendered speechless.

She cried the tears of happiness, but Chisau couldn't tell.

Feeling unable to shut the door on her when she was in such a state, Chisau asked, "Would you like to come in?"

The invitation was like heavenly chorus to Sinyin's ears.

She sat down in his office while he went to fetch her a glass of water. "I don't think you should drink coffee so late at night." He was as caring as before.

"Thank you." She sipped some water. Then she asked, "What has kept you in the office at this hour? Are you very busy?"

For a moment, the Sinyin whom he had known had returned. Her mask was off; in front of him were a genuine face and a friendly smile, with a familiar gentle tone and attentive concern. Chisau was confused.

"When the staff is hardworking, the boss must work hard to keep up!" he laughed at himself. "I shouldn't have been in at this hour but I've dozed off reading some reports! After a couple of late nights, my body is sending me signals."

They chatted like they used to.

"Sorry to have woken you up. I couldn't sleep, so I got up

and took a stroll. I didn't expect to find you here at this hour."

"Were you calling for some urgent help?"

Chagrined, Sinyin looked down, "I know I sounded desperate, didn't I?"

"What was the urgent call for? Are you feeling unwell?"

"Well, I … no, it's my heart; my heart is aching. Does that count?"

Sinyin fixed her eyes on Chisau who did not know how to answer.

"In my defence," Sinyin continued, "I didn't expect anyone to be in. No one was supposed to hear that. It was –" she hesitated. Then she resumed, "It was intended as a little gesture to vent my frustration; my call – you see – was not supposed to be met with an answer, but – I thought – as long as I persisted there was hope. That's what I was expressing. Silly, wasn't it?" She looked at him with expectancy.

There were layers of meaning in there that Chisau did not wish to unpack or acknowledge, so he asked, "How was the charity concert this evening?"

"Everything went smoothly; well, at least I didn't collapse!" Sinyin threw in a self-parody, which evoked a smile on Chisau. "Judging by how much it has raised, I would say it's a success," continued Sinyin.

"If everything has gone so well with you, then why are you frustrated?"

How nice it was to talk like this, heart to heart! She missed being "ordinary". She was glad to see a familiar face from her past before her fame. She sighed, "When I was stiflingly busy, I wished everything would halt so that I could rest a little. But when everything halts, like now, I only feel lost, lonely and empty. Why are we always contradictory? We don't know what we want, do we?"

Chisau registered their couple rings Sinyin dangling round her neck.

"You'll feel much better after a good night sleep. So go back now and take some rest. You seem tired. I also need to go as it's getting late." He got up and moved towards his desk to pack up.

No! No! No! That's too short! Sinyin did not want their sweet moment to end. She got up and embraced him from behind. Chisau was caught by surprise. The more he tried to loosen her grip, the tighter Sinyin held on to him. "Don't move, please," was the desperate request from Sinyin.

Tears started to roll down her cheeks again, and she asked, "Why can't you come back to me like how we were before?"

Chisau could not deny that his heart was stirred. But he was not going to retract his considered decision on impulse! Seeing that Chisau did not resist, Sinyin took courage. She went round to the front and launched a kiss on him; there was such pleasure in satisfying a longing. She wished the world would stop for them. But this moment was almost non-existent to grasp as Chisau pushed her away in an instant, saying, "Sinyin, please don't!"

"Why not? Have you another one on your heart?"

"This isn't the reason."

"Then why?"

"I've already told you thousands of times if only you would listen. If you don't demand more, perhaps we could still be friends. Please don't make it hard for me."

Chisau's unyielding stance shattered Sinyin's hope. She could not bear it anymore; she let herself collapse on the floor. Streams of tears started to flow without restraint! Chisau felt sorry for her but it was a stage that she must go through, the same stage he went through when she left him. Right now, she should cry on someone's shoulder but just not his.

"Why – can't success make me happy? Why – must behind success – be emptiness?" Sinyin sobbed. "What's – the point – of working hard? What – have I gained?"

Chisau helped her to the sofa. She cried like a river for a long while until she fell asleep on him. He lay her down comfortably on the sofa and wiped her tears away. Somewhere deep down in his heart, he would always have a soft spot for her. After all, they had walked together and he had once made a promise to take care of her. At the time, it was regrettable that she chose to walk her way without him. Now that she had to face the consequence of her decision, she realised she was never prepared for it.

Why can't you come back to me like how we were before? Her wish was echoing in his mind. "Can life ever be as perfect?" Chisau sighed.

Early in the morning, Miss Lau rushed into Sinyin's room, only to find her rolling in bed lazily. "What's wrong? Are you feeling unwell?" Miss Lau asked with some urgency.

Sinyin was baffled, "What are you doing? I'm fine. There's nothing wrong with me."

"What happened last night?"

Sinyin quickly sat up, and asked, "Why did you ask?"

"Director Lee called me first thing this morning, instructing me to take good care of you and saying that you might've been exhausted by the busy schedule. He suggested that we should space out your schedule a bit more, so as to factor in time for proper rest and a private life. He particularly emphasised that you should have a social life outside work and encourage you to meet up with friends."

"Did he really call you to say that?" Sinyin could not believe it.

"Yes. He also said that nothing was more important than health, and that it was a false economy to work hard at the expense of health. He said that Sinyin needed to slow down her work and strike a better work-life balance. And he said it's my responsibility to make sure it happens. It was like having a lecture from him on how to do my job!"

"He really said all that?" Sinyin was secretly happy.

"Yes! He asked me to come to see you immediately, and make sure that you eat your meals at regular times and that you have time to relax. Actually what did happen last night? Did you pass out in front of him again?"

Sinyin looked a bit embarrassed and gave an evasive answer, "Nothing happened."

"I think Director Lee really cares about you."

"Do you really think that?" Sinyin's spirit was lifted.

"Yes, I do think so. Why are you so happy?"

"Nothing." Sinyin was secretly pleased as she saw glimmer of hope: *perhaps persistence does pay off!*

"Get up now. We have to listen to Director Lee's wise instructions, don't we?" said Miss Lau.

"All right. I've heard you!" To Sinyin, it was a beautiful start of a beautiful day; nothing was going to dampen her spirits!

Meanwhile this day marked a milestone in Yuetching's work at the Hotel. She rose early and went into work before everyone else to be as prepared as she could for the progress meeting with Samyin and Chisau. Was she a little nervous? Perhaps. Deep down, she wanted to prove her worth even if only to herself; she needed reassurance that she could stand in her own right to have a future in the Hotel. The meeting would decide the direction of the next stage of the project and she would attempt to steer it towards the direction she thought it should take.

Samyin walked up to her desk and greeted, "You're so early! How's the preparation for today's meeting?"

"It's nearly done. I'm transferring data and presentation to the laptop. Can I pick your brain on something?"

"No problem. Come in."

Yuetching grabbed her laptop and followed Samyin into his office. They both sat down on the sofa and Yuetching started asking Samyin a series of questions, which he answered patiently. Having heard Samyin's opinion, Yuetching was pondering how to amend her presentation. Samyin loved watching her deep in thought – how she liked to stare into the distance when she was thinking, brush her hair behind her ears when she was typing. All these little habits of hers had been unwittingly imprinted on his heart. When Yuetching suddenly lifted her eyes from the computer, their eyes crossed and she caught him staring at her. Embarrassed, Samyin quickly looked the other way and got up to find something else to occupy his mind with!

Having worked hard for the whole morning on the album concept, Sinyin returned to her room to rest a little, just as Chisau had ordered her! She could not stop smiling all morning and was sweet to everyone. Her steps were light, almost skipping like a little girl. Nothing was going to dampen her spirits today, she told herself.

As she entered her room, two cleaners were tidying up her bedroom. But that did not irritate her as it would have normally. Unaware of Sinyin's presence, the cleaners carried on chatting while they worked.

"Have you heard that Cheung Yuetching is now the personal assistant of Manager Chiu? She hasn't been here that long. Who knows how she climbs to that sort of position? Is she any different from us? She worked with us here."

"She makes people jealous, doesn't she?"

"Last time, when she was cleaning this room and got injured on the hand, *both* Director Lee and Manager Chiu escorted her to A&E for treatment *personally* and stayed with her there. Haven't you heard?"

When Sinyin heard this, she knew they were talking about the mysterious lady, whose identity she was dying to find out. She crept up to the bedroom door and stood obscure in order to get a better earshot.

"I bet Director Lee and Manager Chiu don't even know who I am or what my name is. But they are so attentive to this girl that they seem to take a personal interest in her. I think this girl isn't as innocent as she seems."

"I'm so jealous – she's like a modern-day Cinderella, being plucked from the obscurity and rising to the top!"

"She's probably very good at worming into people's hearts and earning their affection. She's very thorough, you see. Her attention doesn't stop short with the two direct targets but is extended to Director Lee's granddad. Aren't you amazed at her skills? I've heard that she often assists his granddad with his physiotherapy exercises in the pool. Which one is more likely – that she's simply good-natured or a fawner with some ulterior motive?"

"Really?"

"There's more. You must know Miss Yan's drowning incident in the pool not that long ago. She was the heroine in saving her life." Sinyin's jaw dropped when she heard this!

"She collapsed afterwards," the cleaner continued, "and was put up in a Hotel suite like this one to rest. She was in there for three days and guess who were looking after her?"

"Who?"

"Who else? Director Lee and Manager Chiu took turn to look after her *personally* for three days! It was said that she went mad for three days, could not let anyone see her and was too weak to go home. It's rumoured that she might be emotionally unstable. Even if she was too weak to travel, where was her family? Why must Director Lee and Manager Chiu look after her themselves? If you don't call this favouritism, I don't know what is. She has captured the hearts of both men, I tell you."

It's she again! That was why he wouldn't fire her! That was why he yelled at me! He's defending that scum! A blinding rage arose within her. She stormed out of her room, heading towards Chisau's office for an explanation! She could not stand back and let a woman from obscurity ruin her chance with Chisau like that!

Inside Chisau's office, the three of them spent most of the

morning going through motions on internal policies, including streamlining staff's salary and benefit structures to remove anomalies, extensions of product range in terms of services provided, a pricing framework, possibilities of efficiency improvement and cost reductions, investment strategies and some preliminary suggestions of strengthening the Hotel's social responsibilities. Adding to that, Chisau briefed them on an expansion plan that the Hotel group was considering.

"Let's take a break here," suggested Chisau.

"I'll be back," Samyin popped out.

Yuetching got up to stretch her legs and walked to the windows. Chisau went up to her, commenting, "The concepts are substantial and constructive. The areas of concern you have identified and directions of ways forward are insightful. Now has come the detail crunching time. Are you ready for it? We need to make it realistic with the resources and time that we have. We must prioritise, so that areas we pursue will be allocated adequate resources. I put the whole Strategic Planning Department under Samyin's direction to assist in this project. We must focus on thrashing out the proposals, so that the details are ready for our Annual Meeting."

At this point, Sinyin barged into the office, buzzing like crazy while attempting to break down the door. "Open the door," she shouted. Miss Wei was concerned that the noise might be heard from the conference centre, so she let her in to quiet her. Once on the other side of the door, she couldn't be stopped. She bypassed Miss Wei and walked straight into Chisau's office. When she caught the sight of Chisau and Yuetching standing together by the window, looking pretty cosy, all the rumours seemed to have proven true for Sinyin, who required no more explanation. She rushed in and grabbed Yuetching's wrist. Before she knew it, Sinyin slapped her on the face.

"You shameless flirt," roared Sinyin, ready for a cat fight.

Wide-eyed in horror, Chisau rushed forward to separate them.

"What's gone into you? Have you lost your mind?" shouted Chisau. He turned to Yuetching to see how badly she was hurt, only to find her face red with Sinyin's hand print!

Witnessing how attentive Chisau was towards Yuetching, Sinyin felt her fury or jealousy roaring inside her, "Lee Chisau, you've been lying to me. You said that there was no third person. Then who's she? She was only a cleaner to start with. How did she climb up the ladder so fast and so high within such a short space of time? Work and report is only a pretence, isn't it, to fool people? How could you be so gullible as to fall for her tricks? How could you be so foolish as to be manipulated by someone so cheap and lowly? She's emotionally unstable. You should know that as you *personally* nursed her back to her senses! Or did she just pretend to be sick after saving me to get your attention, because to be honest, I can't see what so traumatic about performing CPR that she was incapacitated to leave the Hotel room for three days? Does she not have a family? Have you ever asked her? Do you know where she came from? Have you ever tried to find out? Aren't you suspicious at all of who she is and what her real motives are? How could you be so easily seduced by someone as despicable as her? How can you be so careless and mindless? Has your brain been scattered or is it just too spellbound to think? Was it because of her that you could not fire the person who set out to ruin my reputation? You roared at me in order to defend HER! How could you stand on her side against me and throw our history away? It's because of her that you can't come back to me; it's SHE, isn't it? ANSWER ME!" Sinyin turned to Yuetching, taking hold of her hand, and slashed at her, "A modern-day Cinderella, are you now? You wish. There's no such perfect fairytale in real life! Go back to wherever you came from, back to obscurity where no one knows you or sees you! That suits you much better than dressing up as Cinderella! You are NOBODY but one – shameless – social – climber! Anything that aids your rise I bet you would do; you're a disgrace! Just LEAVE and move on to your next target!"

There was an eerie sense of déjà vu. One might be able to dismiss what one person said but it was much harder when two people were saying the same thing. There must be some truth in that reflection! Yuetching was defenceless against Sinyin's onslaught. It made her already fragile self-confidence crumble. Her inferiority-complex resurfaced and took control of her at full force, wiping out all her confidence and debilitating her from fighting back. Feeling exposed, she wanted to find a place to hide, for she was too self-conscious about herself. She fled from the confrontation.

Sinyin let out a victorious laugh and enjoyed the moment of her triumph, "The cunning fox has finally exposed its tail. Look, she's so ashamed that she couldn't face people but go hiding. At least she still knows shame!"

Chisau closed his fists in rage. He would have retorted on Yuetching's behalf, but he knew the most urgent matter in that instant was to go after her. As he was about to chase after her, Sinyin blocked him, "You're *not* permitted to go after her. Let her return to her rightful place. How could she even think that she could stay beside you like that?"

Chisau pushed her away, and said, "Yan Sinyin, listen carefully. I don't wish to see you again, and this Hotel doesn't welcome you anymore. Leave."

Sinyin ran up and held on to Chisau. She was angry too and would not let go.

"I'm not going to lose to that flirt!" Samyin walked in and was shocked by the change of scene. It all happened so quickly that Miss Wei didn't know what to do. Chisau turned to Sinyin, retorting, "I don't allow you to call her that. She's a far better person than you've ever been by miles. Look at yourself and listen to yourself. Who's more dignified here? Just leave."

Sinyin was still holding on, weeping. Chisau had to struggle hard to get loose. He ran out of the office, and Samyin followed. "Where could she have gone?" Chisau first tried the rooftop garden where Yuetching said she would go to "have a break from people" and "be alone". But when there was no trace of her, he started to panic.

"Let's go to the Security Room and look at the CCTV footage," suggested Samyin. "What a good idea!" Chisau agreed.

They went into the Security Room with such urgency that the guards were alarmed. They put forward their request without divulging anything of substance. It didn't take long for them to locate Yuetching and trace her exit route. The footage confirmed that she had left the building through the exit adjoining the shopping mall.

The shopping mall was hardly a place to be alone! It was therefore likely that she just walked through it to places that she could be alone. Chisau and Samyin went in different directions to search those likely places, but they were denied the joy of spotting her anywhere in the proximity of the Hotel. They had to admit defeat and went back to the Hotel to regroup.

They gathered at Samyin's office; Yuetching's personal belongings were all there at her desk. "She has no money, no keys, and no phone on her," noted Samyin.

"That means she couldn't have gone far, but it also means that she isn't herself; she isn't thinking straight." They went in and sat down in the office.

"Where would she go or do when she's upset?" asked Chisau. They searched their memories and realised that for the whole time they had known her, they had never seen her upset. As a result they had no clue what she would do as a reaction.

They sighed.

"What exactly happened?" asked Samyin.

"I don't know either. I believe Sinyin has heard some rumours from the staff, rumours that are very damaging to Yuetching. The facts were accurate and provided the catalysts for the rumours. From what I've heard from Yuetching, Sinyin's accusation is along the same line as Szeman's suspicion of her – a shameless social climber. Obviously I'm bewitched by her just like you are in Szeman's eyes."

"That means Szeman's impression was not an isolated case; the staff has begun to notice Yuetching and her movements. Since we haven't said anything to explain the situation, speculations fuel the rumours."

"That sounds a reasonable inference from what's happened."

"Finally I understand how you must've felt when I caused Yuetching to be insulted by Szeman," Samyin said.

Chisau had to eat a humble pie, saying, "Does it mean that you're infuriated with me? I had no right to be angry at you! Worse than you, I couldn't even protect her – she got slapped by Sinyin. How arrogant I was to stand on the moral high ground to judge you and to believe that I could protect her. Because of me, she got hurt by Sinyin, and not just once but twice. What right do I have to censure you? I'm sorry; we're always quick in judging others than ourselves, aren't we?"

"Don't blame yourself too much. Let's go out to search for her again," suggested Samyin who could not sit around and did nothing.

The joy of finding her eluded them and it was getting late. They decided to abort the search and went home to wait instead. As soon as they got into the house, Chisau asked Granddad anxiously, "Has Yuetching come back yet?"

"No, she hasn't," answered Granddad, who was alarmed by Chisau's tone. "What has happened to her? You sound as though you've lost her!" Granddad demanded to know.

"Nothing," Chisau hesitated.

"Don't even think that you can lie to me!"

Chisau and Samyin exchanged a look, wondering if it was wise to tell him.

"Are you going to tell me yourself or should I ring Miss Wei up to find out?" ordered Granddad. He had a point. Chisau and Samyin walked over to sit down with him. Chisau told him everything with no details spared. It was the first time that Samyin heard the full story too. It was déjà vu. No wonder Yuetching was upset. Although she was tough over a lot of things, she did have her acutely sore points, and Chisau and Samyin had a vague idea of what those might be.

Granddad was saddened by what he heard, and blamed himself, "Yuetching has been proven right, hasn't she? It's my fault. Not only have I caused all her hardship, but also for her to be insulted and slandered like that by Sinyin and the Hotel staff." The two young men were upset for her sake too. She had always led a low-key, simple life. She was always averse to public attention especially adverse ones. How was she going to cope?

"Perhaps it's time we made her identity public. Let's make the public announcement and introduce her to everyone at this year's Annual Meeting with the shareholders. During the time leading up to it, the three of you must work hard together to finalise Hotel's medium-term vision and proposals of immediate policy reform. Yuetching has many fresh ideas; you two must assist and guide her to bring them to fruition. Let's try our best to consolidate Yuetching's position at the Hotel by establishing her professional abilities beyond doubt. It's critically important that we establish her position as indisputable, not only because of who she is but also on her own merits. Yuetching above all others needs to know that about herself. You two must assist her to the best of your ability; you mustn't let her give up. Do you understand?" Granddad instructed.

They nodded to accept the charge that Granddad had laid upon them.

They waited till late and Granddad had to retreat for the night.

"It's late. Why don't you go home as well? I can wait for her. I'll let you know when she turns up," Chisau said to Samyin.

"You think I can sleep?"

"Since when have you got so worried about her that you would lose sleep?"

"Do you think you're the only who cares and worries about her?"

"What's that supposed to mean?"

Samyin took a deep breath, and plucked up the courage to announce, "I don't know when it started but I think I've fallen in love with her unknowingly."

Chisau was a little startled by this declaration of love; he was unsure about his feelings – if he welcomed it.

"It was Szeman who uncovered it for me," Samyin continued, "I could not deny what she suggested because I did feel something special about Yuetching even though I wasn't sure what it was at the time. I didn't intentionally leave it as 'a convenient misunderstanding' to drive Szeman away. I wasn't *using* Yuetching as an excuse to gain an easy exit for myself from a sticky situation, as she and you seem to believe. Contrary to what you think, it wasn't a lie but an emerging truth, so I couldn't deny it. I couldn't respond or defend myself at the time, because I was in a muddle. Was it just a short-term infatuation or was it love? I needed time to work out what my feeling was before I could decide how to handle it."

"Are you telling me that you now know what it is?"

"She has become a part of my life now. Even without dating her, she has unwittingly become the girl closest to my heart than any other girls I have ever known," declared Samyin.

Chisau was not exactly elated, and he did not know why. Perhaps he liked to think that he had a special place in her heart and life, and the monopoly right to protect and take care of her. Now he realised that one day he had to relinquish that place to Samyin or someone else, who could love her further and deeper than he ever could.

"Do I have your blessing or not?" Chisau's silence made Samyin uneasy.

"Are you serious about her?"

"She is the first woman I love," Samyin said most resolutely. "She makes me realise I have never loved before. Previously I was living out the girls' expectations of me. With her, there isn't such pressure. On the contrary it's about selflessly care about her without any expectations and wanting the best for her as I know it. Surprisingly that brings me out and helps me know myself better. It's 100 percent genuine. That's most strange to me. I'm like a different person." Chisau felt a sense of loss. Silence ensued. With his eyes closed, Chisau was chasing his memory of the time with Yuetching.

"Where would Yuetching go when she's upset?" Samyin reiterated the same question asked earlier.

Chisau recalled, "Her castle on the clouds." Then he opened his eyes and replied, "Disney."

"What?" Samyin had not a clue, "Disney?"

"She once told me, when she was little, she owned a castle on the clouds – her imaginary land where there were no worries, no sadness, no pain and no hurt. When she was unhappy, she would fly there and no one could find her. Now as an adult, whenever she saw the Disney logo, she would be reminded of that lovely place, which had helped her pass many unhappy days." Chisau's face lit up when he talked about Yuetching. Samyin was moved by Yuetching's narrative while also jealous of the tender moments that Chisau seemed to have shared with her.

"It's a pity that she hasn't had any money on her, so she couldn't have gone to Disneyland!" added Chisau.

At the moment, the doorbell rang. Both rushed to the door.

Chisau opened the door and Yuetching fell into his arms, scaring both of them.

"What's wrong with you?" asked Chisau anxiously.

"Food…Food to eat," Yuetching said weakly.

Chisau asked Samyin to bring some dinner out of the kitchen, while he helped Yuetching inside. Chisau sat her down at the dining table; Samyin served her dinner. She devoured the dinner in no time, and reminded Chisau of the first day they met. He chuckled at the sight, but was relieved that she was home safely. He stood up and poured a glass of water for her.

"Thank you," she said.

Having stuffed herself, she put down her chopsticks and bowl with satisfaction. She rubbed her tummy, saying, "So satisfying!"

Both Chisau and Samyin laughed.

"Where've you run to all day? You made us so worried! We looked for you everywhere and waited for you the whole day. You didn't bring anything, not even your phone! Now these are back to their owner." Samyin handed back her personal belongings from the office.

"Thank you," said Yuetching with her charming smile.

"Where've you been? Today we realise we know you so little," said Chisau.

"The public library. I found a corner by the window. I was not alone but I was not disturbed. It was quiet. I was surrounded by books. It was bliss. I stayed till the closing time and then I walked and walked until I had no more energy."

Samyin asked, "Did Sinyin hit you hard? Does it still hurt?"

"No, it doesn't hurt. This is the least of the issue."

"I'm sorry for what's happened today," Chisau apologised.

"Me too. I'm exhausted; I'm going to bed now," she wanted to escape as fast as possible, so as not to discuss about today!

"You're upset, aren't you?" Chisau stopped her from moving away. "Why don't you tell us what you're thinking?"

"There's nothing to tell. I haven't decided what to do yet. But I'm too tired now and I can't think."

"Granddad intends to introduce you to everyone at this year's Annual Meeting of shareholders," Chisau told her.

Yuetching paused half way up the stairs, and asked, "What does that mean?"

"This means people at the Hotel from top to bottom will know who you are; everyone will know that we are your family and you have every right to be here as we do. Today's incident won't happen again," added Chisau.

"And you think this is the best way forward?" Yuetching doubted.

"You're a member of our family. Sooner or later we'll have to announce this fact to people at the Hotel. Are there any alternatives? Don't tell me you're thinking –" When Chisau contemplated this possibility, he was scared. "No, don't even think about it; I won't let you leave," said Chisau emphatically.

"I've said that I haven't decided what to do." Yuetching hated it when her own thoughts were always transparent to Chisau.

"Running away is not a solution. You can't run away from your true identity. The question is whether you have the courage to live up to what that identity entails. Where's the courage that has enabled you to swim? Promise is made to keep, not to break. Your books are all here. They are a reminder of your resolve and commitment to make this work. " Chisau was firing everything she had said to him back at her to dissuade her from giving up;

he was desperate.

"I've told you I haven't decided what to do yet, so stop pushing me for answers that I don't have!" Yuetching showed her irritation. Chisau was too concerned to stay calm, but Samyin stopped him from hounding on her, "Please don't pressurise her now. Let her rest tonight. We discuss it tomorrow."

Yuetching rushed upstairs to her room.

"Why are you so harsh on her? It's unlike you." asked Samyin when Yuetching was out of earshot.

"Am I harsh on her? It's because you've never tried to find her! I'm concerned that she might sneak out from our life without telling us, and go hiding in the crowd again. Then where do you ask me to find her again?"

"Even so, this isn't something we can find a solution in one night, especially when she's that tired. If you over-pressurise her, she might really run out on us. I'm going home now, and you should get some rest too. Let's talk and think tomorrow," Samyin patted Chisau's shoulder and saw himself out.

Chisau walked past Yuetching's door, knowing that she was on the other side. He had an urge to knock but he restrained himself, on the consideration that she must be exhausted. He returned to his own room, and threw himself on his bed. He was exhausted too, both physically and emotionally. He felt he was losing her – nothing they could do to stop her if she decided to walk out on them.

Why aren't you talking to me like you used to? Why are you shutting me out? Why don't you let me reason with you on the matter? Why must you decide on your own? And, Chisau paused, and resumed in his thoughts, *will you accept Samyin? In your eyes, you've once said you two are impossible. Will that change when Samyin really pursues you?*

Chisau never realised how disturbed he was over the thought of losing her. As Yuetching once said, "life is unpredictable," who knew what was going to happen next. He suddenly perceived how short-lived the current perfect balance would be; it was only a matter of time that their relationship would change one way or another: Yuetching could decide to move out or worse, to walk out on them and cut all contact; she might one day get married and be someone else's wife. None of these was within his control. Perhaps what he could do was as Yuetching said, "Cherish the perfect moments while they last."

On the following morning, Yuetching tried to sneak out early so as to avoid Chisau but he had predicted it and stopped her on her track. "Where are you going so early in the morning?" Despite his suspicion, it was encouraging to Chisau that she was in work clothes, so at least it appeared that she intended to go to work.

"Work. Where else?" she answered tersely.

"Let me drive you."

"No."

"Then let us talk before you go."

As an answer, Yuetching tried to walk past him, but Chisau blocked her. "Please, just spare a few minutes to talk with me. Can you not grant me even that much?"

Yuetching conceded and followed Chisau to take a stroll in the garden.

"Did you sleep well last night?"

"I ate too late and was too stuffed to be able to sleep much!"

"Are you upset? Please tell me what you're thinking."

"This time I feel the whole Hotel is gossiping about me in that common light. I feel everyone is watching me and cursing me. Sinyin did not form her own opinion like Szeman. The details that she was able to recite mean that she heard it from somewhere, most likely within the Hotel. It's not that easy to dismiss it as if it hadn't happened. How am I supposed to walk back in there and face the people, knowing they're talking about me behind my back? I'm so embarrassed that I'd rather die! I just wish the ground would open up and swallow me!" Then Yuetching turned to Chisau and requested seriously, "May I resign?"

Chisau could not say he was surprised. "Granddad's wish is for us to firm up the proposals together and do it well, so that your position at the Hotel is secured not only on the basis of your relationship with this family but also on your own merits. This is an opportunity to prove yourself. You above all others need to know who you are and what you are really capable of if only given a chance."

"I don't have to work at the Hotel. I could stay with the family but work somewhere else. Then we won't face the complicated issues of a public life like you do and I won't bring you troubles."

"Are you going to admit defeat without even trying? What

are you afraid of? Persuading you to stay is not purely because you're family. From a management point of view, you have potential that we would like to help develop. This is my responsibility as a manager too."

"What potential? All that I have come up with are a few naïve ideas, which I don't even know if they're feasible! Who do I think I am?!"

"*This* is the only naïve idea I've heard from you!"

"Let me go now; we can't resolve it here and now."

"What do you plan to do today?"

"I don't know. Don't keep asking me questions that I don't have answers for!"

"At least promise me that you won't run off."

"I'm going in to work. Why are you putting other ideas into my head?"

"Okay. I let you go because I have your words."

"Thank you."

Watching her leave, Chisau wondered: *How do I handle this stalemate with her?*

Samyin had been waiting for Yuetching since very early in the morning. He went up to greet her when she turned up. "How are you this morning? Did you sleep well last night?"

"I'm fine, if that's what you're worried about." She sat down at her desk.

"All right. Let me be direct then. What's your decision?"

"I've already given my verbal resignation to Chisau."

"This is disappointing. I don't think Chisau would accept it."

"If it comes to this, what can he do to stop me from leaving?"

"Are you serious in considering it?"

"It does look very easy and attractive."

"What is the key factor that prompts this decision?"

"I only like focusing on the work and hate everything about office politics. This is the best option for me."

"People don't live or work in isolation. Work and people issues can't be separated. How many times can you run away? You'll have to deal with similar situations sooner or later wherever you go."

Samyin was probably right, so she could not reply.

"If this is the case, why don't you start with the current one and learn how to deal with this kind of situation now?" Samyin continued.

That was a thought.

"If you've decided to resign, why do you come to the office? Is it to pack your stuff?" furthered Samyin.

"I don't know, all right? I don't know what I'm doing. Perhaps it's a habit. Happy now?" Yuetching snapped.

"It appears to me that you aren't resolute about your decision – yet. Something in this post you still relish and it pulls you back."

"You're confusing me now." Yuetching buried her head in her hands.

"What's so powerful about Sinyin's few words that you would consider giving all these up without a fight?"

"Who am I to strive for a position like this and a life that is beyond me? This is all but a dream. One day I'll wake up, and I'd die of humiliation and embarrassment as the worst laughing stock that I've even tried and believed in it. My place is in the obscurity; there at least I have peace and people can't disturb me."

Samyin discerned that Yuetching was facing a confidence crisis and got all melodramatic, so he pulled her away from her desk.

"Where are we going?" asked Yuetching.

Samyin did not answer.

Chisau was in his office, planning how he could best assist Yuetching to regain her confidence. A short break from the Hotel environment might help. The Hotel's expansion plan considered the possibility of investing in ----- Island, an up-and-coming tourist destination. Originally he thought of taking Yuetching on a trip to the Island for a site visit, but now he was contemplating sending Samyin in his place on this mission. If he was to entrust Yuetching to someone, why not Samyin? He should give him his blessing, and perhaps even create an opportunity for him with Yuetching.

This is what a brother should do, Chisau told himself. *That's decided then.*

"Director Lee," Miss Wei buzzed, "Miss Yan is here and requests to see you."

"Let her in. I'd like to settle something with her."

Sinyin demurely walked into Chisau's office. Once the door was closed behind her, she started, "I've come to apologise for yesterday."

"Are you sincere?" Chisau had no intention to conceal his sarcasm, "I guess you are not. Besides, you shouldn't apologise to me. You know full well to whom you should be apologising." Chisau moved quickly on to what he would like to say, "I just want to make it clear to you that you do NOT have a free access to my office and you cannot threaten us in order to gain entry by creating a disturbance. Miss Wei will call Security next time and we won't be held responsible for any repercussion on your reputation or public image. Between the two of us, we have no more personal relationship. Even on business matters, I will avoid having any contact with you. I wish you would respect my wishes. Finally I give you one week to find some longer-term accommodation. A week from now, you MUST check out of the Hotel. I hope I would not need to send someone to vacate your room for you."

"Chisau…"

"This is all I've left to say to you. Everything about us in the past I've put down. Anyhow I feel I no longer know you. If you haven't changed, then I must have, or I've never known you. From today onwards, there's no more you and me, and I also wish that you'll no longer cause trouble for Miss Wei."

"Who's Cheung Yuetching? Why do you treat me like that because of her? Do you think you owe me an explanation?" Sinyin got frustrated.

"It has nothing to do with her. There's no sincerity in your apologise. To you, how things have turned out is never your fault but someone else's. Perhaps it's time you looked into yourself and took responsibility for your own actions."

Sinyin felt rejected and burst into tears. She was now a headache to him, and he wished she would disappear from his sight! He had learnt from his experience that this could be achieved more quickly if he walked out of the room rather than waiting for her to leave.

"See her out when she's ready," he instructed Miss Wei when he was passing.

He walked to Samyin's office and found it empty. He gave Samyin a ring.

"Hello, where are you? Is Yuetching with you?"

"Ah! We're applying for a day off today. Yuetching is with me. Don't worry," Samyin answered hand-free.

"Don't be too late. Drive safely."

"I know. Bye." He hung up.

Chisau sat in Samyin's office and let the idea sink in.

I must let go, he reminded himself.

As they were approaching the destination Samyin had in mind, Yuetching was surprised, "Why do you bring me here?"

Samyin smiled smugly, as if he had some insider information, "When you're unhappy, don't you go to your 'castle on the clouds'?"

"How do you know?" Yuetching then guessed it, "Chisau has told you."

"Yesterday we were pulling our heads together to work out where you could have gone. It came up in the process."

"I see."

They entered Disneyland and soon reached the Main Street that led to Sleeping Beauty's Castle, the iconic symbol! It was the first time that Yuetching got close to her imaginary scene! She took a deep breath as if to soak up the carefree and pain free atmosphere. "This is a town that makes people forget the reality, isn't it?" The child inside had returned to her. She took out the camera that Chisau gave her, and snapped a shot of Samyin when he was not paying attention with the Castle in the background.

"You don't want to miss anything, do you?" observed Samyin, "Otherwise, who would be committed to carry a camera in her bag at all times?"

"I feel I've missed too many days already not registering the colours in life." Simple yet powerful and deep, her words were always substance to chew on. To her, seeing was knowing; she carried the camera because she had promised to be receptive to the blessings in life.

"So what'd be your caption for the photo?" Samyin asked nervously; he would like to get a hint of what he meant to her. He anxiously waited for the clue.

Yuetching paused for thought, and then answered, "The Person who made my childhood dreams come true. This is the second time."

"What? You've never been?" Samyin was astonished.

"No."

"Why haven't you brought yourself here to fulfil your own wish? You could've done a long time ago!"

"If I have to fulfil every wish I had since I was little, then life would be very deliberate and contrived, wouldn't it? Do we live in a way to compensate for our past? Somehow I don't think this is a good way to live because it would be looking backward, constantly dwelling on past regrets and lacks, rather than forward. The clock can't be turned back. Even if I now do everything I've missed as a child, I still can't compensate what I didn't have then. It's meaningless to right the record in this intentional way. I imagine a bit of spontaneity would add to the surprise and joy in life. When it happens it happens, and it will be memorable how it happens in its own right, don't you think?"

Samyin marvelled at what she said, which had the power to change the direction of one's thinking completely. He looked at Yuetching admiringly, thinking that there was so much more about her than met the eyes.

"Do you mean I'll have a place in your memory?" Samyin tried to oblige Yuetching!

"Well, obviously; how can anyone forget you?" Yuetching gave him a smile.

Walking through the Castle, they reached the Princess Courtyard. Yuetching saw the hired "princesses" pacing up and down to greet the visitors, especially the children. They posted with them and signed their autographs as Snow White or Cinderella. This was interesting. These princesses acted as the icing on the cake in this make-believe world; they were part of the set. They grinned as if they had no worries, but to Yuetching, their whole demeanour, even their friendliness, was somewhat plastic and commercial. *When they return to their real life, how many would keep that grin going?* Yuetching wondered. *Do they get tired of looking happy as that is their job? Do they even hate looking happy for others when they are not?* In contrast, the happiness radiant from the children was more genuine. At least for the moments when they were in the Park, all their sadness and pains, if they had any, were forgotten. Their imagination was so powerful that they truly believed they were the princesses. They twirled in their dresses, looking beautiful and feeling special. *They* were the true princesses of this world; *they* made the Castle come to live with their heartfelt laughter! This world belonged to the little ones, while others were present to share their joy!

Samyin studied Yuetching's gaze which was so intense and hungry that her preying eyes were like black holes that nothing seemed to be able to escape. What a peculiar way to "play" in Disneyland! Samyin was bemused! Yuetching's face gradually relaxed and a smile appeared. *Does she project herself onto the children, living her childhood through them?* She seemed to have caught on the fun that the children were having!

They sat down on a bench and watched the children for a long while before Samyin plucked up the courage and asked directly, "Why? Why does finding a way to overcome Sinyin's words so terrifying to you that you're prepared even to change the course of your current life completely to avoid it? Why?"

The question instantly wiped the smile off her face. Her gaze betrayed her and revealed that her mind was no longer there and then with the children in Disneyland. She sighed and began with a tone weighted with heartfelt regrets, "Certain things in life can never be changed, however hard you try. What can you do? Among them are your identity and your family background. Some positions are reserved for people with an immaculate background, connections and a respectable name. They are out of reach for someone without a family or any identity. *I* am someone without a family or an identity. Even if I somehow land on such a position, I'll only find myself out of place and will never be able to convince others anyway. They will always ask, 'Who do you think you are? Do you know your place? You've overstepped your limits.' They ask all these questions before your competence. This is the world."

"Isn't it a bit defeatist?"

"Meritocracy is not a state of affairs but operates along a spectrum. It means that socio-economic background still matters; the difference is only in degree. Besides, what right do you have in making any comment on the matter? You belong to the class of privilege and have no idea. This is the reality for most people. I've been there before, so I know."

"*You have been there before*? What do you mean?"

"Don't want to talk about it."

"Talking it through may help you see through it," Samyin coaxed.

"No matter who you are, at the end of the day, it's what people say and believe about you that stick. They judge you first by your background. If that does not close off the door, you can't do anything right in a position without speculation of your ulterior motive. If enough people hold the same view, it becomes true."

"What bad experience have you had? Tell me."

Judging by how pensive she had turned, Samyin could tell it was an unhappy chapter in her life. But he still encouraged her to open up, "The first step to overcome it is to talk about it."

Looking askance at Samyin, she was questioning his interest in it. Samyin quickly clarified, "I've no other motive except to help you see a way out. You can trust me."

"Usually people who can't be trusted are those most keen to emphasise that they can be trusted." Samyin looked dejected on this remark. "Cheer up! I'm just pulling your leg." Yuetching laughed at him and he was relieved. Fixing her gaze forward, she took a deep breath and began her recollection.

"When I led a shadowy existence, no one cared to bother me. I had peace and freedom to do whatever I wanted. I lived in my own world and was happy there. The family was doing fine until I moved up to the secondary school, when *gujeung*'s business went bust. Financially it became tight. As the retrenchment bit more and more, I was looked upon by my cousins as the extra that they could not afford. They made their unwelcome known to me; only *guje* fought to protect me but not openly. There wasn't much to do except to study because school was free and compulsory. I threw myself into it to occupy my mind and distract my attention.

"I was not out to compete with anyone or trying to secure the top spot in class. It was just a personal choice of how to spend my time. But my effort did show up in grades and test scores. I got attention of the teachers who started giving me commendations in school assembly. Grades give you status at school. I suddenly became the dark horse to watch out for in tests. Some started to befriend me and soon I was brought into a particular group. There were five of us. I was not the leader of that group but a member. I thought I had friends but the group dynamics was just a headache. My concept of friendship transpired to be different from theirs. I was too trusting and naïve while theirs was measured friendship by what you could contribute to their welfare. We were a formidable team and were quite successful in inter-school competitions of various kinds.

We earned fame at school.

"Being a mixed school, we had a Head Boy and a Head Girl elected each year. In my last term at school, it had come to our turn as a year group. Teachers nominated me against the leader of our friendship group to bid for the position of the Head Girl. I went to discuss with the teachers that I didn't really want the limelight, but they insisted that it would be good for my personal development to run a campaign for the visions and ideals that I believed in. They said casually, 'What can you lose if you don't care to win anyway?' In hindsight, it was a misjudgement of my teachers. But at the time, I trusted them, so I threw myself into the campaign. I diligently studied the mandate of the student council, its interaction with the school and the governing body, and the ongoing issues in discussion. Based on my understanding, I drafted my election manifesto, which I thought was the basis of the campaign. I thought the electorate was to be appealed by reason, but I was wrong. Leaders need charisma which I had none. I was deserted by my friendship group who supported their leader. Who used to be my friends now turned antagonistic against me. I had to run my campaign against whom I used to call my friends! An election campaign is quite ugly, isn't it? It is not just about winning but also about taking the other party down by whatever means.

"I was not deterred but soldiered on. Believing in the strength of my manifesto, I thought I stood a chance if people could know it. One day I went to school and saw that all my posters were defaced. Written across them was a question, 'Can an orphan spring to sky?' I thought to myself, 'What has this got to do with the election? Who try to sabotage my campaign?' Subsequently, my family background and living conditions started to circulate on the school ground like news from gossip magazines. When private matters only those who lived with me could know started to surface, I knew my cousins were behind the smear campaign. With this sort of situations, if you provide people with some nuggets of facts, damaging rumours and half-truths about you would just spin out of control and catch on like wildfire. I went to interrogate my cousins of their actions and intentions, but they all denied it. I got really mad and physically fought them, who were my minors.

"When we got home, *gujeung* and *guje*, who knew none of the background, put all the blame of the fight on me. Yes, I was the one who started the fight. They scolded me and hit me. I ran out. I had one person and one mouth. How could I defend myself against the world? At that moment, I understood what it meant to be an orphan. It meant no one stood behind you to support you, to cheer you on or to defend you. Behind me there was no one. In this world, there was only me on my side. At that moment, I felt loneliness like never before. That night, I went to my hideout and did not go home.

"What hurt me most was that those whom I had called my friends did not show any solidarity to defend me. Even though we stood against each other in this campaign, were there values more important than winning the campaign? My enemies were their friends. They stood to gain when I was crushed, so they watched on the sideline if not also capitalised on my sorry state. The teachers did intervene and reprimanded my cousins. I was crazy to carry on. Perhaps I was so mad that I would like to get back at them by winning it and prove them wrong. I was naïve. The damage was done and I was discredited. Something I learnt from that experience was how scary public opinion was; it could have been for you one moment, and turned to devour you the next. On the election day, when I took the centre stage to give my pitch, no one was listening to what I had to say. It was hijacked by the smear around me. I was a joke, a clown, a sideshow; no one took me seriously. When an egg was thrown at me and hit me, I woke up from my fairyland where justice reigned and rewards were impartial.

"Losing was not the problem. What etched on my heart was the tacit rule of the world that an orphan without backing had no chance to lift his head in front of others. Any attempt to do so would only invite people's ridicule, whether it was vocal or silent.

"My teachers were wrong; I had lost much in that campaign. I had lost my friendship group, my beliefs, and my confidence. Feeling bad about what had happened, one of them came to tell me that it had been our leader's childhood dream to be the Head Girl when time came. She had lived and worked for that moment to be crowned as Head Girl. She wasn't to let anyone get in her way. I suppose that was her way of saying sorry for how I had been treated. I nodded and thanked her for explaining, but really it didn't matter. It was obvious where their loyalty lied and moral dilemma revealed our hearts. I came to know the person they were through this campaign. This was my gain.

"Have you ever felt so ashamed and embarrassed that you just want to vanish from the world? That was how I felt then. After the election, I withdrew myself from the world. I didn't talk to anyone as if my mouth were physically sealed up. Whether it was exhaustion or my silent protest against the world, it didn't matter. I channelled all my energy into studying perhaps as my surest way to escape from what I couldn't deal with at the time. It was my only defence mechanism. I successfully transformed myself into a transparent person in a crowd, who would threaten no more. My existence became marginal. Even if they came to poke fun at me, who cared? I didn't. My life was peaceful because my heart was unfeeling. I left school altogether soon after that; I didn't plan it but in a way, it was a relief also. I continued to mingle in the society as a Miss Nobody without any connections, until now I work at the Hotel. Who could've guessed the attention that other people give me is no different from the past when I was at school? You tell me, what should I do? I say just let them have their way; I have no intention to contest."

"You were betrayed by your friends; it was a big blow."

"Betrayed by my friends *and* my so-called family. The egg thrown at me sent me back to obscurity where no one saw me or knew me. It did suit me, just as Sinyin has said. She's also right in that there is no fairytale in real life, isn't she? I've learnt that from my experience, and it would be naïve of me to believe it; there is no Cinderella in life."

Samyin listened attentively and felt he had a better grasp of Yuetching's complicated complex. He made his attempt to encourage her, "Has it ever occurred to you that people could be jealous of you? The problem wasn't with you but with them. Because they couldn't win over you fair and square, they attacked your personal weaknesses, your confidence, and your self-belief. They're threatened by you and they felt insecure. Who wouldn't? Their strategy then was to put you down before you even had a chance to rise. It's jealousy. Don't you see?"

"What difference does it make?"

"So you're to be defeated without a fight? This is NOT the Yuetching whom I know."

"What can I do? You teach me."

"Follow Granddad's plan. Give your all to finalise the policy proposals. At the Annual Meeting, take your rightful place at the Hotel not just as Granddad's granddaughter but on your own merits. This will settle the controversy once and for all. There're no other workable solutions to this. You think leaving will quiet the rumours? Wrong. Rather it'll *confirm* the rumours. You think no one will gossip about you after you've left? Wrong again. The only difference is that you no longer hear it yourself. If you don't stay and give it time for the truth to unfold, rumours will be circulated as facts and will forever attach to you, whether you hear it or not. You can give up your job at the Hotel; fine. But is it worth giving up your new found family as well if and when the situation gets untenable because of malicious rumours? Personally I won't give it up without a fight. Having your family is your right; don't forfeit it for silly reasons. It's not easy for you guys to find each other, so please do not give it up for no wrong that the family has done this time round."

"I persevered till the end last time. What was the result? An utter disaster. What's the point? I do *not* wish to go through the same experience again."

"Yuetching, do you still remember your big dream? Big dreams can't be realised by a *transparent* person in the crowd. They require a face, a voice, a champion and a platform to make them happen. You are someone with visions and ability, which need a certain position to complement for accomplishment, if you are serious about your belief of making a difference to the world around you. Otherwise all your talks will remain dreams which benefit no one. Would you be curious to know how the world would change cumulatively as you work to *implement* all your little dreams?"

"Why would I put myself out as a target of attack?"

"This isn't about yourself but about what difference you could make for the benefits of others. Are you to give up this opportunity? Conviction is costly."

"I…"

"How many times do you intend to run away in life? Is this going to be the pattern of coping with nasty adversaries?"

"…"

"Haven't you once said to me you have a belief: 'Even on my own, and with my negligible ability and influence, I can still make this world a better place to be'? Do you really believe in what you say you believe in? If you do, call upon that belief now."

"..."

"What kind of life would you want to lead: one that is calm without a storm so that you can come and go without leaving a trace of your existence, or one that you work to exhaust all you've got, seeking to make a difference to others because of your existence? This is not a life goal but a life attitude. If you've never had such an opportunity, admittedly this debate would've remained academic. But you have an opportunity right in front of you now, how are you going to choose? Besides, this is your destiny; you can't run away even if you want to. Can you run away from being who you really are? Rise up, and grow into the person you are supposed to be!

"Give yourself an opportunity; stay with us, at least till the Annual Meeting. This is not only for your own sake; it's for Chisau and me. If you leave now, what are we going to do with the preparation for the Annual Meeting? We have only four months to go. After the Annual Meeting, you can decide if you are to stay or to leave. By that time, you may change your mind. Could you do this much for us? Please let me beg you to stay and help us out for now. You can't abandon us at this critical point. Please?"

"Am I really a great help to you and Chisau?" asked Yuetching doubtfully.

"Yuetching, you can doubt all aspects of yourself *except* your competence. You *must not* believe in anyone who tells otherwise," Samyin affirmed.

Yuetching smiled; she seemed to see a light breaking through the darkness. She remembered she had promised herself not to live a life in fear, in cowardice, in timidity. She even forced herself to confront her worst fear in order to find the courage to hold her head high. She recalled the sweet taste of victory every time she swam, and how Chisau asked her the previous night, "Where's the courage that has enabled you to swim?" Perhaps this was the linchpin of the whole matter, and Chisau saw it from the start. In any case, she was not someone who would like to leave things incomplete. Helping out till the Annual Meeting would bring the current phase of work to its natural end, and gave her an opportunity to hand over her work neatly. This neatness appealed to her.

Samyin got a little nervous waiting for Yuetching's decision. He gave his final offer to seal the deal, "All right, when we get back, I promise you to do two things: first, I'll announce formally that we hire you as my personal assistant on merits; second, in order not to fuel any new rumours, I'll get more involved by handling any interdepartmental interactions that are beyond your capacity as my personal assistant in this project. For example, I'll personally request for highly sensitive documents and information, and for co-operation from other departments. You can accompany me to meetings under the pretext as my PA, but we know that the three of us work on equal basis in this project. What do you say?"

Yuetching came to see that Samyin's charm was not hollow; he had people's skills that made things workable and comfortable for people. Moved by his sincerity, Yuetching accepted his proposal and offer. She promised to stay till the Annual Meeting, when she would revisit her decision.

"That's a relief. Mission's accomplished!"

"Mission? Who's sent you?"

"I have!" replied Samyin cheekily.

Feeling relieved, Samyin invited, "We're not going to sit here all day, are we? Shall we go and play?"

Yuetching agreed and they had a wonderful time doing all the things that kids did at Disneyland. As it was not a holiday, they could go round all the attractions efficiently. As with all things that she set her heart to do, she did not hold back and thoroughly enjoyed every moment as if she would never have the chance to come back. She had such capacity to be happy precisely because she had so little in the past.

They did not go home until the Park closed. Chisau was waiting for them. When he saw Yuetching's bright countenance, he knew Samyin had succeeded in dispelling the dark cloud that was overhanging her. Whatever means he had used, it was effective.

"What's your decision, to stay or to resign?" asked Chisau directly.

"Yuetching has promised to stay till the Annual Meeting, when she'll decide her next step," answered Samyin on Yuetching's behalf.

"That's wonderful!" Chisau heaved a sigh of relief. "I'm relieved to see you lighten up and back to your usual self again.

Let's work hard tomorrow!"

Yuetching echoed, "I only need to find the courage that has enabled me to swim!" Chisau smiled with delight. "Sorry for causing your grief last night and this morning," Yuetching apologised. "I'll work hard tomorrow."

"Don't mind it too much. A confidence crisis can hit anyone. When it's my turn next time, I hope you'll encourage me," said Chisau.

Yuetching nodded– it was a promise.

"In order to give you a break from the Hotel environment, I've decided to send you two to ---- Island for a site visit – our new business venture. Should we decide to go ahead, it will be the core of our medium-term business plan. But first, we need to do some information gathering in order to conduct the necessary analysis that will help us make that decision."

Samyin was surprised because it was the first time he heard about this trip himself. He was delighted that he could go on holiday with Yuetching under such a brilliant excuse!

"You're to set off the day after tomorrow," Chisau continued. "We have a holiday home on the island. When you are on this business trip, you can look in there also. You can check that everything in the house is functioning properly for us," Chisau joked. He cleared his throat and instructed, "Use tomorrow to prepare for the trip. Now Yuetching, you can go upstairs to rest, and I'll see Samyin out."

Yuetching was a little startled that Chisau suddenly sent her away, but she was too tired to find out why. She turned to Samyin to thank him once again for the day before she complied with Chisau's request. Chisau walked Samyin out, and asked out of curiosity, "Where did you bring her today?"

"Thanks for your tip, I brought her to Disneyland."

"Then she must be very happy," Chisau only regretted that it wasn't he who brought her.

"Of course! She had never been before today! And today I've become the person who granted her the wish," Samyin could not conceal his delight.

"Really?" Chisau felt like he had just swallowed a very sour grape!

"Have you confessed?" Chisau continued to probe.

"What?" Samyin did not expect the question.

"Then, when do you intend to confess?"

Unprepared for such a question, Samyin was totally embarrassed. "I haven't thought about it yet, given that I'm sure of my feelings for her only recently."

"Don't say that I haven't provided you with an opportunity."

"What? Do you deliberately send us on the trip together?" Samyin was surprised by Chisau's revelation.

"When you told me last night, I was a little startled. But when I think about it, you're not a bad choice if I were to entrust Yuetching to someone."

"*Not a bad choice*? I didn't know your opinion of me was so low!" protested Samyin.

"Have you never heard the saying that to a father, no son-in-law is ever good enough for his daughter? Even though I'm only Yuetching's older cousin, my instinct to protect her is no less than a father has for his daughter. Perhaps it's because she has lost her parents since she was little. Please don't disappoint me, and don't you dare break her heart!"

"Does it mean that I have your permission and blessing to pursue her?"

Chisau nodded, adding, "Even though I have approved, the most important thing is how she feels about you. On this, I can't help and I won't force."

"Thank you," said Samyin with all his heart.

Driving off with his broad grin, Samyin surely would have sweet dreams that night. In contrast, it was a difficult choice for Chisau to let Yuetching go from his care. Unknowingly, he had got so accustomed to having her under his wings that he knew he would feel an acute sense of loss when she one day flew away. That day now seemed to approach much faster than he was prepared for.

Samyin and Yuetching embarked on their seven-day site visit to ---- Island. The island had been made famous as the filming location for a movie franchise which had grown in popularity over the years. It had successfully amassed a vibrant international fan base which underscored the island's potential to become a popular holiday destination. A movie theme park, for example, was in discussion, which would provide a focal point for visiting families and fans alike to live out the movie experience. Tourism however meant commercialism and would inevitably change the local dynamics and outlook, which no economic benefits could directly offset. The tradeoff between development and preserving the local characters and scenic beauty was not always sensitively struck, nor was it ever easy to strike, leaving local residents marginalised and feeling resentful.

"The original attraction of this place is being a tranquil retreat from the world. Now the world is going to come in," Samyin lamented.

"You sound as though you wanted the Hotel to leave it alone," replied Yuetching.

"If it were not our Hotel, there would be others. It makes no difference to the fate of this place, so my regret has no bearing on our business decision."

Yuetching nodded as if enlightened.

"On the contrary if our Hotel is a player, we might lend weight to a more considerate approach than otherwise," he added.

"I see."

"How do you soak up the local characters?" Samyin quizzed suddenly.

"How?"

"Be as inconspicuous as possible."

"Be inconspicuous, as tourists? Is it even possible that locust swarms can be inconspicuous? This is not what they are here for. They think they come here to spend money, so they should get what they are here to buy. I don't think many tourists aim to blend in or discover the life of the locals while they are on holiday! They simply don't have time to do that. They are here to have a good time, whatever it means to them."

"We have to soak up this place first, before we can educate others how to enjoy this place." Wide-eyed, Yuetching did not expect to be constantly surprised by Samyin, who stretched her mind and challenged her with a new way of thinking. Her perspective of this trip had been completely flipped around. Suddenly she felt she had so much to learn – from Samyin. "Lifestyle is about people in relation with their environment. Let's discover it; seven days aren't enough! Let's go! No time to lose."

They worked hard to gather local information while gaining some first-hand experience of the place. Samyin spent the first evening studying the information and planning their itinerary of the trip; it was an absorbing exercise, which demanded Samyin's total focus. Feeling redundant, Yuetching retreated to her room for the night. They rose bright and early the following day. Having travelled widely, Samyin acted as a tour guide; all Yuetching had to do was to follow and enjoy! They started each day by making a working assumption of their budget, ranging from holiday on a shoestring to a luxurious experience where money was not an issue! They employed and assessed a range of tourist services from a tourist's point of view starting with a different accommodation each day. They also moved off the tourist hotspots to gain an insight into the life of the local community. They toured by public transport to see how accessible and affordable facilities were. They even rated the family friendliness of the place and identified where there might be lacks with the existing provisions! The various famous film locations were the must-seen. For them to come to live, they reckoned that reminders of the movie scenes in one form or another would help tremendously. It was an eye-opening experience for a novice tourist like Yuetching. Apart from having a good time, it was also a study trip with Samyin as the tutor. She was seeing the world through his eyes, which was always colourful, fun and delightful, as well as surprisingly sentimental and relational. "To see the people, you need to take time."

Yuetching never knew holiday could be so much fun as well as intellectually engaging; she had *never* enjoyed herself as much as on this trip. Life to her had always been harsh and, at times, exhausting. But through Samyin, she experienced an aspect of life that had largely eluded her thus far – joy. Samyin was inadvertently opening her up by cultivating her capability to see and in turn enjoy the goodness in life. "It's all around us, if only you care to look. To me, *lifestyle* collects the best of human ingenuity; it's a celebration of life steeped in knowledge of the people's story if we are to appreciate it fully."

Throughout the trip, Yuetching was preoccupied with jotting notes. As time was pressing, she could not always afford to sketch. But on those rare occasions where Samyin had built in windows for them to "take time", sketching was a reliable way to "take it all in" – more so than snapping photos. When she was sketching, Samyin would silently engage with the scenery. It suddenly occurred to her that Samyin probably could sketch very well as he was an architect, and she would like to see it. She invited him to do so by passing her sketchbook and drawing pencil to him. Samyin looked at her and smiled. He took his idle hands out of his pockets and accepted the invitation. His hand moved familiarly and skilfully across the page and soon the image began to take shape. To Yuetching's astonishment, he sketched out the space that people could not yet see – a concept of the new hotel! Yuetching had not expected it and was speechless. "Are you so inspired?" "It's an occupational habit. I just see it." Yuetching looked at this rudimentary concept in front of her, and recalled Samyin's dream, which was to make visible the space and surrounding beauty that people could not see. "It's effortless for a talented person to work," Yuetching was almost envious. "Wrong! It takes a lot of work to bring a concept to fruition, *so much* hard work that you won't even imagine!" A man of substance instead of a man of pomp – he certainly was maturing into one, at least in Yuetching's eyes.

It was their last day on the island and Yuetching suggested that perhaps they could check out Chisau's holiday home and try self-catering by cooking their own dinner. Samyin agreed. So they ended their tour by shopping groceries at an open market. Yuetching was prepared with extra carrier bags, which were soon filled up with ingredients.

"Let me carry them," offered Samyin.

"You don't need to treat me like a lady; I'm used to carrying shopping."

"You aren't *like* a lady; you *are* a lady. How do I not treat you *as* a lady when you *are* a lady? Let me carry them."

"Well I can't argue with you on that," so Yuetching complied.

When they got to Chisau's family property, Yuetching quickly checked out the place while Samyin unpacked the shopping in the kitchen.

"Are you not curious at all?" asked Yuetching, when she returned to the kitchen.

"Does it occur to you that I've been here before?" replied Samyin.

"I'm going to take one of the guest rooms."

"Why don't you take the en-suite?"

"Nay, it feels like a master room."

"That's fine, whatever makes you feel comfortable."

"It's a bit dusty. How long have they not been here for?"

"Granddad has not been well, remember?"

"Of course. Let me give the kitchen surface a quick wipe." Yuetching looked through the cupboards for cleaning products. "Why did they buy their holiday home here?"

"It's a tranquil place away from the world – is it not an attraction? It's a scenic place to slow down from the hustle and bustle of city life." Samyin moved out of the way for Yuetching to clean the kitchen.

"But as you say, this place's going to change with the development. Will they be sad?"

"Well, the location of this house is such that I think they will have a choice when they come here if they would like to keep out of the tourists."

"This is a roundabout way to say this is in the middle of nowhere!" laughed Yuetching.

"You may say so!" echoed Samyin.

"You did most of the shopping; are you going to cook for us tonight?" asked Yuetching.

"I can cook."

"Are you a good cook?"

"It depends on the standard you apply, but I do cook. Eating out a lot helps. If you can't create your own, you can always steal!"

"What style of cooking are you 'stealing' tonight?"

"An assorted western style."

"What's that?"

"It means improvisation!" They both laughed.

"Okay, the kitchen is ready for use. It's all yours, Chef. I can be your assistant. How may I help?" Yuetching looked through the drawers and asked, "Do they have aprons?"

Samyin walked up and got the aprons out for both of them.

Yuetching scrubbed up and was all ready for action. Samyin suddenly got all fluttered being around her. He cleared his throat, recollected his thoughts and made himself focus on cooking the dinner. He moved in and took charge of the kitchen as the Chef and began to instruct Yuetching what to do. Working side by side with her in a tight space somehow made Samyin's heart pound. He blushed! He turned his back to Yuetching to hide from her, while she tackled her task on hand with her usual focus and efficiency. When the preparation was done, Yuetching excused herself from the kitchen to make room for his creativity, she said. Samyin breathed a sigh of relief! He regrouped and focused, striving to deliver an unforgettable romantic dinner with Yuetching. Not only must the food be superb, the setting must also be spot on. To complete the presentation, Samyin dressed the table for two, lit the candles, dimmed the lights and even managed to find some romantic melodies to hum in the background. He was pleased with what he had improvised.

"That'll do," he said to himself smugly. *Everything is set perfectly for a perfect evening,* thought Samyin.

He went to fetch Yuetching, but couldn't find her anywhere. He heard water sound from the bathroom, which guided him to look in that direction.

"What are you doing?" Samyin found Yuetching inside the bathtub scrubbing it with the shower head in one hand.

Yuetching looked up and said, "Cleaning the bath; it's dusty if nothing else."

"But we have the walk-in shower."

"But you may wish to have a bath to relax – you know – after a week of hard work? This bathtub is big so I have to climb in to clean it."

"You do this – for me?"

"Yes, I don't take bath."

"You're such a silly silly girl." Samyin did not know what to say, except to rescue his princess out of the bathtub! "My Lady, dinner is served." He extended his hand out for hers.

"What?" Yuetching was a little stunned. "But I haven't finished here yet."

"Leave it. I'd rather have your company than taking a bath tonight," he was speaking princely, but Yuetching wasn't playing along! She was not accepting his hand, so Samyin reached over attempting to switch off the water. Yuetching got to her feet quickly to stop him, saying, "It's dangerous to leave it…" As she spoke, she slipped on her footing and the shower head went flying. In catching her, Samyin fell into the tub with her and his back hit the taps and controls as he went down. "Ouch!" Samyin let out.

Samyin found himself lying in the bathtub with Yuetching in his arms; the shower was spraying on them. "Are you hurt?" She was his only concern in that moment. Yuetching shook her head, "But you are." She felt very guilty. "I'm so sorry."

Although in pain, Samyin did not want this moment to pass – they were so close, so so close. Yuetching tried to move away to reach for the tap, but Samyin tightened his grip as if to say, "don't go, let's stay like this just a little longer."

"What's the matter? Are you in a lot of pain?" Yuetching understood the squeeze as tension from his pain. She explained, "Let me just swi –" Samyin stopped her from finishing her sentence by planting a kiss on her. She froze and was startled. In a split second, as if seeing the nightmare replaying in her mind's eye, instantly she was filled with terror. In a fit of hysteria, she struggled to break free, screaming, "No, No, No!" "Let me go!" Samyin heard her cry and instantly released his grip. He saw a tearful and frightened Yuetching in his arms, the same pallid look he had seen when she suffered from shock. "Are you all right? What's wrong?" Alarmed by what happened last time and by his memory of how sick she got, he did not take this lightly. Yuetching was shivering.

She got up and climbed out of the bathtub as quickly as she could manage. She was sobbing, she slipped and fell. She got on to her feet again and ran out of the bathroom as fast as she could. Samyin was not as quick as he would have liked to go after her because he was indeed injured. He heard the slam of the door. At long last, he clambered out of the bathtub and went after her. He followed the water marks on the floor which led to a guest room, and knocked. There was no reply. He turned the knob. At least it was locked. He checked the front door just to make sure – he was relieved that it hadn't been opened. By all evidence, Yuetching should be safe inside the house whatever was churning in her head. He felt he had to guard the house. Yet he knew there was no stopping her if she was determined to run away as there was always the window. So he went to check the other windows of the house and was relieved to find that they were locked for security reason. He went back to the room and knocked, trying to coax Yuetching to open the door to him. His speech was punctuated by expressions of agony from the pain of his back.

"I'm sorry," apologised Samyin most sincerely. "Please say something so that I know you're okay." He lingered outside her door and kept talking. "I didn't mean to frighten you. I'm too hasty. I'm sorry but it's genuine on my part. Please just give me some indication that you're all right." She was not yielding. He began to feel the chill, so he left his guarding post temporarily to change out of his wet clothes. *What's going through her mind? Has it brought up some past trauma again? What could it be this time?* He returned to her room and pleaded with her to eat something. "Even if you don't want your dinner, you know that it's better to have someone by your side at a time like this." Samyin sighed. He knew it probably would be a long night, so he went to gobble up his dinner to keep his strength up. He put out the candle and turned off the music. *How could a perfect night turn out to be such a disaster? What am I going to say to Chisau? He would be so mad at me. Should I break down the door to make sure that she's safe?*

After dinner, he went back to sit outside Yuetching's door. He knew it's better to own up to Chisau about what had happened or he would be guilty of concealment if nothing else. He texted Chisau:

Samyin: *Really sorry, but you should come at your earliest convenience.*

Chisau: *What's up?*

Samyin: *I might have done something that has triggered some bad memory in Yuetching. In shock, like last time.*

At that point, Chisau picked up the phone and called. Samyin gave him an outline of the event. "If you wish to tell me off, it's fine. But right now, I'm more concerned of Yuetching. I don't know how long it'll take this time for her to get over this. She isn't talking to me at the moment. Do you know where the keys to the rooms are so that I may gain entry without breaking down your door?" Chisau didn't know off hand, so he had to find out.

Chisau told Samyin in a text where the keys were kept in the house, and added: *I'll be on the first flight out tomorrow. Keep her safe for the night.*

Samyin got the keys and opened the door. He found Yuetching curled up like a fetus in a corner for comfort or security. Afraid of frightening her, he edged forward gingerly and invited no response. So he moved forward a bit more until he was in front of her. Her face was totally buried, but he could see that she was breathing and still wet.

"At least dry yourself and change out of these clothes or you'll get sick," he coaxed.

Seeing that she was not responding, he pulled the duvet off the bed to cover her.

"Chisau will be here first thing tomorrow morning." He thought this might bring her comfort. They sat through the night without words. When Yuetching fell asleep, Samyin moved her to the bed. He brushed her hair away and exposed her tear-stained face. *How much sorrow and sadness is your tiny heart storing?* It did seem disproportionate. *How long will it take to drain it all out? I'm so sorry to have caused you pain when I meant to bring your happiness? I'm disqualified to take care of you, ain't I?* Samyin was dejected and regretted how the evening had turned and the otherwise wonderful trip was closed.

His back ached much, so he lied down on the floor in an attempt to find a comfortable position for the night which proved to be impossible.

Chisau woke him up.

"Wow! You're early! What time is it?"

"First flight out at 6.00. Hardly slept."

Samyin could not hide his agony as he moved.

"What's wrong with you?"

"I hurt my back when I tried to catch her from the fall in the bathtub."

"You haven't mentioned it. Let me take a look… It looks you've hurt yourself quite badly on impact. You should have it checked out properly."

"I know, but I can't leave her, can I? The pain has gotten worse overnight," he groaned. "I'll go to emergency, now that you're here."

"How's she?"

"Not a word. No food or drink for the whole night. She sleeps fitfully as if having a bad dream all night."

Chisau walked up to her bed, and saw that she looked contorted with pain.

"What has caused her such pain?"

Samyin struggled to get up on his feet and Chisau lent him a hand.

"You would find out all right," said Samyin.

"Only me and not us?" Chisau expressed his surprise.

"Well, I'm not sure if I'm still qualified in taking care of her. Look what a mess I have made. Have I broken her trust in me? I don't know. Do I still stand a chance? I don't know. I'm confused and ashamed of myself. I'm sorry I've let you down. I've also broken your trust in me. Apart from last night, we have had a very fruitful work trip. It was great fun. But it's all spoilt. This may be the only thing that she would remember about the trip."

"These are all speculations at this stage. It may not be as bad as you think."

"I tried to save her from physical harm only to cause her psychological damage? How ironic!"

"You're feeling rotten."

"How can you not be? I'm grateful you're not adding to that sinking feeling."

"Let's find out the truth about this before we lay blame."

"Whatever it may be, it's likely to be highly sensitive."

Yuetching woke up to the welcoming face of Chisau and she smiled at him.

"A smile! Not a bad start at all. How are you feeling?"

Yuetching sat up and found herself aching all over for no apparent reason.

"Have a drink first, please."

Yuetching was compliant.

"You're still covered in cleaning product. Would you like to have a shower?"

She nodded.

After she had cleaned herself up, she came to the living area and found Chisau.

"Would you like something to eat?"

Yuetching stared at the dining table set up for last night as if studying it.

"It seems that Samyin went through a lot of trouble to impress you last night. It's a shame that it didn't go according to plan."

"Where's he?" were Yuetching's first words since last night.

"He's gone to the hospital to check out his injury from last night."

"Is it bad?" she showed concern.

"It's definitely sore. We'd like to be sure that he hasn't done anything to his spine."

"It's my fault – that he's injured."

She sat down where she should have been sitting last night and wondered.

"He has saved your dinner for you. Would you like to have it now?"

Yuetching nodded. Chisau got it out of the fridge and heated it up for her.

"It's good to see that you want to eat. Last time –" Chisau stopped there as he was not sure if it was wise to draw an association with last time hastily.

Chisau served up the food, and sat down opposite her. Yuetching studied the food as if trying to read Samyin's mind behind what he was making her for dinner. It was only when she was satisfied that she started tasting it. She took time to chew, observing how the combination worked together. She tried to work out the order to take her food as intended and she got it right. Chisau was most impressed. Compared to how she used to gobble up her meals in the shortest time possible especially when she was ravenous, her transformation was remarkable in just one week under the intense tutelage of Samyin.

She cleaned her plate.

"Impressive. He has taught you a lot during this trip, hasn't he?"

She nodded.

"You miss him?"

She did not answer.

"Thank you for coming."

"Not at all."

"Shall we go out for a walk?"

"Sure."

They walked for hours before sitting down to watch the beach. He waited patiently next to her; he was content to be there even if they did not speak a word to each other. They quietly watched the tides together. Whether the sea was her friend or foe, her comfort or disquiet, who could tell? But to be sure, it had a special tug on her.

"The sea is my curse and my blessing... I have never quite worked out to love it or to hate it.... But it pulls me and it calls me.... I'm drawn to it... I've sat by the seaside and pondered many life lessons and decisions." Yuetching spoke intermittently.

"I've never known there is so much in there that need to be sorted through." She put her hand on her heart.

"Darkness can be so heavy, weighing on your heart.

"It can be so dense at times that it does not let light in.

"It's exhausting to have to keep battling through them, but

they keep coming.

"Two battles in ten days; this is intense, isn't it?

"I had no idea how these emotional scars had affected me until they were triggered.

"It surprises me also.

"I'm sorry to have caused alarm and got people worried."

"Don't be silly."

"I'm somewhat damaged, ain't I?"

"Everyone has his own baggage. You're not alone." Chisau tried to reassure her.

"I've never told you why I left *guje*'s home at the age of 16, have I?"

Chisau shook his head.

"The reason is only known to me and *guje*. I've never told a third person. Perhaps it was my deliberate effort to forget. But what happened last night brought back the memory. It makes me realise that no matter how hard I've tried to erase it from my memory, it's futile – I'm still living in the tormenting shadow of my past. I realise now I can't run away from it forever. To conquer it, I must face it head on. I'm trying to find the strength to stand up again. This is also because of my promise to you, remember? *The blessings that you wish me to have I'll try to fight for and experience.* I realise that what often stand between me and blessings in life are the shadows of my past. For me to open the path for blessings to come into my life, I must face up and in turn conquer these shadows, one by one as time has led me. No matter how unwilling my heart is, this is a necessary evolution that I must pass through. I need the courage to be healed.

"I believe Samyin has told you what happened last night."

"Yes, I know broadly what happened."

"When I was 16, something similar happened to me and in Samyin's place it was *gujeung*." Chisau's jaw dropped with shock, but he did not interrupt.

"That day I went home after school. *Gujeung* was drunk as usual. Coincidentally, only I was at home with him. I was doing my homework at the dining table, where he fell asleep, drunk. He woke up, and tried to get on to his feet, perhaps to move to the bedroom for the more comfortable bed. But he was unsteady and kept stumbling. Without thinking, my natural instinct was to lend him some support. I held him for a few steps, but then he lost his balance and toppled over me. We both landed on the floor, and he was on top of me. I couldn't move and had not enough strength to push him away – he was a huge guy. He was looking down at me with his dreamy eyes. My instinct alerted me to danger and I struggled to get free. Suddenly he pushed me down and started kissing me. I screamed, and kicked, and wiggled to avoid him … I was… I was … terrified." It was painful for Yuetching to relive the scene. She was shivering with fright just by recounting the event and thinking what it could have been. She felt the panic anew, and tears started to roll down. Chisau found her some tissue paper. He put his arm round her to give her comfort and security.

After Yuetching had calmed down, Chisau let go of her. She took a deep breath and continued, "Do you believe in God, who watches over you without slumber? He saved me. He sent *guje* home early that day because she felt unwell. She walked into the flat at that critical moment to save me from that monster. Having pushed him over and got me up from the floor, she hit him and fought him and cursed him. He erupted and started beating *guje* up! I grabbed her bag and managed to trip *gujeung*. When he was on the floor, I pulled *guje* away. Both of us ran away. I took *guje* to a pharmacist so that her wounds got cleaned up and dressed. She was so shaken that she could not think or speak. Right there, my teetotalism was sealed. We found somewhere to sit down and pondered about our future. When she came to her senses, the first thing she asked me was if it had happened before. I answered, no. She was relieved. Even so, she was adamant that I could not return home. She took me to a friend of hers whom she could trust and asked her to put me up for a while, until she could find me a place to stay. She came back after two weeks to 'reclaim' me. I'll never forget her parting speech to me. She said, 'Before your *gujeung* commits a crime against you, and makes me ashamed to face your father, I need to send you away from this home. I've rented a little studio flat for you in a nice area far far away from here. I've already paid the rent for two years. In these two years, the landlord can't terminate your tenancy. Here's a little money. This is all that I can spare. Even I'm unwilling, this is the best way to ensure your safety. After you've left, don't contact me, don't come back to visit me, don't even return to this neighbourhood. In short, you must completely cut off from us. I don't want to drag you down, and you mustn't let your *gujeung* find you. You must be strong on your own. Understand? Yuetching, I'm sorry. I can no longer take care of you or protect you. This is the best I can do. I feel ashamed to have to send you away. Please forgive me.' She sobbed as she put the address, the keys to the apartment and the money into my hands, and sent me away with my suitcase that she packed. 'You're sure you can find the place?' I nodded. This was how I started a new life on my own.

"The studio flat that *guje* rented for me was very far from where they lived. It was a completely new neighbourhood. But then my heart was bursting with excitement too. It was after all the first time I had my own space. I was at peace, and deep in my heart, I was grateful for the sacrifice that *guje* had made for me. Although she had given me a new beginning, she hadn't taught me how to live. I had limited money in my hands, which would be exhausted one day. I had to find a way to earn a living. I sat in the flat and thought for a week. I decided that I could quit school but I couldn't quit studying. This was how I started working full-time and going to evening school! I did various odd jobs at weekends. After two years I took the public exams and got into a university; my tenancy expired and I moved into students' accommodation. What happened thereafter you already know.

"Do you remember you have once asked me if I have any longings for love? The truth is that I don't know what it should be. Before I know love, I already have to pick up the pieces from brokenness. You know how things happened in your formative years could screw up your head, even though I know I've been saved from the worst! Still I feel I'm messed up about love. I don't know what it is or how it should be. Physical intimacy terrifies me; the whole concept makes me frigid. It feels like exploitation that I have to defend myself. No doubt I'm curious but I'm also scared as I know how badly wrong it could go. Romantic movies are probably the next best thing for me to observe love from a distance. By watching different cases, I hope to understand more. But sometimes I feel what's been frequently portrayed is also empty and shallow. The answer to what love really is still eludes me.

"It's true that I've never dated anyone. My way to deal with it is not to deal with it! And staying away from boys has been my way to protect myself. I don't know if I can ever overcome this

227

psychological barrier to physical intimacy. Will I ever be able to accept a kiss without affrightment?"

Chisau thought that it was a reflective question to herself, but unexpectedly Yuetching was looking to him earnestly for an answer! That was awkward. He felt it was out of his depth to counsel her on such a delicate matter, but it was not easy for her to open up, how could he turn her away when she placed such confidence in him? Who else could she turn to? If he did not talk this through with her now, there might never be a second chance for her to talk with anyone else. Therefore gingerly he attempted his task. "This – I think – well –" Chisau struggled to find words. He took a breath and restarted, "This – I think – isn't something that you can just use your brain to reason in advance. Rather it's something that you use your heart to feel at the time as well. Sometimes, physical advances of boys are violations. Pushing them away is the absolutely right thing to do. Love is much much more than physical love. If boys are only looking for physical love with no commitment or any sense of responsibility, stay away. Physical intimacy is an expression of love, but it's not love itself. Love comes first if that makes sense."

Yuetching was chewing on every word Chisau was telling her. He continued, "Yuetching, I believe when you meet someone you really love, kissing will be the most natural thing that will happen. Your heart will lead you there. In the meantime, you don't need to worry if it'll ever happen or to rationalise too much if you should let someone kiss you or to rush in just for the experience. If you're not ready, you're not ready. You shouldn't reason yourself into doing anything you don't want to do. Above all, never think that you'll offend if you say no. Any decent guy should care about the girl's feeling and also guard her reputation. Understand? For a girl, it's actually wise and right to take a more conservative approach with boys. Trust me, I'm also a boy."

"Truly?" Somehow Yuetching found Chisau's version of love reassuring.

"Yes, truly." Acting as her guardian, Chisau suddenly felt he needed to reiterate the key points: "Today, people have different opinions of what love is and everything seems permissible. But this is what I think or what I want to find in love. Intimacy is not something that should be forged but progress with the development of the relationship. It should never be taken out of that context. Making physical attraction and intimacy the basis on which love builds, you find your love on a shaky, if not empty, ground. And even within a loving relationship, both sides have to be willing. If there is reluctance on either side, then it should not be. The girl especially should not compromise just to please. If you aren't ready to be hugged or kissed, then say no. If the boy really loves and cares for you, he'll respect your wishes and wait. The bottom line is that you should never force yourself into anything you aren't ready for. You must remember that you are a lady and should demand to be treated as one. Understand?" Suddenly Chisau got all shy and flushed, "Sorry, I'm blushing myself talking about these things." He cleared his throat. "It should've been your mother teaching you about this kind of things. But since you don't have anyone to ask, I just have to step in and play the role, even though it's a little embarrassing and I probably have done a lousy job!"

"No, I thank you for taking me seriously and not laughing at me! What you portray is much better than anything I've watched or read. In your portrayal, love is no longer a fearful prospect, so much so that it may even be something I could handle! Thank you for helping me see this breakthrough even though it's awkward for you."

"In return I thank you for your trust; it's not easy for you ask either."

Yuetching got a little shy, but she plucked up the courage to ask, "In a relationship, how … how far should you go? Should you go as far as *that*?"

Chisau was not sure what Yuetching was asking, so he guessed, "*That*? Oh, *that*. Well, even though I may be the only one in the world, I still believe in the beauty of marriage – one man and one woman committed to each other till death do they part. I would say wait and reserve *that* to happen within the marriage. Speaking from a man's point of view, I believe I should never demand that of a girl, if I'm not prepared to marry her. If I'm prepared to marry her, then I should wait till I've married her. In the meantime I should care about her reputation and purity. No matter how hard it's for me, this is how I'd like to treat my lady as a lady deserves before marriage, while you, young lady, must have self-respect. I know I can't impose my view on you, but as your guardian, I do sincerely hope you would believe in marriage too – it'll grieve me a lot to see you go through the heartache of incessant emotional turmoil or being mistreated in relationships."

Astonished, Yuetching was speechless.

"Why? Do you not agree?" Chisau got a little worried.

"Quite the contrary, I think it's beautiful, simple and straightforward as it should be. I find it so attractive that for the first time I feel a tug of the longing for it, as it should have been all along." Yuetching smiled shyly, "Thank you for recovering that for me." Chisau found it gratifying that his counsel yielded positive result in her.

"Find the right guy who shares your vision and you stand a chance for it to work. Settle for nothing less than that." Chisau wished this blessing be hers one day.

"What happened last night then? Why was Samyin trying to do?"

Chisau laughed heartily at Yuetching's cluelessness! "Can you believe that he likes you; he likes you a lot actually?"

"What?" Yuetching never imagined it.

"Believe it or not, it was probably his confession of love," Chisau spoke for Samyin, "Why I'm helping him to tell you this I don't know!"

"You've known?"

"Yes. He was unsure himself, so we talked about it. Now that you know about this, do you like him?"

"I can't imagine it! How is it possible that a sophisticated guy likes a rustic girl? Doesn't he find me uncouth?"

"Love does not always follow a formula."

"We do get on, however. In fact, I've known him a lot better on this trip."

"I can see his influence on you. You only imitate people you admire."

"Is it how it is?"

"Isn't this logical? He says you are the first girl he loves even though he may have dated quite a few."

"What's the difference between the two?" Yuetching was confused.

"Samyin explains the difference in this way: previously he was living out the girls' expectations of him. With you, there isn't such pressure. On the contrary as he selflessly wanting the best for you, you bring out the best of him and help him know himself better. He is like a different person under your spell. You make him realise he has never loved before. And I suppose he does care for you a lot. He gets serious about you without even dating you."

"What does that mean?"

"I don't necessarily speak for others, but this is what I think. Dates are the initial steps when two people get to know each other with their lives still set on separate tracks. They have their own pursuits and autonomy. Their life may be going in different directions and on different paths, but neither cares at that stage. But when they 'get serious' about each other, both should start wanting the same thing in life, pulling the original two tracks together to become one. In the process, there is give and take from both sides. Independent of how they get there, the two should become one unit, marching out in the same direction and working towards the same goal in life. This forces changes upon each individual. When they make big decisions in life, they no longer think about themselves without considering the other half. Instead, they should discuss and make big decisions together. I judge that Samyin has never moved on from the dating stage with anyone before."

"I guess then you and Sinyin were in the 'serious' stage?"

"I don't really know. I thought we were but of course, she proved me wrong. She went off on her own to pursue her own goal without even letting me know. How serious could she be about me? Now our lives are on separate tracks running further apart from each other, what's the chance of us coming back together again? She's unrealistic to think we could and should. I haven't told you yet. After the last incident in my office, I gave her one-week notice to move out of the Hotel. She's just left! When you go back, you won't see her in the Hotel anymore."

Wide-eyed, Yuetching exclaimed, "You did what? She must've been furious."

"The world does not revolve around her. The sooner she gets that, the better for her really. My tolerance also has its limit. It's best for everyone concerned."

"Have you had a lot of experience being 'serious' with someone?"

"No. In one lifetime, we don't have much time or energy to be 'serious' many times. Yuetching, please remember, don't get into a relationship just for the experience. You shouldn't consider it unless it's with someone you love. Otherwise it'll drain your body, mind and soul, and hurt your heart for nothing. Don't waste your time and mistreat yourself like that. I for one will be saddened if you do that. But when you meet someone you love, then go for it. Don't be afraid. Find that courage in you to love wholeheartedly. Otherwise you would miss out something beautiful and wonderful in life. That'll be a big regret too." No one ever had wished the best for her like he did. He was always sincere in his advice, which was also a blessing. Yuetching held it dear in her heart.

"What am I to do with Samyin?"

"Do you forgive what he did last night?"

"He tried to save me and hurt himself. I think I need his forgiveness and not the other way round."

"And the awkward bit about him trying to kiss you?"

"The moment was a blur. I was too busy reacting to what *gujeung* did than what he did that I did not really know how I felt about him, if that makes sense?" Yuetching was unsure.

"Do you accept his love for you?"

"I honestly don't know at this stage. It's all too new for me. I need time to understand more. Without complicating things, can we keep our status quo till the Annual Meeting so that we can focus on delivering the project first? I mean I can't cope with a new relationship and finishing the project at the same time. Do you think this is a good-enough answer?"

"I think he'll understand. He'll be elated that you haven't rejected him outright, and it's pretty legitimate to request time to work out your feelings. You won't feel uneasy working with him?"

"I'm happy to give it a go. Will he be uneasy working with me?"

"Well, he'll cope."

"Are you on his side in this, I mean on the matter of him and me?"

"Well, it was my idea to send you two here. If you two do get together in the end, I won't object. Samyin is a good guy, honestly; a girl is lucky to have him."

"This is a very high personal recommendation!"

"Well, I'm telling the truth, and I'm sure you see that too." Chisau turned to Yuetching and asked, "Any further questions?"

Yuetching laughed and shook her head.

"You know, I'm grateful that you didn't just run away this time."

"Why?"

"Last week, when you vanished from the office and we could not find you, I really panicked. The feeling was really bad. I can't explain how scared I was." He turned to Yuetching and got serious in requesting, "Yuetching, can you promise me not to disappear again? Not knowing where you are or what you decide to do make me nervous and anxious. Can you promise to come to me if anything happens to you?"

"I'm sorry; I don't mean to worry you. I never need to be accountable to anyone and no one cares anyway. I can't promise you that I'll always remember to report to you on my whereabouts – it doesn't come naturally to me. I'm sorry." Chisau looked disappointed. "But," Yuetching took out her phone and continued, "I can promise you that through this phone, you'll always get hold of me no matter where I am. This is my 'telephone contract' with you. Would you accept?"

Looking at Yuetching waving the phone he bought her, he found it fitting that it now served as the device that ensured his access to her. He was more than pleased in accepting Yuetching's counter proposal.

8 A Preview of Her New Life

Back from the hospital, Samyin settled himself on the couch to wait for the pair to come back. Although he was still physically, his heart was in turmoil. Waiting was even harder when you could do nothing to distract you from the stillness of time. He had no idea what verdict they would bring back on him. Fixated on his mind were the terror in her eyes, the tension in her body, the sadness of her tears and the pain behind her contorted face. Her unresponsiveness rendered him helpless in doing anything for her. But where she had shut him out she had allowed Chisau to go in. Would he always be an outsider to her heart? She just could not be totally honest with him like she was with Chisau. The more he dwelt on it, the more melancholic he became. *Love is long-suffering*, he told himself. *Give her time and patience.* What else could he do?

On the sound of the door, the long wait was over; he was excited as well as nervous! He tried to sit up too quickly and aggravated his injury. As it turned out, he welcomed them back with groans of agony! How undignified!

"How did it go?" Chisau asked.

"Nothing to worry about; it should heal with time and rest."

An awkward silence ensued.

Samyin's searching gaze was on Yuetching, desperate to gauge her mood.

"Your dinner was not wasted; Yuetching cleaned the plate when she got up," Chisau tried to break the ice.

"Really? I thought it was you who ate it all!" Samyin was

glad. He turned to Yuetching and asked, "How was it?"

Yuetching nodded with both thumbs up.

Samyin smiled with pleasure.

"You two have been gone for a long time. You surely had a lot to talk about. Are you sorted?" asked Samyin more directly.

"Half of the time we were just walking and not talking," corrected Chisau.

"Still are you sorted?"

"Sort of," Yuetching answered gingerly with embarrassment. "You see, I'm really messed up and a lot I don't understand about myself. Sometimes I don't know why I reacted the way I did, but there is always a reason somewhere deep inside. I'm really sorry to have caused alarm and worried you unduly."

Samyin blinked in disbelief and wondered if he had heard it right.

Yuetching continued, "I need time to think things through. Talking to Chisau has helped me think in a new direction but I still need time to digest and absorb it."

Samyin looked at Chisau, "Is she telling me something?"

"Well, she's saying that she can't make a decision about you and her right now; she needs time to work things out. In the meantime, she would like to keep the status quo and focus on delivering the Annual Meeting as we have so much to get through."

"Another deferred decision till after the Annual Meeting?"

"Considering, it's not a bad outcome. You have to admit it. I think it's pretty legitimate to request time to work out her feelings. You have to agree that you can't rush these things. Or perhaps you would like me to relocate her to my office in the meantime to make it easier on you?"

"Of course not!" Samyin refuted the proposal outright.

"Then this is settled."

"What happened last night? Are you going to tell me?"

"This is not up to me," answered Chisau.

All attention was on Yuetching, who diverted the subject, "To have caused you injury, I'm truly sorry." She walked up to him and asked, "May I take a look?" Samyin didn't object. "It looks pretty sore. I'm really sorry to make you suffer. Are you sure you don't need some pain relief? Would you like a hot bath, for example?"

"I don't mean about my injury – I mean –"

"I'm going to run a bath for you. How ironic that the same bath both caused your injury and gives you relief now!" and she left the room.

"But —"

Chisau went up to him and put his hand on his shoulder to stop him from pursuing. "I know you're dying to know, but if I were you, I wouldn't press her on the subject. Wait till she's ready to tell you. Patience especially in this case will be handsomely paid off; trust me."

Love is long-suffering …Give her time and patience — the only thing you can do.

"We should be grateful that she seems to have gotten over this fair quickly compared to last time," Chisau added.

"How am I supposed to treat her?"

"As before."

Samyin was forced to take some time off because of his injury. On his return, he found everyone was working full steam that there was no space and time to think of anything else. Yuetching and Samyin worked well together. They also held regular meetings with the Strategy Department to fill out the details. In her spare time, she was busy organising materials gathered, making observations, and structuring the reports. She also planned work schedules for others, constantly feeding the team and departments clear instructions. When Yuetching focused on work, she was single-minded and professional. Samyin had learnt from her a work ethic that was second to none. She never hesitated to bounce back anything that was perfunctory or not up to her standard, and demanded Samyin to redo — no excuse accepted! Samyin had never worked so hard for the Hotel before! But she had made the work far more interesting than before and she did lead by example in her dedication. She would always do her best with her heart, whether she liked a job or not. Very often, Yuetching would do another shift at home with Chisau and Granddad after work. Samyin could never understand where her endless flow of energy originated from! To Samyin, though, the priority during this period was never work *per se* but to take care of Yuetching: he worked hard so as to share her workload; he stayed in the office for long hours in order to keep her company; he stayed close to her so that he could ensure she ate well and took regular break. How clueless was Yuetching about boys that she did not pick up Samyin's attentiveness! But to Samyin, this only added to her charm!

Samyin walked up to Yuetching, whose eyes were fixed on her computer screen, working with her usual intense focus.

"What's up?" Yuetching asked without taking her eyes off the screen.

"I need to go out. My dad visits every year for the Annual Meeting. This year, the whole family is coming as a holiday, so they arrive earlier than usual and will stay longer. I'm going to the airport to pick them up now. I'll return to work after picking them up."

Yuetching gave him an arch glance, suggesting, "You don't need to rush back. Take time to be with your family. Don't worry about work; I grant you leave today, all right?" Yuetching pulled his leg. "You're the boss here, Samyin. Why do you behave as if I were the boss?"

Samyin liked Yuetching's playfulness. He replied, "Then I'll see how it goes. Say, if they're tired and would like to rest, I'll come back to work. I'm leaving now."

Yuetching worked intensely and time flew without her noticing it's already lunchtime. Feeling a little tired, she got up from her desk to take a break in Samyin's office. She stared out of the window aimlessly while munching her sandwiches.

"Why are you on your own without company?"

Yuetching turned round and found Chisau walking into the office, "It's you."

Chisau sat down in front of her, asking, "Where's Samyin?"

"He's gone to the airport to pick up his family; they're arriving today."

"Ah, I've heard from Granddad that they're arriving early this year." Chisau noticed that Yuetching looked a little dim, so he inquired, "Are you all right? You look quite tired today."

Yuetching blew out a heavy breath as if going out of steam. "I suppose you're right; I do feel quite sluggish today. Is it really possible to finish all the work before the Annual Meeting?"

"Don't worry about this. In fact, I believe we're making good progress. What we've achieved has already surpassed my initial expectations, so don't be too harsh on yourself. Don't be over demanding either. You must know that work is never-ending; you can always improve it if you have more time or know more.

I know you like to do your best in every job you take on, but a mature work attitude is also to know when is good enough and when to stop, given the objectives of the project, the time limit and the physical limit of your team. Understand?"

Yuetching nodded and suggested, "Perhaps it's time to start wrapping up the findings and constructing the final report."

"Agree!" That settled the matter with work and Chisau changed the subject, "Yuetching, we must let Samyin's family know who you are. How do you feel about it?"

Yuetching looked puzzled, so Chisau explained further, "Uncle Chiu has been Granddad's friend and business partner for decades. Every time he returns, he comes to us for dinner and all of us will meet him. Among other things, Granddad and Uncle will talk about the business and the Hotel. We probably could not and should not hide from him what we've planned for the Annual Meeting. Furthermore you work in the Hotel, live at home and are Samyin's secretary; for you not to meet with them is too deliberate. If they find out the truth afterwards, it's very awkward for us to explain ourselves. Would you take this occasion as a rehearsal for the Annual Meeting?" Chisau entreated earnestly.

That was a bit sudden; Yuetching had not prepared for it at all.

She composed herself and replied, "Sooner or later, this day will come. Let it come then. Having a foretaste of what it's like before the Annual Meeting may not be a bad thing."

"Good. They'll be staying at the Hotel. In all likelihood, you'll bump into them very soon."

"Thank you for giving me a heads-up of what to expect," Yuetching smiled, thinking that Chisau was always looking out for her.

Normally Yuetching's work pattern was not dictated by the office hours, but today her brain had been really slow. No matter how hard she had tried to push, her brain would not give anything. It was a signal to take it easy and call it a day. When Samyin returned to the office at the close of day, he was surprised to find Yuetching's computer switched off and she was ready to leave.

"Is there something wrong with you?" asked Samyin out of surprise.

"I'm a little tired and efficiency's low. It makes no sense to stare at a blank screen just for the sake of it. The time is better used if I go home and rest, and be refreshed for tomorrow."

"Is there anything you would like me to help out?"

"What? Now? Don't you need to be with your family?"

"If I've got work to do, they won't disturb me."

"Since when have you cared so much about work?" Yuetching was baffled. "There's nothing that can't wait till tomorrow. Chisau said today that we should start wrapping up the reports. This was the only decision concerning work today."

"I see. Let me tell you the big news I've learnt today." Samyin was excited.

"What's it?"

"My little sister's engaged! And they're planning an engagement party at the Hotel. This is why they return early and plan to stay a while."

"You only learnt this today?"

"Yes, to give me a surprise, they say."

"Who's the fiancé?"

"He's a senior from the same university. He's already working, so he can't afford the time to stay that long with them here, and will come only for the engagement party."

"You haven't met him?"

"Of course, I have, a few times."

"And what's your impression of him?"

"He's easy going, friendly and gets on with my sister."

"No qualms then?"

"Of course not. If my dad isn't objecting, how can I have any objections?"

"Time's really tight. Will the Hotel have any openings to fit it in? It's clashing right into the Festive Season." Yuetching's mind jumped to the logistics naturally.

"We just have to find an opening somehow!"

"You'll be very busy," Yuetching predicted.

"Wrong. *They* will be very busy," corrected Samyin.

"Understood." Yuetching smiled. These days they had acquired a tacit understanding of each other that not everything needed to be spelt out in full between them.

"We'll be going round to your place for dinner tomorrow."

"Ah right. That soon."

"Before we meet, I'll tell them a little bit about you, so

there'll be no embarrassment," furthered Samyin.

"Perhaps an aspect of being part of a family is having to sit through 'political dinners', those that you would rather not attend but can't escape," Yuetching spoke her mind bluntly.

"Sometimes I feel like that, so I understand. But I do sincerely hope that you'll get to know my family and over time, it'll cease to be a 'political dinner' when you dine with us," smiled Samyin full of hope!

Samyin noticed that Yuetching was looking quite languid, so he asked, "Are you all right? You're not ill or anything, are you?" Samyin put his hand on her forehead to feel her temperature.

Yuetching gently brushed off his hand, replying, "I'm fine. I'm entitled to be tired, you know. I'm just sleep deprived! I'll go home and sleep all night. Then I'll be fine tomorrow."

"Let me drive you home."

"There's no need. Go and be with your family instead." Yuetching was getting annoyed with all the fuss.

"After I've dropped you off, I'll return to my family," insisted Samyin.

"It isn't proper for the boss to give his secretary a ride home after work. I don't permit you to give me a lift. Is that clear?" Yuetching instructed.

At that moment, there was a buzz at the door.

"Who could that be?" asked Yuetching.

Samyin looked through the glass door and answered, "It's my family."

Yuetching unlocked the door and let them in.

"Samyin, we've come to pick you up for dinner," said his dad.

Yuetching greeted them.

"Ah, are you Miss Secretary? How do you do? We've heard about you," said Mr Chiu. This introduction came as a surprise.

"What have you heard about her and from whom?" asked Samyin.

"I've just been talking to Uncle Do," answered Dad.

"He told us that you and Szeman were no longer an item because of your new secretary," Mum continued. "We're curious, so we came here to your office, hoping to catch of glimpse of the girl who is better than our Szeman. How could you be so secretive? You know your mother is very anxious about you settling down and starting a family. How can you hide this big news from us?"

"I've found it strange that my brother would take on a secretary willingly. How about we introduce Miss Cheung to everyone at my engagement party? You know, I'm getting married before you and everyone will be pestering you. But if you take Miss Cheung to the party arm in arm, the answer is already there for everyone to see before they can bother you. I'm being thoughtful for you," Samyin's sister, Huentung (萱彤), suggested playfully. Samyin looked shocked and embarrassed.

Yuetching began to feel a headache, as she did not expect to be besieged like this. She took her leave, saying, "I think you have misunderstood. I will let Manager Chiu to clear up the misunderstanding. Let's be clear of one thing though – going to the party arm in arm with Manager Chiu will not happen. If you would excuse me, I'm just on my way out. Please enjoy your evening together." Yuetching took a little bow and made her way to the exit.

Everyone's eyes were following Yuetching until she was out of sight. "She's unfriendly," declared Huentung.

"Thanks to you, I'm in deep trouble," Samyin showed his displeasure.

"What? Manager Chiu? Isn't she your girlfriend?" his mother was disappointed. Samyin was speechless. He could only say, "Let's go to dinner and I'll explain it all. Let's go."

At dinner, Samyin outlined Yuetching's story to the family. "Her story is so pitiful; you can't mistreat her, understand?" Huentung commanded her brother.

"Don't say she's pitiful; she doesn't like it. Don't treat her well out of pity; she'll hate it even more," explained Samyin.

Huentung sat up and took him seriously, "You really know her, don't you? You care for her a lot."

"Why wouldn't I? She's Chisau's cousin."

"But if you're not an item, why would Szeman say so?" asked Mum.

"Is it a convenient misunderstanding? Can you explain please?" urged Dad.

"Don't mention it again. This misunderstanding cost me a great deal. I wasn't allowed to speak to her or Chisau for three whole days! I was nearly ruled out from attending Chisau's birthday gathering too. So please, may I beg you not to allure to it or do anything that will embarrass Yuetching!"

"Although you aren't a pair now, do you like her? Since you see her everyday in the office, have you developed feelings for her?" tested Huentung.

"Are you implying that Chisau should also have developed feelings for Miss Wei then? Don't be silly," Samyin dismissed the possibility.

"I know you, brother. With your temperament, if you don't get along with her, you wouldn't have let her stay by your side for so long. I say YOU LIKE HER," Huentung was convinced.

"Son, you aren't getting any younger. Don't play around and be indecisive. Miss Cheung looks nice. Have you considered her?" urged Mum.

"Mum, don't try to push me on this subject every single time you see me! This is getting irritating!"

"Getting you two together shouldn't be that difficult," Mum was already planning regardless.

"Please don't intervene. You can only cause me trouble. Right now, we have a lot of work to get through, and you mustn't distract us from the task. We've put in a lot of hard work, especially Yuetching. We mustn't fail her. We have an agreement that we're to focus on work – discussion on private matters is banned …"

"See, he has admitted it. There are *private matters* between the two of them! They are only temporarily put on hold to make way for work. Since when has my brother been so concerned about our Hotel business anyway?" Huentung teased.

Samyin could not find words to dispel the situation and blushed.

"Ah! Look, he's blushing. Miss Cheung really is *the* one on his heart! He's serious this time. But right now, it looks as if it's one-sided. Does she even know you like her?" inquired Huentung.

"……" Samyin's speech had failed him.

"Oh! It looks like he has already tried, but got rejected. Brother, how can you fail to woo her – the one who matters most of all when you brag about girls all the time?" Huentung was getting excited at piecing together her brother's love life.

"Do you need us to create some opportunities for you two?" Mum joined in.

"Please don't. If you intervene, then it's really game over for me," Samyin could not conceal his concern.

"Leave it to us. Don't you worry. We won't make things worse for you," Mum tried to pacify. But Samyin shook his head, as if his worst nightmare was only about to begin.

Chisau and Samyin arrived home roughly the same time. Surprised not to see Yuetching tag along, Uncle Chiu asked, "Where's Miss Cheung? How come she hasn't come with you?"

"Yuetching makes her own way home. As her identity is still not public knowledge, it's not advisable for her to come home with us," explained Chisau.

"I see."

Chisau and Samyin sat down on the couch to join the party. They chatted away while waiting for Yuetching, who stepped through the door about half an hour later. As she entered, she greeted everyone.

"Miss Cheung ..." Samyin's mother was about to address her, but was interrupted by Granddad, "Miss Cheung? It sounds so formal. Call her Yuetching. I don't think Yuetching would mind, would you?"

"No, not at all. Please call me Yuetching."

"All right. Yuetching, we'd like to apologise for mistaking you as Samyin's girlfriend yesterday," said Auntie Chiu. "Samyin has already cleared the misunderstanding."

"That's good."

"Have Samyin and Yuetching been mistaken as an item?" Granddad was curious what happened to the youngsters, "How come? I'm interested to know."

"Granddad, since misunderstanding has just been cleared, why do we want to rekindle it again by talking about it?"

"Rumours always have some truth in them as basis, even if it accounts for only 30 per cent," Granddad teased.

"Granddad, please don't tease us. You're going to embarrass us," Yuetching made her stance clear.

"Granddad, please let this pass," Chisau added his weight.

Granddad obliged and changed the subject, "Have you got a date for the engagement party yet?"

"Oh, yes, we have. Six weeks from now, and less than two weeks before the Annual Meeting," answered Auntie Chiu.

"So soon?"

"There's no other date available."

"Will you have enough time to prepare?"

"Should do. We don't intend to make it big. It's just an excuse to get the family and friends together," answered Uncle Chiu.

"Yuetching, you must come to my party too," Huentung insisted.

"What? Me?" Yuetching was startled by the unexpected invitation.

"You're a member of the Lee family, so you must come."

"But I –"

"If you can't appear as Chisau's cousin, then you can pretend to be my brother's girlfriend and attend the party arm in arm," suggested Huentung cheekily.

"Miss Chiu is kidding, right? What's the advantage of covering up a real identity by a false one? Do you think it great fun to clear misunderstanding once rumours start to circulate? Your suggestion is not going to work," Yuetching counter-argued.

"It's not necessarily a *false identity*. Rather, it could be a presage of a future identity," Huentung was carried away with her dream.

"Miss Chiu, most things in life proceed in a certain order. To act as if something that may or may not happen in the future had happened is simply reckless!"

"All right, then. If not as girlfriend, you could be his partner for the evening. How does that sound? I've invited Sinyin to perform at my engagement party!" This was like a bombshell dropped! No one had expected it!

"When did you see her?" asked Samyin.

"Today! Who'd have guessed she'd have time and even agree to come? When I first got acquainted with her through Chisau, I already knew she was very talented. I've never dreamt that she'd remember me even after she's become famous. She's even willing to make a guest appearance at my engagement. I can't believe I'm so much favoured!" Huentung recounted the event with excitement. She then turned to Chisau, and asked directly, "Why did you two break up? You were like a couple made in heaven. It isn't too late to change your mind; it appears that you still have a chance to save the relationship." Huentung tried to be helpful.

"Stop it right there and speak no more," ordered Samyin.

"Don't put your nose into other people's business."

"No matter what identity you take on, everyone here has to come to my engagement. If it doesn't work as my brother's dance partner, then you could be my best friend!" Huentung winked at Yuetching as if she were the cleverest of all. Yuetching wondered if she was sincere in requesting her presence or plain evil in making things difficult for her.

At this moment, dinner was ready and Puiyin gathered everyone to the dining room. The Chius hustled Yuetching and Samyin together, leaving them with no choice but to sit next to each other. Chisau could only sit opposite them at the table.

After everyone was seated, dinner was served.

"Huentung, what's your plan for the future?" asked Granddad.

"I'm interested in interior design, but it's difficult to get into the business right now. Then I discover that I like furniture design too. Hence, I've enrolled on a carpentry course, through which I hope to gain some experience of working with wood. I believe this knowledge is invaluable as a furniture designer. By the time when I finish the course, I hope the business climate would've turned and it wouldn't be a problem to get into the industry."

"Carpentry for a girl, will that work?" Granddad was concerned.

"It'll work. My goal isn't to be a carpenter. I only want to know more about how to work with wood and the characteristics of different kinds of wood. I believe this is basic knowledge for a furniture designer."

Yuetching thought, it was such a blessing to have the time and space to dream, and in turn have the resources to work towards realising it. In comparison, her life had been savage and coarse. In order to survive, she could not afford to be choosey. She ate so as to avoid hunger, and not for the taste of the food. She worked so as to earn a living, and not for her interest. She dressed for comfort and practicality, and not for the style. This was the difference between their worlds, the difference between Samyin and her. Once again, she silently suffered from an attack of her inferiority complex.

"Will you come back to work eventually?" continued Granddad with his line of questions.

"It's unlikely in the near future; my fiancé's in the UK."

"How about *lo* (老an address for an old friend) Chiu, Will you return?"

"I can't say at the moment. It's true that when Huentung is married, we are officially released from our responsibility for her. We have the freedom to consider a new way of life."

"Yes, perhaps we should return to irritate Samyin instead, until he finally settles down. This threat may just work to put some pressure on him to find a wife," joked Auntie Chiu.

"Mum, you can't be serious!" objected Samyin.

"Is England a nice place to live?" asked Puiyin.

"It's not bad. The weather's gloomy all year round though! It's suitable for people who like peace and quiet. But if you're after some livelier lifestyle and love company, then here is better."

"Yuetching…" Uncle Chiu suddenly called her.

"Yes, Uncle Chiu," answered Yuetching.

"Have you got used to working at the Hotel yet?"

"Yes, I've got used to it now."

"I've heard that you're an excellent worker and a great asset to the team."

"I only try my best; I'm new to the sector and still have a lot to learn."

"I've never seen Samyin so focused and diligent on anything before. I think this significant change in him can be accredited to your influence."

"This isn't true. He too is an asset to the Hotel."

"Is the preparation for the Annual Meeting going well?"

"Yes, we're making good progress, but we still have a lot to do."

"Then we must rely on your good effort and hard work for a little longer."

"It's not only I who work hard. Chisau and Samyin plus the whole of Strategy Department are on the forefront of this work too."

"You're too modest! Yuetching, do you have any hobby or interest?"

"Sorry?"

"Outside work, what do you like doing?"

"I only like working," Yuetching tried to keep the conversation clinical and short. But others knew this was not true.

"That's not true," Granddad cut in. "She's a brilliant swimmer. She assists me with my physio exercise in water, so I know. She even saved Sinyin from drowning in the Hotel pool not that long ago."

"What? Sinyin nearly drowned?" Huentung was eager to pick up the gossip.

"Huentung, that's none of your business," Samyin restrained.

"Then Yuetching is not only a filial granddaughter, but also a heroine, who is a great help at work and saves people too," Auntie Chiu piled on compliments, which made Yuetching feel exceedingly uncomfortable.

"That's correct. The fact that I can recover so well and so quickly is all thanks to her," Granddad was more than happy to join in praising his granddaughter.

"Please, Granddad, this isn't true. *Kaumo*'s (舅母 whom Chisau's mother was to Yuetching) attentive care is also very important," added Yuetching.

"After the Annual Meeting, why don't you take leave and go on holiday with us?" asked Uncle Chiu.

"Ah? What?" Yuetching was shocked by this proposal.

"Dad! Oh please, no!" protested Samyin.

Chisau shook his head as their intention was too obvious. He decided to help Yuetching out by diverting the attention and conversation, "Uncle Chiu, where have you planned to go on holiday?"

Uncle Chiu was a keen traveller. Once he was on the subject, he could go on for a long time, and Chisau encouraged him. Yuetching breathed a sigh of relief and sent her thank-you to Chisau across the table via her little gestures.

What a long night it was for Yuetching! She felt emotionally drained after the evening. She went to sit down in the garden for some quiet time to herself.

"May I sit down?" Chisau walked up to her from behind.

Yuetching turned and saw him, replying, "You haven't slept yet?"

Chisau sat down next to her on the bench, saying, "No, not yet. What are you thinking on your own here?"

"Political dinner is tiring, and I don't envy you that you have to sit through many of those. When I was on my own, I never needed to waste time on entertaining people whom I didn't want

247

to entertain. I could choose to go or to leave, or not to go at all! So tonight, I felt both uneasy and irritated that I had no choice but to sit it out! This again was a new experience for me."

"I understand."

"What was their intention tonight anyway? Why did they keep pushing Samyin and me together? It's so annoying," complained Yuetching.

"I see that they would like to get you two together."

"It's annoying," reiterated Yuetching.

"Sometimes, parents are like that, doing things that are vexing to us! I believe that tonight Samyin was himself a victim too."

"And Huentung's engagement banquet – what am I to do? If you ask me, I don't want to go. Before tonight, Huentung was just a complete stranger to me. After tonight, we were like a family, as if I should care about her engagement! How does this work? If I'm honest, she was nobody to me yesterday, and she's still nobody to me today. Why should we behave as if we had known and liked each other for life purely because we're related via some convoluted network of friendships, business partnership and family? All look so fake that I have difficulty in accepting them as genuine. Is this what family means?"

"Perhaps we can look at it this way. There are nearly 7 billion people in this world. In our life, we're only ever going to meet a tiny handful of them, and get to know really well an even smaller number of people. For all those people we meet in life and can further establish some kind of relationship on whatever basis, call it *yuenfan* (緣份). People often think *yuenfan* only refers to those magical moments of chance and coincidence in life, and overlook the fact that blood ties are also one way to bring people together. People whom you meet because of your family ties are connected to you by another kind of *yuenfan*, but it's *yuenfan* nonetheless. You once told me that your world was empty. But you must have brushed shoulders with some people before you met us. The difference was that there were no bases for you to make connections with these people, and in turn your world was empty. Yes, you could be carefree and did not give a damn about anyone or anything, but this is a world after its perfectness has been broken in one way or another: it's cold, lonely, colourless, no laughter and no warmth. It is not a world to be preferred, to fight for, or to preserve. Blood ties are one basis among others to make connections with people. You're right in discerning that we have happy days as well as bad days when we're irritated! But these are colours of life. The wonderful part of family is that as time passes, and when we look back, even the times when we fought and annoyed each other could become humorous and funny moments that bring us laughter through our memory of them."

"Really that magical?" Yuetching was bewitched by the vision set before her.

"Yes. Furthermore, wedding, with our best intention at heart at the time, is once-in-a-lifetime event. It's an important milestone in anyone's life, and for this reason, most people would like to etch the sweetest and most unforgettable mark in their memory. Therefore we invite the most important people in our life to share the moment together. This is why when we receive an invitation to someone's engagement or wedding, we shouldn't fret but feel honoured. This person requests my or your presence to witness her reaching an important milestone in life – this is also *yuenfan*."

"Aren't these just beautiful words you use to persuade yourself to go through something vexing with a smile?" Yuetching was sceptical.

Chisau smiled, "Wrong. Invitations I receive because of business is business; I attend them as my job. All invitations I receive outside work are honours. I really think this way."

"Then is Huentung's engagement banquet business or a private matter?"

"Private."

"Even if you have to bump into Sinyin?"

"Yes. Samyin will have to see Szeman too. In life, there may be unpleasant encounters that we can't avoid. Then we must face them with courage."

"How about me? Should I attend?"

"Yes, you should."

"Then from what capacity should I attend? You should know the guests will most certainly ask."

"Perhaps as Samyin's personal assistant to ensure that the evening will run without a glitch? That's to say, use work as a disguise to attend for private reasons. Will that work?"

"But we already have the whole Special Events Team to oversee everything, and I'm not involved."

"Discuss it with Samyin. I'm sure he can find you a title and something that you can help out with."

"That means I've to go and request extra work for myself to do!"

Chisau laughed, "Yes, you can say that."

"I still have one more concern," said Yuetching.

"What's it?"

"I – I've never dressed up for any formal occasions. Glamour and I are like chalk and cheese – we don't go together. I'm apprehensive just by thinking about it. Can I attend as a waitress instead?"

"You certainly cannot and must not!" Chisau was adamant! "Don't worry about this. I can help you. We have a beauty salon at the Hotel, which will look after your hair and makeup on the day. We need only to find an evening gown for you. Even that I can enlist some help," Chisau assured Yuetching confidently.

"You see, how much trouble this invitation has brought me!" Yuetching fretted.

It had been decided that all the paperwork for the Annual Meeting had to be finished before Huentung's engagement banquet, to allow time for proof-reading and printing. As the deadline drew closer, Chisau, Samyin and Yuetching spent all hours finalising all reports. They met regularly to discuss key points, proof-read and edit each other's work, leading a regimental life in the final month of this project with only one focus. Even though it was tough, it was worth the effort as all the hard work in the previous months came together into coherent proposals, and the final reports began to take shape. Although everyone was a little exhausted, they spurred each other on, encouraging each other that they must not run out of steam when the finishing line was in sight. Instead, they threw in their all and their best in the final leg in order to finish the race with a bang, determined to bring all their hard work to a perfect conclusion for everyone to see.

During this period, everyone was marching towards the same goal and the team spirit was wonderful. Meanwhile, Chisau enlisted his mother to help Yuetching choose her evening gown for the banquet, whereas Samyin was made MC of the evening. He was also charged with producing a slideshow on Huentung to lighten up the evening.

Today was Yuetching's birthday. But to Yuetching, it had always been just another normal day. She had no memory of ever having a birthday party. Over the years, she had learnt not to have any expectations, so that she would not be disappointed. In recent years, she subconsciously made herself exceptionally busy on her birthday, so that it was physically impossible for her to think about it. She worked herself to the ground so that when she got home, she fell asleep without having the slightest chance to feel miserable. That she was busy became a convenient excuse why she did not celebrate her birthday. Then a new day would come and it was not her birthday anymore.

Today is my birthday … the thought crossed her mind like a flash, but Yuetching stopped herself from dwelling on it, and changed the direction of her thought, *Today is another working day, and these are the things I must finish today* …

She got into the office nice and early, focused on work and made really good progress. Chisau stopped by and initiated a conversation with her, "How late will you be tonight? Mum asks if you're coming home to eat tonight."

"Please don't wait for me. I'll look after myself."

"Please don't work so hard. Mum and Granddad haven't seen you for a long time and they're complaining to me for working you too hard. Come home early tonight, so that they can see you," Chisau coaxed.

Yuetching paused from her work and looked at Chisau, saying, "It's not the first time I work late. Why do you worry all of a sudden today? You know how I work. When today's work comes to a natural conclusion, I'll go home. Don't worry."

"Aright, I don't want to force you. I'll tell mum that she doesn't need to save you dinner," Chisau was disappointed that he had not succeeded in finding a way to bring Yuetching home early without making her suspicious.

"Thank you." Yuetching turned back to the computer and resumed working. As Chisau could do no more to change her mind, he left.

Around 10 o'clock in the evening, Yuetching dragged her fatigue body home. The lights were already out, and she could not be bothered to switch them on. The darkness suited her well as it calmed her senses to the slumbering mode. She dragged herself to the lounge in the dark, and tumbled into the couch.

She closed her eyes as she leaned back against the head rest. Her nerves began to relax and her fatigue quickly surfaced to lull her to sleep. Soon her body became too heavy to move...

With her eyes still closed, she heard people singing Happy Birthday. She thought she was already dreaming and was not in a hurry to wake up. Even if it was just a projection of her fantasy, she was not to deprive herself of a sweet dream – she deserved that much. The singing was getting closer and closer, as if it was just next to her ears; and there was the flicker of candle flames on the other side of her eyelids to toy with her senses. She laughed at herself, "This dream is getting real!!" She opened her eyes, only to find candle light really flickering in front of her and dimly outlining Granddad, Chisau and his mother behind the birthday cake. Startled, she sat up.

"Would you like to make a wish?" asked Puiyin gently.

That was too much to take in. For a moment, Yuetching could not respond.

"The candles are nearly burnt out, if you aren't quick!" Chisau teased.

Obediently Yuetching closed her eyes and made a wish silently to herself, *I wish this warm feeling will remain in my heart forever. Thank you for today.*

Yuetching opened her eyes and blew out the candles, while the others clapped their loudest to add to the atmosphere. Yuetching smiled most timidly and asked, "How did you find out?"

"From your application form. Have you forgotten?" Chisau looked smug.

He went to switch on the lights while his mother passed a knife to Yuetching, inviting, "Come, cut the cake." Yuetching was happy to comply.

"Today, you are treated like a VIP. You've made us all wait up for you, including Granddad!" complained Chisau.

"I'm sorry, but I didn't know," apologised Yuetching.

"Chisau, stop making her feel guilty. It's not her fault. It's because we wanted to give her a surprise, so we didn't tell her," Granddad defended Yuetching, and then turned to her, "This is your first birthday with us. Chisau said that a simple celebration suits you best. I hope you don't mind it too simple."

"Of course not. Simple is good; Chisau was right," said Yuetching.

While Yuetching was transferring the cake onto the plates, Puiyin took out a present and said, "This is little something from all three of us. We hope you'll like it."

Yuetching put down the knife to receive the present. Her hands were shaking; she could not be more surprised. She held the present tight to her chest, saying "thank you" in a way that no one would doubt her sincerity.

"Open it, and see if you like it," urged Puiyin.

Yuetching unwrapped the paper slowly, refusing to let the moment pass without extra care! As the wrapping paper came off, it revealed a jewellery box. She opened it and greeted her eyes was a glittering jewellery set, comprising a necklace and a pair of earrings. She looked up to her *kaumo* Puiyin with an expression of disbelief.

"We guess that you wouldn't have any jewellery to wear for Huentung's banquet. On the day, please wear them," explained Puiyin.

It all suddenly became a blur as Yuetching could no longer hold back her tears. This was the most valuable present she had ever received in her life – not just in terms of the price tag but in terms of what it meant. Valuables and she were like two polar concepts, and she had never dared to hope that one day the two would be linked together. But today, on her 25th birthday, was the first day when she felt she was valuable to someone, and her existence mattered to them. Suddenly she felt expensive – she was no longer other people's inconvenience and had other people's leftover. Finally, she had someone sparing some thought *especially* for her, choosing a present *especially* for her, and owned a gift which was truly hers *first hand*. This affirmation was like tempestuous waves that hit against her inmost being. Her defence crumbled against the force and tears rolled down like rivers without any restraint – she was literally washed out!

Puiyin, representing the two men, went over and gave Yuetching a motherly hug. She rubbed her hair, while lamenting, "It's been tough for you…" In the warmth of the motherly arms, Yuetching cried all her tears out. The plangent cry conveyed most truthfully the rending wistfulness that she had stored in her heart across the years for all to feel.

Finally, the waves subsided, and sob turned into sniffle. Yuetching apologised for losing control. "Don't be silly. If you don't cry at home, where are you going to cry?" comforted

Puiyin. In that moment, she wished she could pour out all the motherly love she could give to her in order to moisten her parched soul.

"Thank you for everything that you've done for me today. I'm very grateful."

"It's our pleasure. We can feel it. I believe *loye* and Chisau would agree also," responded Puiyin. The two men nodded in agreement.

"Well, now let's eat our cake, shall we?" suggested Puiyin.

This was the sweetest cake Yuetching had ever tasted!

While they were eating, Puiyin mentioned in passing, "I had no idea you were such a premature baby."

"What do you mean?" Yuetching did not understand.

"When Chisau told me that today was your birthday, I was surprised. You must've been premature by at least three months! It follows that it must've been very hard for your mother to take care of you when you were first born. Seeing that you're healthy now, I can imagine how much work your mother must have put into caring for you in the first year of your life! Therefore, Yuetching, even though your mother isn't with you here and now, her love is always with you – it's embodied in your health and sturdy constitution. This love will never leave you, understand?" Puiyin tried to encourage her. Yuetching was given one more way to cherish her mother.

Two days before Huentung's engagement party, all the preparation work for the Annual Meeting was drawing to a close at last! There was lightness in Yuetching's footsteps as she made her way to the office on this last day of the project! All that was left for her to do was to go through the final checklist before sending all the documents off to the Communication Department.

When she arrived at work, she was surprised to find Samyin sleeping on the office sofa. He did not seem to have gone home at all. Yuetching was puzzled. She went in and woke him up, asking, "Why didn't you go home last night? What have kept you in the office all night when we've finished all the work?"

Samyin opened his eyes, and muttered, "I was working on the slideshow and fell asleep without even knowing. I have only two days left, what am I to do? I'm wretched!" Samyin sat up and put his forehead in his hand as if having a splitting headache.

Yuetching sat down next to him and switched on the computer, saying, "Let me see how far you are with the slideshow." Samyin logged on. Yuetching flicked through his selection of pictures and smiled every now and then when she saw something nice or funny. "How far off do you reckon you are from completion?" asked Yuetching while going through the photographs.

"Do you know how many photos Huentung has?! It's countless! It will take days just to screen through all of them," Samyin expressed his despair.

Yuetching turned to Samyin and looked straight at him, advising him in an official tone, "Samyin, haven't you learnt anything yet? You don't have the time to *aimlessly* screen through *all* the photos. You need first to decide on the structure and main points of your slideshow, the story you want to tell. For example, it could be about some memorable moments in her life, her milestones, or the Huentung whom you know and so on. Once you've got your theme and outline worked out, *then* you search *purposefully* for the photos to support your story. Though you risk missing something, it's a far more effective way to compile the slideshow with the limited time you have...."

Yuetching carried on giving him concrete suggestions on the slideshow, but Samyin could not hear a single word. His full attention was on how close Yuetching was sitting to him, so close that he could smell the fragrance of her hair. She was most animated when she talked about work. The slideshow was no exception, even if it was only for private use!

For a moment, Samyin was deeply attracted to her and was spellbound by her mesmerising movements and demeanour. The impetus to lean forward and kiss her was rising within him. He managed to refrain himself this time, while Yuetching stopped in the middle of a sentence, having sensed the awkwardness. He stood up and walked away abruptly to cool his head.

Watching him pacing up and down the room, Yuetching asked, "Are you all right?"

Losing his patience, Samyin turned to face her and asked directly, "Do you have any feelings for me? Just tell me once and for all."

"Samyin ..."

"I beg you, just tell me. Seeing you everyday without an

answer is driving me mad!"

"…" Yuetching was a little stunned.

"Please don't hold me in suspense any longer; please don't torture me like that. Please end my misery," Samyin begged.

"…" She didn't know how to reply.

"I can't see you just as a friend. You have totally taken my heart captive," Samyin spilled out his heart content for the first time without rehearsal, without a game plan, without pretence and without inhibition. He had triumphed!

Yuetching had heard the confession through Chisau before, but it was nothing like hearing it from Samyin himself! It was the first time she heard a declaration of love for her! Her heart seemed to have stopped. She was flabbergasted. She was flattered by his affection, as well as shocked by the power of love which seemed to have inflicted so much pain on him. She did not know how to respond. The truth was that she did not have an answer to his question. When she searched for an analytical framework to process the question, she found none! She was lost.

"How much longer will you have me wait?" Samyin was disappointed with the nil response.

"I'm sorry, Samyin. I don't mean to cause you pain but I don't know about this thing called love. That's the truth. I don't intentionally hold you in suspense. I – I need to process it – but I don't know how. I need to find a way to think it through."

"Will you consider it?" entreated Samyin.

"Yes, I will. When we're no longer as busy as we have been, I will consider it *thoroughly*." Yuetching gave Samyin a lovely smile, and he was frustrated no more. At least, he could hope.

Seeing that Samyin had softened, she walked up to him, saying gently, "You go back to your work, and I to mine. When I finish, I'll come and help you. How does that sound?" By then, Samyin's heart had totally melted. He could only respond by nodding his head, agreeing to whatever Yuetching had said!

The big day of Huentung's engagement banquet had finally arrived. Everyone was busy with the last minute preparation. In the end, Samyin did not assign to Yuetching any special task. Instead, as the host of the evening, he told Yuetching in private that she was attending the banquet as a VIP to the family, and it was his sincere wish that she would enjoy herself without any worry. Regarding the seating plan, Yuetching insisted *not* to sit with Samyin or Chisau, but to sit with the Hotel's event organisers. Samyin had no choice but to respect her wish.

Although it was not Yuetching's big day as such, she was getting nervous too, because it was the first time when she had an excuse to dress up. She had no idea how she would look like. She was apprehensive, "Would I look out of place? Would I look the part?"

Chisau had booked an appointment for her with the Hotel's beautician from 3pm. She never realised it could take as long as that to get the hair and makeup done. She later found out that she had to get her nails done too! She was glad that she did not need to look immaculate every single day!

It was Sunday, so Yuetching did not need to go to work. After a late lunch, she was about to set off for her appointment. Puiyin met her at the door, trying to settle her nerves by saying, "Have you got everything you need? Don't be nervous; just relax and enjoy. Dressing up for different occasions is part of the growing up process. It's great fun for girls to dress up and look pretty every now and again. Embrace this new experience and be pampered with an expectation to discover something new about yourself. Have fun and be excited."

Yuetching took a deep breath and thanked her for the advice.

"Why aren't you coming to the beautician as well?" Yuetching asked.

Puiyin smiled, "Well, I will wait till the day when Chisau gets married to do that! For today, I can look after myself at home. Besides, I have to take care of *loye*. You go now, and have fun!"

Watching Yuetching leave home, Puiyin ached for her, feeling her vulnerability on the one hand and being comforted to be in a position to play the mother's role on the other. It brought her tremendous pleasure to help dress her for the occasion and in turn build up her confidence. She realised that during this period, she had grown to like her very much and unwittingly treated her as if she were her own child.

Chisau and Samyin were at the Hotel overseeing the final preparation for the banquet. For both business purpose and private reasons, it had to be perfect! Everything was set to their satisfaction and they could relax a little before the guests arrived. They stood by the entrance of the banquet hall, jesting to help each other relax and kill the time.

Right at that moment, the lift doors slid open; an elegant lady stepped out and glided towards the gentlemen in her floor-length gown. She was like a shining star that dazzled and naturally attracted attention. Both Chisau and Samyin were enthralled by her beauty.

Yuetching's gown was maroon in colour, which complimented magnificently against her warm complexion. In texture it was as soft as silk which effortlessly outlined her well-proportioned and slender figure. The shine of satin gave her the glamour. The earrings and necklace (which Yuetching received as her birthday present) glittering under the light together with her sparkly silver clutch bag completed her outfit. Her hair was curled into ringlets and tied up loosely at the back, leaving the fringe and ringlets on the sides to complement her oval-shaped face. The hair style reflected Yuetching's lively and cheeky personality. Together with the makeup which aimed to accentuate the natural beauty without exaggeration, the real Yuetching was allowed to shine through, rather than disappear under the artificial veneer of glamour. Everything from head to toe complemented each other to perfection. Tonight, Yuetching commanded attention, not because it was loud but because it was quiet – quietly beautiful, naturally captivating and irresistibly charming.

Yuetching walked up to the gentlemen, looking shy. She was self-conscious as she did not know if she could carry the look.

"Do I look all right? Will it pass for the occasion? Is it over the top? I hope they haven't overdone it with the hair, the makeup AND the nails!" Yuetching asked nervously.

Chisau knew she lacked self-confidence for this kind of occasion, so he walked up to her and reassured her, "It's spot on, perfect in fact. Everything works perfectly together, and it's not over the top. Mum has chosen well for you. You look stunning this evening. Don't feel uneasy. Just enjoy yourself."

"Really?" Yuetching was relieved. Chisau never failed to reassure her. Suddenly there were the flashes. Yuetching instinctively turned to look, and found Samyin was snapping pictures of her! He walked towards her, and said, "Chisau only praises you with words; I do it with action! Miss Cheung, you look very beautiful today. I regret that you are not my partner for this evening."

Yuetching returned the compliment with a subtle smile, saying, "Stop firing at me with your usual adulation!"

"Can't you just take it as my sincere compliment for once? It's not adulation. When will you believe me? Why do you always believe Chisau and not me?" Samyin felt a little dejected.

Yuetching was beginning to think if she was a little unfair to Samyin. Rather than waggling on the subject, she dismissed it by saying, "Don't sulk. You look pretty handsome yourself in your formal attire."

As a consolation, Samyin thrust his camera into Chisau's hand and requested, "Could you take a picture of us please?"

Chisau was more than happy to oblige. Samyin pulled Yuetching away and put his arm round her shoulder. Yuetching looked at him with suspicion but then decided not to object. Instead she cooperated with a lovely smile for the camera.

Having taken the pictures for Samyin, Chisau handed over his camera and swapped places with Samyin. When Chisau walked up to Yuetching, he deliberately copied Samyin and put his arm round her shoulder. This made her laugh brighter and more naturally in the pictures than the previous ones with Samyin.

Seeing that the organisers started to turn up before the arrival of guests, Yuetching excused herself from the gentlemen, "You're busy; I'll look after myself."

She went into the banquet hall to see how she might help.

"Is Manager Chiu sending you here to supervise us?" the person-in-charge of this evening, Miss Cao, joked. Yuetching had worked with her in the Special Events Department during her work experience.

"Of course not. I'm only a spare pair of hands ready for your assignment," replied Yuetching.

"Then I'll take up the offer. Here is today's seating plan. Could you go round and check again that all name plates are correctly placed according to the seating plan please? The hosts have spent a lot of time and thought behind the plan, and we can't afford to make mistakes on fine details like these. Please do the final check. Sorry to trouble you."

"Not at all. It's my pleasure."

Yuetching took the seating plan and quickly got on with the task. She started with Table No. 1. This was the table for the Chius – the hosts of the evening. Granddad was also at this table, reflecting his status and friendship with Uncle Chiu. Yuetching moved onto Table No. 2, and discovered that Samyin had seated Sinyin here. Yuetching laughed at his intention to feed her ego, so that he could put Chisau and his mother at Table No. 4. It was obvious that Samyin avoided seating Chisau and Sinyin together for Chisau's sake! But she was not sure if it would go down well with Sinyin! Szeman and her parents were at Table No. 8, while she was seated at the last table with all the other Hotel staff.

After all the final checks had been done, Yuetching and Miss Cao joined the party in the reception room. It appeared that most guests had arrived. Miss Cao breathed a sigh of relief. All the hard work was done and from now on, the evening should be running like clockwork! Miss Cao sipped some fruit juice, offering one to Yuetching at the same time, "Aren't you thirsty too or is it just me?"

Yuetching thanked Miss Cao for the juice and the two of them started small talks to amuse themselves. On the other side of the room were Chisau, Granddad and his mother. Among all the guests, Chisau could only see Yuetching. She was the one who stood out for him this evening. He was watching her every move and was totally enthralled by her gracious demeanour. Her friendly persona was very approachable and there were no signs of any uneasiness when she was chatting with Miss Cao. Her laughter was infectious, and her wit entertaining. This was the confident Yuetching at her best when she momentarily forgot her background and her defeatist talks. Chisau was determined to slowly chisel away the shackles of her past, no matter how long it would take, in order that this confident Yuetching could shine without restraints. He would have loved her to see and believe what a gem she was. He could not resist but take out his camera to capture her. Curious, his mother followed the lens of the camera and found that the subject of interest was Yuetching. This was also the first time when she saw Yuetching in her full frock! She was pleased with the outcome. Even Granddad had to say, "Wow! Our Yuetching looks very pretty tonight. Puiyin, you've done a great job. Chisau, do you agree?"

Chisau nodded eagerly to give his approval.

"This is not all down to me though. The most important element for the look is the person who carries it!"

"How regrettable she can't sit with us tonight! But we need

only to wait for ten more days, and then her relationship with us will be public," Granddad comforted himself.

Meanwhile, Sinyin arrived at the Hotel, trailing a group of paparazzi frantically snapping pictures of her. She pretended to be shy and slightly annoyed, but she never forgot her smile in front of the cameras.

"What function are you attending, Miss Yan?" someone shouted from the crowd. Sinyin smiled without replying.

"Can you disclose what the occasion is? Are there any other celebrities in the party?"

"Please respect our privacy," requested Sinyin courteously before walking into the Hotel. She was followed by her assistant who among other things looked after her violin for her. Samyin was there to greet her. He was concerned about the paparazzi, so he suggested, "Should I call security?"

"There is no need. I deliberately leak my whereabouts to them. They're harmless."

"Why would you do such a thing?" Samyin was shocked by the revelation.

"They ensure that I'm on the papers constantly."

"Is your life on show now?" retorted Samyin disapprovingly.

"I've decided any news is good news. No news is bad news."

"Be careful that this may backfire on you one day."

"Oh well, what have I got to lose? Wooing the public is fun. They are so gullible. They believe anything you wish them to believe."

Samyin could not believe what he was hearing. "Well, this is a private function. I hope you will respect that and won't bring your game with the media into it."

"Oh well, I know. Don't worry! A bit of enigma actually adds to my appeal!" she winked at Samyin, and she had never flirted with him before.

"Are you on drugs?" asked Samyin, noting the subtle change in her behaviour.

"What? I'm offended that you even suggest that. Take it back. I'm going to perform, am I not? Why would I throw my career away after I have sacrificed so much for it? I haven't totally lost my mind yet." She threw her coat into Samyin's hands and walked into the reception hall. Samyin was shocked to see how Sinyin had turned out – she was even worse than before. He sincerely hoped that this evening would pass without incident!

As she entered, she immediately searched for Chisau. After she had located her target, she changed into her demure persona and walked up to them. She bowed and greeted the seniors.

"Sinyin, long time no see. You've become a lot prettier than the old days," greeted Puiyin politely. "You've been busy, haven't you? We see you are very active. Are you keeping well?"

"Yes, I am well, thank you. This has been my dream and I have worked hard to achieve it. I always have a passion for music. Performing helps me understand the pieces I am playing even more deeply. It is a blessing to be able to use music to express all different kinds of emotions. On the one hand it provides a vent for my own emotions, and on the other hand it helps me understand myself more. It is wonderfully therapeutic. This personal journey is just like a piece of music itself – with its ups and downs, variations and dynamics. It's just amazing. I feel fulfilled that I can share this experience with the audience."

Chisau wondered if she had done too many interviews; her answer sounded well-rehearsed and automatic. It had grandeur but no sincerity whatsoever. He adopted an official tone with her too, "We are honoured with your presence this evening, Miss Yan."

Sinyin squeezed a smile, replying, "Not at all. Huentung has been my follower even before I got famous. It's my honour to be invited here at the engagement party of my first and loyal fan!"

Chisau scratched his head, thinking, *How did she just turn this evening into something about her again? Ah right, Huentung is her loyal fan!*

The guests were moving towards the banquet hall.

"Right, we are being seated now. I am at Table 2. Where about are you?"

"Granddad is at Table 1 while mum and I at Table 4."

"But why …"

"We shall move now," Chisau pulled ahead with Granddad and mum, leaving Sinyin behind to find her own way.

After everyone had been seated, Samyin stood up and welcomed the guests as the host as well as the MC of the evening.

"Welcome everyone. Thank you for coming and we are honoured with your presence this evening. Tonight we gather to celebrate the engagement of my dear sister Chiu Huentung to Cheng Chunshek (鄭俊碩). Let us welcome the couple." Applause erupted as Huentung and Chunshek entered the banquet hall arm in arm. They stood and greeted the guests before taking their seats at the table.

Samyin continued, "If you are like me, you would be dying to know when the wedding day is going to be." The guests responded with laughter. Samyin paused to create some suspense. "Unfortunately," Samyin resumed, "I am none wiser than you on this matter! All I know is that they have *not* started preparing for their big day yet. Together with my insider knowledge of my sister who has cherished high expectations of her wedding since she was little, this is sufficient to rule out the possibility of their tying the knots within the next 12 months. When a date is set, we will surely notify you.

"This evening, we are also honoured with the guest appearance of Miss Yan. After dinner, she will be performing three pieces of music, two of which, I have been told, are chosen by my sister. But before Miss Yan's performance, I have prepared a slideshow to embarrass – no, to celebrate my sister's life and the person she is. By that point, my responsibility for this evening will be complete. Thereafter, I have been told, my sister will take over. She has organised the entertainment for this evening, the nature of which has been kept under wraps. Even I have no idea what it is going to be. I just hope that we will all have a wonderful and memorable evening.

"No matter how exciting all the line-ups are they are only secondary. The most enjoyable aspect of this evening must be your company, which we are honoured to have; we are grateful for your presence with us this evening. Without further ado, let us first enjoy the food we have prepared for you."

Guests were complimentary with their applause. Samyin took a few bows before returning to his seat. Yuetching thought he was handsome tonight, and the role of MC really suited him. The lights were dimmed, while dinner was served, accompanied by a string quartet in the background.

When guests were enjoying their last course before the desserts, Samyin got up and prepared the slideshow. The background was still dim, so when the projector was on, it would become the focus of the audience.

Desserts were served and all was set for Samyin. Spotlights

were on him. He began by an acknowledgement, "Before the slideshow, I would like to acknowledge the assistance I've received from my secretary – Miss Cheung Yuetching – in preparing this. Strictly speaking, this was beyond her official duties but generous as she is, she volunteered to help her boss who is never good at organising materials and information efficiently. So pivotal was her contribution that without her assistance, there would have been no slideshow. I just wish everyone to know that."

Samyin's tone however had betrayed him. It seemed to have an undertone that carried a sincere personal message to Yuetching, which made her feel uneasy. She did not understand Samyin's intention. Even Miss Cao could discern it and tease her for that matter. She was glad to have darkness as her shield. *This is embarrassing!*

"Brother is so hopelessly in love," whispered Huentung to her mother.

Samyin started the slideshow, which Yuetching spent the whole Saturday editing, experimenting with different visual and sound effects with the aim to enhance its dramatic impact. The main theme of the slideshow was the little sister through the eyes of her brother. It did express Samyin's tender brotherly love for her. It had adopted a humorous angle to tell each of Huentung's milestones in life, her character, the relationship between the brother and sister, and finally his blessing to her, now that she was engaged. The journey was dotted with ups and downs, tears and joy, vexations as well as laughter. His penetrating perception of his sister and how well he had remembered everything reflected the brotherly love he had for her. He had always been there for her and noted everything. This love itself was moving. Samyin was excellent in his delivery. He had the charisma to command the stage, if he chose to, and he could be very funny with grace and taste – perhaps this had been how he was always successful in charming the ladies. Watching the slideshow in the audience, Yuetching felt even more acutely the loss of not having any record of her childhood. She could not help but feel a little envious of Huentung, who was so blessed to have a brother like that. Huentung watched it the first time with the audience; and what she saw far exceeded her expectations. As Yuetching turned to look at Huentung's reaction, she was not surprised to find her in tears – who wouldn't?

Samyin concluded with a blessing and a warning, "Before today, I probably was the man, who was closest to her and knew her best. But my little sister has grown up. After today, I have to let go of that role and hand her over to another man in her life to take care of her, to love her, to make her laugh again after playing pranks on her. After today, the person to continue making this slideshow and to know her best is no longer me, but Cheng Chunshek. Cheng Chunshek, my parents and I wish Huentung and you every happiness, and that your love for each other will only deepen and mature with time. We command you to treat her well, and to cherish her; anything less will not be acceptable to us. Be warned that we will surely be on the case and won't let you off slightly. I hope our expectations are clear to you." Cheng Chunshek nodded as hard as he could as a promise to love Huentung well! Chisau on the other hand could totally relate to Samyin's sentiment. He felt he could be making the same speech on Yuetching one day.

"The part that I play this evening is coming to the end ..." Samyin was interrupted by an eruption of applause for his slideshow and presentation. That took him by total surprise. He did not expect such an overwhelming reaction from the guests. In the midst of the applause, he told how he felt, "You are all too kind to me and making me feel very embarrassed, because I should not be taking all the credit for the success of the slideshow."

The applause died down a little because the guests would like to hear what Samyin was saying. He continued off the script, "To be fair, I did not do much. All the hard work including the spectacular visual and audio effects was down to my secretary. She knew that we as the hosts would be very busy with the final preparation the day before the banquet, so she offered to help. She spent the whole of Saturday – her own time – to work on this. As with everything else she does, she never fails to deliver quality beyond expectations. She is –" Samyin paused and then spoke a heartfelt truth, "She is simply amazing; there is no other word for her really. Your appreciation should go to her as well." Samyin intended this to calm the crowd's reaction towards him. Instead, it got them on their feet to applaud and cheer. Now everyone would like to meet this *amazing* woman! Samyin was even more embarrassed; they were out of control. Chisau on the other hand was taken totally by surprise how Samyin managed to turn the occasion into a time for his own confession!

Samyin spoke through the microphone again, "At this rate, I'm afraid I have to invite my secretary to come up to share the appreciation you have kindly bestowed on me." The guests liked that idea a lot and clapped even harder; Huentung was the loudest cheerleader! Yuetching got really anxious, and chanted in her mind, *No, this is not true; this is not happening. Please don't take me away from my comfort blanket* (i.e. darkness). Chisau was getting a little nervous for Yuetching too.

"Miss Cheung, it seems that the guests would like to thank you in person. Would you mind coming up to the front and meet the guests?" Samyin

Commotion ensued at Yuetching's table. Miss Cao was leading the team to pull her off her chair. In the end, Yuetching had no choice but to go along with the wish of the vast majority present that evening. She walked up to Samyin elegantly, smiling. As she approached Samyin in the front, there were a few seconds to communicate to him her very complex emotions with her facial expressions for this awkward situation he had got her in before turning round to face the guests. Samyin whispered to her, "Sorry and thank you." Yuetching whispered back jokingly, "You owe me one." She stood by his side, courteously acknowledging the applause and appreciation that the guests showered at her enthusiastically. Meanwhile Sinyin was standing by to make her appearance next just outside the banquet hall. She was shocked to see Yuetching so remarkably transformed in just a few months. She was elegant, classy and presentable, even attractive. She was stealing *her* attention from the crowd. A rage that originated from envy overcame her.

For Samyin though, it was like a dream. Standing side by side with Yuetching, both dressed up for the occasion, in the thunders of applause, Samyin could be forgiven to fantasise for the briefest moment that it was their engagement! Even though it was just a fantasy, he could not have enjoyed anything more!

When the applause finally died down, Yuetching returned to her seat. Samyin began his last task of the evening, which was to introduce Sinyin, "Our special guest tonight requires no introduction. She is the rising violinist in the world of classical music. We are all familiar with her work and news. We are honoured to have her with us amid her busy schedule. It is an even bigger honour that she agrees to perform for us. We are in for a treat. Let us put our hands together for Miss Yan Sinyin."

Sinyin made the grand entrance to take the centre stage, while Samyin retreated. All lights were on her. She spent time to compose herself. Her concentration was intense. She closed her eyes and started narrating a story through her music. It was a solo performance without any accompaniment. It was a showcase for her techniques and variations. The range was wide, the rhythm was fast and slow. Her performance was expressive and tantalising. She was a born performer, who naturally drew the audience in and captured their attention! A chain of fast notes which built up to a crescendo ended the piece in a climax! The audience responded with their generous applause. This was the moment that had never failed to thrill her.

Huentung got into the spotlight and gave Sinyin a big hug. When the applause died down, Huentung spoke into the microphone to unfold what she had got in store for the guests.

"Tonight, we are really honoured to have Miss Yan performing for us. Words are not enough to express our gratitude."

"It's my pleasure," responded Sinyin.

"What is the next piece of the music you are going to perform for us?"

Sinyin was puzzled by this question, "How come you are asking me? This piece is chosen by you; you should know."

"Can you tell us what kind of music it is?" asked Huentung.

"It's a waltz," answered Sinyin.

"Do you know why I choose a waltz?"

"No idea; is there a special meaning to your choice then?"

"Do you know how Chunshek and I met?"

Sinyin shook her head, answering, "No."

"Chunshek and I met in ballroom dancing class; we were classmates. After a few lessons, we became exclusive dance partners to each other in class. You could say that ballroom dancing was our match-maker." Huentung pulled a cheeky face, and the guests responded with their laughter.

"So if we have to tell you about our love story," continued Huentung, "we have to tell you about our ballroom dancing. Since tonight we are here to celebrate us and our decision to step into the next stage of our life together, if you would not mind, Chunshek and I would like to dance a waltz for you to mark this occasion. That Sinyin is going to play with the string quartet for us is just going to make this experience electrifying! Many thanks, Sinyin *jeje*, for making this occasion memorable for us." The guests all clapped and cheered on this idea!

"Thank you for your support!" Huentung put down the microphone, and went up to take her place on the dance floor with Chunshek. There was silence.

On the beat of the music, the couple started to move elegantly and artistically across the floor. Huentung's poise was gracious and confident. Her steps were light, leading her gown to swing musically in the air. They glided from one corner to another effortlessly as a couple, and worked perfectly to dovetail each other's moves. They were communicating with their dance moves, and love was the subject. They twisted and twirled in harmony; no one could doubt they were one unit. They were simply exquisite to watch!

The music came to the end, so was the dance. It was romantic and fitting for the occasion. The guests enjoyed it enormously and the standing ovation belonged to the couple! Huentung and Chunshek held hands and bowed to the guests. They could not stop smiling. That was a picture of happiness. They shared the applause with the musicians too.

Chunshek and Huentung went up to Sinyin with the microphone in hand. "Sinyin *jeje*, what is the next piece you are to perform?" Huentung panted.

Sinyin smiled and shook her head, "First I must commend your dancing skill! What a treat! What a surprise!" The guests clapped to concur with Sinyin.

Then Sinyin went back to the music, "The next piece is also chosen by you. Perhaps you would like to explain to us why."

Huentung put on her cheeky look and asked, "Can you tell us one thing about this piece?"

"Well, it has been used in the UK's television adaptation of 'Pride and Prejudice'."

"Precisely. Do you know how people danced at balls at that time? They did not dance as couples individually but together! Apart from dancing with their own partners, they had to dance in team formation too. It was a little like folk dance we did at school.

"On our invitations, we specify the dress code as formal. We are not going to have a disco this evening! Oh, no. Instead, I am going to bring a bit of Britishness to you by a bit of ballroom dancing. I hope you will support us and give it a go. It's great fun. I have hired a teacher to give you a crash course!" That created a stir among the guests.

"This is the entertainment I have prepared for you this evening. I hope you will enjoy the experience. Now please first find a partner, and then two couples in a group for our group dance." Samyin could not believe that was what his sister had arranged for them. But of course, he had to support her and join the dance!

Chisau looked at his mother, who said, "Don't look at me; I am not going to dance. Go and find Yuetching. Don't let her sit it out."

Chisau therefore got up and went to invite Yuetching as his dance partner. Yuetching declined at first but Chisau persuaded her, "We are not going to disappoint our hosts, are we?" This left her with no choice!

Samyin went to invite Szeman as she had not got a partner. He still felt like an older brother to her and also a little bit guilty about what had happened between them.

Therefore, Samyin and Szeman, Chisau and Yuetching formed a group. Seeing how cosy they looked as a couple, Sinyin was furious. Subconsciously she still acted as if Chisau belonged to her; if she could not have him, no one should either.

With Chunshek and Huentung on hand to demonstrate the moves, the teacher taught them a simplified version of the dance which kept repeating the basic elements again and again. It was not difficult to get the hand of it quickly. Between the two couples, they have to keep changing their partners and then go back to the starting position. As a group of four, though, they moved up the line after each round! After a few practice rounds, the teacher called, "Let's do it for real with the music this time. Get into position." Suddenly everyone was a bit nervous, worrying that they might make mistakes! Everyone was concentrating hard, and tried their best in memorising and executing the steps. Sinyin got ready to play.

The music counted them in, and everyone was trying their best not to mess up. They did really well at the beginning but then mistakes started to creep in and mess up the rhythm for others, creating more mistakes. In the second half, they just could not stop laughing while dancing because they kept making the wrong steps. The hall was filled with laughter from the dancers as well as from the guests who were watching. One must admit it was pretty entertaining. Yuetching had never felt as ecstatic in her life! For that moment, nothing troubled her and she laughed till her stomach ache and could laugh no more. The music came to an end; the gentlemen took a bow while the ladies curtsied. They then clapped to express how much they enjoyed the dance – Yuetching had her first taste of how social dance worked to bring people closer to each other.

Huentung took up the microphone again and first thank Sinyin, "Please put our hands together for Sinyin and the musicians!" Sinyin waved goodbye to the guests in their applause.

"Was it great fun?" asked Huentung of her guests.

"Yes!" her guests shouted back!

"It's great to hear that. Ballroom dancing can really bring delight to our hearts and draw people closer. I'm glad that we're able to share with you the reason we love ballroom dancing." Huentung paused, and then resumed, "Tonight, I've prepared one last item on the programme. But before that, I would like to say some thank-yous. First, I have to thank my parents, for their love and care for me all these years. Without them, I will not be the person I am today. I also have to thank my brother. You all have caught a glimpse of how he has spoiled me with his attention over the years through the slideshow, which is very sweet and brings back fond memories. Thank you, brother. I wish that you will catch up with me soon and find my future sister-in-law in no time." Everyone turned to Samyin and laughed out loud. He was not surprised she would throw that one in, but today was her big day, so she could get away with anything!

"We must also thank the Hotel staff, especially Miss Cao, for their professional advice and service. Under the guidance of their capable hands, the preparation for this evening has been surprisingly stress-free for us. It has been a pleasure to work with such an efficient and capable team. We have to thank the string quartet and our dance instructor, who provide the entertainment of the evening. Last but not least, we would like to thank every one of you; your presence has made this a memorable and joyous occasion for Chunshek and me." Applause filled the hall.

"Now the last activity I've prepared for you this evening is to shape you up for a waltz! Our dance instructor will teach us some basic steps. I wish you will be as engaged and interested as before. Please don't be shy. Do come forward, young or more senior. I hope you enjoy the experience. Thank you."

Chisau stretched out his hand in front of Yuetching, asking for hers. Yuetching gave him a lovely smile and accepted the invitation. Samyin did the same to Szeman, calculating though in his mind that he would invite Yuetching for the next dance.

The dance instructor gave them a crash course on waltz. Yuetching stepped on Chisau's toes a few times in practice. That seemed to be an inevitable part of the learning process. Actually it was rather amusing and Chisau did not mind it at all. Then the lights were dimmed once more; the couples were getting ready for a proper dance. With one hand in Chisau's and the other on his shoulder, Yuetching had never felt closer to him. At that moment, she saw him for the first time not as a brother, but as a handsome, respectable, and attentive gentleman, who knew her better than anyone in the world. This thought startled her. Suddenly, she got nervous and felt this tightness in her chest. A beautiful melody started to float in the air. Chisau and Yuetching moved naturally to the beat of the music. One, two, three; one, two, three, the beat magically linked up their pulse, and locked their gaze at each other. Time seemed to have halted. In that moment, everything in the world faded into the background, and in her eyes she only saw Chisau. He let go of her to twirl on her own before returning to his arm. Yes, it was this familiar arm which had always been waiting for her, to catch her when she fell, to comfort her when she was sad, and to give her a sense of security when she was scared. She went away from that arm again to twirl on her own, but in actual fact, every time she was out there, all she wanted was to return to his hold, and be close to him once more. Suddenly, this wishful thinking crossed her mind – how nice would it be if she could own this space in front of him as marked out by the embrace of his arms? Her heart was pounding with excitement; every nerve was electrified. She felt a surge of warm current from within travelling all the way up to her cheeks, and making them burn. A panic attacked her, and she could look at Chisau no more. She turned to avoid his gaze. She seemed to have lost all her senses; her legs only managed to follow Chisau's lead mindlessly.

Meanwhile, Sinyin returned to the banquet hall after the

waltz had already started. What a merry party, she thought. But her smile was wiped out by her jealousy when she saw Chisau and Yuetching dancing in each other's arms. She saw all the tacit exchanges that went between them. Every touch was electrifying, so highly charged that could have produced sparks!

How could they not be a couple? This is a blatant lie. Who do they think they can fool? thought Sinyin. A rage surged within her.

In Sinyin's vision, she saw herself dancing with Chisau when they were still a couple all those years ago. Chisau was a proficient ballroom dancer himself, so his steps were always crisp and sure, his lead confident and his frame secure. Above all, anyone in his hold would look elegant, graceful and beautiful.

"It should have been me right there in his arms, and not *her*," Sinyin simply could not resign to this proposition that they were an item.

Regrettably the dance came to an end. Yuetching curtsied and Chisau bowed. Couples left the dance floor one after the other. As Samyin brought Szeman back to her father, he stayed to chat with Uncle Do. Meanwhile, Chisau and Yuetching were standing on the other side of the room, feeling a little awkward towards each other after the dance. They could not look at or speak to each other. Both were suffering from the aftershocks of the quake that had just hit them emotionally. Yuetching's heart was still pounding. She had never felt like this for anyone before. What had just happened? What was that feeling? She was confounded as well as scared.

Trying to show off to Yuetching her place in Chisau's life, Sinyin approached Chisau with the familiarity of an old couple and slipped her arm into his, and launched her attack, "Seeing you two dancing together, who would have believed that you are not an item?"

Chisau politely withdrew his arm. Sinyin was offended, "What did you do that for? Our past really has no meaning to you? Are you afraid that Miss Cheung would misunderstand?"

"I am not worried that Yuetching would misunderstand; I am more worried that *you* would misunderstand," Chisau was direct.

"Lee Chisau, you –" Sinyin was angry and decided to attack his weakness, which was Yuetching. After the electric shocks on the dance floor, Yuetching was still a bit dazed, defenceless and in turn made an easy target.

"Miss Cheung, see that you're all flushed. Was it your first experience? Don't mistake it for anything real or special for dancing has this magic of transporting a couple to the fantasyland that does not exist. This is just the nature of the activity. This often happens especially if you are in the arms of a proficient dancer like Chisau who knows the art. The whole thing is just a make-belief – this is the rule of the game. The better you are as a dancer, the more believable the experience is. If you don't believe me, you can ask him; I'm sure he won't lie to you."

Was it really what it was – a make-belief manufactured by a proficient dancer? It would be a relief if it was. She looked at Chisau in search of answer; she wished he would once again reassure her when she was confused. But the answer was not forthcoming.

"A make-belief means that you have to wake up eventually. I see you have made quite an effort on your part in today's make-belief too. I have to say, you are very pretty today – stunning even. Even I as a lady have to pass you compliments. You must have turned many heads tonight. As a woman myself, I *know* for a fact how much effort you have put in to achieve this look – the hair, the makeup, and the dress. You even completed the look with some nice borrowed jewellery. I see no expense spared for this evening. You are making your best effort to play modern-day Cinderella, aren't you? Who is your fairy Godmother? Perhaps you should introduce her to us. You do look like the part tonight. For a moment even I was fooled and deceived. But then I remember last time when I saw you in a similar setting, you were wearing a waitress uniform, waiting tables. Do you seriously think that by putting on an elegant frock and an expensive look, you can change the reality of who you really are? You can change your appearance but how about the rotten core underneath? Can you change your lowly upbringing with a family background that you need to hide, and the fact that you were nobody as a cleaner, and a waitress before without any family? You don't seriously believe that by putting on a robe, you would be turned into a crown princess, do you? You must be commended for trying hard to be somebody. But if you do not know how far to go and when to stop, you are inviting ridicule. Let me give you some sincere advice: wake up from your Cinderella dream before it's too late, quit while you are ahead, and go back to your reality in obscurity, from there, work hard and live well; try not to climb the social ladder that is beyond your reach, and enjoy your peaceful and quiet existence. You don't fit in here."

"Stop it," Chisau reproved.

When Samyin caught Sinyin's move at the corner of his eyes, he quickly rounded up his conversation with Uncle Do and excused himself. When he arrived, Sinyin was giving Yuetching her "sincere advice".

"Miss Yan, please don't be rude to our VIP. If you are determined to cause trouble, as the host, I have no choice but to kindly ask you to leave," Samyin stood up for Yuetching.

"What? She is your VIP and you are asking me to leave? This is ridiculous. I am going to complain to the Hotel for your treatment."

"This has nothing to do with the Hotel. This is a private matter between the Chius as the hosts tonight and Miss Yan. Please leave now," Samyin stayed firm on his stance.

"Chiu Samyin, you –" Sinyin knew that she could not win the argument, so she stormed out in a rage.

Yuetching suddenly felt that everyone was staring at her, and laughing at her for pretending to be someone whom she was not.

Noticing that Yuetching had turned quite pale, Chisau inquired, "Do you feel all right? Don't mind what Sinyin says. She is like that, blasting out anything when she doesn't have her way. We've heard that and we've been there before. Just erase what she has said; it's not even worth the memory space."

"That's right. Let us dance the next waltz; I've been waiting for the whole evening. May I have the honour for your hand?" smiled Samyin innocently.

She looked at Samyin and then Chisau. These two gentlemen made her so confused that she did not know what was real and what was not. Right now, she could not face them or have another dance with either of them. She must find an inconspicuous way to leave; she must be on her own.

She pretended as if everything was normal, and said, "I'm fine. I just need to go to the washroom." She moved away from the gentlemen with a smile, grabbed her clutch bag on the way out, and walked as calmly as possible out of the banquet hall. Once she was out of sight of the others, she hurried her pace to the cloakroom and picked up her coat. Then she rushed out of the Hotel and left in a taxi.

Samyin and Chisau waited for her in the banquet hall for a little while. But Chisau's instinct was telling him that something was not right. He told Samyin, "I'm going to look for Yuetching." He ran out of the banquet hall and straight to the cloakroom, asking, "Did you just serve a lady in a maroon dress?"

"Yes," the staff replied.

"Where has she gone?"

"I saw her heading for the exit."

"Thank you."

When Chisau got to the exit, Yuetching was nowhere to be seen. Chisau's phone rang; it was Samyin.

"Hello," Chisau answered.

"Have you found her?"

"No, she has left the Hotel. I will go and find her. I know you have to stay for the guests. Please don't worry," Chisau tried to be reassuring.

"Then I am relying on you. Please find her," requested Samyin, knowing that he could not leave the banquet.

Chisau tried to think where Yuetching could have gone. Then he remembered Yuetching's "telephone contract" with him. On this promise, he rang her, but there was no answer. Then he texted her: *Where've you gone?*

There was no answer.

Chisau reminded her of her promise: *Remember our "telephone contract", my exclusive access to you.*

Yes, of course she had promised, and a promise was for keeping, not for breaking. She therefore replied: *I'm fine. Don't worry. I just want to be alone.*

Chisau: *Where are you?*

Yuetching: *In a taxi.*

Chisau: *Where to?*

Yuetching had no choice but to disclose: *Heading home.*

Chisau: *I'll be heading home then.*

Yuetching: *No, don't let me spoil the party.*

Chisau: *I'll keep you company.*

Yuetching burst into tears when she read this text.

When she got home, she rushed into her room and locked herself in. She took off her evening gown and changed into what Cheung Yuetching should be wearing. She sat in front of the

275

mirror, and within seconds, her hair was down and makeup washed off. The traces of this evening were erased, and she was back to her normal self. *Dressing up is just a game; it is a make-belief; it is not real.*

Chisau arrived home and was relieved to see Yuetching's room lights on. He went in and knocked on her door, saying, "I'm home." But at that moment, Yuetching could not face him. "I'll be in my room. If you need anything or a listener, come to find me, anytime." Why was he always so tender and attentive to her? Yuetching found it hard.

Yuetching said nothing. Chisau felt he had been in a similar situation before. He knew it was best to leave her some space. When she was ready, she would talk. He returned to his. But actually, he was in the same boat as Yuetching, asking the same question, "What to do?"

The phone rang. It's Samyin.

"Hello," Chisau answered.

"Have you found Yuetching?"

"She has come home and I'm home with her."

"Is she all right?"

"I don't know. I haven't seen her. She has locked herself in her room. In situation like this, it's best to give her some space, right?"

"Agree."

"Is the party still going?"

"Yes."

"Please take care of my mum and Granddad."

"Sure, I will."

After he had hung up, Chisau sent his mother a short text to say that he had taken Yuetching home as she wasn't feeling well.

Then he could not help but text Yuetching also: *Are you all right?*

Yuetching: *I'm fine.*

Chisau: *Where are you?*

Yuetching: *Next room to you.*

Chisau: *How can I be sure? I haven't seen you or heard you.*

Yuetching: *I really am.*

Chisau: *Has another shadow from the past been descended on you?*

Yuetching: *I don't know yet. Give me some time.*

Chisau: *All right. But don't forget our "telephone contract".*

Yuetching: *I won't forget. Thank you for everything. Goodnight.*
Chisau: *Goodnight. See you tomorrow.*

The banquet hall was finally empty and Samyin was the last to leave. He was exhausted; the previous few months had been extremely busy for him. At last, he could relax a little before the Annual Meeting. As he drove past the bus stop near to the Hotel, he noticed a lady in her gown waiting. He recognised her as one of their guests of the evening and he did not feel right to leave his guest waiting at the bus stop on her own deep into the night.

He stopped his car and wound down the window, calling out, "Hi, are you all right? Are you waiting for the bus?"

The lady had a peep into the car and recognised Samyin from the banquet. She was relieved that he was not a stranger. She replied politely, "No, I'm waiting for my dad to pick me up. He has got a bit lost but he'll be here soon."

"Then I'll wait with you till he comes," Samyin stopped the engine and got off the car. He went round and sat next to her on the bench.

To break the awkward silence, Samyin first tried to strike up a conversation, "Are you my sister's friend?"

The lady smiled, and answered, "No. I'm to Cheng Chunshek as you to your secretary."

What an unexpected answer! Samyin was intrigued, "What do you mean?"

"We were really good workmates. We worked well as a team and enjoyed working together, perhaps a little too much on my part. You know, I never had a chance," the lady lamented. Talking from her own experience, she had this advice, "If you like your secretary, you should tell her. Don't let the chance go."

Samyin laughed at himself, "Was it so obvious to everyone?"

The lady smiled, "Look, you do not even deny it. You're more hopelessly in love than I originally thought."

"No, not really. Whatever happens, she is and will remain a good friend."

"That's the way to go, I suppose." The lady said no more on the subject.

Samyin then asked, "You must've been a really good friend, to have come all the way from the UK for his engagement party."

"No. I don't live in the UK anymore; I have resigned. I have been back for a little while, so he invited me along to the party. I believe I was the only guest who was acquainted to him tonight."

"Why did you resign and come back?"

"I felt it was time for a change, so I took the bold step. I'm still deciding, so I'm taking time out to study in the US. Do you think two years will be long enough for me to make up my mind?"

"Should – be –" Samyin was unsure how to answer.

"You believe what I said! No, I'm not that aimless. Two years are an investment towards my goal."

"Which is?"

"Not telling you."

"You must have been a little lonely tonight then," Samyin changed the subject. "Did we look after you well as hosts? Did you feel welcome?"

"It's all right. I didn't expect much since I knew nobody except Chunshek. The guests were friendly enough and we had a good time, didn't we? I was thoroughly entertained." The lady paused and recalled her night. Then she said, "What you did for your sister was very sweet. It was personal and sincere. I like it a lot. Well done. You were cute up there."

"Cute?" Samyin frowned.

"All right. If not *cute*, how about *charming*? Is it better? I bet you can charm any girl if you so wish."

"Don't say that," Samyin had been fighting this image to people, thinking how much trouble this reputation had caused him.

"Except perhaps your secretary."

"Oh please!" protested Samyin.

The lady laughed, and apologised, "Sorry, I'm unkind. I do apologise."

Samyin found her intriguing, so he asked, "What's your name?"

"Dung Yiksze. (董亦詩 *Yik* means also and *sze* means poetry.) A strange name, I know. People have frowned at it all my life. My dad's wish for me is to *also* have the same depth as a *poet*."

"Wow! It's a good name then, as it embodies your dad's blessing he wants for you. It's very meaningful."

"Thank you, but I'm not sure if I have fulfilled it." Just then, a car was pulling up, and Yiksze said, "Ah, my dad's here. Thank you for waiting with me. I really appreciate it. Goodnight."

Samyin waved goodbye as Yiksze jumped into the car. She certainly had left an unforgettable impression.

"Who's he?"

"Someone from the banquet," answered Yiksze.

"It's nice of him to wait with you."

"He certainly is nice, Dad."

Chisau woke up in the morning. The first thing that came to his mind was to check on Yuetching, only to find her door was still shut.

"She's still not up yet?" Chisau wondered.

He returned to his room and got ready for work. His phone beeped to signal an incoming text. He picked up the phone, which showed text from Yuetching: *I'd like to take a week off. I've something I'd like to do before the Annual Meeting. Don't worry.*

He rushed to Yuetching's room and found it tidy and empty. He went into her bathroom, and confirmed that her toothbrush and other toiletries were all gone. He frantically texted her: *Where've you gone? And for how long?*

Yuetching: *In preparing for the Annual Meeting, I suddenly have one thing I'd like to do. I don't know how long it'll take, but have allowed for one week.*

Chisau: *When will you stop running away on your own like that?*

Yuetching: *Perhaps never. I like time to myself. Sorry.*

When Chisau arrived at the Hotel, he went straight to Samyin's office to complain!

"Where's Yuetching?"

Chisau sat down on the sofa and shook his head in disbelief, "She has run off yet AGAIN! She is taking a week off. What am I to do with her? She didn't come out of her room the whole night, and was gone before anyone got up this morning! She sent a text this morning to formally take annual leave for a week."

"Why?"

"She says she has something she would like to do before the Annual Meeting."

"What could it be?" Samyin put his thinking hat on. "But from her point of view, the Annual Meeting will be a turning point in her life. Perhaps she does need some time to prepare herself psychologically for such a milestone in her life."

"I just hope that she wouldn't think too much, get cold feet and decide to return to her previous life."

"Four months ago, she promised that she would come back and finish the work in hand at the time. What she has NOT promised us is to stay on indefinitely. Instead she said she would then reconsider her situation and decide her future direction. Perhaps we should let her be. Her final decision may not be what we've hoped, but we must learn to accept it. After the Annual Meeting, her status as a member of the Lee family will be sealed and cannot be refuted. Even if she subsequently decides to work somewhere else, it isn't that bad, is it? I can't see how the outcome can be worse than that, so this is our bottom-line. The impact of that decision on us will be losing an excellent worker to someone else, and we will have to work harder. But as long as Yuetching is happy, I can accept that. We can't deny that our wish for her to stay at the Hotel is partially for our own selfish reasons. But we should think what's best for her. Let's give her complete freedom to choose, and respect her decision, whatever it may be." Chisau agreed with Samyin's analysis, which had put his mind at ease.

"Besides work, she has another decision to make," Samyin hesitated to add.

"Another decision?" Chisau was puzzled.

"She has promised me to think about us when she is not as busy as she has been. I'm waiting for her answer. I sincerely hope it'll be good news for me," Samyin looked a little embarrassed and shy.

"Have you two made progress in the relationship?" Chisau tested.

"You can't say there is a *relationship* between us, but I have confessed to her – properly this time! I've asked her not to make me wait any longer; waiting without knowing has been a torture. She's promised to consider *us* and give me an answer."

"This is progress."

"You call this *progress*?"

"Even if she does have a lot to consider, she doesn't have to run away every single time! It gives me a scare every single time!"

"Perhaps it's you who aren't used to her way. You have to remember that she has lived on her own for a long time. To you, it's like running away; to her, it's as normal as going on a holiday on the spur of the moment. The fact that she remembers to notify you is already showing you remarkable consideration. We should be grateful."

"How come all of a sudden you seem to know her so well?" Chisau sensed that Samyin and Yuetching had gotten closer.

"By now, I should have known her a little. After all, we've spent quite a bit of time together – even if only working!"

"All right, then, as Yuetching is on leave, we have to work even harder to do her share as well. We should follow up on the preparation for the Annual Meeting tightly. We must not let her down. Understand?"

"Of course. But I still regret the missed opportunity."

"What missed opportunity?"

"To waltz with her last night! If not because the trouble Sinyin had caused, I would've danced with her and carried on in my dream."

Chisau was reminded how it was to dance with her last night. He comforted Samyin, "You two stood side by side, being congratulated by the guests in the raptures of applause last night. If this sweet memory is not enough, then you are greedy indeed."

"Okay, I've got the point. I'm going back to work now," protested Samyin.

"Wow! Looks like Yuetching really has changed you. I've never seen you willingly get to work like you are now."

Samyin smiled with pleasure. He never knew how sweet it could be to willingly bear the influence of someone you liked until now.

9 All Crumbling Down Once More

Yuetching was not upfront about where she had gone or what she was doing. But following Samyin's advice, Chisau had decided to let her be; he was not going to ask if she was not telling. Everyday they only texted each other once to make sure she was safe and sound. What was surprising to Chisau was the fact that he could really concentrate on work. He felt good to be able to trust Yuetching and not to worry.

It was Wednesday, the third day of Yuetching's leave. At lunchtime, Chisau was surprised to get a text from her, saying: *Could you spare the time to come and find me?*

This unexpected text got Chisau a little worried, so he immediately responded: *What's wrong? Has something happened?*

Yuetching replied: *Don't worry; nothing's wrong. I need to do something but can't face it alone. You're the only one whom I feel I could ask to help. Could I trouble you once more?*

Chisau frowned, while gauging the gravity of the situation: it was not normal for Yuetching to ask for help. It meant that whatever she was contemplating doing must mean so much to her that she could not bring herself to give up; whereas for some reason not yet known to him, facing it alone scared her stiff. The only way to resolve this conflict was to bring in help, and she had decided to trust Chisau.

Chisau: *How to find you?*

Yuetching: *When can you come?*

He checked his watch, while estimating how long the meeting in the afternoon would take.

Chisau: *Can I come after work?*

Yuetching: *Can you stay overnight then?*

That sounded serious. Chisau checked his schedule for the following day. As he was taking Friday and Monday off to accompany his mother home for her father's 85th birthday and the Annual Meeting was taking place from the following Wednesday to Friday, he had a lot of work planned for Thursday before his long weekend away. But Yuetching seemed to need him urgently, what should he do? He could not abandon her when she called for help.

He therefore replied: *It's fine to stay overnight, but I'll have to delegate work to Samyin. Can I let him know the rescheduling is due to you?*

Yuetching knew Chisau was a dutiful manager, so she responded: *Sorry to trouble you. Perhaps you can't really afford the time.*

Chisau quickly convinced her: *No trouble at all. I only need to make some arrangements. Samyin wouldn't mind it. Both of us would like to see you back for the Annual Meeting.*

If she had a choice, she would not have asked. She decided to be selfish for once and took up Chisau's offer: *Then tell him that I need your help, but not where I am?*

Chisau: *Of course. How do we meet up?*

Yuetching: *Let's have dinner together. Address — . Text me when you set off; then I will know when to meet you.*

Chisau: *Got you. See you later.*

Yuetching: *Thank you.*

Chisau approached the restaurant which Yuetching had specified, and from a distance, saw her pacing up and down at the entrance. It was the first time he saw her after the dance. His stomach fluttered with excitement and he hurried his pace.

"Why didn't you wait inside?" Chisau surprised her on approach.

Seeing Chisau standing in front of her, she conjured up an image of her very own personal *Superman*, who would always turn up in front of her whenever she called for help. Even now, she still found it hard to believe that someone would have cared about her so much to make himself available at such a short notice.

"How have you been? I haven't seen you for three days. You must have been busy at work?" Yuetching started with the basic greetings.

"No busier than usual. Let's go in and eat, shall we? I'm hungry," smiled Chisau.

After they had ordered their food, Chisau was direct to the subject, "Now, tell me, how can I help? What makes our usually fearless Yuetching so scared?"

Yuetching took a deep breath, and began telling Chisau her long train of thoughts, "This is where I grew up. I came back to remind myself who I am. My chosen way to deal with most of the things that happened here has been to escape by running away. The day when I left here and started my new life, I was in effect walking away from my identity here at the same time. I faked an identity as someone with no family to cover up the pain I had endured. Subconsciously, I packed up my life here, sealed it and never wished to reopen it. At the time, I did not know my chosen way to deal with my past would cost me all my friends. In order to prevent people from asking unwelcome questions, I must lead a lonely life. However, the day when you came to find me has forced open my closed-up world. You thrust in front of me my past which I thought no one knew; I had no escape but to confront it! Your appearance in my life has told me one thing – my past has never ended. All that I cherish now is nothing but a continuation of the past that I so wished to erase from my life! You came to find me *because* I was my parents' daughter, *because* of who I have always been, the identity from which I have been running away!"

The dinner was served up.

Yuetching continued while eating, "In fact, I'm very grateful to you and Samyin, who have opened up my past and helped me face my demons that have been menacing me. Before then, I thought I was doing fine and coping the best I could with everything. I was proud and didn't want to change my way. But in reality, I was a patient who was blind to her own ailments, and in turn unaware of what healing she desperately needed. I'm grateful that you two are such good listeners to me, patiently use your own experience to point out my various biased presumptions, lovingly coax me away from my cosy little corner and bring me to a spacious place where I'm constantly challenged, fascinated, inspired and excited by all the new perspectives about life that I've never seen before! It was as if the knots in my heart have been loosened and eventually untied under your loving care. You may not know but having known you two has been a great blessing in my life. Our daily interactions have unwittingly bound up my broken heart little by little, like a balm that has been applied to sooth the pain and the tightness of my heart which have been smothering and immobilising me. I feel deeply blessed in life to have someone to whom I can freely pour out my heart content without any reservations or hindrance. I have never known that I could talk so much and have so much to say, that I too could guffaw and enjoy some fun. It has been a surprise too to discover my sense of humour! Spending time with you all has helped me discover a lot about myself which I did not know before. At the same time as you are getting to know me, I am getting to know myself. During this time, I have changed."

Yuetching paused to eat her food, while Chisau was chewing on every word that she was saying! She was always thoughtful and reflective; she always surprised.

She continued, "I've come to realise that the identity after the Annual Meeting is in effect *not* a new one. Rather, it's a continuation of who I've always been. Then I realise that if I were to accept my identity now, I *must* at the same time resume my identity of the past – the one that I've tried so hard to shake off throughout my adult life! This is my conclusion. Therefore, I came back here to take a turn, even just to remember things that I've tried to forget. Standing where I'm now today, what seemed a curse yesterday has now miraculously become a blessing. For the first time in my life, I believe my life is full of blessings and not cursed. This is a major turning point in my thinking and I have never felt so much at peace with myself and with who I am as now."

Chisau was curious, so he asked, "You seem to have everything thought out. You don't seem to need help in any way."

"There is a place, and a person, from my past that I would love to visit, but my fear has stopped me from getting close."

Chisau had a thought and guessed, "Is it your *guje*'s home?"

Yuetching nodded, adding, "*Guje* instructed me to cut off all contact with her. But right now, I really want to see her, to thank her for all that she has done for me. My steps unfortunately are hindered by my anxiety of not knowing how this family has turned out after all these years. At the time when I left, this family was a mess. The last time I saw *guje*, when she sent me off, she didn't look good. I'm not sure. They could have carried on their path but equally they could have made a decisive turn for the better. I just don't know, but I would like to find out. Would you go with me tomorrow?"

"Of course, I would. You don't even need to ask!" affirmed Chisau of his willingness. Finally he knew what his mission was for this trip. He felt privileged to be by her side at this tender moment in her life.

"Why did you ask me and not Samyin though?" asked Chisau.

"You're family and he isn't, although he is also very dear to me. Does that make sense? My choice goes with what my heart tells me on this."

"Samyin cares a lot about you and has instructed me not to fail my mission in bringing you back before the Annual Meeting. In fact I think he's crazy about you."

"He's a special person to me too; he's been exceedingly kind to me, I know."

"Will you accept him?"

Yuetching looked at him, puzzled. Chisau explained, "He has told me that you are considering about the two of you."

"I still haven't an answer to this. As a matter of fact, I also wish my heart will give me a clear answer very soon."

After dinner, they walked out of the restaurant. The air was fresh. Chisau took off his scarf and wrapped it round Yuetching's neck. She was taken by surprise, but Chisau said casually, "It's getting chilly. Be careful."

"How about yourself then?"

"Don't worry about me; I'm fine with a shirt, a tie and now a turned-up collar of my coat!" Chisau turned up his collar against the chill.

Yuetching suddenly had an idea and asked, "Would you like to see my hideout?"

Chisau was curious, so he agreed.

They stopped under a structure in the local park.

"Do you see at the top of the climbing frame is a lookout point? I called it a tree-house – my hideout," disclosed Yuetching. "Would you like to climb up?"

"How exactly do you climb up there?" Chisau was unsure.

"Like this." Yuetching demonstrated the way and reached

the top in a flash!

Yuetching looked down from above, offering her invitation with a broad grin, "Are you coming up?"

The way up was actually not as easy as it seemed with his overnight bag! When he was nearly there, Yuetching reached out to lend him a hand! Yuetching said cheekily, "Welcome to Cheung Yuetching's hideout. You are her first visitor ever! Come and sit down on this side; I have just wiped it clean for your nice suit!"

Chisau smiled and sat down as told, while Yuetching curled up opposite him. They exchanged a glance and Chisau noted, "It's not easy to climb up here."

"It can't be a hideout if it's easily accessible," Yuetching pointed out the basic criterion of a hideout.

"What kind of memories do you have in here?"

"I came here when I did not want to return home. I had been here working through my homework under torch light. Sometimes I would stare out and watch the stars in the night sky. I had even slept here. It was modest but it provided me with a most needed breathing space in time of pressure and pain."

"You were never discovered?"

"No one had ever tried to find me! No one has ever been more concerned about the whereabouts I am than you!" Then Yuetching changed her tone and joked, "Luckily I had never had unwelcome visitors either. All the memories here are good ones."

"I think the height has protected you."

There was nothing else to say, or they did not want to disturb the peace. They sat and enjoyed each other's presence in silence.

"Let's go. Tomorrow is an important day for me. Thank you for coming and face it with me," said Yuetching wholeheartedly.

"I'm going down first, and will catch you if you fall," Yuetching showed her cheeky side again. Deep down, perhaps she was a child that she had never been!

She went down in record speed just like how she got up. Chisau threw his bag down for Yuetching to catch, so as to make climbing easier. But he was as clumsy and awkward as he was on the way up. Looking up from the ground, Yuetching was feeling anxious for him. He struggled to find his footing but somehow managed to fumble down half way. Then he slipped in his leather shoes and was left dangling. Yuetching rushed forward instinctively to his rescue, and ended up being his cushion as he fell. Chisau got up and asked worryingly, "Are you all right? Are you hurt in any way?"

"I'm all right; you didn't fall that far. My foresight is good," bragged Yuetching, getting up and dusting off her clothes.

Chisau was relieved that Yuetching was not hurt, but it didn't make him look any better! He exclaimed, "Oh dear! This was embarrassing."

"Shhh… I promise this will be our secret! You can of course blame it on the shoes!" teased Yuetching.

Yuetching led the way to a little guest house. She took Chisau to his room, explaining, "There is no six-star hotel here! I hope you don't mind. I have booked this room for you, while I'm over there – room 201. If you forget, just text me. This is your key. Breakfast will be served from seven in the morning, but we do not need to be that early. Let's meet at eight for breakfast. Any questions?"

"No further question! You've done us proud as a trainee from Arlando!"

"Well, that means its training is good! See you tomorrow."

They parted for the night.

After breakfast, Chisau and Yuetching set off to her childhood home, and she had chosen to walk there. It was as if she was prolonging the journey to get there. Along the way, she shut herself in her own thoughts and said nothing. Was she preparing herself or was she summoning up her courage? No one knew precisely what went through her mind, except herself. Her pace was steady and thoughtful but not in a hurry. She navigated the streets with a great deal of familiarity, and decisions on which way to turn required no conscious thinking. She was so absorbed in her own thought that at times, it was unclear if she even remembered Chisau was there with her. But he did not mind at all for his role was here to protect and assist her; he felt fulfilled just being by her side at a critical moment of her life such as this.

After a 45-minute walk, Yuetching stopped in front of a building and said, "We're here." She looked at Chisau as if to say the moment that she had been dreading as well as feeling excited about was finally here; this was it! She took a deep breath and marched into the building, a step she had failed to take in the past three days on her own. She was grateful to Chisau for making the time to be here with her today, or she would have never been able to come this far! Chisau followed her up the stairs to the third floor, only to find himself in a maze! It was a bit daunting for him but not for Yuetching, as she meandered through the twists and turns of the corridors, and finally stopped outside an apartment. She took a deep breath again, and wondered who would be greeting her on the other side of the door. She plucked up her courage and rang the doorbell; her heart was pounding with anxiety.

The door swung open, and a stranger came in view. She was relieved and surprised at the same time.

"Who are you looking for?" asked the lady who answered the door.

"I'm looking for Cheung Meiying. Is she here? Is this the Wong household?"

"Cheung Meiying? She no longer lives here. They moved out of here three years ago." The lady was about to slam the door shut but Yuetching put her hand out to stop her.

"Do you have her contact details?" she was desperate to find her.

"Sorry, no. We can't help you." Then she closed the door, slashing Yuetching's hope for finding her *guje* at the same time.

Having geared up for nothing in the end, Yuetching was disappointed. Where was she going to find *guje*? It seemed impossible now. Chisau felt her disappointment. They walked down the stairs and exited the building. Yuetching lingered and would not leave, as if by doing so, she could somehow find a link to her *guje*. After all that was the last contact point she had of her and her family. Chisau observed the surroundings and spotted a store across the road.

"It has never occurred to me that they could have moved. Silly me. Perhaps it's for the best. Perhaps *gujeung* has sobered up and started up again. Who knows? Perhaps they're doing very well." She turned to Chisau and apologised, "Sorry for begging you to drop everything and come here for nothing."

"There's no need to say sorry. Let's go across the road to that store." Chisau pointed it out to Yuetching; his detective instinct from the days of finding her suggested that it might be a fruitful avenue for inquiry.

As they were approaching the store, the storekeeper already

ran out to meet them outside. She circled Yuetching and then screamed with joy, "Cheung Yuetching! Right? Are you really Cheung Yuetching? Thank goodness, you've finally come back. I've been waiting to meet you again for five whole years!"

Yuetching could not express her shock. How could it be possible for anyone on earth to spend five years waiting for her? She asked suspiciously, "And you are?"

"You used to call me Auntie Cheung! Don't you remember me?"

"Auntie Cheung?" Yuetching began to recall some hazy memories of her.

"I dropped by every now and then to see you. I bought you sweets and clothes. Do you remember?" the strange lady tried her very best to jog her memory.

"Ah –" memories were slowly coming back. "I remember. You were – the auntie who turned up randomly from nowhere," exclaimed Yuetching with a bit of excitement.

"That's me! I've opened this store specifically to keep watch on who are coming and going from that building in case you come back one day. This day has finally come. I saw you – it was you, wasn't it? – linger around in the past few days but I wasn't sure. It has made me more vigilant to look out for you. I'm glad that today I have a closer look at you. Come in. We can sit down and have a chat. I have a lot to tell you. I've waited five years for this day to come." Auntie Cheung could not conceal her excitement of seeing Yuetching.

Yuetching was baffled though and a little scared. *Why has she been waiting for me and what does she want to say to me?* She was suspicious. Seeing Yuetching fixed on the spot, Auntie Cheung grabbed her wrist but Yuetching withdrew from her grip in a reflex. Auntie Cheung tried to convince her once more, "Look, you have come all the way to see your *guje*. Have I guessed wrong? Do you wish to know where she's now and what's happened to her and family? If you do, then follow me. I'm not going to eat you. I've waited five years for you, so please just hear what I have to say. I'm not going to let you go until I've told you everything I want to say. Got it? After I've told you everything, at least I can move on in my life one way or another. If you're scared, your boyfriend can tag along."

Yuetching looked at Chisau, who nodded to say it was a risk worth taking; after all she was offering exactly what they were here for. They followed Auntie Cheung inside. When they got in, Auntie Cheung closed the store. This was ominous. For some reason, Yuetching felt uneasy and anxious – all signs suggested that this was NOT going to be a general social chat. She was so glad that Chisau was by her side. Seeing that Yuetching looked nervous, Chisau reached out and held her hand into his to give her a physical reminder that she was not alone.

Auntie Cheung led them to the back of the store where she lived. She sat them down in the lounge and poured them some tea. Yuetching thanked her.

"You'd like to know what happened to your *guje*, and I'll tell you all. Mr Boyfriend, you know it's right to hold her hand. She's in for a shock today." Yuetching exchanged a look with Chisau, who tightened his grip on her hand to give her courage.

Auntie Cheung took a deep breath and began, "Your *guje* died three years ago."

"What?" this was Yuetching's first shock of the day.

"She had a brain tumour. From diagnosis to her passing away was only six months. She had been the one who kept the family together. When she was down, the family fell apart. Even when she was ill, there was no one to take care of her. I was near at the time, so I looked after her a little." Yuetching felt the wrench of her heart and tears started rolling down silently. Auntie Cheung passed her some tissue paper, and addressed Chisau again, "I've told you that it's a smart idea to hold her hand. This wasn't a happy ending."

Yuetching calmed down a little and Auntie Cheung resumed, "When she breathed her last, all the family finance had dried up also. They opted for the *Simplicity Package*, which meant direct cremation with no mourners present and her ashes to be scattered in their garden of remembrance. I couldn't accept it, so I interfered. I paid out of my own pocket to arrange her ashes to be put in the columbarium. This was the least I could do not only for her but also for you, thinking that you would find comfort in having this little place of memorial kept for her when you returned.

"They were evicted from the apartment not long after as they were behind in their rent. Your *gujeung* is now homeless on the street in the neighbourhood, leading an aimless life. All his children disowned him a long time ago. Alas, your *guje* worked hard all her life, trying to support and keep the family together.

She would have been heartbroken to know what has become of it. I felt sorry for her, I really did. It was mercy for her to die young so that she didn't have to work herself to the ground for people who showed no appreciation of her whatsoever. They were all like leech sucking off her. She drained her life supporting them, I tell you."

Yuetching broke into sobs; her sorrow for *guje* was beyond words. Thinking that it might take a while for Yuetching to calm down, Auntie Cheung left them alone when she went into her bedroom to search for something. She emerged again with an old tin box in her hands. Yuetching feared that there might be more to know.

"Why are you so concerned about me? Who are you? What's in that box?" Yuetching fired her direct questions at Auntie Cheung.

"Would you like some more tea?" Auntie Cheung was trying to delay the moment when she opened up the box. Yuetching sipped some tea as told in order to hasten her disclosure.

Auntie Cheung took a deep breath and pronounced, "This box holds the secrets of your birth. This is what I've waited for five years to tell you." This time Chisau was shocked as well as Yuetching: what could have been more to be known about her birth?

"What – what do you mean? What secrets?" asked Yuetching anxiously.

"Simply put, *I* am your biological mother," declared Auntie Cheung.

Yuetching jumped onto her feet, and knocked over the stool she was sitting on, in shock. Auntie Cheung also stood up, looking nervous. "Please sit down and I'll tell you all about it," requested Auntie Cheung. Chisau picked up Yuetching's stool and brought her to sit down. He continued to hold her hand – firmly. Auntie Cheung went back to her seat only after Yuetching looked more settled.

"Mr Boyfriend, I'm glad that you're here today. She needs you very much," repeated Auntie Cheung.

"Please tell what you have to tell now," hurried Chisau.

"Then let me begin:

"Lee Oiyee and I were classmates at school and best friends. I didn't study, so I didn't get into university, whereas Oiyee progressed to university without a glitch as expected. From then on, we led very different lifestyles, and met up rarely. On and off I heard news about her from different sources, so I knew she was dating a guy called Cheung Saiyuk. I made a mental note that she seemed to have a preference for people with the same surname! After I had left school, I did everything that a good girl wouldn't do. I worked during the day and partied at night. I lived for my nightlife, and roamed bars and discos. In the early days, Oiyee urged me to quit such a self-destructive lifestyle, saying that I was abusing my health and youth with alcohol and soft drugs. At the time, since I didn't even listen to my parents, why would I listen to her? I was fed up with her disapproval of my lifestyle, and I broke off the friendship. Back then, if you didn't play with me, you weren't with me. I accused her of being nosey and judgemental, having an air of superiority. I distanced myself. It's human nature, isn't it? You hate those who tell you that you're wrong.

"The life as a party animal ran its own risks. A few years into this lifestyle, and being careless once, I got pregnant with you. I was scared and did not know what to do. My parents had disowned me a long time ago, and I was too proud to ask for help. I had no one to depend on. All the guys in my life were out to play – they didn't know what commitment or responsibility meant. In fact, I didn't either. Despite that, I couldn't bring myself to abort you though; I must admit I did contemplate it, but I couldn't do it; my conscience would not allow me. My hesitation gave you time to grow inside me and suddenly you were nearly full-term, a full life in me! When I was in labour, I went to the hospital on my own. Who would have guessed I would find Oiyee there! I heard her name mentioned by the staff. For my peace of mind, I went to make sure it wasn't the Oiyee I knew. This was the first time I met Cheung Saiyuk, who was by her side. Oiyee looked as if she was in a very critical condition. I asked him directly what the matter was, and found out that they had lost their baby. That was not it. Because it was an ectopic pregnancy, Oiyee had lost a lot of blood and almost died. She was in a critical condition. And that was not it either. She could not have any more children. Oiyee suffered three blows in one attack! Her life was hanging in a balance. No one could be sure if she could pull through or indeed if she wished to live. I looked at their situation: she had a man who loved her, committed to her and was willing to take responsibility for her, whereas in my arms, I had a baby, of whom I didn't know how to take care when I left hospital. Then a thought crossed my mind in a flash: if Oiyee pulled through, they would provide a stable family for you. It would have been far better than following me. Therefore, I went over, casually sounding the idea to Saiyuk, who took it as a God-sent offer, leaving me with no room for second thought! He took you on as his own child and encouraged Oiyee to fight so that she could get better and take care of *her* baby. Yes, he lied to her that her baby lived albeit in intensive care. Oiyee did pull through and *you* were the reason why she lived.

"Of course, I was discharged from the hospital with you much earlier than Oiyee. I stayed at their place to care for you. During that time, Saiyuk looked after me to look after you and was also taking care of Oiyee. This was how I came to nurse you the first five months of your life, and fulfilled a bit of my maternal duties towards you. Oiyee did get suspicious why I suddenly came back into her life – I was the last person on earth to be the mothering kind! But Saiyuk just brushed it aside to say I was her best friend and in turn stood by her in times of needs. At her fragile state, she would believe whatever you said to her. She either wasn't thinking straight or didn't wish to know. Saiyuk and I struck a deal that if I was not to tell Oiyee or you the secret until you were 18 years old, he would let me keep in touch. If I broke the promise, he would run and I would never see you again. This deal actually got sour in the early days. It was never easy to give up a child, but as a new mum, I didn't appreciate that. As I bonded with you as your mother, I got cold feet and would like to call off the deal. I talked to Saiyuk about it and he panicked. Snatching you from Oiyee and telling her that you were a lie probably would have killed her in her weak condition at the time. That was his main concern. To my horror they really ran away and cut all contact. I could have called the police, I suppose, but I didn't; I worried about you as a newborn and my concern was to find you. Luckily I did. I asked Saiyuk not to run away but let me honour my original promise. He warned me that I could have my second chance but not the third chance. He demanded a more formal arrangement, so I named them officially as your legal guardians. I continued to nurse you, but used the remaining time to sever my tie with you. I kept telling myself that it was in your best interest to leave you with them.

This was how I came to be your Auntie Cheung who turned up every now and then to see you. "

Auntie Cheung opened the box and took out a pile of old pictures. Looking at the first one, she said, "This was your first picture. Oiyee was holding you in bed. I sat next to you two. I gave you the name Yuetching (*Yuet* means delight and pleasure; *ching* means sunny and bright), as you were always sunny and made people around you happy. They loved it, so this was how you came to be called Cheung Yuetching. To mark the occasion, we took this picture together. The rest of these were taken when I came to visit you at different times. Would you like to take a look?"

Yuetching was overwhelmed by a tsunami of mixed emotions that she did not know what. She was shaking uncontrollably. She burst in tears seeing the pictures of her growing up, pictures that she believed she never had. Although they were only sporadic records, they were priceless and precious to her.

"This is your birth certificate. This is the proof that I'm your mother."

"And she was never adopted?" asked Chisau.

"No, they intended to but never got round to for whatever reasons. Then they died. Both died," sighed Auntie Cheung. "It was tragic!"

"You had never thought of me for all those years. Why did you come back to find me five years ago, even to the extent of opening a store here? Why?" questioned Yuetching; she wanted some answers.

"Alas, call it old age. I was getting old and could not live like a party animal for ever. Men did not treat me well. Foolishly I even followed one to live overseas for a few years, leaving you behind. It didn't work out, so I returned on my own and found that my dad was dying. I nursed him in his final days. Our disagreements were put aside and his heart became softened towards me. It's in no doubt that he disapproved of me but in his death, he wished to do his last bid to save me from self-destruction. He left me with all that he had – a sizeable sum, commanding me to *turn away* and here's the funding to wean me off men. He asked me to promise him to live with decency and dignity as a woman, and not to squander his lifesavings on useless men. How could I dishonour his memory and not live according to his dying wish, especially when it's for my own good? At that turning point, I naturally thought of you as my only remaining family, so I looked for you. You were 20 then. Here was my first port of call five years ago, but your *guje* said that you had started your own life away from the family, and didn't keep in touch. I didn't believe her; you were not that kind of girl. I sensed that she wasn't telling the whole truth. Therefore I used my dad's money to open up the store, which would give me a living while I kept watch on the family at the same time. I've lived on the belief that I'll see you one day. But you've disappointed me, you know. I didn't believe that you were heartless but you didn't visit even when your *guje* was dying. I lost hope a little after that, thinking that you probably were heartless and might never return. But then I had nothing to lose to wait, so I stayed put."

This judgement pierced Yuetching's heart. She was too overcome by her grief and sadness to defend herself, and Chisau felt for her.

"Why did you come only five years ago to call me a family? Why not when I was five years old?" Even in emotional turmoil, Yuetching did not lose her sharpness. With flashbacks of her chaotic life back then, Auntie Cheung blushed with shame.

"You can't answer, can you? Perhaps let me answer in your stead. You couldn't give up the freedom of your single life. You saw that a family was happy to take me in unconditionally, believing that I was a relative, and you let it be, you let this lie continue for your convenience. Was that right?" Yuetching was relentless in her pressure for some truths.

"With men that would hit me, it's simply unsafe for a child." Auntie Cheung blurted out the truth about her hellish life.

Yuetching interrogated further, "Who is my dad?"

"Well, on that, I honestly don't know –"

In her anger, Yuetching sprang to her feet. "What? YOU DON'T EVEN KNOW WHO MY DAD IS!" bawled Yuetching, distressed and insulted. Auntie Cheung was shaken by her roar! She then laid down her charges forcefully, "I was only an accident, an inconvenient byproduct of your pleasure. You didn't want me; you even contemplated to murder me while I was still forming in your womb. From the day when I was born, you already planned to get rid of me. All along you were thinking about how to shuffle the responsibility for me from one to another, so that you could continue your carpe diem lifestyle. My non-biological mother sacrificed her life to save me. How about you? What have you, who boldly claim to be my biological mother, ever done for me? My non-biological mother has given me self-respect, and even to the extent of sacrificing her life to tell me that I was precious. This was her love for me, on which I have built my life. Because of her love, I find the strength to live positively and take good care of myself; I try my best to live well and do well FOR HER. How about you? In one stroke, you have taken it all down, and torn my life apart! You have done NOTHING except to insult ME and MY VERY EXISTENCE with your EVERY sentence, EVERY word and EVERY decision that you made. Instead of saying I'm worth it, EVERYTHING you do says that I'm indeed unwanted! You make me feel I am nothing but dross to be discarded, and mud to be trampled on. How could you destroy me and all my beliefs so utterly in one blow? How could you be so merciless as to hollow me out from within? How could you trample over my every self-belief that I have just like the others? How can I ever lift my head up high from now? How DARE you claim to be my MOTHER AFTER ALL THAT YOU HAVE DONE TO ME? Do you have no shame? You don't deserve to be my mother! I HAVEN'T A MOTHER LIKE YOU!" howled Yuetching.

"But – you're my only remaining family," pleaded Auntie Cheung nervously.

"I am NOT your family," Yuetching denied it outright.

"I nursed you for five months."

"But you chose your party lifestyle over me every single time."

"I visited you and checked on you."

"But you never admitted you were my mother or played that role."

"It's simply unsafe to bring you with me!"

"It's because you chose not to face up to your responsibility."

"I bought you sweets and dresses."

"Those were for you, not for me, to ease your own guilty conscience."

"I gave you your name."

"That was my tragedy."

Auntie Cheung was utterly defeated in this exchange, and

could list no more. She was ashamed of how quickly she had exhausted all that she had ever done for her own daughter, who in turn had every right to despise her. Seeing that Auntie Cheung had retreated in her defence, Yuetching said in her favour, "The only good things you have ever done for me were two: taking these pictures and giving *guje* a resting place. For these, I thank you. Now, may I keep the box and its contents please?"

Auntie Cheung dared not say no! "Yes, please take them."

Yuetching returned all the pictures and documents to the box, picked it up and was leaving. Auntie Cheung grabbed hold of her, begging, "Will you come back to visit me again?"

"Don't expect too much," Yuetching was honest and firm.

Auntie Cheung let go of her and quickly jotted down her number. She held it out and requested, "Please take my number. If you change your mind, call me or text me. I'll wait for you." Yuetching would not take it, so Auntie Cheung thrust it into Chisau's hand. "Keep it for her, please," she begged. Yuetching walked out through the store without turning. Chisau followed suit, picking up some chocolates on his way out from the store and leaving some change for them.

Yuetching walked away from the scene as quickly as her feet could take her, while Chisau had a hard time in keeping up with her. Her thoughts were miles away and she was not alert of her surroundings. She constantly walked into people and dashed across the roads without looking! Chisau worked hard to keep her out of accidents! She looked as if she was wandering around aimlessly, but habit automatically took her to her hiding place in the park; that was what she did in the past when she was distressed. She climbed up in a series of agile moves, leaving Chisau with no choice but to follow. When he reached her hiding place, Yuetching had already settled down, with her head leaned back and eyes closed. Pain was written all over her face and too many times he had seen it. Chisau sat down opposite her; he did not demand her to talk but was content just being there for her. He wished if only he could share her suffering in some ways.

After a long while, Yuetching sat up and opened the tin box. She took out the pile of photos; there were about 200 of them in all. They were mainly snapshots covering the first five years of her life with her parents; during that time, Auntie Cheung must have been a rather regular visitor. Thereafter the photo record of her got more spaced out. Perhaps it was because she was avoiding the camera as she grew older, or it was simply because Auntie Cheung did not visit as frequently. It was more likely to be the latter; according to her memory, she visited probably once a year or less. When she was little, she would go out with her to play or to eat. But when she grew older, she retreated to herself and probably refused to interact with strangers. Perhaps that was why Auntie Cheung visited her less and less; she was not sure as memories of her were really hazy. She went through the pictures, delighted to see some visual records of her happy memories for the first time. When she was with her parents, she was full of joy and laughter. Those were days when she was not sad, she thought. How carefree she looked at that time! Looking at these pictures, she could believe that she was once happy, although happiness was never in her memory. Yuetching smiled at her own cheekiness and cute expressions. Being able to own some memories comforted her. These were snapshots that she would like to remember well.

She passed the photos to Chisau, saying, "Finally I know how I looked like when I was little, and why your mother thought I was a premature baby!"

"I also understand why my aunt suddenly vanished." Chisau looked through the pictures with great interest, and smiled at some funny ones. Those indeed were sweet memories. "It's nice to retrieve some memories, isn't it?" Chisau reflected.

Yuetching nodded, "Yes, these photos have filled a big hole in my life. Retrieving some records of my childhood is the only good thing in this mess; everything else – the lie, my conception and the repeated abandonment by my biological mother – everything else is to destroy me without mercy. Before today, I thought I finally knew who I was and in turn my position in life; I was preparing for this new role and a new beginning. Who would have thought –" Yuetching had a lump in her throat and paused.

"Who would have thought," she continued, "I'm not whom I've believed I was, and have to start all over again – yet again? I was not born out of love but as a careless byproduct of some adult game; I AM an unwanted baby, and subsequently a bean bag to be passed around! I feel my origin was utterly meaningless and filthy. I'm nobody, unwanted. All those who were closest to me died or left me," she began to cry. "Alas, what am I to do?

I'm – exhausted…" With arms wrapping round her legs, she curled up into a bundle and rested her head on her knees.

"Yuetching, my aunt's love for you was real and unchanged," Chisau tried to assure her. "Where you came from hasn't changed my opinion of you either. You are still the Yuetching I know – you have self-esteem; you are positive, diligent, effective, efficient and above all, honest, kind and sincere towards people. Isn't that you? Has your nature changed just because you had a different birth from the one we knew?"

Yuetching looked up with tear-stained eyes, snivelling, "I don't know anything anymore. Everything I believe is a lie. What's true and what's false I can't tell. I am exhausted… I don't know from where I can muster the strength anymore."

"Yuetching, don't give up. You must be a tumbler once more – resiliently bounce back after you've been pushed down. If you become dejected, and lead life like a deflated balloon, I'll be very sad."

"Why do you care – I'm not related to you anymore! In fact I'm nobody, related to no one. I'm nothing but a stranger to your family. I have no right to stay at your home anymore." Yuetching saw the life that had been perfect begin to tumble down right before her eyes as an inevitable consequence of this newfound truth. She had got used to the warmth and security that this family had provided her; she was frightened to leave and be on her own again. She didn't want to let go, but she knew full well she could not possess what was not hers.

"You've said that blood ties are one basis to make connection with people. This basis has just been dissolved between your family and me. The past year was just a dream, a misunderstanding. Sinyin has been right all along. I'm out of place, and it is a status beyond my reach," Yuetching sighed heavily. Why, with all things and with all people, had fate elected to prove Sinyin right?

"It wasn't a dream," Chisau refused to accept the reality, "Aren't you a real person, who loves, cries and feels just like anyone else? We have worked, lived, eaten, laughed, fought, stood, and shared our joy and sorrows together, as a family and as a work team. Can you say this is *nothing* but a dream? Although these have happened because of a misunderstanding, we have NOT been lying. Everything that has happened has been based on honesty and done in good faith. There is no shame in it."

"Your granddad won't accept me," Yuetching was realistic in her expectations.

"You haven't cheated him. You WERE the girl whom his daughter died in order to save. To her, you were her daughter from the day you were born and till the day she died. This is an unchangeable fact. You WERE the girl Granddad was looking for at the time. That wasn't a lie. Most importantly, you must remember your life is precious."

"Of course, I remember. Without her, I don't know what I would have become. I probably wouldn't have been able to stand up! But still I don't want to hide this secret of my birth from Granddad. Lies are a rotten basis on which to build a relationship. They only breed more lies and condemn us to a life of fear – fear that the truth will one day come out. I don't want to live like that. He should know the whole truth, not the partial truth. Letting people believe what they want to even if we know they are wrong is deception on our part."

Yuetching had a point, but he was scared of the outcome.

"All right, we'll tell but we must plan and consider carefully how to proceed before we act. We can't afford to be rash. We need to think up the best possible way and find the best time to disclose it to him. We'll go to see Granddad together after my weekend away with my mother. This'll give us a bit of time to think it through and plan the way forward. Could you promise me not to say a word until then?"

Yuetching hesitated, "We don't have a lot of time; it must be told before the Annual Meeting, that is, next Wednesday."

"I know; we'll do it by then. Please promise me not to do anything until I'm back." Yuetching was forced to agree.

"Are you hungry? Would you like some chocolate?" Chisau offered and got some chocolates out of his bag.

"I'm surprised you're so well prepared," Yuetching lightened up a little.

"No. I grabbed these from the store before we left. I was afraid that you might be hungry and faint."

Yuetching was touched by Chisau's attention, but she declined his offer, "I don't want to eat chocolate. Let's go and eat a late lunch/ afternoon tea, shall we? Let's go."

Chisau was happy that Yuetching had not lost her appetite. He got up quickly and got down more skilfully this time. He bragged, "See, I didn't fall this time! I'm getting better at this!"

"I can see – yes, much improved!" Yuetching approved!

When they were making their way towards an exit through the park, a homeless person was just waking up from his nap on the bench. After a few stretches, he got up and hobbled in the direction towards Yuetching and Chisau. Seeing him, Yuetching halted as a panic had gripped her and immobilised her. Before Chisau had the time to work out what had happened, the homeless person was already in front of them, begging for money, "Sir, Miss, please have mercy and spare some change."

Yuetching avoided his gaze but he would not let go. He was so close to her that she could smell his breath, a familiar smell which had not changed for the past nine years! As they scuffled, the man recognised her, "Yuetching? You're Yuetching! Wow, how pretty you've turned out and all freshened up. Look how cool and posh you look now. Look at your clothes! You must've been doing well. How nice of you to come back to the neighbourhood! We're very proud to have produced such a fine specimen like you. Are you visiting us?"

"Let me go!" shouted Yuetching.

"I see you've got yourself a posh young fella too. It's regrettable that Meiying isn't here to see this. Have you heard she died three years ago?"

Piecing everything together, Chisau began to work out who this man was. He intervened to protect Yuetching.

Yuetching's *gujeung* got angry, and turned into a thug, "Yuetching, I raised you, you know. What you owe me far exceeds the change in your pocket that I'm demanding. I took you in when you were an orphan. You should repay my substantial kindness to you, and give me a generous lump sum to show your gratitude. How could you stand back and not lend a helping hand when your *gujeung* is in such a pitiful state?" He tried to grab Yuetching's bag. In their struggle, *gujeung* lost his balance and fell, pulling Yuetching down with him. It was déjà vu. Yuetching struggled frantically to free herself from him. Chisau quickly pushed *gujeung* away and helped Yuetching up.

Chisau imagined that Yuetching must be rather frightened, and was solicitous, "Are you all right?" Yuetching nodded; she was much stronger this time!

Gujeung finally stumbled back onto his feet. He rushed towards Yuetching to terrorise her. Yuetching went to hide behind Chisau. Chisau got furious with this man and defended themselves by pushing him away. *Gujeung* fell down again, as he was always unsteady on his feet.

"Serve you right for being rude to Yuetching in the past and present!" yelled Chisau. He turned and pulled Yuetching to leave. Feeling ashamed of himself, *Gujeung* started to cry and had a fit of self-pity.

Yuetching halted her steps, requesting Chisau, "Wait just a moment." She opened her bag and emptied her wallet of cash. She ran back to *gujeung* and Chisau followed close behind. She knelt down to his level, and counselled, "With this habit of yours, money is only going to harm you, not help you. Here is all that I have on me. Take it; buy something good to eat and warm to wear. If you don't help yourself, no one can help you. Do you understand? If you don't kick this habit, you have only one outcome, which is that you'll be dead on the street one day. It's your choice, as it has always been."

Gujeung took the money and was moved. With more tears gushing out, he said, "I believe you're the last person in the world who would care to counsel me." He reached out and grabbed her hands, saying, "I've wronged you. I'm sorry." He cried even louder.

Yuetching withdrew her hands, and settled the score, "From now on, I owe you nothing." She stood up and left him on the ground.

On their way out, they walked past a public toilet. Yuetching went in and washed her hand thoroughly as if to wash off everything she had to do with her *gujeung* and his family.

Sitting in the restaurant, Yuetching stared at her food in a daze. Her mind was obviously elsewhere or in a shutdown state.

"Eat something," coaxed Chisau.

Yuetching shook her head.

"Aren't you hungry?"

For Chisau, she forced herself to eat. Even with her best effort, she could only swallow a few mouthfuls. Seeing Yuetching in such a state, Chisau bought some takeaway and paid the bill. Then he brought Yuetching back to her room. He shut the door and said to her gently, "Now you can cry. Don't bottle it up inside."

Yuetching sat on the floor and leaned on the edge of her bed. In no time, she curled up into the foetal position again. It seemed to be the posture that gave her most comfort in time of distress. Her head was pounding with a splitting headache; it ached because it had been overloaded with too much to process in one day. She felt she was a mess, who had lost all her directions and knew not where to go or which way to turn next. She was exhausted. The life she had been working hard to establish was once again shattered into pieces in one stroke, and she did not even have a say; she could not even object. That pain and disappointment of brokenness came to strike her yet again. It was like an old friend who would not leave her alone, but familiarity did not make it any easier; it hurt just the same. Why must life be so hard and merciless? Could she have some breathing space? Why couldn't she have the right to enjoy the fruits of her hard work? Why must life be so cruel to her? She was angry, at all the injustice and unfairness that had happened to her in her life. Her heart ached terribly, as if every wound it had ever borne had cracked open once more and released excruciating pain of all sorts in a cocktail! All the unhappy memories rushed back to her mind to torment her all at once, mocking her that this was how it had been and would be! She was trapped in this repeated cycles of torments that she could not escape. No matter how hard she tried to build herself up, she always ended down at the bottom of the pit. Why happiness was always short-lived? Was the bottom of the pit where she belonged? Why couldn't she get out of it? A flood of tears finally broke through its dam. Yuetching cried out uncontrollably; this was the sound of her accusation towards her life and fate. Chisau sat down next to her, and let her tremble and abreact in his arms. Her shriek pierced right through his heart.

At long last, tears had dried up. Yuetching calmed down, not because she felt better but because all her strength had been drained. Chisau passed her a towel to wipe her face. Then he gave her water to drink and food to eat. Like a robot, she followed obediently all that Chisau had asked her to do, because at that moment, she was unable to think of anything. Before she could finish her food, she dozed off on Chisau's shoulder. Chisau took away the food box from her hands and tucked her in bed.

He brushed away her hair, so that he could see her face clearly in her sleep. She still wore the pain on her pretty face. Her eyebrows were locked up tight. Chisau thought to himself, *are you having a nightmare? How can I ease your pain? If only I could share your burden…* Chisau laid his hand on her forehead and started to gently rub out the knot between her eyebrows with his thumb, hoping that he could ease the tension. It was as if he were ironing out the rugged path in her life. Even though he might not be able to make it easier for her in reality, he wished she could at least rest peacefully in her sleep.

Chisau pulled the duvet up for her and started clearing up the rubbish in the room. When the room was tidy, he switched off the lights on his way out. But he froze at the door; he felt he could not leave her. What if she ran off somewhere again when he spent the night in the other room? Where was he going to find her? He went back into the room and sat down on the empty bed next to hers, and stared at her silhouette in the dark. His fear of losing her was brought to the forefront to confront him. He just could not let go of her. He was distraught even having to contemplate the possibility of losing her! If she was not by his side, he knew he would be miserable. He would miss her terribly, and would want to know if she was safe, if she encountered any bullies, if she was happy, if she was sad, if she was tired… that is, everything about her he wanted to know! In the past, he believed this desire originated from the fact that she was his long-lost cousin, and in turn he had a duty towards her as her big brother. How about now? Why did he still care when it was no longer the call of duty? How did he rationalise this strong desire for her well-being? Fate had this mysterious way of linking two unrelated strangers together. He might not be able to present some grand reasons why he cared, but having been through so much together, he knew he could not let her go alone again, no matter what happened in the future. Under no circumstances would he let her go back to her previous life like no one ever cared!

Chisau took off his shoes and lay down on the bed. As he closed his eyes, he saw in his mind the scene when they waltzed together. That evening, she was as if she had put down all her baggage, and freely enjoyed every moment like a horse without its rein. On the dance floor, she was radiant with her infectious smile. For the first time, he saw who Yuetching could be when she was free of restraints and her unhelpful complex; and she was breathtakingly beautiful as a person when she was carefree. *The magical power of dancing is to make you momentarily forget – that was*

305

true. But when the atmosphere skilfully lulled them to momentarily lay down all the scruples, their naked feelings for each other unexpectedly collided and sent shockwaves straight through to their hearts! *Was it just a make-belief as Sinyin had said or were the feelings true?* He had dismissed it as a make-belief as it had happened before on the dance floor, which was true. At that moment, he was confused too. Chisau suddenly sat up, his heart pounding. He confronted himself with a possibility that he dared not toy with before, "Can I – can I love her?"

This possibility shocked him to his core. He turned to look at Yuetching, who was still fast asleep. He was very clear what his wish for her was: "Only to see you happy ever after."

Chisau woke up bright and early. Yuetching was still sleeping; she must have been exhausted. He went back to his own room and quickly packed his bag before coming back to Yuetching's room to wake her up.

"Wakey, wakey," Chisau called.

Yuetching slowly opened her eyes. Her head was still aching, while the excessive crying the night before made her eyes sting and puffy! Thinking about the state she was in, she was too embarrassed to face Chisau. She pulled the duvet over her head and hid.

"What are you doing?" Chisau had not a clue!

"Too embarrassed to face you!" Yuetching mumbled from under the duvet.

"Then this made the two of us."

Yuetching pulled down her duvet and asked, "What do you mean?"

"I was clumsy on the climbing frame and needed you to catch me on the ground. Was this not embarrassing for a man?"

"Ah, that one," Yuetching smiled.

"We're equally embarrassed, so you don't need to hide!" Chisau then changed into his serious and sincere tone, and said, "Thank you for asking me to come. I'm glad to be by your side yesterday when you faced another major setback in your life. I haven't helped much; you're still the one who feels the pain. But I'm content that at least I was able to take care of your physical needs."

"Please don't say that. I'd have been in a worse state had it not been for you. You have kept me safe, so it should be I who thank you."

Chisau was happy to hear that.

"Will you ever come back here again?" Chisau was curious.

"I'll come back one day to visit the columbarium."

"Then you must be careful not to bump into your *gujeung* again."

"Yes, I know; I'll be careful. I don't want to bump into him either."

"Are you hungry? I have to bring you home because I have to go away for the weekend with mum. That's why I have to wake you up."

"If you're in a hurry, you can leave first. I can take care of myself."

"I'll feel more at ease if you come home with me. Would you let me take you home?"

His care and attention for her had not changed at all, and in response, she must learn how not to worry those who worried about her! Out of her consideration for Chisau, therefore, she got up briskly and was ready in 20 minutes.

After breakfast, Chisau drove Yuetching home. When Chisau pulled up, he reminded her, "Remember to wait till I come back before we explain everything to Granddad." He paused to pluck up his courage before finishing, "No matter what happens I won't let you go. If Granddad doesn't let you stay, I'll go with you and take care of you."

Yuetching was shocked by what he said, "What do you mean?"

Without any ornate speech, he declared simply and tenderly, "I love you."

Yuetching choked and trembled at these three words! Chisau continued, "Wait for me; I'll deal with this. I'll explain it clearly to Granddad and mum. Don't worry if you don't like me. I'll still protect you as your brother, until the day you find someone with whom you're going to spend the rest of your life. When you have come to care for someone so much, you can't just stop caring for her suddenly, can you?"

"Chisau, I –"

"Let's use these three days to consider the situation carefully before we make any decisions or take any actions."

Chisau got off the car, while Yuetching had lost her senses and managed only to follow Chisau like a robot!

"You've come back," greeted Granddad. "Did you have a good break? Did you have fun?" Yuetching forced a smile and tried to look as normal as possible.

"Chisau, you've come back. It's about time for us to set off," said Puiyin. "I've packed your bag, so we're ready to leave. Yuetching, did you have a good time? You've been working so hard lately; I'm glad that you took a break!"

Yuetching nodded robotically.

"*Loye*, Chisau and I set off now. Please look after yourself. Yuetching, please keep an eye on him."

"Yes, I will," promised Yuetching.

Before he left, Chisau whispered into Yuetching's ear, "Remember to wait until I come back." Then he left with his mother.

Yuetching spent most of the day taking Granddad out for some fresh air. He was in high spirits and talked about everything under the sun. He entertained Yuetching with his wit as well as looked forward to the future when they officially became a family. Yuetching was silent on that subject and looked uncomfortable rather than pleased! Yuetching was lousy at pretending!

At dinner, Granddad's appetite was particularly good, perhaps due to a day of fresh air. He had noticed that Yuetching had been unusually quiet all day, so he asked, "Yuetching, why are you downcast? Is there something bothering you?"

Oh dear! Her moods were too easy to read especially to people who were close to her! She quickly dismissed, "No, there's nothing the matter."

"Are you a bit nervous about the Annual Meeting?" suggested Granddad.

"….." Yuetching did not know how to respond.

"Samyin has explained to me that you lack confidence. Together with the fact that you are not used to this kind of occasion, you feel a little frightened. This was why you took time off just before the Annual Meeting to calm your nerves and prepare yourself for the occasion. Is that right? Actually there is nothing to be nervous about. That you are a member of this family is already an established and unchangeable fact. Whether the public knows about it makes no difference. Making you known in the public is simply following the natural order of things. This will settle the score and root out all future rumours and gossips. This is a good thing, so you don't need to fear."

"....."

"Personally, I look forward very much to that day to come. As I have such a nice and capable granddaughter, I can't wait to tell people how proud I'm of you. Yuetching, Granddad is very glad to have found you, and got to know you. I'm grateful that you let me repay some of the debt I owe to your mother through you. To officially welcome you into our family with people present as witnesses, it's the last thing I could do for your late mother to honour her."

Granddad went on and on about it excitedly, inviting Yuetching to dream along. Inevitably she did picture it and for a moment she forgot where she was. As she was mindlessly stirring her food, she utter mournfully to herself, "But that day will never come now …"

"What did you say?"

Granddad's stern question made her jump. "Nothing."

"Did you say, 'That day will never come'? Why?"

Yuetching bit her lips and couldn't answer.

"Why?" Granddad was sensitive because he too had his nightmare.

"…"

"Are you keeping something from me? You haven't been yourself since you came back. What's happened during your time away? Where did you go?"

"…"

"Spill it out!" Granddad was getting sterner and sterner. The longer Yuetching hesitated, the more suspicious Granddad became. Yuetching's acting skill was non-existent and she was terrified.

"Spill it out!" bellowed Granddad. Yuetching jumped to her feet. "You're not leaving this room until you tell me the truth!"

"…" Yuetching was getting scared.

"If you won't talk, I'll call Chisau and ask him dir–"

"No!" interjected Yuetching. Chisau should be allowed to enjoy the joyous family occasion without more trouble from her. Besides she wanted to keep her story contained as much as possible.

"Then you speak the truth." Having found the hostage to hold against her, Granddad pushed his demand for the truth once more. His face got redder with rage and Yuetching was worried about his health.

Yuetching took a deep breath. *Sorry Chisau, I can't keep the promise of waiting till you return before we tell Granddad. So sorry; please forgive me.*

"I – I am not your granddaughter."

"What? What did you just say?"

Yuetching plucked up her courage, lifted her head up, and declared clearly, "I am not your granddaughter. Your daughter was not my biological mother. We are not in any way related."

"I knew it! I knew it!" Granddad shook his head, "You're too good to be true! I've spent all these years regretting my natural suspicion towards people which drove Oiyee out of this family in the first place. I told myself I had to change in order to mend this wrong. But when I'm trusting, you've treated me like a gullible fool! Why do you have to prove my instinct right when I so wished it to be wrong!" He slammed his fist on the table in anger. "Who has laid this guilt trip on you that you care to tell me now, just days before I make myself out to be the biggest fool? After we've expensed so much time, effort and considerations to make this happen in the nicest possible way for you, you care to tell me now that you are NOT my granddaughter? Is the occasion too daunting for you or do you worry that your lie has grown out of hand and you are about to be exposed as the greatest fraud?"

"I'm sorry –"

Granddad interrupted, "Chisau has been the schemer behind this, hasn't he? He couldn't find my granddaughter, so he plucked you out from nowhere to play the part and deceive me, right? You couldn't have been here if he isn't the mastermind!"

"No, it's not like that –"

Granddad barged in, "Can you deny that he has known about this and has not uttered a word about it?"

"Yes, he does know, but it's not like that. We've never knowingly deceived you –"

Granddad slammed on the table and cut her short again, "Who have you taken me for – an old fool? I resent being fooled and humiliated! How could you have acted so well? I must admit you play into this role superbly. I can't fault your acting skill. This is all that it is, isn't it? We live on your acting skill! It's all a lie! All the tears, the birthday, the sudden disappearance every now and again that got us all worry sick, the nerves and the fear were nothing but acts! You wrote a perfect script! And we genuinely believe it! What would have been your motive, I wonder? I could think of none other than cheating an inheritance out of us! You must have thought that we were gullible and laughed your head off. How could we be so totally deceived? You could've gone through the Annual Meeting and sealed your part in this family; if you did not tell, we would have never known. After all you even went through Huentung's engagement party with such marvellous performance. Why do you break your silence now? Perhaps you still have a tiny bit of conscience left in you or your business deal with Chisau has expired and you want out? Yes, playing my granddaughter for a short time is a job but playing it for life will be slavery. No deal can demand that. Now, PLEASE LEAVE MY HOME IN THIS INSTANT; I DO NOT WANT TO EVER SEE YOUR FACE AGAIN, YOU LIAR AND DECEIVER! YOU MAKE ME SUCH A FOOL TO HAVE BELIEVED IT! There are no good and honest people around; they just want your money, just like the father in your script that came before you!"

Granddad slammed the table again to show his frustration and disappointment before leaving the room. He was unsteady on his feet, so Yuetching went up to support him. But he brushed her away in disdain. "Don't touch me! Leave me alone, you liar! It's worse than a scam when you toy with people's hearts." He felt humiliated, and his heart was torn. He was in such pain of losing her that no words could describe his sadness and disappointment but the person he was so fond of did not even exist! He had foolishly loved a fake! He was stricken by grief.

Yuetching watched him stagger out of the room, full of sorrow to have hurt him so. She saw the irony of the situation: *Only if I were a brilliant actress as you've believed, then at least I could've done a better job in pretending until Chisau returns.* As she was deeply wounded herself, she could summon no strength to carry other people's wounds as well. She retreated to her room. Her heart wrenched and tears rolled down once more. Alas, she thought they had dried up since the night before. *A liar, a deceiver, a fake and a scammer!* She did not realise false accusation could be so piercingly hurtful. She was sick of crying. Could she cry no more? Her chest tightened, and she panted for breath. She wanted to wail for she was so frustrated with all the unfairness hailed on her. She wanted to scream at the top of her voice so that the whole world would know. But who would listen to her cry? It's not important anymore. Her phone beeped; it was Chisau's text: *Arrived safely and Grandpa was in good spirits as he has all generations gathered for his birthday. How about you? Did you have a good time with Granddad at home?*

It pained her to think about Chisau. She remembered his parting words, *If Granddad doesn't let you stay, I'll go with you and take care of you.* She believed him. Precisely because she did not doubt that he would do it, she had decided for him that mustn't happen. She could not let history repeat itself in this family that she had come to love so much. She could not bear the thought that this time she was the reason in splitting the family. The painful consequences of family fallouts she had lived through and she refused to be the cause for one. Chisau would be an exile from his family; no, she couldn't do that to him. Right now, this battleground was too personal for her to hold as she was badly injured herself. Retreat was her only chance to survive before she was completely destroyed. *I leave to protect this family. It's the best way to love him; I'm not worthy of his love that would cost him so dearly. I won't destroy him.*

She put up a pretence and replied to Chisau as if nothing had happened: *Went out all day with Granddad for some fresh air. He was joyful then.*

Chisau was assured, and replied: *That's wonderful. Remember not to tell until I return. Goodnight.*

Goodnight. Yuetching wrote. It's so easy to lie behind the screen. She clutched her phone into her chest, thinking that this might well be the last *Goodnight* she said to him! The pain was almost unbearable at the thought that she had to leave this phone in order that he knew not to look for her. She wept bitterly as if in mourning.

In her tears, she started packing. She left all the clothes that Chisau had bought her, the evening gown and the jewellery set that she wore to Huentung's engagement party. These were all for Lee Oiyee's daughter, whom she was not. But she kept the camera Chisau bought her, and the big soft toy that Samyin won for her. Those were good memories that she would like to keep.

The phone beeped again. It was Samyin this time. His text said: *It's late, so I didn't call. I'm the only one left holding the fort! I'm overwhelmed! You've returned with Chisau, right? Are you all geared up for the Annual Meeting? Have you made the decision about us yet? I miss you a lot. Hope to see you soon.*

Yuetching smiled; Samyin was always sweet. Could she just pretend that she was sleeping and not reply? But that seemed too cruel, so she said: *Back home. Sorry to leave you with all the work. Rest well; I'm in bed already.*

Knowing that Yuetching was not asleep yet, Samyin immediately replied: *Shall we meet up tomorrow?*

Oh no! How should she reply? Let's find an excuse quickly: *Sorry, my date is with Granddad this weekend.*

He was disappointed, but certainly he could not compete with Granddad for Yuetching's attention, so he could only say: *Then see you in the office on Monday.*

Sweet dream. Yuetching replied.

Yuetching set off early the following day to look for a place to live. She returned late at night and hence did not catch a sight of Granddad at all. She went straight to bed, so that she did not have to think too much. She would only be sad if she contemplated the fact that this was her last night at this home. On Sunday, she woke up bright and early, and started clearing her room. She had rented a car for the move. When everything was loaded in the car and she was ready to go, she went to see Granddad for one last time. She handed in her keys and said, "Goodbye, Uncle Lee. Sorry to have caused you pain and trouble, but thank you for taking care of me in the past year. These are the keys to the house. I'm leaving now. Please take care of yourself." She bowed and left.

Granddad was grieved; the gloom had come back like an old friend. He had wished Yuetching to defend herself, but she did not. To him, this acted as a silent admission to wrongdoings and guilt. He therefore had to resign himself to the fact that she was only a mirage and wasn't real. He let her go without saying a word. Actually he did not know what he might say if he opened his mouth. He did not want to do anything to betray his emotions. He asked if it was divine punishment after all. Lost-and-found was uplifting while found-and-lost was most crushing! He told himself what she did was unforgiveable; he was mourning a loss that was not real. Yuetching could easily fool him again and worse, he would probably have fallen for it! This was how very fond of her he was! This made Yuetching very dangerous to him.

On the following day Chisau and Puiyin returned home; Granddad was waiting for them in the lounge, looking stern.

"Where's Yuetching? She hasn't picked up her phone or replied to texts. Where's she?" was the first thing that Chisau said as soon as he stepped into the house.

"I've kicked her out, and she has left," Granddad deliberately said in an authoritative tone, and put on a straight face to make it sound as convincing as possible.

Chills went down Chisau's spine. His nightmare had been realised. He confronted his Granddad angrily, "You've kicked her out? Why didn't you wait till I came back and discussed it with me? How could you just kick her out?"

Puiyin was shocked and sensed that the matter was serious, "Actually what's happened here? Why did *loye* kick Yuetching out?"

"You think your opinion deserves to be respected on this matter? You're her accomplice. You've been colluding with her to scheme on us from the beginning. Why should I trust your opinion?" Granddad defended himself with conviction.

"What're you talking about? Was that what you said to Yuetching?"

"She's a liar, a deceiver, and a fake with brilliant acting skill to fool others in her scam! She's just like the father in her perfect script that came before her."

"What? You said that to her and you kicked her out for that reason?" Chisau was getting more panicky by the minute.

"I asked her to leave and never to show her face again!"

Chisau was so angry that he felt he was about to explode! He was so frustrated that he had lost his cool and did not know how to debate with Granddad, who could not be more wrong! He rushed into Yuetching's room, only to find it empty. He took out his phone and called upon their "telephone contract", hoping that it was still upheld. He dialled Yuetching's number, waiting anxiously to hear her voice. Instead he heard a soft ringing tone coming from inside one of her drawers. His heart nearly stopped, when he realised the implication. He went towards the ringing tone, and opened the drawer. When he found her phone ringing and jumping with vibration inside the drawer, it was as if he was walking into his worst nightmare. He hung up, and picked up Yuetching's phone. Tears just came rolling down.

His mum walked in and inquired anxiously, "What's happened? Where has Yuetching gone?"

Beating the lump in his throat, Chisau uttered, "This –" Chisau raised Yuetching's phone in his hand, "represents how disappointed and disheartened she is with this family. She – is asking us never to look for her."

Samyin had just arrived as Yuetching did not turn up for work and was not answering her phone. He was greeting Granddad when Chisau rushed out of Yuetching's room in a fury.

He confronted Granddad, "Before you ordered her to leave, had you given her a chance to explain? Of course not, because YOU ARE ALWAYS RIGHT! You must've been slamming the table, scolding her for keeping the truth from you with the intention to deceive you. Am I wrong in assuming this? You've said everything that Yuetching minds the most. She might be able to shrug it off if those words were from someone outside, who could've easily mistaken who she was. But it's completely different when these false, unfounded, unfair allegations came from one of those whom she had trusted most. Do you know how much you've hurt her? When you asked her to leave, did it cross your mind that she would go to a place where we COULD NEVER FIND HER?" Chisau was pacing up and down the room in despondence with arms akimbo. "We've lost her forever!" he uttered in despair. He snarled a retort at Granddad, "Don't you think I at least have the right to be consulted before you kick her out? After all I spent TWO years of my life looking for her!"

Samyin was stunned and could not quite work out what had exactly happened.

"At the beginning," Chisau continued, "she didn't want to have anything to do with this family, fearing that people would gossip about her motive. Today her worst fear has come true, and the perpetrator was none other than the very person who begged her to come and live with us in the first place! YOU have betrayed her trust in us. When you were busy slandering her, did you give her a chance to tell you that she was also a victim in this, that she had been deceived and lied to? She didn't know her biological mother until last Thursday. She was as shocked as you were when she was told that my *guje*, your daughter wasn't her biological mother, whom she had thought to be her real mother

ALL HER LIFE! Isn't it ironic that while you so readily called her a liar, a deceiver, telling you the whole truth was among her first reactions after she had found out about her birth? Do you know that your daughter almost died of blood loss due to an ectopic pregnancy, that her child did not live and that she could never have children again? At that time Yuetching entered her life to be the child she had lost, and gave her a reason, if not *the* reason, to live and fight. She fought hard to get better and came out of her critical and, what seemed at the time, hopeless state. She saved your daughter then. Perhaps you have conveniently forgotten that in the same way, Yuetching came into YOUR life when you were critically ill and lacking the will to live. It was SHE who gave you a new lease of life too. Have you forgotten how she patiently walked and exercised with you? Now that you can lead a more or less normal life, may I ask, to WHOM is the credit due?

"Back then, you were full of regrets, and you begged and begged. At last she found the heart to forgive you, and you were greatly comforted by that. Today, how could you dismiss her so lightly and carelessly as if she were any stranger from the street? Do you have a heart? When you saw her leave, did you even ask her to stay? How could you trample over a person's delicate feelings with so little concern and care? Who gives you the right to ask someone to come and go as you please? How selfish you are! Thanks to you, I feel the pain, the guilt and the regret that you felt back then, because I was the one who'd found her and brought her into this family, only for her to experience abandonment by people closest to her once more. It's me who has brought her this latest episode of unnecessary pain. The fault is *mine* indeed! And I will live to regret it for the days to come!

"Your daughter never knew Yuetching wasn't her real child. To her, Yuetching WAS her daughter, and she did die in order to save her. I can't be sure why she avoided you and deliberately cut off all the contact. They might be moving around at the time in order to conceal this secret, or she might be angry with you for all that you did or did not do. Perhaps the real reason was a bit of both. I've always wondered how you could do it, turning your back on your daughter. Today I finally experience your heartlessness. Even though Yuetching isn't related to us by blood, can you seriously wipe out everything she has done for you and this family? She put her heart into *everything* she did, whether at work or at home, and there was not a thank-you! She has been through so much since little; how could you be so brutal as to add another stab in her heart, which is already heavily scarred? How could you have the heart to send her back to her previous, lonely life? Back in those days, if your daughter was angry at you and decided to sever all contact with you, I can fully understand now because right at this moment, I feel exactly the same way!"

"Chisau, there is something that should never be said," Puiyin reprimanded.

"Really? I think it's time Granddad heard some truths of the pain and hurt that he's inflicted on people with his reckless and inconsiderate acts. These are people, not robots; they have feelings to be hurt.

"Do you know how Yuetching found the courage she needed to move in with us? It was hard for her to forgive but she did. She believed that reconnecting with her family might be the treatment needed for her wound to heal. She wanted to get well, so she took the risk with this treatment we *eagerly* recommended to her! She has trusted us but, look – how – spectacularly – we – have – failed – her –" Choked with emotion, Chisau was unable to carry on. The thought of Yuetching's disappointment in this family and in him personally was unbearable to him. He left the house and drove off to clear his mind, leaving Granddad, his mother and Samyin to work out their reaction to the bombshell he had just dropped on them. The unexpected turn of events had stunned them into a state of disbelief.

Chisau got home late that night, and headed straight to the stairs. His steps were halted by his mother's call in the dark; apparently she had been waiting up for him.

"I don't want to talk right now. We'll talk some other time. Please go to bed," Chisau pre-empted his mother's move. He returned to his room and had a shower to cool his head. He was exhausted. He was living through his worst nightmare and it was only the beginning. Looking back, he used to live in fear – fear that his worst nightmare would one day become real. Now that this event had taken place, at least he was liberated from this fear. This was his only consolation.

After the shower, he felt languid but not tired enough to fall asleep. He sat down in the comfy chair and played with Yuetching's handset. It indicated the number of missed calls, voice messages and texts that had not been opened in the past two days. He guessed that most of these were probably from Samyin or him!

What could be her passcode? Chisau wondered. He thought of some obvious combinations. He tried her birthday which was wrong. Then he tried his birthday – and bingo! It was a surprise – he did not expect to have ever guessed it right!

Will the phone hold any clues as to where she has gone? He started searching through the phone but to his disappointment, there were no unknown numbers or anything that might be of use. But when it struck midnight, the network signal went down. It was obvious that Yuetching had made a prior arrangement to terminate the contract. Chisau's heart sank. If Yuetching did not want to be found, it would not be easy to find her! It was as obvious as one plus one.

Alas, Yuetching, where are you? Why are you so uncompromising that you've left NO clues? Chisau was despondent.

He got up and went to Yuetching's room to see if there were any clues. He opened the wardrobes and found that she left all the clothes that were given to her. The evening gown she wore to Huentung's engagement was actually paid for by herself; she had left it probably because she thought she had no chance to wear it again. Everything else was gone, including all her books; he knew she was not returning. *How long, Yuetching, did it take for you to pack up all those books and load them into the car?* He went over to her dressing table, and found the jewellery set which they bought her for her birthday not that long ago. He then looked through all her drawers and found them empty. Chisau felt defeated, *Sinyin at least left me a letter when she left; but you did not even leave me a word…* Suddenly, he understood Yuetching; he heard her silent goodbye: *she was too distraught and heartbroken to know what to say. Not in any words but in silence, she said her goodbye.* Chisau sat in her room for a long time, to soak up this silence that Yuetching had left him, to feel the heaviness of her heart, to sense her presence and in turn to connect with her. *Yuetching, this is so plangently poetic that my heart aches!*

At least, she's brought with her my camera and Samyin's huge snow-white bear. Chisau found some comfort in that fact. He could not help but ask, "Yuetching, what are you going to do from now?"

10 Getting Used to the Life After

Tuesday was the first day after. Chisau left home early without breakfast to avoid seeing Granddad or anyone. He went back to the Hotel and focused on the last minute preparation for the Annual Meeting. Samyin was equally early and came straight to his office.

Chisau was not surprised at all, "I've expected you to come and find me."

"What's this? Are you going to pretend that nothing has happened? Have you not thought of finding Yuetching?" Samyin questioned.

"Of course, yes, I've churned over in my head all the possible ways to find her, but right at this moment, what would Yuetching have wanted us to do if she were here?"

"Can you be so rational?"

Chisau put down the work in his hand, and analysed for Samyin, "First, we should not patronise Yuetching. She's a very capable person. Before we found her, she had been leading a very orderly life without our intervention. In terms of daily life, I believe that she can look after herself far better than you and I can look after ourselves! In this respect, we don't need to worry about her. Second, we know she is NOT in a state of emergency that requires us to find her immediately. She's mentally tough and I trust her not to do anything stupid even in time of distress. Third, finding her is a long-term project. The first time I spent two years to find her, and even then, it was through a coincidence. This time, luck may not be on our side, especially when she's trying to avoid us. She has left and terminated her phone, and cancelled her email accounts. These are actions to show us her determination not to be contacted. This will make finding her even harder than last time; this is just being realistic. Fourth, even if I would like to find her, I have no clues at the moment to follow up! This is also being realistic. Fifth, apart from memories, the deepest marks that Yuetching has etched on our life are through her work. On the one hand, I don't want to see all her effort in the past year get wasted. On the other hand, I would like to live out her spirit and do her proud at the Annual Meeting in honour of her influence on the team. Focusing on work now is for her; I don't want to disappoint her."

Chisau paused and then resumed to tell his heartfelt truth, "Samyin, the normality you see on the outside can be deceptive; you don't see the turmoil inside and I'm far from being rational. But what good does it make to pace up and down the room and look worried? The reality is that we have no concrete leads to follow up on right now! While we wait, I would rather channel the negative emotions into positive motivation for something constructive. How about you? Are you willing to assist me or do you want to go around finding Yuetching like a blind fly?"

"Even so, can you really concentrate?"

Chisau nodded, "Yes, I can. Work is a very good distraction, or I'd have gone mad. Then what? Even if I go to tell Granddad off again, would it bring her back?"

Samyin laughed at this joke. More relaxed, he went to sit down in front of him across his desk. He asked, "What has actually happened?"

Chisau outlined how they came to find out about Yuetching's birth.

"That's to say, Yuetching knows who her real mother is. Could she be a lead?" suggested Samyin.

"I don't think so. Not only that, I don't think Yuetching would want her to know she has cursed her life! I think she wants to be able to hold her head up high in front of her, and we should respect her wishes and not to get in touch with her."

Samyin was disappointed that this was not a lead.

"What was Yuetching's reaction when she found out?" asked Samyin.

"She looked perfectly normal and calm initially, and then came the delayed reaction when the truth sank in. She cried like a river for the whole night until she was exhausted and could cry no more. You can kind of feel for her, can't you? She thought at last she had found out who she was and a niche in life. Then that life was all shattered in a flash, just like that, and she had to start all over again. Life can be really cruel, as we have seen so many times in her life."

"I could never have guessed, at Huentung's engagement party was the last time I saw her! How am I to live with that?"

"Thinking about it, it isn't too bad, is it? At least it was a beautiful memory, and she looked stunning that night."

"Please don't speak as if it's a life and death separation. I AM confident that I'll see her one day."

"But you must be prepared that this may not happen in the foreseeable future."

"Did she ever mention me? She still owes me an answer."

"On that, she said she was still considering and you were very dear to her. But now she's no longer my cousin, has your feeling towards her changed?"

"The person I like is Cheung Yuetching, not Lee Chisau's cousin. Whether she is your cousin or not is not important to me, although I can't say the same for my parents."

"You're quite honest and determined too. Will that be a hindrance?"

"Yuetching is worth fighting for."

"Do you really love her that much? Will you wait for her indefinitely?"

"Why do you ask such a question? Is the chance of finding her really that slim?"

"I don't know. But I have a feeling that Yuetching works to make us forget her and deter us from finding her."

"Will you respect her wish?"

Chisau shook his head.

A realisation suddenly dawned on Samyin, prompting him to ask the same question, "Now that Yuetching is not your cousin, has your feeling towards her changed in any way?"

Chisau had not expected this direct question. On the spot he did not know how to answer. He got up and walked to the window.

From his hesitation, Samyin surmised his answer even though he did not speak it. He walked up next to him and said, "It looks like we are now rivals in winning Yuetching."

"I have no desire to compete with you. My deepest wish for Yuetching is to see her happy. I've told her it's all right that she doesn't like me that way, but I will not relinquish my role as her brother until she finds someone with whom she's happy to spend the rest of her life."

"You have already confessed to her?" Samyin was shocked.

"At that moment, I only wished her to know no matter what happened she wouldn't be on her own. But she obviously has rejected my motion to her. In spite of what I had said, I still failed to make her stay; she still decided to go alone." Chisau turned to face Samyin and continued, "At the moment, we're on the same side, and not rivals, because we want the same things. They are first to ensure the success of the Annual Meeting for Yuetching's sake, and second, to find out whereabouts is Yuetching. All other decisions are immaterial until these two have been accomplished. Do you agree?" Chisau held out his hand, Samyin shook it as he believed Chisau was right, and the gentlemen sealed a deal of cooperation.

The three-day Annual Meeting came to a successful conclusion. Most of the proposals had been accepted. A lot was down to Yuetching's impetus, her thorough preparation and watertight analyses, so that all proposals read thoughtful and convincing. Amendments, if any, were on the fine details. For the two who worked most closely with Yuetching, the whole Annual Meeting was full of her shadow. The shareholders heard the main points, whereas Chisau and Samyin saw the process and hard work that went behind them – the initial brainstorming, data collection and organisation, numerous discussions about the key points and many late nights to get it all done! They missed her terribly. In the concluding speech, Chisau acknowledged the contributions of Yuetching, but this did nothing to fill the emptiness and regret caused by her absence. At the Meeting, Chisau did not speak with Granddad except for business purpose. Puiyin was deeply saddened to see the ongoing cold war between them without any signs of relenting.

At the gala banquet, both Chisau and Samyin felt terrible. The tension building up to the Annual Meeting had passed, and there was nothing else to occupy their minds with the same intensity. Grief suddenly gripped them almost in full force. In this same hall, Chisau danced with Yuetching and Samyin saw her last only two weeks prior, but now the distance between them seemed immeasurable! Wherever they turned, whatever they did, they were reminded of her. A joyous celebration was turned into a mournful service for them. Today Yuetching should have been here celebrating with them the fruits of their hard work, as well as her new public status as a member of the Lee family. They had never thought the situation could be so much worse than Samyin's original bottom line!

The banquet concluded the three-day conference; it's finished!

"Would you like to go for a drink?" Samyin asked Chisau.

"No, thank you. I'd like to go home. Also I'll take next week off."

"Why? Have you found some clues to locate Yuetching?" Samyin got excited.

"I wish. No, I think it's time I moved back to my own flat."

"Are you so angry with Granddad?"

"When I moved back home, it was only a temporary measure. I stayed because the family needed me at the time. Now, it's time to go back to my independent life."

"Does it hurt that badly? I guess both of us have to find our own way to mourn for the loss. Remember, as soon as you have any clues on Yuetching's whereabouts, you must first tell me."

"Yes, I will. You've worked hard too in the past few months. Should you take some time off too?"

"I probably should spend some time with my family before they head back to England." Chisau gave his permission, "Then you do that. I'll keep an eye on the business remotely."

Chisau was sorting out his belongings in his room to prepare for the move. In the background, he played the slideshow of recent photos. These days, Chisau found himself looking at Yuetching's pictures more often than when she was around. He took out the drawing she gave him for his birthday and recalled how he watched her make the cake in the kitchen. In his ears, he seemed to hear Yuetching's voice ringing, "The blessings you wish me to have I'm willing to try, to experience." *Where are you now? How are you adjusting? Are you sad as we are?*

Chisau's thoughts were interrupted by a knock on the door.

"Come in," answered Chisau. His mother entered. She sat on his bed. Seeing that he was packing, she sighed, "Is it that painful?"

"What?"

"Still want to deny it? Ever since Yuetching left, I haven't seen you smile. You wear a sad face all day long."

"Really?" Chisau did not realise it, but it was true that life seemed to be less cheerful after Yuetching had left.

"Are you still angry at Granddad?"

"He's stubborn. There is no use to be cross at him. He'll never change and will never admit that he was wrong."

"He is an elderly; it's not easy for him to say sorry or to admit mistakes in front of others. Call it pride. I think he does feel bad about wrongly accusing Yuetching. These days, joy seems to have eluded him, and he doesn't speak much. Knowing that you're moving out, he has become even quieter. Yuetching seems to have stolen something from this family. Since she left, it hasn't been the same. In this sense, we have all missed her."

"Mum, the fact that I'm moving out is not directly related to this. You should know that."

"I know, so I'm not stopping you. When your father died, you moved back to look after this family. I'm grateful for that. But first Yuetching and now you're leaving home, it'll take a while for us to get used to a half-empty house with no youngsters to enliven our life!"

She then noticed the picture on Chisau's lap, and was curious, "Who drew this of you? It captured you very well!"

"Yuetching did this; she copied it from a photo she took of me. It was her birthday present to me. Because it was the first time she sketched a person, and she was afraid that she didn't do it well, she asked me not to unwrap it in front of the party."

"I see; this was a very personal present, with a nice thought behind it."

There was silence, as they recalled their respective memories of Yuetching.

"Chisau, can we find Yuetching? Even though we're not a family, I still wish to know how she is. She was like a daughter to me too."

"She doesn't intend to be found. To find her won't be an easy task."

"It leaves you a bad feeling the way she left. It's strange to have someone so close one day only to leave our life abruptly the next without any prior warning. The finality of the break paralyses us from adapting. Among all the people, you must be the one who feels it most acutely. After all, you spent two years finding her in the first time round."

"To tell you the truth, this is not the saddest part for me. The saddest part for me is how right she has been in her prophecy, and I, who have been told her prophecy, could do nothing to stop it from happening. Slowly watching her prophecy fulfil without the ability to do anything has been the hardest part for me."

"What prophecy?"

"Yuetching once said to me her life here was almost perfect. But because of her experience, she naturally asked when and under what circumstances this perfect life would be shattered. To her, she was almost certain that this was how it would end. Given the near certainty of a tragic end, she felt she was living in a bubble at the time. Her attitude was to cherish every moment before the bubble burst for whatever reason. As a response, I naïvely promised her that her newfound perfect life would not be shattered. I'll never forget what she said afterwards. She said that life was unpredictable, and there was no need for me to promise her anything; cherishing the time together was enough, and who knew what tomorrow might bring. Looking back, she was full of wisdom and insight at the time. Since that day, I've wished so hard that she would be proven wrong. But sadly she has been proven right yet again! In the end, I really can't do much for her. Having been through so many upsets in life, how can we still expect her to hope about her future? This is the saddest part for me."

Puiyin began to understand more of Chisau's sorrow.

He continued, "Not only has this period when she stayed with us failed to make amends to her life, I fear that it might have deepened her wounds. She was repeatedly abandoned by her biological mother, separated from her parents by death, asked to leave by her *guje*, albeit out of good intentions, and finally kicked out by Granddad. If she has not left us under that kind of circumstances, I wouldn't have been so mad and so sad."

"Now I understand why you were so angry with Granddad that day."

"It was just wrong, and we didn't even have a chance to say sorry and don't know if we ever would." Chisau sighed.

Looking at Yuetching's photos on the computer screen,

Puiyin said, "She was very pretty that day, wasn't she?"

"Yes," Chisau had to agree. Then he remembered the jewellery set Yuetching had left behind. He took it out of the drawer and passed it to his mother, "Yuetching didn't bring our present with her. Please keep it safe for now."

"Oh! It's so regrettable! I still vividly remember how overjoyed she was in receiving this! Do you miss her?"

"Yes, I do. Perhaps it has become a habit. As the saying goes, I've grown accustomed to her. Both at work and at home, it's full of her presence. Plus the two years before that, it's a long time to have someone constantly on your mind."

"Is this the reason why you're moving out?"

"Not totally. I just want to change the environment and give myself some breathing space. Actually I can't pinpoint the precise reason. When she isn't around, life seems a lot duller, and nothing seems to spark my interest."

"Son, this is called love-sickness," teased Puiyin.

Chisau was shocked as well as embarrassed, "What?"

"Do you think you can hide it from your mother? Or don't you realise your feeling for her?"

"What are you talking about?"

"You love her, don't you?"

"Mum –"

"I thought you two make a nice couple."

"Mum –"

"But what are we going to do with Samyin?"

"Mum, that decision isn't in our hands. At the moment, we're in the same boat."

"And he agrees?"

"Yes, he agrees. Mum –" Chisau stopped.

"What's the matter?"

"If – with the most unlikely probability – we do get together, will you object?"

"Object?"

"Her family background is – well, non-traditional – even scandalous. Feeling ashamed of who she is may be why she slipped away from us without saying goodbye. Her family connections are liabilities, not assets."

"Life is unfair, isn't it? Her background closes rather than opens doors for her. But life is also unexpected, isn't it? In a most convoluted way, we have come to know her heart-to-heart.

Like you, I suppose, when you have come to care for someone so much, you can't just stop caring for her suddenly. Although her background is chaotic, her life is not. On the contrary, she is pure at heart and a remarkable fighter, isn't she? All the battles in life have worked to refine her into an admirable and adorable person with empathy. She is nobler than many. I can't reject her person; that means I just have to accept her background too."

Chisau was relieved to have his mother's blessing, and said, "Thank you."

"Wow, I earn a smile from you! This is the first recently. Although you can be sure of my blessing, Granddad may still need a lot of persuading."

"I still thank you."

"Oh well, I believe the best remedy for your dejected heart is to assign you the task of finding Yuetching. From now on, this is your mission outside the responsibilities of your daily life and business, understand?

Having the support and understanding from his mother, Chisau felt much better. He said one more time, "Thank you, mother."

Before she left, Huentung met up with Sinyin to say farewell. "At the engagement party, you left so early that I didn't have a chance to express my personal gratitude to you. Here I am today to say thank you and goodbye. Here's a small token of our appreciation for your presence at our party." Huentung presented a small gift to Sinyin.

"You shouldn't have," Sinyin leant forward to receive the present, and continued, "Don't be so formal each time you see me. No matter how busy I am I still need to ringfence some private time. You are the only friend who keeps in touch from before I was famous. I do miss those days when I was anonymous and had the freedom to do anything. I miss the friends from those days too," Sinyin was sincere in what she said.

"If this is so, why did you leave so early at the engagement party? You should have stayed longer to catch up with your friends from yesteryears!" Huentung was puzzled.

Recalling her exit that night, Sinyin was irritated, "I couldn't stand the sight of Chisau and that Cheung Yuetching together. I felt sick and I was angry, so I left."

"Then Sinyin *jeje* has misunderstood everything! Has no one ever told you the truth?"

"What's the truth?" Sinyin was most intrigued.

"Yuetching was invited to my engagement party as the granddaughter of Uncle Lee. But as her identity had not been made public, she attended as one of the Hotel staff in disguise."

Sinyin was shocked at this news but all began to make sense.

"Are you saying that Yuetching is Chisau's cousin? But where did this cousin come from? I've never heard of her existence. Does it mean that they're close because they're cousins, and I've completely misunderstood their relationship? Oh my word! How could I be so wrong? And all the horrible things I said about her! No wonder Chisau was furious at me."

"Well, this is a long story. In short, Uncle Lee had a granddaughter whom he had never known. Chisau *koko* spent two years in locating her, and after all the effort, he found Cheung Yuetching. She then started working at the Hotel, and even moved in to the family home. Because of the special attention she had received from Chisau *koko* and my brother, unfavourable rumours started to circulate about her."

"I've been wrong!!! What am I going to do? I must go to Chisau and apologise. I've been insulting his cousin. But why must they keep it secret? Why can't they make it public?"

"Indeed, they had planned to make their family tie public knowledge at the Annual Meeting. But between my engagement party and the Annual Meeting, they discovered that Yuetching was NO granddaughter to Uncle Lee after all, and she got kicked out by Uncle Lee. Now no one knows where she has gone! I don't know the ins and outs of the whole matter. My brother is reluctant to divulge more than necessary."

Sinyin was stunned by the twists and turns in this story. She could not help but gloat over Yuetching's current misfortune. She felt justified now to have said all those words to her, and she took pleasure in that she had been right in her judgement of her at the outset! She emerged victorious in this contest while Yuetching had fallen from her height! That was very pleasing indeed!

"Chisau must be very upset to have been deceived and cheated by Cheung Yuetching. I see that he was really sincere in his kindness to her. I've known all along there was something fishy about this girl. Now that her motive has been exposed, she has gone hiding. How typical! Perhaps she's looking for her next victim to con!"

"Oh, please don't say that. I don't think Yuetching is that kind of person," Huentung put forward a feeble defence for Yuetching.

"One can never know one person completely. If she has not some skills, she wouldn't have been able to put up the act for so long. She's plain evil when she got everyone so sincerely kind to her and to like her, including your brother!"

"This is only a misunderstanding. She isn't like that at all," Huentung started to regret; she should have never told, especially she only had half the truth! She knew she had got herself into deep trouble with her brother about this.

"Thank you very much for meeting me today, and help me understand *everything* that I haven't understood before! This is the best way you've returned my favour! Thank you very much. I'm going to his office right this minute, so that I can comfort him in time of his distress." Sinyin was revived by the sparkle of hope.

"You won't find him there; he's on leave to move home."

"Really? Where to? Hmm… Back to his own flat? It must be!"

Sinyin got up and was ready to leave.

"Where are you going?"

Sinyin was put in really good mood on hearing the turn of events that she could not help but gloat, "Haven't you said that it was regrettable that we broke up? Chisau broke up with me because of Cheung Yuetching. Now it's exposed that I've been right about her and he has been wrong, he may feel so ashamed to face me. But I don't mind – I'll go and apologise first. This is a golden opportunity for us to get back together, I tell you."

"You're going to pay him a visit?"

"Of course! I would say my farewell now and you have a safe journey back. Love you, little sister." She left in a flash.

"Why do I feel so uneasy? Have I done something wrong? Do I have to confess to my brother? Will he be angry?" Huentung was full of doubts!

The intercom buzzed. Chisau was very puzzled whom it could be since his mother had come and just left. *Has she left something? Or could it be Samyin?* He wondered. The last person whom he expected to see was standing in front of the intercom. Sinyin slowly took off her sunglasses and cracked a signature friendly smile at him. She asked with all her charm, "Why? Are you not going to invite me in? Are you asking me to stand outside?"

Chisau was unmoved. He gave her no illusion that she was welcome here.

"I know you're cross with me. It's understandable. I've come to apologise. Let me come in first before we talk in greater length. May I?"

Chisau was still unmoved.

"Oh, please don't make me stand at your entrance. If it appears on the papers, then I'll have the trouble to explain."

"In that case you may leave right this instance, as we don't have anything to say to each other."

"I know I was wrong in hurling all sorts of insults at Cheung Yuetching but you can't blame me. Who ask you not to tell me she was your cousin!"

Chisau was surprised that she knew. *How did she know?* He decided to let her in to find out what and how she knew about Yuetching. Chisau shut the door behind her, while Sinyin had already ventured inside to see the place. She made a turn, "It's like coming home, isn't it? I know this place." Chisau stopped her on her track; he only wanted to know how much and how she knew.

"I see that Cheung Yuetching still holds a spell on you. To get your attention, I just need to utter her name. Oh, Lee Chisau, since when have you become so foolish that you can't tell right from wrong, and good from bad?" Sinyin continued to suggest, "I've brought with me today some wine as a peace offering. I was wrong in getting cross with you over Cheung Yuetching and wrongly assumed that you two were an item. But it could also be used to celebrate your liberation from her lies and deception. You must feel terribly foolish and cheated right now, but looking on the bright side, it's much better than living in her lies forever. Now you can start all over again. I'm so happy for you. And maybe you'll reconsider the matter between us."

"What rubbish are you babbling?"

Sinyin put down the bottle on the coffee table, and then looked around, trying to find some wine glasses.

Chisau stopped her on her track again, saying, "This is not your home. Where did you hear all these rumours from?"

"I have my source."

"Spill it out."

"Look at you; why do you let Cheung Yuetching make you so pitiable? All right, let me put you out of your misery! Huentung came to explain everything to me! Everything makes perfect sense now. Why didn't you tell me earlier? Why did you break up with me and let me misunderstand?"

"You know Yuetching was not the reason why we broke up."

"I don't care if it was because of her or not. Today it has proven that I was right about her at the outset! That's why I feel victorious and I'm very happy. Would you drink with me?"

"You have come here to gloat?"

"No, no, no. I'm offended that you even think of me that way. I'm here out of my concern for you. I've come to nurse your wounded heart and pride. I'm here to comfort you." Sinyin moved closer and whispered in his ears, "Just like when your father passed away."

Sinyin had succeeded in reminding him of some tender moments between them. That was special at the time.

Seeing her impact on him, Sinyin continued, "This is sincere. Although we have been fighting ever since I came back, in my heart of hearts I still care deeply for you. If you're willing to let me walk close again, anything's possible," Sinyin was suggestive.

She got all gentle and soft, reminding him of why he was attracted to her in the past. "I don't want to waste time over stupid fights anymore. Can we maintain a normal relationship? Can we march forward together again?" Sinyin moved closer yet. She wrapped her arms round him gently, and rested her head on his chest, speaking softly, "Does this give you some comfort?" Chisau's heart began to pound.

Sinyin lifted her head and looked Chisau in his eyes. She continued to test him, "Are you rather lonely these days?" She saw that Chisau was not resisting, she got bolder. She got onto her tiptoes and pressed her red lips on his. Chisau didn't expect it but he closed his eyes and responded. But in his mind, he saw that he was dancing with Yuetching. Only then did he realise his hidden desire to kiss her then. In his fantasy he thought he was kissing Yuetching. He was shocked by this revelation himself. When he realised what was going through his mind, he opened his eyes and pushed Sinyin away. His heart was pulsating…

Sinyin was proud of her power over him and encouraged

him, "Why? Don't be shy. It's all right to be honest with our feelings."

Chisau heard an irony in that, so he explained, "My reaction is towards Yuetching and not you. *This* is my honest feeling."

"What?" Sinyin was shocked in hearing this.

"When we broke up before, it was not because of Yuetching. But the reason why we can't get back together today *is* because of Yuetching."

"What?" Sinyin could not accept it.

"Has it ever occurred to you what the implication could be now that Yuetching is NOT my cousin? If I am honest to myself, I would prefer Yuetching *not* to be my cousin. All that is left for me to do is to find her."

"She is a cheater and a crook!" Sinyin simply wanted to slaughter her!

"She is NOT a cheater! Let me warn you not to ever again slander her!"

"She has no family, no connection. She is nobody from nowhere. She is savage in her upbringing and she has no class, and no culture!"

"So what? I don't care."

"Without all these, who is she?"

"She is Cheung Yuetching; and that's enough."

"Are you out of your mind? She will bring scandal to your family."

"I know, so what?"

"You've gone crazy!"

"Ding dong, ding dong, ding dong…" the doorbell rang in urgency.

Chisau opened the door and Samyin asked anxiously, "Sorry, Chisau, Huentung confessed to me just now that she had told Sinyin about Yuetching and she's heading here …" Samyin got the hint from Chisau's expression, "She's already here, isn't she?"

Chisau moved away and let Samyin in.

He saw Sinyin stand in the middle of the room. The atmosphere was tense, and he apologised to Chisau, "Sorry, I'm *so* sorry."

"It doesn't matter. Sinyin is about to leave, are you not?" Chisau kept the door open for her. Sinyin fixed her angry stare at Chisau and would not let go.

From the tension, Samyin guessed, "You two argue again?"

"We have nothing to argue about. Both of us have understood something now," explained Chisau.

"Of course, we didn't argue because we were busy kissing!" Sinyin attacked.

Wide-eyed in astonishment, Samyin exclaimed, "What? You two?"

Seeing Chisau hot under the collar, Sinyin continued her attack to embarrass him, "Can you deny it?"

"Sinyin, please leave. We shall never meet again. I apologise for what happened today." Chisau pointed to the exit.

"Lee Chisau, you –" Sinyin grabbed her bag and walked towards the front door. She stood in front of Chisau and slapped him hard on his face, saying, "This is for the insult you hurl on me today!" Then she left. Chisau slammed the door shut.

"Are you all right?" asked Samyin.

Chisau walked to the sofa to sit down, his hand rubbing his red cheek, saying, "Thanks to Huentung for this."

Samyin went to sit down next to him, and asked, "What's happened? Did you two really kiss?"

Chisau looked at Samyin and considered hard if he was to tell or not to tell. In the end, he decided to tell. He nodded to admit the act, but explained, "It's only because she was a substitute of love."

"Do you mean she was a substitute for Yuetching?" Samyin wanted to clarify.

"Without realising it, I projected my feelings for Yuetching onto Sinyin at that moment," Chisau added. "When I told her, she said I insulted her. She came, thinking that Yuetching had left the scene, and we would have a chance of getting back together. Now we *both* know that it's impossible. Even to myself, it was quite a revelation. I never knew the intensity of my feeling for her until today. Perhaps I've been thinking and worrying about her too much. This was what had happened here today."

"Ah…" Samyin was a bit dumbfounded, not knowing quite how to respond.

Looking at Samyin's silly face, he sighed, "You and I are doomed! It's not worth thinking about something that has no answer at the moment. Before you decide to see and treat me as your rival, let's go out to eat."

"Fine…" Samyin was still a bit confused.

Chisau stood up and got ready to go out. On this matter, he advised, "Please counsel Huentung to be more circumspect about what to tell people especially regarding others' private business. Today she has violated Yuetching's confidentiality. This is unfair on Yuetching. The matter is made worse especially when she knows only half the truth."

"I know. I'm sorry for her act," Samyin apologised sincerely.

Unsettled by a piece of news this morning, Chisau made his way to the office full of thoughts.

"Good morning, Director Lee," greeted Miss Wei, "Have you heard – "

"Yes, I've heard; it's headline news," interrupted Chisau, passing Miss Wei's desk without stopping. He shut the office door behind him, and went to sit down at his desk. Head buried in his hands, Chisau was busy analysing the optimal course of action to take, when Samyin stormed open the door in distress, asking, "Have you heard –"

"YES, I've heard! Must the whole world come and bother me with this?" answered Chisau, frustrated.

Samyin stopped in front of his desk, and continued, "And?"

"*And* what?" asked Chisau.

"What are you going to do?" Samyin asked in urgency.

"Must I do something?"

"You do not plan to do anything?" Samyin asked doubtfully.

"Perhaps it's best. I have NOTHING to do with her now. Perhaps it's best to stay that way."

"And you can live with that?"

Chisau looked away.

Sensing his heart, Samyin encouraged, "You should go and see her, you know. Even I, further related to her, couldn't sit still. If I could do something for her, I would have."

"What good can I do? Will it make matter worse if I visit her?"

"You think too much. Just GO."

On the speaker, Miss Wei relayed, "Director Lee, Miss Lau is on the line to speak to you."

Chisau hesitated to take the call, so Samyin made the decision for him and said, "Miss Wei, put her through please."

"Hi Director Lee, sorry to bother you," Miss Lau greeted.

"Not at all. How's Sinyin doing?"

"She has been saved. She is now resting."

"That's good, a relief to us."

"I know it may be too much to ask, but I wonder if you would visit her?" requested Miss Lau.

"Are you sure you would like me to visit her?"

"She's very down, you know. She needs someone to talk to, and I think of you."

"Does she specifically ask for me?"

"No, she hasn't said a word. This is why it's worrying."

There was silence as Chisau considered.

"She's very shaken," continued Miss Lau, "who wouldn't if you have been so close to death and back? I'm shaken myself, discovering her in such a state. I nearly had a heart attack myself. She needs a friend right now, someone who really connects with her. I know how she has been behaving, but in a crisis, we put down our differences, don't we? I believe she'll listen to you – only you."

"All right. I'll visit her," agreed Chisau.

"Thank you," Miss Lau could not hide her relief, and hung up.

"Come with me, Samyin," requested Chisau.

"Sure."

Sinyin saw them enter and approach her bed. Little energy that she had, she could not muster a reaction. She looked dazed and physically weak. She was pale and in shock. Her visitors pulled the chairs over and sat next to the bed.

"How are you?" inquired Chisau tenderly.

"I am as well as can be," whispered Sinyin.

"What happened?"

"I overdosed." Feeling ashamed, she turned away to hide her tears.

"Did you attempt to kill yourself?" There was no condemnation in his voice, just compassion.

Sinyin turned and looked at Chisau in the eyes, cursing his probing and direct question. It fired her up though, and she shouted, "What difference does it make if I intended to kill myself or not?"

"If you did, then my next question is why?"

Sinyin let out a mocking laugh. "Why indeed? If only I knew, perhaps I wouldn't have been lying here."

"Would you like to talk about it?"

"No." She turned away.

"Would you like us to leave?"

She turned round and grabbed Chisau hand, "Oh no, don't leave," Sinyin begged, "You don't know how lonely and terrifying it was to face death with a conscious mind. Oh no, please don't go." Tears streamed down when she relived the fear. Chisau held her hand into his to steady her. The warmth of his hands that conveyed care and compassion was comforting, and soon relaxed her.

"I felt – I felt life was so empty that I wanted to die, but when I was really dying, I didn't want to die... Miss Lau rang to check on me, so I told her what I had done ...I scared her to death ...," she murmured.

"When I'm lying in this bed, your words come back to haunt me," Sinyin blurted out, "They were ominous and are now fulfilled prophecy. How much you do know me, only if I would listen more carefully!"

"What was it that I said?"

"You once said to me, 'If you carry on with your reckless ways, blaming others for everything but yourself, it's a matter of time that you WILL kill yourself, I can assure you.' Do you remember those stern words? How those words had taunted me! I set out to prove you wrong, only to accelerate on my course of self-destruction to prove you right. How ironic is life?"

"And you too, Samyin," turning to Samyin, Sinyin continued, "You asked me if I was on drugs. Do you remember? Why couldn't I see what everyone could see?"

"Don't judge yourself now," Chisau tried to find words of comfort.

"Lying here, my whole life flashes back in my mind like a movie. I can see it now – how I rose and fell, how I lost my soul and grew proud. How unbearable and insufferable I have become! I understand now why you hate me."

"I don't hate you," corrected Chisau.

"Yes, you do. Don't deny it. I've lost you forever, haven't I? There is no turning back for us, right? Although it pains me to think about what it could have been between, at least now I know why and can begin to accept it." Tears continued to roll down Sinyin's cheeks. Chisau pressed her hand tighter.

"I thought I was in control of my life, only to discover that life was slipping away from my grip. In the end, I'm nothing but a mortal – a helpless mortal." Sinyin let out a shriek. "I seem to have everything I've wanted but why wasn't I satisfied? In the end I was nothing but a slave to the life that I had set up for myself to sustain. The very things that I had been striving for were slowly killing me. How did that work? I haven't a clue! Now I know *clueless* is my name, and my head throbs when I try to unravel this riddle!"

Samyin was listening attentively. Sinyin was like a different person. There was something poignant about it – wisdom and insights gained through a near-death torment. Solemnness was in the air, to which the only possible response was humility.

"Then unravel it some other day, when you're feeling stronger. Rest now, Sinyin. Don't think too much. Your focus now *must be* on getting better," Chisau comforted her.

"What will people think of me? What will they say in the press? I must look stupid and foolish. How do we deal with shame?"

"If you have the courage to face death and pass, you have the courage to face anything ahead. What do you fear now?"

Sinyin sighed and asked, "Today, I've had a narrow escape. Will this bring blessings? Will I have a new beginning?"

"I'm sure it will and a new chapter in your life dawns."

"Then what will fill those pages of the new chapter? What should I do now? Will you be in it?"

"These are not questions for now, dear. Rest."

Sinyin closed her eyes. She was drowsy, "Thank you for coming," she managed to whisper before falling asleep.

There was silence between Chisau and Samyin for a while. It was as if they were soaking up the occasion. At long last, Samyin reflected, "She has turned some corner, hasn't she?"

"Yes, she has," Chisau concurred.

Samyin looked at Chisau and was puzzled, "Why do you look so uneasy?"

"I don't know why I feel so responsible for her."

"What do you mean?"

"There seems to be a tie between us that can't be severed completely," Chisau admitted honestly. "I have once promised to take care of her, and I can't just walk away from this situation, can I? Not until she is back on her own feet again."

"Oh no! Are things going to get complicated for you?" asked

Samyin.

"I don't know."

"Hello," Samyin picked up his phone and answered.

"Hello, Manager Chiu. This is Hui Onchi from Personnel. We would like to clarify the status of your secretary Miss Cheung Yuetching. She hasn't been at work for two months, and has far exceeded her entitlement. We would like to consult Manager Chiu how we should handle her case?"

"What are the options?"

"We can't pay her indefinitely."

"I understand, but how about applying an unpaid leave for her?"

"This is an option. What's the duration?"

"Six months."

"Reason?"

"Personal."

"Is Manager Chiu the person who authorises the leave?"

"Yes."

"Could Manager Chiu then please fill in the relevant forms and send them to me? I will email the forms to you."

"Many thanks."

"In the meantime, would Manager Chiu like a temporary secretary to cover for Miss Cheung?"

"There is no need."

"Understood. If you have any further questions, please do not hesitate to give me a call. Thank you."

"Thank you." Samyin put down the phone.

He lifted up his head and surveyed his office, which had gradually gone back to its chaotic state as in the past. Subconsciously he had been relying on Yuetching returning to tidy it up for him once more. But because he did nothing, Yuetching's marks in his office were inadvertently fading under the mess that had been building up as time went by. Worse still, he had been forgetting his meeting times lately and could not find the relevant documents. Work was getting harder, because of the lack of order and organisation. Everything was a mess, and he was coping much worse than before having Yuetching as his secretary.

He suddenly realised, "I've grown so reliant on you that I can't do anything on my own now! You have spoilt me rotten!"

He was laughing at himself. But psychologically he was not ready to find a replacement for her yet. If he had a choice, he would like to freeze this relationship with Yuetching unchanged. Reserving this position for her was his way to remember her; it also represented his undying hope that she would come back one day.

He got up and said to himself, "Let me temporarily do your job for you." He started organising his documents according to Yuetching's filing system. When he followed closely what Yuetching had been doing, he stumbled on a surprise! He suddenly understood more of Yuetching's thinking process that had underpinned her organisation and working methods. In an unexpected way, he felt he'd got closer to her! Finally, he filled in his calendar. Now all his appointments and meetings were clearly listed, just the way how Yuetching would have wanted it. He was proud of himself and was sure that Yuetching would be too. In this way, Samyin felt as if he had worked a full day with Yuetching.

Thinking of her, he sighed, "Oh Yuetching, where are you now? Do you have any idea how much we miss you?"

In the subsequent months, this business with Sinyin had distracted Chisau a little and occupied his mind. He was generous with his time and his support during the immediate aftermath of her ordeal. She had to go through counselling, psychiatric assessment and rehabilitation for her addiction. The press of course was not kind to her nor did it show any compassion. As Chisau frequented the rehab centre, he got dragged into the story and their history had been dug out. Speculations were rampant that they were back together. He too was swamped by harassing media attention but he handled it with class. "Anyone in the situation would have done what I'm doing, or you're a subhuman. There is no need for further justification other than that." "A life-and-death situation puts things in perspective and transcends differences." "The focus of our effort should be on the well-being of the patient and rebuilding her life; the media attention should do the same." "Being imperfect is commonplace; the real story is in how she addresses and overcomes it." Chisau was a wonderful life coach who worked wonders in picking Sinyin up when she was down. Under his care and protection, she came through rehab and was embracing her second chance in life. Chisau had been cautious not to mislead her that there was anything beyond friendship.

"I've lost to someone who isn't even physically around! How lame I am!" Sinyin laughed at herself.

"You're growing more adorable each day," praised Chisau. "Having the capacity to laugh at yourself is very healthy."

"And yet it's too late for your affection," Sinyin lamented.

"I'm sure you'll find someone soon enough and he is a very lucky guy."

"Truly, thank you for everything you have done for me."

"Don't mention it."

"I'm moved that you stand by me in crisis even at the risk of having your reputation tarnished by your association with me."

"Doing the right thing is important."

"How you handle the media makes you look so cool!"

"Really? Whatever, I don't notice."

"Your soundbites were masterclass. You defended me resolutely in the press. How can anyone in my position not fall for you?" Sinyin looked at him wistfully.

"I'm happy that we can part amicably as friends."

"My regret is to have mistreated you and taken you for granted." She took out a jewellery box and put it on the table. "I was wrong in accusing you of breaking this promise. You've kept this promise despite our official status. I'm grateful that you stayed by me when I most needed you. You didn't retreat or moan when keeping the promise cost you and inconvenienced you. This love is so pure that it is nourishing and invigorating. Among other things it has taught me how to love you back. Today I would like to do one thing for you." She paused and took a deep breath before announcing, "Lee Chisau, I formally release you from this promise. You are no longer responsible for me. I promise I will take good care of myself, so that you don't have to. At long last, I'm ready to take this ring off. Would you be happy to keep both of them as a memento?"

That was totally unexpected! Although it was the outcome that Chisau had been hoping for, he had not anticipated the path it had taken.

"Why don't you keep them?"

"I don't want to hold onto the promise, so you should keep them."

Chisau nodded, "In that case, yes, I'll keep them then."

He reached out and put the box away.

Finally this relationship had its proper closure.

"Cheung Yuetching is lucky to have you."

"Perhaps I'm jinxed. People whom I love keep running away from me, and leave me stranded."

"Hey, I didn't disappear from the face of the earth!" protested Sinyin.

"Still, I must endure the pain of separation yet again. Both times I had no say in the decision. Both times, my wish did not count. It's not funny at all."

"I'm sorry for what I did to you back then, truly," Sinyin formally apologised from the bottom of her heart. Chisau nodded to acknowledge it.

"How long are you going to wait for her?"

"For as long as it takes."

"What if during this time, she has got married and has an army of children?"

"Then I can move on, but until then, I have to hold out my promise to her."

"She can't expect that of you, surely?" Sinyin protested.

"Why not? Haven't we owed her that much? I can't bear to be yet another one, who has come close to her, only to break her trust. I can't bear to pain her heart in this way. I just can't let her down. Until she releases me from my promise, I will be here for her, whether she knows it or not."

"What if you *never* see her again? Are you going to remain single for her? That sounds ludicrous!"

"I *will* see her again."

"How can you be so sure? Have you found out her whereabouts?"

"It's just faith. My heart knows it."

"Your unwavering faith and love is naïve *and* endearing at the same time. I hope Yuetching deserves you."

"She does."

"Then you deserve each other. I can't say I'm not jealous of her."

Visiting the seashore and staring at the sea was like a ritual that Yuetching observed. However, this was the first time she came here since meeting Chisau. It felt like only yesterday; the whole episode came and passed in the twinkling of an eye. How fleeting was anything that happened in life!

She used to walk this shore with smothering sorrows weighing down on her, but this day, for the first time she could remember in her life, she felt warmth in her heart. To her surprise, she did not focus on the pain of what she had lost but the joy of what she had gained! Perhaps she was not greedy. Although it turned out that the Lees were not her real family, the experience while she was there was genuine. There was no regret. For a loner like her, to have tasted happy family life, even if only for a short while, was like morning dew in the parched land. She did not know how it had come to be. Again, she was just being swept along by the events in life like waves.

She walked along the shore and the symphony of nature sounded so much softer and mellower today. She had changed as she was no longer cursing life! Instead, her heart was filled with an unspeakable joy, the source of which she knew not. She looked far out at the sea, and whispered to her mother – the sea was her because it was where she had gone into and was never to return. Her mother not only saved her life but also prepared a wonderful family for her, where she experienced the tender love of a mother, the protection of a loving brother, the care of a sincere friend, who would do anything to make her laugh, and the wisdom as well as foolishness of an elderly family head. Chisau once said, "The wonderful part of family is that as time passes, and when we look back, even the times when we fought and annoyed each other could become humorous and funny moments that bring us laughter through our memory of them." It did appear so to Yuetching. How could she thank her mother enough, for all the blessings she had bestowed upon her? Did she deserve them all? Yuetching could not answer; she only wanted to be a grateful recipient.

The truths had healed her, even the unpleasant ones. It was better to know the truth than not, she had decided, no matter how painful it was. There was an amazing positive power in the truth, which made her strong. She was glad that she had finally found out who she was. Whether or not she liked her beginning, she had no choice over it. But knowing how she came along at least permitted her to reconcile with her personal history. That was the start of accepting herself, she thought. No, she could not say life was nothing but a curse now. The goodness that she had tasted was real, and that gave her hope. She smiled.

She let herself fall back onto the sand, and flail her limbs to draw angel. She laughed. For the first time in her life, she felt free. She could not explain it, but she felt all the knots in her heart had been untied. She felt she could die any time now because she had no regrets! She had nothing but she was content. How many people in the world could say that? This made her one of the richest persons in the world! It was a wonderful feeling. She looked at the sky, and laughed. It somehow looked brighter and clearer than any other day.

Suddenly she stopped laughing, because her mind sketched out the faces of Chisau and Samyin in the sky. Not seeing them again made her heart ache so much that she wanted to cry. Did they love her? Perhaps they had loved her once, in their different ways. But now she was not whom they thought she was, they must not love her still; she had no doubt about it. She was too scared to find out; she did not want to tarnish her memory of them in any way; she could not bear the thought that they thought ill of her because they were too important in her life, both of them. She ran away before they felt obliged to treat her as nicely as before because they were such gentlemen, or before they grew cold on her because she was in fact nobody to them. By running away, she would not burden them; it was the best she could do for them. As she was free, they should be free too – that was her thinking.

Looking back this latest chapter in her life, she had to pinch herself before she could believe how wonderful it had been. Somehow even the future looked brighter. Although she seemed to have gone back to where she was, something had changed; she had changed. How was it that she became a different person? She sat up on the sand and stared out on the sea again. That urge came to her again, to meet her parents where they perished, to be physically close to them, to say her goodbye properly and present her gratitude for all that they had done for her most wholeheartedly. A decision was made right at that moment; England she was to go!

She got up and walked to a nearby café. She sat down by the window and ordered her hot chocolate. A guy walked up to her and asked, "Mind if I sit down?"

Yuetching looked up, trying to register his face properly.

"Mind if I sit down?" the stranger reiterated.

"Oh! Sorry," answered Yuetching, coming out of her own

thought, "Of course not."

He sat down opposite her, and said, "You're different from last time I saw you."

"Have we met?" Yuetching was surprised at his comment.

"Yes, here at this same table over a year ago. You don't remember?"

"No, I don't…" Yuetching hesitated. "And you are?"

"And I met you even before that. I'm Tony who used to deliver pizzas with you once upon a time…"

Yuetching frowned and tried to recollect. Some vague images were starting to emerge, but nothing was sharp in focus.

"I saw you here last time you were here. I came up to you like today, but you were … well …. let's say, not impressed at all. You snapped at me and stormed out of the door, without drinking your hot chocolate. I thought I would never see you again."

Yuetching's hot chocolate was served up. "Thank you," Yuetching said to the waiter. "Really?" Yuetching was embarrassed that she could not remember it at all. "If I was so horrible and inapproachable then, why did you still approach me today? Were you not afraid that I would treat you in the same way again?"

"So be it then," Tony was determined.

"Why are you so persistent with me?" Yuetching found it a little disturbing.

"I've always been intrigued by you, and interested in knowing how you are doing. Without taking the risk, how can I ever find out? If I miss the chance, I may really not see you ever again, and I will never find out."

"Why are you so interested in me?" Yuetching was getting suspicious.

"When we were delivering pizzas together, you were always there as if you were not there, if you see what I mean. You were over 100 per cent focused on work and nothing else got into you. You worked with brilliant efficiency and accuracy, but on anything outside work, your mind was on another planet. No one could get a word out of you about your personal life. We did not know if you really didn't hear us or pretended not to. It was clear that you wanted to be left alone. Other co-workers soon isolated you just as you wished, but I kept watching you. I noticed that you were studying very hard in your own time. You always had a book or notes in your hands whenever you had a moment free. You never wasted any time for nonsense! I had never seen anyone approach life in such a clinical manner and at such a young age! And these eyes of yours," Tony leaned forward and pointed to Yuetching's eyes, "were burnt with the fire of determination that was unbreakable. As your peer, you were truly special, to say the least. I watched over you too, you may not have noticed, and arrested a few pranks played on you. Then one day you were gone; you resigned and did your last day without even telling us! Slightly over two years ago, I opened this café –"

"What? This café is yours?" Yuetching could not conceal her surprise as well as admiration, for Tony was young!

"Yes. And this was partly owed to you."

"What? How?" Yuetching was even more surprised.

"I can never forget your determination and your work ethic. I worked hard too. Before our lives crossed paths, I had never tried hard on anything. But your attitude towards life had changed me. You taught me life was serious and determination made things happen. We could never really say that we couldn't do something until we had tried – not just tried flippantly but tried real hard, so hard that our effort hurt! That was what I had learnt from you. And this café is possible because of that spirit you have imparted on me. This is what I have been wanting to tell you if I have a chance. And today finally is the chance."

"To put it simply," Tony tried to sum it up for Yuetching to understand, "you are my inspiration, my mentor without ever saying a word. This makes you a special person in my life. You are unforgettable!"

"Oh!" Yuetching was bewildered. She found life was ironic; to someone she was *unforgettable*, while she thought all along she was *invisible*.

"How are you anyway? I've been dying to know where that determination of yours has brought you to. Please do tell me," pleaded Tony.

"Oh! Me? Well, at this juncture in life, I've just lost everything. I'm jobless, homeless, and family-less, although not penniless."

"You're kidding, right? What happened? Has your business venture gone bust?" Tony could not believe it.

"No, nothing as grand as that."

"Are you all right? Do you need somewhere to stay?"

"No, I'm all right. It's not difficult for a single person to start up somewhere again."

"Strange, you don't look like someone who has just hit the trough of his life."

"Why?"

"You don't look – despondent. Instead, your countenance oozes serenity, which I've never thought possible with you."

Yuetching smiled, for she thought life was so weird that she could not comprehend. She thought she had no friends but here was someone, a complete stranger to her, who seemed to have known her for decades!

"What's it? Have I said something stupid?"

"No, on the contrary, what you've said is so true and very insightful about me too. You're very observant. Perhaps this is what has brought you to where you're today. I'm sorry that I've passed you by at the time we worked together. Thank you for your forbearance with my bad manners and never giving up faith in me. Thank you for working hard in life, but for which I cannot take credit."

"Is that all you can say to an old friend from your past? Are you determined to remain an enigma to every person you bump into? Why do you choose to live this way?"

"Hang on, I hardly know you. It's too early to call yourself a friend, let alone an *old* friend! As a stranger, you're quite forceful. Don't say that you've learnt it from me because I never push people to divulge their personal life." Yuetching was keen to set out the boundary.

"I'm sorry if I've been intrusive. But why must you live like an island? I want to build bridges to link this island to the mainland, and the first step is to talk." Tony wore this innocent grin on his face that it was difficult to doubt his sincerity. Without knowing, he had already pushed Yuetching onto the new territory where she had never been before with people.

"Are you proposing to be my therapist on social behaviour?"

"Why must you be sharp and offputting with people?"

Yuetching was intrigued. She wondered what would happen if she deviated from her usual course of action. Why not make him an experiment? Perhaps she was responding to his invitation. Alas! How did he manage to persuade her? No, she was not to be persuaded; it was because she had changed.

"Tony, sometimes ignorance is bliss, and you're asking for trouble here."

"What? Are you a mafia?" Tony was a little apprehensive.

"No, nothing like that." Yuetching took a deep breath and told a stranger for the first time in her life, "I spent most of my life living as an orphan, only to find out that I have a living biological mother who does not know who my father is. That is to say, I have spent most of my life grieving for the loss of whom I thought to be my parents, only to find out a few months ago that what I should have been dealing with was the pain of abandonment!"

Tony for once was speechless.

Yuetching was enjoying the shock on his face, so she continued a little bit more, "I'm pretty screwed up psychologically. If you think that my social behaviour is a little strange, I could explain the origin of every detail. Would you like me to write you a report?" Yuetching teased him; she continued, "And you thought my eyes were burnt with the fire of determination? That was the primal instinct for survival when I started living on my own at the age of 16. I was focused because I could handle only so much on my own that I had no choice but to prioritise, and at the time we crossed paths, my focus was to get into university. I worked not for pocket money to buy things I desired but for necessities. I didn't care what job I did, as long as it was honest labour earning enough for me to live on, and I did many jobs."

Tony was humbled to a silence.

On a more serious tone, she said, "I suppose you're right though; there was time when I could not even talk about it."

"I – I'm very sorry for being presumptuous," Tony apologised in a demure tone.

"No, not at all. You've meant well. Thank you for noticing me; that means a lot to me. I mean it. Thank you."

They chatted more on subjects more general! Tony ordered a big meal for them on the house, while Yuetching had learnt not to fight if someone insisted on being kind to her.

Four months elapsed since Yuetching had left. Chisau had settled back in his bachelor life. This night he thought of her, and wondered how she was living. Hotel had stopped paying her salary for two months and he wondered if she had enough money to spend. Suddenly an idea popped into his head. He remembered that he had Yuetching's account details somewhere. Where had he put them? He started looking through his drawers and files. It could be with his banking details. He got everything out and after searching meticulously, he found them! He switched on his computer and sent Yuetching some pocket money through internet banking. In the blank which said *Reference*, he wrote: *A goodwill gesture.* "I hope she will get it," he said to himself.

Three days later, when he routinely checked his account on the internet, he discovered that Yuetching had sent the money back with a message *Thanks but no thanks.* Chisau nearly had a heart attack. This was the first correspondence he had with Yuetching in four months! He was not to let it pass, so he sent her the money again with the message: *Still looking for you.* Two days later, Yuetching returned the money with a message: *Don't look.* Chisau repeated the transaction with a bold message this time: *Meet?*

Three days, four days, five days later, Yuetching still did not respond. Chisau nearly went crazy. He sent some more money to her, saying: *torturous wait.* Another five days had passed; there was still no news from Yuetching. Chisau was so frustrated that he had to get up and do something. He went back to where Yuetching grew up, visited the same restaurant where they had dinner, and then he went to Yuetching's hideout. He climbed up and sat down where he used to sit. He remembered clearly all the things that had happened there. He did not think he was going to bump into her for she had said never to return... But hang on! Did she really say that she would never return? He then remembered vaguely that Yuetching was going to return for a reason because he remembered telling her to be careful not to bump into her *gujeung*. But what was the reason? He searched hard through his memory for an answer till his head ached. He went through what happened on that fateful day for clues and he got it! Her *guje*'s memorial! She was to return to visit her *guje*'s resting place. He could not contain his excitement. He jumped down from the hideout and started looking up the nearby columbaria. There were not that many and it did not take him long to locate where Cheung Meiying's ashes had been placed. The person-in-charge told him, "Her niche was rarely visited until recently a young lady who came and made inquiry just like you do. She spent time and effort to clean her plaque. She brought flowers too. She even asked us if we could upgrade it. But as she was not family, she had no authority to change anything. She comes quite often, so I remember her."

Chisau was excited that he finally had a link to her, so he asked, "When does she normally come?"

"She will not come for a while."

"Why?" Chisau was disappointed.

"She said she was going overseas and asked if we could do her a favour by taking care of Cheung's niche while she was away and asked if there was a fund that she could contribute to for that and for flowers. Her pensive look has made quite an impression on me. Whatever her relationship with Cheung was, she has been deeply affected by it."

"Do you know where she has gone and when she will be back?"

"I am not sure where she has gone, or when she will return."

Chisau was disappointed.

"But," the person-in-charge had not finished, "I know she will come here in three months' time, on Cheung Meiying's anniversary. She has told me that she will come that day. She said that when Cheung Meiying died, she regretted that she could not be here. This year on her anniversary she will *definitely* be here."

Chisau thanked the person-in-charge, and went on to visit Cheung Meiying's niche. He had to squat down to get to its level. He observed silence to show respect, while the date of her anniversary was firmly imprinted on his mind.

For the following three months, Chisau lived in the countdown of days! He made a selfish decision not to tell anyone about what he had found out, not even to Samyin. He felt guilty about it, but he wanted to be the *first* and *only* person to find Yuetching. After their first meeting, then he would tell.

Besides playing tennis with Samyin, he had picked up a habit of going to the musical *Les Misérables* regularly. He remembered his promise to bring Yuetching to see it one day, but they had never got round to it. He did not know if he still had the chance to do so in the future, so his heart brought him to the theatre often as a way to express his regret of leaving this promise outstanding when he had a chance! He was reminded of her every time little Cosette sang *A Castle on a Cloud*, and somehow he found he could relate surprisingly well to Marius when he mourned the loss of his friends in *Empty Chairs at Empty Table*. Overall, the story was poignant, just like Yuetching's, albeit for different reasons. In the theatre, he felt this inexplicable connection with her that kept drawing him back.

It was the final week in the countdown. He took himself to see the musical one last time before the big day. During the performance, though, he could not focus much, for he happily preoccupied himself with his dream about meeting Yuetching again after eight long months! At the end of the performance, he visited the washrooms as usual before leaving, and often met the long queue outside the Ladies. Tonight was no exception. But as he walked past the queue, he caught someone familiar. He paused and walked back up the queue, for he could not let pass any chance of finding her, no matter how minute it was! But it was Yuetching. He stood in front of her; neither could believe their eyes. Before he could say anything, Yuetching took to her feet and ran. She was so quick that Chisau failed to grab hold of her. She ran straight into the crowd which became her cover. She dodged the people skilfully and made her way down in a flash. Chisau was held back by the crowd while Yuetching was disappearing right before his eyes! He panicked at the thought of losing her again, but physically he could not move forward any faster! At long last, he cleared the crowd and got out at one of the exits. He turned in all directions desperately hoping to catch the sight of Yuetching's back in one of them. But he was disappointed. He frantically circled the whole block but still failed to spot. As time wore on, he knew his chance of finding her in the proximity was diminishing fast. They were so close and yet so far! Finally, he had to abandon the search and admit defeat.

Yuetching, you can be cruel, was his thought.

He went home in a mood of melancholy.

11 Found and Lost and Found

It's weekend. "Tennis tomorrow?" Samyin asked Chisau in the lift.

"My Aunt's family has come to visit us, so we will be spending time with them. Sorry," Chisau prevaricated.

"Not to worry. See you next week. Have a good one." Samyin left with a cheerful smile. He was always bright and had never suspected that Chisau was up to something. This made Chisau feel even guiltier!

Sorry, Samyin, but I will tell you where Yuetching is after this weekend, if I do get to see her. Chisau said to himself.

Having waited for three months, the day when Yuetching was expected to visit her *guje*'s resting place had finally arrived. Chisau kept this tightly under wraps, for he wanted to monopolise the time of their reunion. He had so much to say, so much to catch up and so much to ask that he could not afford any distraction. He must give himself time.

He was too excited to fall asleep that night, so he got up at the crack of dawn and made his way to the columbarium. "I must NOT let her slip past me this time," he urged himself.

He went to Cheung Meiying's niche, and approached it solemnly. He put down the flowers he brought with him and paid his respect in silence. After that, he went to find a place comfortable to sit down for this could be a long day of waiting ahead of him. But no matter how long today was going to be, it could not have been longer than the past eight months.

He had packed some reading to kill the time, but he could

not concentrate. He was staring at the page but not reading it. In the end, he gave up. He let his mind wander, let himself get uncomfortably anxious and excited at the same time, and let the seconds go slowly by counting them! He was otherwise well prepared with food and drinks. He was determined to minimise his time away from his post!

Time was moving torturously slow. At long last it was lunchtime, but there was still no sight of Yuetching. Chisau was getting more anxious, thinking, *Yuetching, how much longer are you going to torture me? But it doesn't matter that I wait for a long time, as long as you do turn up and let me see you. Don't send me home today without seeing you, please.* This could have been his prayer!

Time was ticking. As the day was slipping away, the probability that Yuetching would not turn up was rising. This knowledge made Chisau feel uneasy, *Oh Yuetching, what would you have me do before you will see me? Would I have to work here and wait for you everyday and all day?*

Just after 3 o'clock in the afternoon, Chisau's patience was rewarded. He saw Yuetching walking slowly up the hill with her head down, as if she was deep in thoughts. He rose to his feet but did not rush forward to intrude into her space. Rather, he waited and stayed away, but he did not let her out of his sight. He was happy just to see her in the flesh. Rapt in her own thoughts, Yuetching was oblivious of her surroundings. She did not notice the presence of Chisau until she was near the columbarium where her *guje*'s niche was situated. She slowed her pace to a halt, and fixed her gaze at Chisau. She would have liked to be able to think clearly but a sound mind had eluded her. Her senses were too busy at dealing with all the mixed emotions that Chisau had stirred up. She was immobilised for her mind was blank and there was no decision on what to do next. Chisau kept his distance, so as to give Yuetching time to come up with a reaction. He was grateful that she was not running away like she did at the theatre. If she did, she could be sure that he would chase after her till the ends of the world this time as there was no crowd to block his way!

Yuetching remembered why she was here in the first place with flowers in her hand, so she went inside the columbarium. Chisau did not go in but he did not let Yuetching out of his sight either. Yuetching noticed that flowers were placed on *guje*'s plaque, so she squat down and put hers in a vase on the floor close to her. There she remained in silence, with her mind full of reminiscence of *guje*: *Sorry,* guje, *when you were gravely ill, I wasn't by your side and didn't do anything for you. In fact I didn't learn about your passing until last year. Although you were not my mother, I know you did the best you could for me within your limitations. You had worked hard your whole life for others. I wish to tell you today that I have lived well, hoping that this will at least bring you some comfort. Thank you for taking me in when I didn't have a home, protecting me by being my shield and giving me an independent life, a start that I was able to cope with at the time. I owed a lot to you. May you rest in peace.*

Having spent the time she wanted with *guje*, she came out and stood in a distance from Chisau. Neither moved as if in a duel, both unsure what would be the right move and both waiting for the first move. Although Yuetching did not move forward, she was not running away either. That was a statement of hope which Chisau read, so he moved up to her, held her into his embrace, and would not let her go. She succumbed to her own emotions and Chisau's wish, and stayed. She remembered the warmth of those arms; within them, it felt like home. In fact, she had missed him terribly, someone who would listen to her thoughts and care for her feelings. She had been fighting her desire to get in touch with him. That in fact had been a tough battle and required a lot of will power. It was not easy going back to a life on her own, but she had to find a way to come to terms with her new status and identity. It was a reality now Chisau had no more obligations towards her than any other strangers in the street. She dared not expect or hope that she would be accepted; she had never wanted anything more in life that disappointment would really have broken her heart. At the time when she was fragile, she did not know if she could ever recover from that, so she left without hoping or demanding, to protect herself as well as him.

Tears trickled down her cheeks in a controlled manner. They were tears of joy! She was moved by the fact that Chisau was unchanged in his manners towards her although now she was back as Miss Nobody, and that he had never given up finding her! She had not made it easy for him, and the way how they met again showed how well he had known her. Unlike the coincidence at the theatre, this was a deliberate search which spoke volume of his effort and sincerity. To be known so deeply by someone was a lifelong desire fulfilled. How else could one respond except being happy! His manners reassured her when her confidence was the lowest. She had felt so ashamed of herself that she went hiding from all people. But she felt within his arms, she could be completely honest. He was a very special person in her life.

After Yuetching had calmed down, Chisau held on to her hand and would not let go. He was not letting her run away and his worst nightmare replay! He led her to a nearby café. They sat down and ordered drinks. Finally Chisau had the time to study her face.

"You've grown thinner," Chisau observed, "Is life very hard on you?"

Yuetching shook her head.

"Is it possible," Chisau summarised the pain he had gone through in the past eight long months into one request, "that you won't let me go through the experience of losing you again? The thought of having to find you in the vast sea of people brings me unspeakable panic and anxiety. Could you – could you promise me never ever again to leave without a word? Could you let me know where you are, and have your contact details at all times? Please do not leave me on my own to worry and feel the hurt. Could you promise me?"

Yuetching looked down and did not answer.

"Are you still angry with me?" Chisau was disappointed.

Yuetching looked at him, eager to deny, "Why would you think that? How could I be angry with you? You're the closest person I have in my life!"

"Then why did you leave without saying goodbye, without leaving contacts?"

"I could not bear to be a family wrecker, let alone the one that has been so kind to me and given me so much. I left to keep your family intact. I don't want you to have to choose between your family and me. I don't want history to be repeated in your family, knowing the pain that it breeds. Do we seriously want the same regrets to perpetuate down the generations? We don't; I certainly don't! Cutting all the ties is to reflect the reality that there is indeed no tie between us. I was the one who shouldn't have been there, so I should be the one to leave. The more my heart refuses to accept, the more ruthless I have to be in order to make myself accept the reality."

"If your heart refuses to accept, then why don't you stay and

354

work things out?"

"We were family before but no more. You were my brother before, but no more. There was a reason, even an obligation, for you to care for me, but no more. There is no basis to work things out, don't you see? Not only do I have no right to stay in your family, I don't want to oblige you to care for me because I'm a charity case. I left, so that I would not fantasise a life that is beyond my reach, or make demands on you beyond my right. I left because we all needed the time to cool our heads, straighten our thoughts and know what our muddled emotions really were. I left so as to expand our options to include what we thought as impossible at the time – that is, back to our previous lives before we met! We need to clear the cloud in order to know our hearts."

"In all this, have you ever thought of me and how I feel?"

"Of course, I have! I would bring scandal to your family name and split your family. You might be ostracised and become an outcast like me. Why would I wish my cursed life for anyone, especially not you, your family or Samyin who are so dear to me? You would want the best, not the worst, for those you love, wouldn't you? I don't want to be a curse to your life."

"Why would you think that people won't accept you? When they get to know you, they will like you. Don't you believe that?"

"You are biased and you can't see clearly. I tell you, Szeman and Sinyin's view of me will be the mainstream opinion of me. People do not believe true love or Cinderella anymore. Before people get to know you, they already form a pre-judgement about you based on your upbringing, achievements, education, connections and so on. What chance do I have to impress people? Even I myself feel embarrassed by my own background and birth, and wish to hide it from all people if I can help it, how can I expect others to accept me?"

"I'm the one who knows everything about you and I accept you as who you are totally and completely. Who says it's impossible?"

"That's because we were family and you were trying to make amends!"

"Mum has said that she'll accept you," Chisau told her to boost her confidence.

"Accept me as what?"

"As my girl. She even encourages me to find you, saying that it's the best way to cure my dejected heart."

Yuetching was gobsmacked, "You've told her!"

"I didn't; she guessed it. What was I to do? Denied it? She's my mother; I can't lie to her, you know."

"Were you really that obviously dejected?"

"What do you think?"

"How about your Granddad?"

"I haven't tested his reaction. Mum agrees that where you came from works against you. But this is irrelevant with us because we have come to know your person first! And what we have known about you is not changed by the new revelation about your birth. This is our *yuenfan*. So have confidence in yourself, and give people time. We can patiently work to dispel prejudice and people will come to accept you."

Yuetching did not answer.

"Yuetching, please don't abandon me. Otherwise searching for you will become my life. Why should we waste the time in this way that we could have spent together?"

"Do you really mean that – you will not give up searching for me?"

"Why do you doubt? You're right in that time apart helps us know our hearts. So thanks to the decision you imposed on me, my heart has been tried and I know it even better now than before." He grinned and Yuetching simply found him adorable.

"Let's deal with what's going to happen tomorrow," Chisau continued to reason with her. "Things that have not happened may never happen. Isn't it a bit silly to make a present decision on things that have not happened and in turn may never happen? Your life experience has proven that life is unpredictable. On the surface, that you got kicked out by Granddad looks like a bad thing, but there is a silver lining, which is the possibility that it has opened up for us! There are always two sides to a coin; it depends on the angle you choose to look at things. Yuetching, I'm not going to give up on you. Please don't run away again."

To Yuetching, Chisau was always persuasive. To avoid answering, Yuetching changed the subject, "I'm hungry. Let's order something to eat, and talk more after we have eaten!" Chisau was happy to see the Yuetching he had remembered gradually coming back. He was also happy that she was willing to stay and eat with him.

During dinner, Chisau was curious about where she had been, so he asked, "What have you been up to since you left? Have you found a job yet?"

"Currently, I'm unemployed! After I got kicked out, I felt drained and exhausted. I felt like taking a long vacation from trying hard in life, and from a race that had no aim. I had saved a lot during the year when I stayed with your family, as you did not accept my contributions to rent or food. Together with my past savings, I allowed myself an indulgence of doing nothing for a while. A lot had happened in my life in just one year. I need the time and space to digest my lessons, think about the meaning of life and find a new direction. I lived an aimless life for three months doing nothing, met Tony –"

"Tony? Who is Tony?" Chisau was alarmed; Yuetching never had friends and never called someone's name with such familiarity.

"It's a long story, but it turned out that he had known me since I was 16 while I didn't notice him at all. We were co-workers delivering pizza. We bumped into each other again by chance. He remembered me while I didn't. He approached me and we chatted."

"You – chatted to – a stranger?" Chisau was unsure.

"Yes, I did," replied Yuetching.

"Do you know how strange it sounds?"

"Well, what can I say? I'm a changed person, hopefully for the better, thanks to you and all the others who worked tirelessly to open me up to the outside world. I can't help it. I thought you would be pleased!"

"I should be – no, I mean I am. Just that I wish your first friend were not Tony. You know how insecure I feel right now."

"I didn't seek him out, he did. I suppose we have some *yuenfan* between us. How else could we have met up after all these years? He said I was *unforgettable* back then when I thought I was largely *invisible*! How bizarre!"

"Don't even say that; it really freaks me out! Have you been seeing him?" he was getting concerned.

"Yes, we met up a few times."

"Does he like you?"

"Yes, I suppose so. He tries hard to draw me out; he's really persistent and forceful too."

"Oh dear!" Chisau thought that was the worst news possible.

"But then I went to England, and haven't seen him since I came back." Yuetching tried to ease his concern.

"Is there anything between you two?"

"He did come to see me off at the airport."

"He's keen. And he did not come to pick you up?"

"I didn't want him to. I had an open ticket and didn't inform him when I had decided to return."

"And he didn't bombard you with texts and emails?"

"He couldn't for at the time, I was uncontactable. I survived for a few months like that – it's therapeutic. He asked for my contact details but I had none to give."

"Will you see him again?"

"I suppose I will. Otherwise it's too cruel."

Chisau looked disappointed.

"How about you? For a time, I thought you and Sinyin were getting back together. It made such a juicy story to read!" Yuetching teased.

"I thought you would agree that I should help her in that situation, or I would have been *a subhuman* – this was among your first words to me, remember?"

"Of course, I remember, and I heard you repeat them to the press." She laughed. "But still, speculations about you two were all over the place. It was the hottest gossip in town at the time!"

"We are just friends."

"So there you are; similarly Tony and I are just friends. You have to trust me." Yuetching continued, "Someone has once said to me, in one lifetime, we don't have much time and energy to be 'serious' many times." It was Chisau who had said this. "At this point in time, I have no interest in being 'serious' with Tony. Whether there is potential is immaterial, because my heart doesn't want to." Yuetching finally released Chisau from the suspense, and he had to trust her word.

"Sinyin gave back the couple rings to me."

"What does that mean?"

"She has finally released me from my promise to her and does not want to hold on to it, so I should keep the rings, she said. She promises to take good care of herself so that I don't have to."

"She's transformed! You've worked wonders on her."

"No one can come through a life-and-death crisis without change, for better or for worse. *You* have worked wonders on

358

her."

"What do you mean?"

"I taught her what you have taught me about life. It's very weird. Spending time with her physically was in actual fact spending time remembering you, so it was a pleasurable thing to do. I don't think anyone would get that except you."

"I've thought the soundbites sounded familiar," Yuetching admitted.

"I know you would have picked it up if you were listening or reading," Chisau looked terribly smug about himself. "It's like our secret codes." That evoked a laugh.

"Tell me about your trip to England," Chisau changed the subject.

"In England, I stayed at two places. I first went to the beach where my parents drowned. Walking the footsteps of my past was a process that I started with you here. When I was tending my *guje*'s memorial, Auntie Cheung's account of how she died kept playing in my mind. It suddenly dawned on me that the reason why *guje* sent me away was not only because of *gujeung* as she had told me. I now understand that it was also her effort to save me from the burden of her family. Should I have stayed with them, I would soon have to share her burden to support the family as I grew older. Even if she didn't ask, I would have offered. I might even give up my education to do that. I sensed that she didn't want that to happen. I seemed to hear her say, 'I didn't want my fate to fall on you; this would have been unfair on you.' It was a moment of enlightenment and I understood my past more. The only way not to burden me with their troubles was to cut off all contact between us – so that I didn't see their needs and they didn't see me as a source of help. That was to free me. I cried having understood her thoughts for me. She did love me in her own way.

"I felt a sense of release when I finally had taken care of this unfinished business and reconciled myself to my past more. The feeling gave me an urge and courage to face another unfinished business, which was to say a proper goodbye to my parents in the UK. This was why I decided to go to England.

"That day, I walked along the beach. I was there from dawn to dusk. I watched the tide ebb and flow, and the sea changing according to the hours. I imagined I must have been very happy playing on this beach when I was five years old; the sand was so soft. I almost could hear my own laughter! But the tide came in really quickly, so quickly that it caught people by surprise. The big wave pushed in one after the other, washing the defenceless little five-year-old girl off her feet. She got swallowed up by the waves! Mum heard her cry, and turned to see what happened. She jumped into the waves and pulled her out in the first instance. She passed her to dad, who passed her to his sister. Then he went back to the sea, trying to rescue mum who was struggling to stay afloat. This was how they disappeared into the sea and never returned. They were never found, so they were *presumed* dead, and the sea was their grave. I stood there and watched my parents being swallowed up by the sea. I did not understand it at the time. I thought if I sat there long enough, they would come back and waved at me when the tide ebbed. I was pretty stupid, wasn't I? But they never came back. I sat on the beach and replayed the scenes, tracing the moments. I didn't cry when I was five years old; twenty years later, in the midst of bitterly cold wind, I cried as if I was watching a tragedy unfold. The tears were not because I was sad but because I was moved. This was how I said goodbye to my parents. I solemnly promised them that I would continue to live well, so that they did not die in vain."

To Chisau, it was pure bliss being able to listen to Yuetching's thoughts and take on life again. Yes, this was what he had missed.

"I regret that I wasn't there with you."

"Why? Must you see me cry every single time?"

"No! It's my wish to be by your side at every important moment of your life."

"Thank you for having that wish," Yuetching said from the bottom of her heart. Then her tone changed, "After I had finished that unfinished business, I went to the Lake District. Have you heard of Beatrix Potter, the creator of Peter Rabbit?"

"Of course."

"I went to the Lake District where she lived and loved! I lived there for three months. I was free during the day and waited tables in the evening, leading a very simple life which was not trying on my brain! That was my retreat. It was great to soak up the aura of the place. I hiked and sketched or read, took joy in the simplest things. Life was carefree. I have only just come back. This long vacation has come to an end, and I must find a job!"

"You went to see *Les Misérables*."

"Yes," Yuetching was a little chagrined for running away.

"Why did you go?"

"I guess it's for the same reason why you went."

"Why did you run?"

"I panicked, so I took flight."

"Was I so frightening that you had to take flight?"

"No, perhaps you can say I wasn't ready to face you."

"In what way do you need to be ready?"

"When my new life is established and I don't look pitiful, then I'm ready."

"I thought you were cruel. What if I didn't have another chance to find you today here, how was I supposed to live after missing you like that?"

"Who knows? I might feel so guilty about it that I got in touch with you to say sorry? This is possible, if you haven't found me already."

"Did you feel guilty after running away from me then?"

"Yes, very."

Chisau was relieved that she wasn't heartless.

"Did you use the money I sent you?"

"Don't worry. What you have sent me I will return in full!"

"I don't mean that. Why did you respond twice and then stop? Do you have any idea how much that tortured me?!"

"You asked me to meet! What was I supposed to say? I needed to be firm in order to dash your hope! But still you've found me!"

"You can be brutal at times!"

"This is called *determined*!"

After dinner, when they were ready to go, Chisau asked Yuetching to hand over her handbag. "Why?" Yuetching was surprised by this unusual request.

"I need to go to the washroom."

"So? What has it got to do with having my handbag?" Yuetching failed to see the link here.

"I hold your handbag in hostage so that you can't run away."

"Are you kidding me? Why would I let a man take my handbag into the toilet with him?" Yuetching was unwilling to comply, so she made him an offer, "You go, and I promise I won't go."

"No, it won't do. Give me your handbag. Even if you do run away, I'll have your personal details to find you again. If you have no intention to run, it doesn't make a difference to you if I take it temporarily. If you are unwilling, it can be an indication of your intention to run away, and then I *must* take it to prevent it from happening! In either case, I should keep it."

What a watertight argument! To indicate that she had no intention to run, she had to give Chisau her handbag! "Please don't get it dirty," Yuetching found the thought slightly repugnant but she had no choice!

Chisau took hold of the handbag and felt secure. Like a happy little child, he promised cheerfully, "I will take good care of it."

When Chisau came out of the toilet, he could not see Yuetching! He frantically looked around, trying to spot where she had fled! He could not believe his nightmare was starting all over again! Neither could he believe that Yuetching had become so untrustworthy! He started panting in panic and asked himself, "She shouldn't have gone far. Which direction would she go?"

When he was thinking of his next step, Yuetching walked out of the Ladies leisurely. Why did Chisau suddenly get all anxious again? She walked up to him and inquired, "What has happened? Have you lost something? What are you looking for?"

Chisau could not tell how relieved he was to see her. Even he found himself ridiculous and mocked himself, "Yuetching, you have successfully turned me into a madman! I'm doomed." He pulled Yuetching into his arms and said solemnly, "Please don't run away again. I can't take this another time."

"I only went to the toilet —" explained Yuetching. But Chisau did not care, and would not let go. He said, "Even if you eventually decide not to be with me, please do not disappear into the crowd and be transparent to my eyes. Please do not abandon me like what your parents did to you on that beach."

"Chisau —" Yuetching was moved.

Chisau held on to her hand all the way and led her to his car. He opened the driver door for Yuetching.

"What? Do you want me to drive you home?" asked Yuetching.

"No. I want you to drive me to *your* home."

"What?"

"I need to see where you live before I believe I have really found you. You can still drive my car legally; you are still on my insurance as an extra driver! Besides, I'm way too tired to drive as I didn't sleep last night; I was far too nervous about today."

Yuetching reluctantly moved into the driver seat. Chisau was happy that he got his way. Yuetching started up the car and tried to set up the satellite navigator. Chisau asked, "What? You don't know how to get home?"

"I don't know the car route!"

Having input her address, Yuetching teased Chisau, "Even your navigator has a record of my address; you don't need to worry anymore."

After a long drive, Yuetching stopped the car and said, "We are here."

"You live so far away again."

"Of course. After all I'm running away from you and others! Do you think I should have moved next door to the Hotel instead?" Yuetching switched the engine off, handed back the car key and got off the car. Chisau followed.

She had rented a little apartment. She opened the door and said, "Welcome, my first visitor! Please make yourself comfortable. Would you like a drink?"

Chisau walked into her home and replied, "Water please."

He looked around the lounge, which had been kept as tidy and simple as before, but with a subtle difference. It was no longer faceless and void of personal traits! Instead, there was a cluster of photos on her shelves. Chisau walked up to the photos and studied them to see what about Yuetching they reflected.

In total four photos were displayed. The first one was a family portrait of her and her late parents, which she retrieved from her biological mother. The second one was another family portrait of her with the Lee family taken at his birthday party. In the photo were Granddad, his mother, him and her. The third picture was the one Yuetching snapped of him when she first got the camera. This was the same picture on which she later based to sketch him. The fourth one was Samyin with the Disney Castle in the background.

Yuetching came out with the water. Chisau moved to the sofa and sat down.

"You have changed; your inner world is no longer empty."

Yuetching smiled with happiness, "So you can tell."

"I thought we only inflicted deeper pain and wounds on you.

363

I have assumed that in your memory of us are our heartlessness and the sadness we have brought you."

She fain smiled and fain shook her head.

"Why? Didn't we walk you through another episode of a happy life being shattered? Are you not traumatised by the experience? Granddad was wrong in what he did and said."

"When Granddad asked me to leave, I was very sad; who wouldn't when a happy time came to an end? But after I had calmed down and returned to a life on my own, I realised that I didn't harbour any anger towards you and the family. On the contrary, whenever I thought of my time with the family, my heart glowed with warmth, and that feeling never failed to make me smile. I had never expected that and my reaction surprised me as well. Perhaps it's because I'm not greedy. This was a family I never had and, as it turned out, never should have had. But it had given me a sweet period of happiness, a taste of a life which I hadn't had and the warmth that I had never felt. I feel blessed to own such fond memories. Towards you and the family, I'm only grateful for the wonderful and beautiful experience that I should never have had in the first place! Even though it was short-lived, I'm content. Regarding this chapter of my life, I hold no regrets. Therefore you shouldn't mind and blame yourself too much. Instead, I thank you for being the very person who opened that chapter for me. Also, don't be too harsh on Granddad. He was disappointed too, I can tell. He only asked me to leave a home that I had no right to stay. I didn't even put up a fight."

Chisau was relieved as well as touched by what Yuetching had said. She was always someone who saw the best of everyone and everything, and never would let any negative feelings to rot her soul.

"How about Samyin? Who is he in your world?" Chisau referred to the photo displayed with his glance.

"You mean the photo? You would like to know why I put his photo out, right?" Yuetching rephrased Chisau's question, and answered, "Samyin is my first and best friend. This photo epitomises what he means to me – fun, colourful and delightful. He is the person who makes me laugh and help me learn to enjoy life. Remember that before I met you, I had no family or friends. My friendship with Samyin is also what I cherish from this period of living with the family."

"But to him you are more than a friend, and you know it."

Yuetching nodded.

"What do you plan to do?"

"Plan? That you found me was not within my plan! My original plan was to rely on everyone forgetting me over time. I guess this plan is not going to work now!"

"You know after today, I must tell him that I have found you? He has been waiting for you as anxiously as I have. He doesn't suffer less than I do."

"I know."

"It's also high time you gave him an answer."

"I know."

"Then the answer is?"

"If Huentung's engagement party had never happened, I probably would have said yes."

"What happened at the party?"

"I danced with you."

"And?"

"And I experienced that loving feeling, which I had never known or felt for Samyin or anyone before. Sinyin said it was just a make-belief, skilfully manufactured by an experienced dance partner, so I thought it was and I dismissed it as so."

"And now?"

"A make-belief will fade with time, right? Many months have passed since then, right? I've had a lot of time to think about this, right? But that feeling hasn't passed, so it isn't a make-belief. Then I know my feeling for Samyin is never the kind he asks of me."

"Are you – saying that – we are –?" Chisau's heart was pounding with excitement as well as nervousness.

"Chisau, whether a couple should be together, mutual feelings from both parties are of course necessary but not sufficient! There are other factors in deciding whether a couple should or can be together besides their feelings for each other. I fear that I'm not good for you, and will hurt you, and end up hurting myself. What if it doesn't work out in the end? I don't want to stack my hope in it in case I lose everything. I want it so much that I'm scared of ending up with a broken heart that can't be put back together –" Chisau stopped Yuetching from further rationalising by pulling her over; and sealing her lips with his. Yuetching was taken by surprise at first but began to relax in his arms. Gradually she was melting and the experience was as electrifying as they were waltzing together.

When Chisau let go of her, she looked embarrassed and shy, with burning cheeks! She didn't know where to look, but he settled her and said, "At least you did not push me away, and at least you know one of your shadows from the past has no hold on you anymore. You can start longing for love. For all the other factors that have been bothering you, let's face them together. You will pain me a great deal if you run away again."

How could I ever escape from him; he knows me so well!

"If you are not saying anything, I assume you agree. Now let's renew our 'telephone contract'." Chisau took his phone out, and asked, "Please give me your number."

Yuetching smiled. She snatched the handset from Chisau and input her number directly. Then she passed it back to him.

"Now, please get your phone out and let me test it."

Yuetching was a little offended, "You don't trust me."

"I just want to make sure."

Yuetching went to get her phone and placed it in front of him. He dialled her number and her phone rang as expected. He was happy, while Yuetching shook her head! He then noticed that his number was known by her phone!

"How come?" he asked.

"Even if I've left behind my phone, it doesn't mean that I've left behind your number too. Something is on the heart forever and you can't forget it, even if you try."

"Even when you have had my number at your fingertips all this time, you've resisted calling me or texting me!" Chisau found this incredulous.

"Once I've made the decision, I will stubbornly stick to it till the end."

"Then what is your decision about us? Are you going to stick to the decision till the end, no matter how difficult it is?"

"So far I'm passive in this decision."

"What do you mean?"

"It's a big commitment! If it doesn't work out and I have to leave you for your good, I am not sure I can bear it and overcome it. I'm afraid I may not be able to stand up again. You see, I have never wanted anything so badly in my life. The more I want it to work, the more it will hurt when it doesn't. It's too good to be true for me and it probably is! Right now, my fear has the better of me."

Chisau held her hands into his, and promised, "Yuetching, if I have the honour as your heart's keeper, I will cherish it and will not let it break for any reasons that are within my control. Will you trust me on that?

"Haven't you once said that you are in effect cursing your own life if you deliberately shut out all the good things that could have happened to you because you fear the possibility that they may be shattered? Haven't you said that a positive attitude towards life is having the courage of a tumbler who will always spring back upright after being pushed down, and then at least your life will be fuller? On love, I wish you will think that I am worthy for you to invest your courage, and to give both of us a chance. Is it worth a try?"

Yuetching was moved to tears. Yes, of course, she remembered her struggle all her life. She dared not hope in fear of being disappointed. She had not loved because she could never believe anyone would ever see her, know her, cherish her and love her wholeheartedly in return. In the midst of her sobs, she nodded to say yes!

"Then this is no longer a passive decision on your part, but a *joint* decision; you and I have to *obstinately* stick to it till the end."

Yuetching nodded to give her commitment.

Chisau took out the handset she had left behind, and said, "I have kept this handset so far. Now I return it to you. I would like it if you use it again, but this time I won't impose on you like the first time."

Yuetching took it and said, "Thank you for returning it to me."

She went to the kitchen and made some tea. When she came back, Chisau was already sound asleep on the sofa. She put down the tea, and sat down to study his face. He looked exhausted, and her heart hurt. She could see from his face how hard this period had been for him and how tired he was today. Yuetching went to fetch a blanket for him, before she retired to bed herself. This had been a long and emotional day. She realised that this was the day she had made a decision which marked an important turning point in her life; she was excited and delighted, while slightly scared at the same time for once again it was too perfect.

It was nearly noon when Chisau woke up. He sat up on the

sofa and felt like he had had a dream. He got up and could not find Yuetching anywhere in the apartment. Where had she gone? Chisau started to panic again.

When he was about to ring her, Yuetching went through the door. Seeing that he had the phone in his hand and looking anxious, she guessed, "You are looking for me again! Last night, you asked me to trust you, so when are you going to trust me again? You are now paranoid! It's unbearable." Yuetching repeated one more time with emphasis, "I – WILL – NOT – RUN – AWAY – AGAIN! Do you hear me? Is that clear?"

Chisau was made to realise how ridiculous he had become. Perhaps he was really insecure! He understood that he must overcome his paranoia and give them a fresh beginning.

Having put down her shopping, Yuetching walked up to him and put her arms round his waist. She whispered an apology to him, "Your insecurity is totally my fault. I thought no one really cared about my coming and going. But I was wrong. I'm sorry to have caused you such grief. Please forgive me by trusting me again. Please do not live in fear." Her words relieved him from such tension that he cried. He held her tightly, only managing to say, "Thank you! Thank you so much!"

At this moment, Chisau's phone rang and he answered, "Hello, mum."

"Please remember to come home this afternoon. Don't be late. Don't make people wait for you," Puiyin said on the other side of the phone.

"I know. I'll be there at around 3pm. All right – understood – see you later." Chisau hung up.

"Are you in a hurry?" asked Yuetching.

"No, I have a lot of time!" Chisau smiled.

After he had a wash, Chisau sat down to have lunch with Yuetching. He chatted casually, "Auntie and her family have come to visit mum. I have to go home for dinner in order to see them."

"Aren't they staying with you too if they visit your mum?" something did not quite add up for Yuetching.

"They do stay with mum, but I do not. After you had left, I moved out."

Wide-eyed with surprise, Yuetching asked, "Why?"

"There were many reasons. First, the family home was full of your presence which made it hard to bear. Second, I wanted to have a break from my overbearing Granddad. Third, I would like to copy what you were doing and feel closer to you! I know I was silly and lame, but at the time, I would do anything to feel connected to you."

"Are you used to living on your own?"

"Don't look down on me! I had lived on my own before! I moved back home only to look after the family after my father passed away."

"I see. Are you planning to leave after lunch then?"

"I can spend a bit more time with you before I leave. What do you plan to do today?"

"Nothing much. After seeing you off, I shall look through job ads!"

In the meantime, Chisau's family and visitors left the restaurant after finishing lunch. They unexpectedly bumped into Samyin in the shopping mall, and he was puzzled, "Why is Chisau not with you?"

Puiyin was surprised to hear this, "Why is Chisau not with you? He says he is at a business function with you and isn't free until three o'clock!"

Chisau arrived home before three o'clock, and found everyone was waiting for him, including Samyin.

"You have come," he addressed Samyin.

"I've come to see for what important reason Lee Chisau lies to his mother and his best friend simultaneously," Samyin did not sound friendly.

Chisau looked guilty and was thinking how best to answer it. The tension was building up and everyone was nervous.

"Can't you answer it? Don't you know where you have been? Shall I have a guess? You have found Yuetching, haven't you?"

Chisau could not deny it, so he nodded to admit. Samyin got angry and went forward to give him a punch, which shocked his mother! She rushed to see if her son was hurt.

"You have broken my trust! How long have you found her?" yelled Samyin.

Chisau got up from the floor.

"Are you all right?" inquired his mother.

"I'm fine," answered Chisau.

"WHEN DID YOU FIND HER?" Samyin yelled again.

"Yesterday," replied Chisau.

"How naïve I was to believe that you had had no clues! Is

that what you mean by us being in the same boat? Where is she now?"

Chisau looked away and did not answer. Samyin saw the hesitation and got annoyed. When Chisau was not paying attention, Samyin went up near him, grabbed his car key that he dropped on the floor and dashed out of the door. He jumped into his car and drove off. Chisau could not catch up with him, and he realised he actually did not know precisely what Yuetching's address was – he just followed the navigator! He rang Yuetching but she was not picking up! She just had to face an unexpected visitor without any prior warning!

Yuetching dosed off while looking through job advertisements and working through her applications. The day before was too eventful and she felt the strain too. The doorbell rang and woke her up. She thought, "Who could it be? It couldn't have been Chisau again."

She opened the door and found Samyin standing in front of her. She was a little startled. They looked at each other for a while, before Samyin asked, "May I come in?"

"Oh! Of course." Overcome by the shock, she had forgotten to invite him in.

She closed the door. No one spoke. Samyin was not himself; he was clearly struggling with his emotions.

"Please come in, and sit down. Would you like to drink anything?" Yuetching started with the usual greeting to break the ice.

"Did you find him or did he find you?" asked Samyin.

"He found me."

"How did he find you?"

"He worked out that I would go to visit my *guje*'s resting place on her anniversary, so he waited for me there."

He fixed his gaze at Yuetching's face, a face that he had longed to see. She looked a little unfamiliar. Was it because he had forgotten the fine details of her face or she had changed?

"Have you lived well?" asked Samyin.

"I'm starting out all over again, another new beginning."

"You and Chisau are also having a new beginning, right?" Samyin's instinct had made it plain to him.

Yuetching nodded.

He moved into the lounge and looked around. This felt familiar, and yet it seemed to have more life and happiness in it than her previous place. Perhaps the photos had helped. He went to look at the photos closely. He was pleasantly surprised that his photo was there among the handful that had been selected for display. He was both comforted and honoured that he had a place in her heart. He picked up his own picture and asked, "Is this your memory of me?"

"Whenever I think of you, the thought that comes to mind is always the happiness you brought me."

"To you I only know how to play. You don't choose me because I am not serious enough?" Samyin would like to know why.

"No. You're a class of your own. You have taught me an important lesson about life which is to enjoy life. What a gift this is! It's nothing about you not being serious enough but what you mean to me. You're my best friend."

"But we are only friends," Samyin lamented.

"A very special friend," Yuetching tried to comfort.

"May I ask why Chisau, and not me?"

"I'm not going to lie. I have no experience about love at all and this is all new to me. But I don't think it is a matter that can be fully explained by reason. It isn't like as if one were the winner and the other the loser – it's not like that at all. But in my heart of hearts, it so happens that I have a deeper connection with Chisau, and I can't explain why this is so. This does not mean that you come up short in any way but that I'm not your destiny. You are a lovely person and you are still very dear to me."

"Is this a consolation prize?"

"Don't be bitter. I believe that the love of your life is only just round the corner waiting for you. For future, you must always be full of expectancy."

"Yes, I should encourage myself that I will find another Yuetching round the corner," Samyin engaged in a bout of self-parody.

"Samyin, don't sound so sour. I believe that *yuenfan* will give you a pleasant surprise, if you will let go."

"Because you believe, then I have to believe too?"

"Yes," Yuetching answered without hesitation.

Samyin sighed. "I don't know which is more tortuous: to be dangled in suspense for months on end or to have a *no* answer. Perhaps I've had the raw deal of being put through both."

"I'm *so* sorry…. I have been unkind to you."

He looked at her, feeling sorry for himself too. "I've missed you much, you know. It's very sore right now, but I'm also very happy to see you again. Please fill me with your chatter just like how it was. How have you been? Are you still sad with everything that has happened? Have you accepted the turn in events?"

"I'm coping well. I've done some soul-searching, and found the rightful place for everyone and everything in my life. In that sense I'm doing really well."

In this way, Samyin and Yuetching chatted for a long time, just like the time when they worked together in the office. Yuetching invited Samyin to stay for dinner; it was the first time he tasted Yuetching's cooking.

"How is it? Is it all right? You are such a marvellous cook. What I can offer is in no comparisons with yours in details or in taste," said Yuetching.

"Simplicity is a kind of beauty. This beauty permeates everything about you, including your cooking. Don't put yourself down," Samyin never forgot to encourage her. Suddenly melancholy returned, and he said, "Yuetching, I've kept the position of my secretary vacant for you. Besides you, I'm reluctant for anyone else to fill it. But I believe you won't be coming back and be my secretary again. Then this position will be vacant forever. You're the only one who has managed to tame me. Now, if it's not Yuetching's way, then it's the wrong way! Who can replace you in my life? What do you say I should do now?"

Yuetching could find no response to that.

"But I'm not doing too badly myself. I invested time to learn your system and methods to organise my office. Now I've graduated and am proud to be tidy and organised! Then I realise you've changed me quite profoundly. Unwittingly I'm carrying your influence in me. In future, no matter where I go, I'll always carry the marks of our time spent together. This has become a reality that can't be erased."

"It's my honour that you bear the marks of my influence," Yuetching smiled proudly. "I also bear your influence in me. Don't you notice at all? We all grow up together and bear each other's influence."

"Yuetching, don't look down on yourself. I believe that

everyone who has a chance to interact with you will be influenced by you to some extent. You're a unique and an outstanding girl with a lot of to give! You MUST have self-belief. Understand?"

"Samyin…" Yuetching was moved.

"Don't be afraid to have big dream, because you have the ability to make it a reality. The question is on you – whether you will fight for, create or grab hold of the opportunities. I wish to see your influence extend in scope to benefit many more people! Yuetching, please don't aim to be a transparent member of the crowd. I wish to see you find a mission in life and work hard at achieving it."

"Samyin, thank you. Thank you for believing in me, thank you for helping me dreams stay alive!"

Samyin gave Chisau a call when he was in the car, asking, "Where would you like me to deliver your car?"

"I'm at home."

Samyin went to see Chisau and returned the car key to him. His cheek was still a little red and swollen from the impact of Samyin's punch. Samyin apologised for his act, "I'm sorry for punching you. Does it still hurt? Your mum must be very cross at me."

"What do you expect? You punched her son right in front of her!"

"And how did you expect me to respond? I was betrayed by my best friend!" defended Samyin.

"I'm sorry; I've wronged you. I was going to tell you, but you found out before I could. I just wanted to give Yuetching some time to get herself prepared. She must have her reasons for not wanting to be found. Finding her was going against her wish. I wanted to hear her reasons first before overwhelming her with our attention."

"I understand. I would have done the same if I were in your position."

"Have you cleared things with her?"

"There is nothing to clear really. The day when you entered this race, I already knew I had lost, but I didn't want to admit it. Still it hurts when this inkling is confirmed to be the reality. It's good to have a clear answer; now I can't live in denial anymore. This will help me move on; I have to. If I'm so generous as to put on my rational hat, you two are very well suited. I mean it and you two have my best wishes."

"Thank you, Samyin."

"This is my turn to say to you: if you don't treat her well, you know whom you need to be accountable for! I'm on her side and I'm not going to let you off easily. Don't say that I haven't forewarned you!"

"I've heard you loud and clear. I'll treat her well; don't worry."

"I have a favour to ask."

"What is it?"

"May I take Yuetching out for a day? Would you grant me that wish, for closure?"

"Why don't you ask her?"

"I've asked her of course, but she says she won't go until I have your permission."

Chisau burst into laughter, "What did she say?"

"You've heard me! Although you haven't yet married, you already behave like a married couple. What am I to say?"

"This is very good news for me," Chisau was enjoying his new status in her life.

"So may I?"

"Yes, you may for one day only as an exception, but you may not kiss her."

"You need not worry; I don't think she would let me even if I try!"

12 Towards a Perfect New Beginning

Ding dong, ding dong, ding dong…. Yuetching was woken up by the noisy doorbell. She fumbled for her phone by her bed to find out the time; it's only seven in the morning. She put the phone down and went back to sleep.

Ding dong, ding dong, ding dong…

Half asleep and half awake, she thought it did not sound like her alarm. It was the doorbell. Who could it be so early? She wondered. She got out of bed to check the door, and found out who woke her up through the spyhole.

"Ding dong, ding dong, ding dong…." the call was not going to relent!

Reluctantly Yuetching opened the door and let in an unusually energetic and eager Samyin. As soon as he walked in, he greeted, "Good morning, these are for you!" He presented a lovely bouquet of roses to Yuetching.

Yuetching was bemused, "The reason why you woke me up so early is to give me roses?"

"Yes, but no, this is *not* the only reason. We have only this one day together; I wish I could have more but you've turned me down. This day is special but time is limited. This makes every minute and every second precious."

Samyin had a gift to make all the girls feel special. Although he said this jokingly, Yuetching finally began to think Samyin might be sincere at the same time. She accepted the flowers and said, "Thank you, but you shouldn't have –" Samyin

375

put his finger on her lips to stop her from carrying on with what she was about to say.

Instead, he said, "Today let me indulge myself and be very selfish. Today let me bring you to places that I have wanted to bring you, do things that I have wanted to do with you, and treat you in the way that I have wanted to treat you. I've been in love with you for so long that I've dreamt up many places I want to bring you and things to show you. I have to really select in order to squeeze everything in one day. This isn't for you, but for me. Would you kindly accommodate my wish just for today?"

This request took Yuetching by surprise. She thought they were just going out to have a meal and a movie like most couples did.

"May I?" Samyin entreated. Yuetching nodded to agree.

Samyin gave her the brightest smile to show his heart's delight! He hurried her, "Now, go and wash and get changed quickly. I will be waiting here."

By then, Yuetching was totally awake and her cheeky self returned. She eyed Samyin from head to toes, making him feel most uncomfortable, "Why are you eyeing me?"

"Nothing," replied Yuetching, thrusting the roses back to him.

"Why? Are you returning the flowers to me?" protested Samyin.

"Since when have you become so slow? I'm going in to get ready really quickly. Please take care of the beautiful flowers. We don't want them to die through our neglect, do we?"

Samyin laughed once he understood what Yuetching meant, "Understood now, Miss Secretary!"

Yuetching was ready in ten minutes. It was Samyin's turn to eye her from head to toes! She was in casual wear and trainers, matching him perfectly. Suddenly he realised what she was doing a while ago, "You were eyeing me up and down to find out what to wear?"

"What do you think? I've no idea what you've planned for today! How else do I know what to wear? Let's go; there is no time to lose." Samyin just liked her spirit – once she agreed with your goal, she would help you with total commitment!

After a simple breakfast, they were on the go. She did not ask any questions about where they were going. This was against her nature, but today she wanted to trust Samyin totally. Even though the day ahead was completely unknown to her, she was not anxious like she would have been. Instead, she had peace. Not only that, she was even excited! She was excited about discovering who Samyin really was by following the steps he was going to take her. All she had to do was to trust him, be patient and obedient.

Yuetching had been staring out of the window without saying anything. This reminded Samyin of the first time he gave her a ride, which made him smile.

"What's so funny? Have I got some crumbs on my face from breakfast?" she guessed, rubbing her mouth with her hand.

"Your face is clean; there is nothing to wipe! I'm only thinking about the first time I gave you a ride, how you silently stared out of the window just like now. You even sat in the passenger seat to avoid me. Now even when we spend time in silence, I don't feel uneasy anymore. Would you say this is an improvement?"

"……"

"Do you know you are a person whom people can read like a book? You are honest with your likes and dislikes and why. To know you, all people need to do is to hover around you and observe carefully. The reason why you have no friends apart from Chisau and me is because you have deliberately been shutting people out and never let anyone get close to observe you and in turn to know you."

"Wrong, no one was really interested until you and Chisau came along."

"Wrong, I'm sure that this was only *your assumption*."

"If I'm plain to know, all the more I should keep a distance from people in order to protect myself."

"Have you regretted that I get to know you a little?"

"Of course not. I'm *honoured* to be known by you!"

They stopped at a nature park. It was greeneries for as far as one could see. The lake was glittering under the sun, as if countless diamonds were dancing in a party. It was a peaceful surrounding, which worked well to clear one's mind.

Yuetching turned to ask Samyin, "What's so special about this place? Why do you bring me here?"

Samyin was glad that she asked, so he told his story, "When I was 14 years old, I had a crush on a girl two years older than me! One day I followed her all the way to here and discovered that this was the place where she met up with her boyfriend, who was very tall and imposing! From that day onwards, I stopped having a crush on her. Instead, I fell in love with this place. This has then become a special place for me. Whenever I'm unhappy or want to have some time to myself, I come here."

Something was not adding up for Yuetching, so she asked, "This should be a place which made you sad. How come it has become a place to make you feel better?"

"It's precisely because this should be a place which made me sad, but it didn't! This made me realise the healing power of this place on me! How is it? Can you feel it?"

Yuetching closed her eyes and tried to soak up its aura. Then she gave her comment, "Yes, it's calming and peaceful. I like this place. Is this why you have wanted to bring me here?"

"During the period when I was waiting for you indefinitely, I came here often. As time passed, the disquiet in my heart was gradually replaced by an uneasy calm. I couldn't say I was unhappy, but I wasn't happy either. My mood was perfectly reflected by this place – there was no excitement from the hustle and bustle of life, but only a subtle beauty of peace and calm. In this place, I've left a lot of my different emotions about you. Can you feel them?"

Yuetching listened attentively to what was on Samyin's heart. It was heavy as well as sincere. She was cheeky, so she asked, "What were the many different emotions that you've left here about me?"

"Well, first is love of course, then there is anger, sadness, worry, anxiety, frustration, longing, adoration, admiration, compassion, and regrets, lots of them."

"Wow! I had no idea!"

"Have you thought about us?" asked Samyin.

"Of course. But unlike you, I didn't have expectations of restoration. I had decided in my heart that what I had had before was a reality that I could no longer own. I compliantly put that chapter behind as my treasured memories of the sweetest dream I had ever had. I was determined to preserve everything of that dream in a special compartment of my memory."

"Like exhibits in your memory museum?" Samyin conjured up a funny image.

"What a lovely metaphor! Yes, that was my intention to have you as a *treasured* exhibit in my memory museum but no longer!

We have reconnected and you do not exist only in my memory but in my life still!"

"Had it ever crossed your mind to contact us, even if only to say you were safe?"

"Yes it had crossed my mind, but I had not acted on it."

"And you could endure it?"

"I wasn't sure if you cared to know. The world did not revolve around me. Would it be presumptuous of me to assume friendship? What if now you treated me as a real social climber and felt harassed if I called? What if you saw me as an annoying petty fly which wouldn't go away but you were too gentlemen to deter? Both of you are very dear to me but what if it was not reciprocated? Rejection would be too painful for me to cope as I was messed up at the time. I'd rather hide and not know than face the truth! It was cowardice, I know."

"You've suffered," said Samyin with compassion.

Yuetching shook her head, saying, "No, it's not suffering. It's the lesson of love. There is also pain with a heart that is sealed up by ice – pain from the cold and frostbites, not to say loneliness and bitterness! Having someone dear to my heart, I feel I've been healed. Deep down, I thank Chisau and you for giving me an opportunity to learn this lesson."

Samyin nodded to say he understood.

"Let's go. How about we hire a boat to go round the lake?" suggested Samyin, and Yuetching concurred.

They hired a pedal boat to go out, and they stopped in the middle of the lake to soak up the sun, to experience its power to dispel all worries and negative thoughts! Yuetching closed her eyes to enjoy the moment, while Samyin preoccupied with capturing her every move in his memory. He could have used a camera, but he worried that it might make her self-conscious.

"Let's go. It's about time to return the boat," Yuetching reminded. Samyin opened his eyes, and looked at his watch, saying, "How can time run away so quickly?!"

After returning the boat, Samyin suggested, "Let's hire bikes now."

"Is today a sports day? But I'll go along with it."

"This is not to torture you, but cycling is the best way to see the park! Let's go!"

The cycle paths were lined by trees. They cycled fast and there seemed no ends to it! Yuetching enjoyed the feeling of wind brushing her face as they cut across it at full speed. It lightened her spirit as she flew through the air! They took a break beside the stream. Samyin passed some water to her. She took the bottle and was thankful, "You're really well-prepared today, aren't you? You can graduate as a secretary now!"

"Don't tease me. This apprentice is in no comparison with the master!"

After drinking some water, Yuetching was tempted to play in the stream as it looked so clear and pristine! She walked up towards it and stuck her hand in to feel the water. It was cool and clean.

"Look, there is a lot of fish swimming in the stream!" exclaimed Yuetching with excitement. Samyin took out his camera and captured the Yuetching he liked so much from a distance. She took a stride and stood on a rock in the stream. She knelt down and studied all the different shapes and sizes of pebbles! She hopped from one stone to another along the stream, as if it was a game. Then she invited Samyin to join her in a competition to see who could stay on for longer!

Samyin got up and joined in. They were like practising *kungfu* in water with their complicated steps! When they got wobbly on their feet, they turned from being rivals into allies who supported each other in time of crisis! They ended up jumping on to the same rock. When Yuetching slipped and was about to fall, Samyin quickly pulled her back and she landed in his arms, just like the time when he caught her from slipping in the bathtub. They stood so close together that Samyin's heart was pounding. He would have liked to freeze that moment if at all possible!

Samyin let go of her and reminded her, "Please be more careful."

"Let's go back then; it's getting more dangerous now," Yuetching turned back along the way they had come.

They carried on cycling, and stopped in the green this time. Samyin opened his bag, and took out water and lunchboxes, saying, "This is your lunch. I made rice balls for you. Please try."

Stunned, Yuetching expressed her disbelief, "You made these? Did you sleep at all last night?" Samyin returned a smile and did not answer.

Yuetching continued, "You're really spoiling me today! When I'm on my own, I've to plan, pack and carry everything by myself. Today I walk around empty-handed! How carefree!"

Samyin replied pensively, "Then please enjoy being spoilt. After today, you won't have the chance to be spoilt by me anymore. Let's me try my best to treat you well today."

"What do you mean by this? Are you going away?" Yuetching sensed sadness in his tone.

Samyin pretended to be normal, and said, "Of course not. After today, Chisau won't let me take you out again. He was very clear, you know? There'll be no exception after today."

"Is that really what it is?" Yuetching was suspicious.

"Yes, that is it," Samyin tried to reassure her. To distract her, he said, "Although I look normal on the outside, you must remember I'm currently nursing a broken heart from losing the girl I like to someone else. I try my best to look as if nothing has happened, so as not to make you and Chisau feel bad. But that doesn't mean that I feel nothing inside. Give me some time, and I'll feel better."

"Samyin….."

Samyin cleared his throat and continued, "Sorry, I've indulged myself again. I shouldn't have become a burden on your relationship with Chisau. Sorry."

Samyin looked at Yuetching and gave her a smile to reassure her, "I'm fine, really. Now eat your lunch."

Yuetching took time to study Samyin's handiwork before eating it. It was very tasty and prettily presented too. Samyin was delighted! After lunch, he asked, "Let's race, from here to the tree over there." He was pointing at the proposed finishing point.

Yuetching pretended not to see, "Which one?"

"That one, over there," Samyin tried to point it out more clearly.

"Which one exactly? How can I run with a full stomach? It's not recommendable."

Samyin realised that Yuetching was making fun of him, so he said, "I'll start. You can sit here and lose."

Yuetching of course would not lose without a fight, so she got up to race. But in the end, they did not seriously race. Rather it was more like a game of catch and they used the trees to dodge the other person. They laughed heartily like kids in the playground.

Yuetching was the one who surrendered, declaring that she

was too tired to run any more. They sat down by the bikes and panted for breath.

Having rested a while, Samyin said, "Let's go and return the bikes now."

"Are we leaving now?" Yuetching was surprised they were leaving so soon, given how anxious Samyin was to start early.

"This is only the first stop of the day," Samyin disclosed.

"What?"

Samyin stood up and pulled her to get up too. "Come on, let's go. It's a long way back."

"I can't move."

"Even if your body really can't move, I'm sure you can *will* yourself to do it. I've seen you apply your super will-power time and time again in work situations. You can't trick me."

Yuetching was struck by how well Samyin had grown to know her too. She could not argue against something so blatantly true about her, so she had to get up and go as told!

After returning the bikes, they sat down by the lake for a rest.

"I've decided to move my castle in the clouds from Disneyland to here," Yuetching muttered, as she grew more attached to this lake.

"What did you just say?" Samyin did not quite catch it.

"I said, 'I've decided to move my castle in the clouds from Disneyland to here.' I feel the ambience here matches my castle better."

Samyin was elated by Yuetching's decision, even though it concerned only about her imaginary world! "Do you really like this place that much?"

Yuetching nodded hard in proportion to how much she liked it. Samyin could not stop smiling.

"Are your dates always so physical?" asked Yuetching.

Samyin shook his head and replied, "No. This is the first time."

"Really?"

"When I dated girls in the past, I was always afraid that they might be bored. So, I always packed the date with all kinds of entertainment, which often took the focus away from each other. Perhaps deep down, I lacked the confidence. Afraid of rejection, I tried hard to please the date and lost myself. Looking back now, these pleasure-seeking dates were not defining."

Samyin turned towards Yuetching and continued, "My time spent with you has made me realise that getting to know someone deeply isn't through entertainment. From now on, when I date someone, I'll bring her to this kind of place to see if we can hear the voice of our hearts and minds."

Yuetching then recalled, "Chisau has said before, you've probably dated many but have never been serious. It sounds as though this is true."

"What? Chisau teased me in front of you?"

"No, not like that. He didn't mean any harm. It was his inference from what you had told him about me. He told me on ----Island," explained Yuetching.

He looked away and sighed, "That day was the biggest regret in my life so far! I've asked myself 'what ifs': What if you didn't wash the bathtub for me, what if you didn't slip, what if I didn't try to kiss you. What if I could have a chance to confess my feelings for you, what if the candle-lit dinner went as planned, what if there was no four months of focusing on work before the Annual Meeting? Would I have stood a chance when Chisau was still your cousin? If we were a couple before you knew you were not Chisau's cousin, we would probably still be together and unaffected by the truth surrounding your birth." Samyin turned to face Yuetching again, "Would we?"

Yuetching thought that it was just a mental exercise, and did not expect Samyin would really direct the question at her!

"Would that be a possibility?" Samyin reiterated his question; he wanted an answer from Yuetching, who was caught up with the awkwardness.

"Those actually were not the critical points in my decision."

"But I felt we had wasted so much time."

"The critical point in my decision was your sister's engagement party."

"How come?"

"The waltz; and I knew something about my feeling."

"Well, then I should ask, what if I danced with you then, and not Chisau?"

"Yeah, that might be the turning point. Sorry for sounding formal here," Yuetching lectured, "but asking 'what ifs' about our past is a hypothetical exercise we derive to learn from our mistakes. The focus is on influencing the future by avoiding the same mistakes, and not on rewriting our history. My experience has told me that what's in the past has already happened. Asking 'what ifs' won't change it; rather it works to torment us even more. To the series of 'what ifs' you ask me, I hold no answers, and I won't start thinking up the answers for you either. You'll need to go to a parallel universe to find out."

Samyin reluctantly nodded to acknowledge Yuetching's wisdom, and reiterated after her, "The focus is on the future and not the past. I'll try to learn this lesson well, and hope I can do it! We should get going now for our next stop."

"To where?"

"Dinner. By the time we get back to town, it'll be dinner time."

Samyin drove Yuetching back to the city and parked the car. They walked along the street and stopped in front of a restaurant. He quizzed Yuetching, "Do you remember this place?"

"Of course I remember. This is where we had Korean Barbeque."

"That's the first time we had dinner together. Am I right in thinking that you like the food?"

"Yes, you're right. I haven't been back since, I like that you bring me back here tonight."

"Then let's go in. I've already reserved a table."

After they had settled to eat, Samyin asked, "Do you remember anything special about the day we came here last time?"

Yuetching scratched her head but still could not work it out.

Samyin reached out and took hold of Yuetching's left hand. He opened up her palm and used his forefinger to trace the scar, saying, "This is the answer. You had six stitches the night before. I asked you if you're angry at Sinyin. You said, no, your injury was not her fault; the fault was in your faulty equation in situation assessment. Do you know why I remember that day so well?"

Yuetching shook her head. Then Samyin revealed, "While most people are quick to see faults in others, you are the opposite. That was the day when I began to see you as a very special girl." He let go of her hand and they carried on eating.

Samyin paused for thought, and then asked another question, "Do you remember the huge snow-white bear I won for you?"

"Of course! I took it with me when I left."

"When you received it as a gift, you were so happy that you had tears sparkling in your eyes. I was surprised why you're moved to such an extent by a common thing like this. You said that was because you hadn't had one before. At that moment, my heart melted for you. These are my fond memories of our time together. They all happened on the same day as I brought you here. I hope this place brings you fond memories too."

"That day," Yuetching joined in the reminiscence, "That day, my impression of you was changed too! You talked about your dream and your passion for architecture. I saw another side of you. From that day on, I started sketching buildings!"

"Really?" It's the first time Samyin heard of that.

"Yes."

Then there was silence. In the end, it was Yuetching who broke the silence, "Why are we reminiscing? The atmosphere is poignant and makes me feel uncomfortable. We still have many opportunities to meet and dine in the future. It's not as if today was the last day we saw each other."

Samyin forced a smile. She had sensed the truth – after today, he didn't know when they would meet again. But Samyin did not tell her. After today, he would tell Chisau his future plan and Chisau would naturally tell her. But for today, he did not want goodbye to taint the happy atmosphere.

"Let's eat up quickly. We have our final stop," Samyin hurried.

"What? We still have one more stop. I thought we're going home after dinner."

"No way am I letting you go home so early!"

"Where else can we go?"

"If you want to know, then eat faster!"

After dinner, Samyin brought Yuetching to a dance practice room. Yuetching was baffled and hadn't a clue why.

"Why here?" asked Yuetching.

"Do you remember you owe me a dance? Ever since Huentung's engagement party, I've been looking forward to waltzing with you. This was before I even knew about the significance of that missed opportunity in my chance with you. Would you be kind enough to grant my wish?" Samyin entreated.

Yuetching hesitated, and didn't want to, "Samyin...."

"That day, you left without a word. Originally I was full of expectations but it turned out to be my last memory of you before you disappeared from our life. You didn't say goodbye and gave no explanation. You vanished without a trace. Do you know how hard it was for all those you left behind to cope with an unannounced separation like that? I had so much to say but suddenly I had no chance to say it; it was as if I had to swallow every word I wanted to say back into my stomach. I had a lot of feelings but couldn't express. They were all bottled up inside my heart. One minute we were having so much fun dancing, whereas complete darkness and total silence engulfed us the next. The two states were so extreme that for all those who were affected by your decision, we had trouble in finding a response, let alone coping with it. I didn't know if I should ask myself to wait or not to wait. The longer we didn't hear from you, the more heartless you appeared to us. I was smouldered, and the pain in my heart was unbearable. You didn't owe me just a dance; you owed me an answer, which I had been waiting for months on end. Do you remember? You left without telling me one way or another. It was as if my life was suspended in mid-air, and I couldn't find anywhere to rest my feet. I believe this probably was the most selfish and coward decision you had ever made! I asked myself if I should set myself a limit: I would wait for you up to a certain date, after which I waited no more. I just had to live as if I had never met you or you had disappeared from the face of the earth! But you had left indelible marks in my life. How could I erase ALL my memories of you? It was impossible. Then I returned back to the state of waiting for you. On the surface, everything was back to normal but in my heart, there was always a chip, with an unfinished business being held up in suspense."

Sad for inflicting so much pain on him, Yuetching could find no words to say, except "Sorry". She began to sob, and Samyin was startled by her reaction. Was he too harsh on her? Everything that he said was true. He just wanted a listener. This was not supposed to be an accusation against her.

Yuetching could not stop crying. Up till now, she was always the one who was hurt. This was probably the first time she hurt someone dear to her through her action. Samyin felt bad about making Yuetching cry so much. He had not expected what he said would have such an impact on her. He went over and embraced her in his arms. He tried to comfort her, "Don't be silly. Why are you crying? If Chisau knows I make you cry, I'll be in deep trouble again!"

"So – r – ry, I – have – p – pained you. Woo…. wooo….. wooo…"

"Don't be like that. This isn't a charge against you. I'm grateful to you for spending a whole day with me, walking a bit of the path that I've walked, giving me an opportunity to say what I've wanted to say and to express my feelings that I've wanted to express. I'm much better now. I feel that my heart is not knotted up anymore. Giving this chapter a proper closure helps a great deal in achieving that. It was fortunate that I had waited for only eight months till you returned, that you've returned safe and sound, and that I can see you again. Having spent today with you, I'm content and can go away happily. I don't need to wait for you anymore, and I've got my answer. Although you've wounded me, it's been through you that I get healed also! Now I've only one wish remaining, which is the opportunity to dance with you. Would you grant me my last wish?"

Yuetching nodded to agree, and began to calm down.

After she had calmed, she said, "I don't know if I can still dance. I'm afraid I might have returned everything I learnt that evening to the instructor!"

"Don't worry, we could practise first. Let's get changed."

"What?"

Samyin took Yuetching to the locker, from which he pulled out two outfits in bags. The long one he passed to Yuetching, who opened up the zip and found the evening gown she wore at Huentung's engagement banquet! She looked surprised as well as puzzled, so Samyin explained, "Although I can't book the banquet hall at the Hotel for tonight, I hope to see you in the gown, and have my memory refreshed!"

She was moved.

They went their separate ways to get changed. When they met again in the practice room, they were transformed into a lady and a gentleman! Yuetching felt awkward in such a gown now, but Samyin reassured her that she looked just fine, actually not just fine, but perfect if she stopped fidgeting!

Samyin switched on the music and returned quickly to Yuetching, whispering, "This is practice."

387

Samyin had been practising a lot for today, so he could teach and lead her. After three trials, it began to feel familiar.

"Shall we dance?" Samyin invited.

Yuetching took a deep breath and replied, "Yes."

Samyin went to set the music and quickly slid back to get into position. He bowed and Yuetching curtsied. Then they moved towards each other, with Yuetching's hand into his and his arm round her waist. They gazed at each other and were ready to waltz.

Finally the moment I have been waiting for is here, thought Samyin.

I wish to pour out my blessings to you through this dance, thought Yuetching.

The music began to play. Samyin was so familiar with the steps that he did not need to think consciously of what he was doing. Instead, he could focus on feeling and absorbing every second of this magical moment. His confident lead was making it easy for Yuetching; she too could relax and enjoy the moment. Soon they left the reality and travelled to their fantasyland. A rigid, dull practice room became a sumptuous ballroom and they were the protagonists in this fairytale. For Samyin, Yuetching tried her best in playing the part and put her heart into the dance. Samyin on the other hand felt he was dancing on cloud nine! For this moment only, let him believe that they were a couple happy together, and let him express freely his admiration for this girl in his arms through the dance.

The music drew to a close. They observed the usual etiquette in finishing the dance, so as to wrap up this memory with a perfect seal. Both laughed heartily as both had a magical time. Samyin held Yuetching's hand tightly and expressed his gratitude, "Thank you very much for granting my wish. I feel content now."

But as the music stopped, his dream came to an end. Just like Cinderella, when midnight struck, Yuetching had to leave and could not stay in his arms. That was really the end. He indulged himself once more in saying, "If we had been together before Chisau entered the race, would it be possible that we were still together?" It was not a question but a thought. Yuetching did not answer; she just continued to smile sweetly.

Finally this day had soon turned into a day of the past! No matter how much Samyin packed into this day, it was still not long enough. He stopped the car in front of Yuetching's apartment block. She was fast asleep. She must have been exhausted and Samyin felt bad in waking her! No matter how reluctant he was, he had to go back to the reality. He woke her up gently, helped her get into her apartment and settle her in bed. Once she touched the bed, she fell asleep again. Samyin tucked her in, and whispered to her, "Goodbye. You have to live well." Then he walked away from her with sorrow.

In the following morning, Samyin went to see Chisau early in his office.

"Surprised to see you at this hour," greeted Chisau. "Did you have a good time with Yuetching yesterday? Where did you go and what did you do? Please report everything in details!" Chisau jested with him.

But Samyin did not seem to be in the mood to jest. He walked up to Chisau and took the seat in front of his desk. He forced a smile and said in a serious tone, "Thank you for granting me the permission to have one day with her. It felt really good to have a proper closure on this and now I can move on." Samyin put a letter on the desk and slid it in front of Chisau.

"What's this?" Somehow Chisau could already guess what it was!

"My resignation."

"Why?"

"Why? I believe you know why. Please don't ask me to stay or try to change my mind. Just let me go."

"Samyin –" Chisau started and then stopped, knowing that he would only make it difficult for him. Instead, he asked, "Where are you going and what are you going to do?"

"I'm going to America, and return to the company where I did my internship. My performance mustn't be that bad, as they're happy to hire me again after a good number of years. It's a good thing to pick up my dream again. Let's see if I can be as dedicated as before and hopefully achieve something. You should feel happy for me. Don't see this decision as a sad ending but a challenging new beginning and a blessing! Understand?"

"Samyin –"

"I don't want to hear any tear-jerking stuff from you. Let me send you blessing for your future; take good care of the Hotel AND Yuetching for me, will you?"

"I'll try my best. But without you around, looking after the Hotel will be much harder work on my own! When are you setting off?"

"I'm leaving tomorrow."

"What? So soon!"

"Don't be so surprised. I've been planning it for a while, just that I haven't said anything until now. Today, the removal company will come to clear my apartment, and then I'll spend my last night here and fly tomorrow."

"And you think we'll let you go in this manner?" protested Chisau.

"I don't want any farewell party."

"At least, we should have a meal together. You can even stay overnight at my place. How can I let you leave as if you had no friends who care? I can't do that."

"I've said my goodbye to Yuetching yesterday."

"You've told her?"

Samyin shook his head, clarifying, "I've said my goodbye, but she doesn't know."

"What's it then, a unilateral goodbye? This doesn't count; this isn't fair."

"I wish to be on my own tonight."

"If it isn't a sad ending, why go in such a sad manner?"

"I haven't been sleeping much in the past few days. I'm looking forward to resting tonight," Samyin was finding excuses.

"Samyin –"

"I'm leaving now. I need to go back for the removal company. I've already cleared my office and I hope that I've left it in order for whoever is going to take over." He stood up and stretched out his hand, "We'll definitely see each other again. Take care and send my regards to Granddad and Auntie. Finally, thank you for everything."

Chisau stood up and shook his hand, saying, "No, I should be the one who thanks you! You take care of yourself too. Keep in touch."

Samyin nodded to say that he would. While he walked out of Chisau's office, he realised he was walking out of the Hotel where he had worked for four years, and the part of his life which he had shared with Yuetching. At the same time, he was opening his steps towards a new milestone in life.

After Samyin had left, Chisau tried to call Yuetching to pass on the news, but she was not answering! Chisau therefore sent her a text before starting his busy day ahead!

Yuetching slept through the night and morning till noon! She was exhausted from yesterday's activities while there was no pressure to get up! This was the joy of not having a job – for a while. She was still in yesterday's outfit! She got up, had a shower, and then had something to eat. After lunch, she went to search for her phone in her bag. Only then did she see Chisau's text: *Samyin handed in his resignation this morning. Tomorrow he'll fly to America, and return to his previous architectural company. Today he stays at home and oversees the removal.* She was stunned by this message, but it started to make sense to her. She grabbed her bag and ran out of the door like a flying arrow! She was in such a hurry that she waved down a taxi and did not even consider public transport; she wanted to see him NOW!

The removal men had just left, leaving an impersonal space as defined by the four walls. Seeing a home emptied out was eerie. All that was left in his apartment was his luggage. He was not thinking about the time or anything in particular. Rather he let his mind wander and fall into a reverie. It glowed with a warm feeling about family, friendships, team spirit and love.

Yuetching arrived in a rush and found the front door wide open. She walked in and found Samyin standing in the middle of the lounge. She ran to him, clasped his waist and burst into tears! Her reaction came as a complete surprise to Samyin.

"What's wrong? What has happened? You've never hugged me. What have I done now to deserve such attention and favour?" Samyin tried to make Yuetching laugh, but she did not find it funny!

"Don't go! Who says you can go …..woo … woo …woo…"

Samyin had never seen Yuetching behaving in such an emotional way towards him. She cried like a little girl who didn't care about decorum or etiquette. She cried so honestly and without any restrictions that Samyin was touched by her naked emotions as well as finding her rather cute.

"Yuetching, why are you like this? I've never seen you like this before. Tell me, little girl, what has upset you so much to make you cry like this?"

"I don't know what kind of feeling this is. I only know that I'm sad to see you go. It's the same feeling when my parents left me behind on the beach and never return. It's like someone who is very close is leaving me. You can't go – let alone sneaking away without even saying goodbye! Woo .... woo ... woo ...."

Yuetching tightened her hold on him! Only then did Samyin believe he was indeed a special person in her life. He suddenly remembered he was among the four photos displayed in her new home, a little gesture that could have been easily overlooked! It suddenly dawned on him that those four pictures represented the closest people in her life, and he was one of them! How could he have slighted Yuetching's gesture when it meant a world to her! Although he could not be her lover, he seemed to have become her brother! Because she had lost so much and so many people before, she had come to cherish everything and everyone in her life. He found life was such an irony sometimes! The one who originally played the role as her brother had become her lover; the one who could have been her lover now had become a brother to her! Chisau's and his roles had been fatefully swapped! But at least he found comfort in that finally Yuetching could be true to him without any reservations!

At that moment, Chisau walked into Samyin's apartment, and saw them embracing each other. He stopped where he was, so as to give them some space.

Samyin tried to coax Yuetching, "Yuetching, don't cry. Brother and sister don't have to be together all the time. Even when they're apart, it doesn't mean that they cease to be brother and sister. Look at Huentung and me. After we have grown up, we're rarely in the same place. Even if I'm in America, we'll still meet up, and I'll still care about you. If you're in deep trouble and need my help, I'll be by your side. Or if Chisau doesn't treat you well, I'll go and fight on your behalf. But when things are normal, you must let me chase my dream. Weren't you the one who encouraged me to do so in the first place? Do you remember you once asked me, 'How about five years later? Would you go back and chase your dream?' Now I'm going back to start from the bottom again, and I'll live out your spirit towards life and work, which I admire. I hope to do you proud. Will you give me your blessing?"

Yuetching was listening. She began to understand her emotions more. Samyin was surprisingly quick in working it all out! He really did know her. She began to calm down, as the strong feeling of being abandoned ebbed and she understood that this kind of separation was only normal. Samyin let go of her and wiped her tears dry. At the corner of his eyes, he caught Chisau standing by the door. As their eyes met, Chisau walked forward to greet them.

Full of compassion, Chisau comforted Yuetching, "Look at you. You must be feeling very sad that Samyin's leaving us."

"How come you're here?" asked Samyin.

"Do you seriously believe that I'll let you sneak away quietly? I've come here to see if I could help with anything, and to kidnap you so that we can send you off properly. Any objection?"

Samyin laughed.

He walked over to his luggage and fetched a file and the car key.

He came to Yuetching and asked, "Miss Secretary, may I trouble you one last time?"

"Of course."

"These are the documents concerning this move. When I find a place in America, and have an address, will you be happy to liaise with the removal company for the delivery should I need someone at this end?"

Yuetching nodded, "Yes, no problem."

"This is for my little sister Yuetching," Samyin put the car key in her hand, "Please look after my car for me, so that I can have a car to use whenever I come back to visit! You have to drive it every now and again, understand? In fact, how about never to take buses again? Use it as much as you can! It'll be more convenient for you."

"Samyin, I can't accept this." She tried to return the key to him.

Samyin closed the key into her hand, and said, "Keep it. Please don't say no on this one. It's not worth that much. It may cost you even more to maintain it. I'm doing it as a bargain here! Will you do this as a favour for me?"

Yuetching therefore accepted it.

"That's good. Let's go now."

That was how Samyin didn't manage to spend the night on his own. Instead he was surrounded by his two best friends in the world and a lot of laughter. So he did not close this chapter with a sad ending.

After finding a job, Yuetching's life was back on track with a regular routine and responsibilities. Chisau was not used to her not being by his side or being so busy that he could not see her often. He also complained that she lived too far away, making it even more difficult to meet up. Together with the fact that Samyin had gone, Chisau's desire to hire her back at the Hotel was even stronger. But Yuetching refused his offer every time.

Sinyin was a transformed character and continued her music career. She made no pretence in front of the public, and to her surprise, she gained another and even more loyal following. She and Yuetching were reconciled. Although they were not the best of friends, they were on good terms. She was genuinely happy for Chisau, if not also a little jealous, that they were finally an item, after all the difficulties. To promote her latest album, she gave a concert, to which Yuetching took Chisau. This was to help him fulfil his role as "an onlooker who had no demand on her but to admire her elegant flight high up in the sky from the ground"! After the concert, Sinyin left the country to explore work possibilities abroad.

Yuetching also returned to visit Auntie Cheung. People had asked how she could have forgiven her. She did not at first but neither did she rule it out as a possibility. She wanted to give both of them a chance. She went back to see her in order to get to know her. That day Auntie Cheung served her tea and a slice of homemade cake! The cake was so exquisite that she had never tasted anything quite like it before! Auntie Cheung told her that she worked as an apprentice in a famous bakery for many years in her youth and in her years overseas she continued to learn the art in Paris! This discovery about her inadvertently united them in a project. Yuetching brought her to the Hotel, and asked the permission for her to use the kitchen to bake. She made a few cakes for the Hotel chefs to try, and they were impressed. Armed with this recommendation, Yuetching suggested Auntie Cheung to sell her little store, moved to the city and started her own bakery. The business picked up really well and quickly exceeded everyone's expectation! Fame was a funny thing that caught on like fire and then grew on itself. A long queue outside the bakery was now a common sight. Together with orders from hotels, Auntie Cheung had to hire extra hands and started an apprentice scheme herself! She remained an auntie to Yuetching and nothing more.

As expected, Granddad found it impossible to accept

Yuetching's background. Her insistence not to split the family meant that Chisau had to learn patience from her! Secretly Granddad was very happy to see her back into their life and enjoyed their visit every time. The gloom of death that had been overhanging the family for so long was dispelled by the joy that Yuetching brought. Granddad was pleased that his blunder with her did not seem to spiral out into more regrets in life. He could not deny the fact that he was very fond of her as a person! Puiyin added to their voice, "How long do you want the youngsters to wait? If you are sincere in your sorry for what happened to *muimui*, then you should not stand in the way of their marriage now. Are you denying my happiness in seeing my son get married too?" When Auntie Cheung redeemed herself with a promising bakery business, he grabbed it as a good excuse to soften his stance and finally approved the marriage between Chisau and Yuetching!

So this was how two and a half years came to pass. Chisau and Yuetching were busy getting ready for their wedding. Giving Yuetching a proper status was also the only way to get her back at the Hotel to assist him. Samyin returned especially for their wedding. They were excited to meet his fiancé for the first time.

"This is Dung Yiksze," Samyin introduced.

"Many congratulations on your engagement! Nice to meet you, Miss Dung... how did you two meet?" asked Yuetching.

"We met the first time at the bus stop near the Hotel after Huentung and Chunshek's engagement party.... I subsequently went to the States to study. When Chunshek and Huentung came to visit Samyin, Chunshek came to visit me too. This was how Samyin and I got to meet again in America, and discovered that we actually lived quite close to each other! This is *yuenfan*," answered Yiksze, glowing with happiness.

At their reunion, judging by the fact that Samyin could not stop talking about architecture, Yuetching knew he was happy and had made the right choice. Chisau sincerely invited him back to take charge of the new hotel project on ---- Island.

"I've shown them your sketch of the new hotel all the way back then, remember?" Yuetching added.

Obviously tempted, Samyin replied, "Maybe you can consider hiring my architectural firm?" As if she could foretell the future, Yuetching passed back his car key to him, saying, "Yes, come back to 'make visible the space we can't see' for us.

Your car is waiting for its rightful owner."

On her wedding day, Yuetching, along with Puiyin, had her hair set and makeup done by the Hotel beauticians. Huentung made a trip back specifically to be her maid-of-honour. Among the guests were also Tony, her only childhood friend she did not remember initially, and his wife. On her wedding day, Yuetching put on the jewellery set that Puiyin had been keeping for her. When this was first given to her as a birthday present, her identity was a little mixed up. But on this day, there was no doubt about who she was or rather who she was going to become! No one could barge in and said that she was only pretending to be a modern-day Cinderella! This was because this day was *not* a fairytale, but her reality. This day, when she walked down the aisle, she stepped out with the confidence that Chisau had expended years and much effort to nurture with love and care. She was no longer embarrassed by her birth, upbringing or her background. She did not mind how others would see her. Instead, she found her courage to be herself in meeting with new people and relate to others. In her life, there was nothing to hide! How liberating! And in her world, it was full of colours and warmth. She felt she was home at last, and she was never going to run away. This day, she stepped out with confidence into the role that had been prepared for her at the outset. And to the mother who died to save her life, she could heartily respond by saying, "Thank you for my blessed life!"

Auntie Cheung sent her blessing in the form of a personally designed wedding cake for the couple! Thanks to Yuetching, she had found a niche through which her talent could shine and contribute to the society. It gave her a sense of pride that she had never had before, fulfilling her father's dying wish for her to live with decency and dignity as a woman. At the wedding, Yuetching invited her to take photos together. To decide where to place her, the photographer asked the bride, "How is this lady related to you?" Yuetching blabbed out, "She's my mother." Once that came out of her mouth, everyone was shocked, including Yuetching herself. But this was the truth, admit it or not, like it or not, a bad mother or not, and Yuetching could not say otherwise. She realised that as she had worked hard on people not to judge her by her past, who was she to judge her mother by her past? Auntie Cheung was so moved that she burst into tears! Yuetching went over and gave her a hug, whispering softly in her ears, "Don't cry, mother." On hearing that call, Auntie Cheung cried even more.

At last, Yuetching was officially a member of the Lee family as Granddad's granddaughter, not as the daughter of Lee Oiyee but as the wife of Lee Chisau. She was no longer a transparent member of the crowd. After they were married, Yuetching went back to Hotel to assist Chisau, finally taking on Samyin's challenge to her, which was to put into practice her vision to benefit others from the platform she was given.

At times life looks so broken that we believe it can be perfect no more. But working through brokenness in life can be a way of perfecting, leading us to a higher perfection that lifts us up from the abyss of darkness, battles with our worst demons and wins, and conquers hopelessness with the Morning Star of hope, leaving us to fear not.

The End

Epilogue: From the Author

The worth of a fiction is not in its realism but in the message it conveys and in its artistry of conveying it. Assuming that you do not read the book back to front but have come to this point as the natural course of the book has taken you, I wonder if you have enjoyed it or it has invited your scorn. Do you think it's naïve as it reads like a fairytale with an element of being too good to be true? I wonder what your overriding impression of the book is. Would it be sarcasm because it is unreal and therefore untrue, indifference because it is unrepresentative of reality and your way of thinking, irrelevance because it speaks of yesteryears' values, or resonance because you hear echoes in your own life, encouragement because it convinces you of your own beliefs and longing because it gives words to your heart's desires that you have been unable to word?

There are two levels of reading a novel – what the story means to you and what the author tries to say. The former focuses directly on what you take away from the work and enjoy it or not for your pleasure, having little or no regard for the author's existence or intention. In contrast, the latter requires you to make a connection with the author's mind in order to distil the message from her words. In today's fast pace life, most often we are content with adopting the first approach to consume a novel as the latter approach takes more effort. It is also possible that the author's intention may be inaccessible to you even if you try because her experience is not shared with yours and as such, there is no common ground for you work it out. I fear that this may be the case with some of you.

This novel has been ten years in the making and has gone through four or five revisions before it reaches you. There has been no epilogue until now. A handful of friends have read the earlier versions. To one, the key theme of the story was forgiveness. (Perhaps it was a difficult subject for her in her life.) She asked why I did not tell reader where to find the forgiveness as seen in the novel. It is indeed my intention of your reading of this work to challenge yourself if you wish your life to be any different from how it has been, to help you see light in the most impossible situations and to help you desire something better than you think possible. If my novel has worked as intended with you, it is only natural for you to ask me the same question as my friend did. I realise not to point you to the source of life would make this work a cruel mockery. It would be unloving to leave my seeking reader dangling in mid-air with nowhere to rest your feet; I cannot treat you in this way. Therefore telling you the foundation on which every word of this work is built is to make it complete. In this epilogue, I am breaking the enigma of an author and her creative process by explaining this work to you because I weigh that your eternal salvation is far more important than guarding my author's aloofness!

The Morning Star of hope is Jesus Christ of the Bible.

It excels all other stars in brightness, and is the forerunner of the day.

He launched His earthly ministry by proclaiming that these words of prophecy in the Scriptures have been fulfilled in Him:

> *The Spirit of the Lord is upon me,*
> *because he has anointed me*
> *to proclaim good news to the poor.*
> *He has sent me to proclaim liberty to the captives,*
> *and recovering of sight to the blind,*
> *to set at liberty those who are oppressed,*
> *to proclaim the year of the Lord favour* (Luke 4:18-19).

I wrote this story primarily as an act of worship, to give Him glory for who He is, as manifested in His work and His great love for us. (Good intention however does not necessarily imply success in delivering it – I am very aware of my inadequacies compared with Christ's immeasurable excellence and brilliance!) He came to this world to give us the gospel – the good news, and its transforming power is witnessed through the life of Yuetching. Not everyone receives this good news as only *the poor,* as opposed to the proud, are receptive to it.

Most people would find forgiveness difficult, so much so that one friend has said that it is a supernatural act. But unforgiveness is bitter and allows the infliction, whatever it may be, to enslave us for as long as we cannot forgive. We are trapped and there seems to be no escape. To be able to forgive is to first acknowledge that we ourselves are infinitely greater debtors to God than anyone on earth can be indebted to us by wronging us. To reconcile with anyone on earth is to first be reconciled with God through Christ. If you do not think or know that you have a broken relationship with God, this is evidence that you have sinned against Him. The Bible tells us that *All we like sheep have gone astray; we have turned – every one – to his own way* (Isaiah 53:6*). In the pride of his face, the wicked does not seek him [God]; all his thought are, "There is no God"* (Psalm 10:4). *They have all turned aside; together they have become corrupt; there is none who does good, not even one* (Psalm 14:3). *Transgression speaks to the wicked deep in his heart; there is no fear of God before his eyes* (Psalm 36:1). Whatever you may think about yourself, this is the verdict of God, the Judge, on you – you have sinned against Him because you don't acknowledge Him let alone seek Him or fear Him; instead, you denounce Him, despise or curse Him. From this root sin comes all sins – the sinful deeds. And you are not alone – *for all have sinned and fall short of the glory of God* (Romans 3:23, added emphasis). Therefore, we stand condemned under God's law already and God's justice requires us to face His wrath. Sins make us enemies of God.

The basis for Christian forgiveness is in us being forgiven by God who in His mercy remembers our sins against Him no more. This greatest act of forgiveness does not compromise God's justice as He sent to the world His one and only Son, Jesus Christ, who being divine, took on the likeness of our human nature, was sinless but made sin, to die for us on the cross, take the punishment that our sins deserve, and redeem us from the curse of God's law by being a curse for us. Our debt to God incurred by our sins is paid in full by Christ on the cross, so that we may go free. *For freedom Christ has set us free* (Galatians

5:1). As God's justice is satisfied by Christ's sacrifice, our sins have been dealt with satisfactorily in God's sight (as proved by His resurrection) and as such Christ reconciles us to God. *This is the gate of the LORD; the righteous shall enter through it* (Psalm 118:20).

If you think that your sin against God is nothing, compared with how others have wronged you, this is because in your view, God is too small and insignificant. The extent of our sins is proportionate to the worthiness of whom we sin against and in turn His command in our obligation to treat Him otherwise. Indeed, theologians say that we have committed cosmic treason in our rebellion against God, as we are under infinite obligations to love, honour and obey Him in proportion to His loveliness, honourableness and authority. Eternal damnation is what our sinfulness deserves, but Christ saves us from God's wrath proportionate to our sin. Therefore, in place of justice, we have mercy. Against mercy of such an epic proportion, what injustice can't we afford to bear from the hands of our fellow men when God has forgiven us so much and commanded us to be likewise merciful to others? That we can't forgive is a position held from a moral high ground that we can't claim as we are all sinners and needing God's mercy. Who are we to hold others accountable when God Himself has forgiven their trespasses as ultimately all sins are sins against God – are we in the place of God? God commands us, "love your enemies and be merciful even as I am merciful (Luke 6:36)" and "never to avenge yourself, for vengeance is mine, I will repay (Romans 12:19)." In this sense, forgiveness is indeed a supernatural act. This is what underpinned Yuetching's generous heart towards others and her reasoning for forgiveness is to count the benefits that can flow from it when we obey God's command. It is not the enabler but reflects the truth that when we obey God's law, we will come to see God's practical wisdom too.

Jesus says, "Those who are well have no need of a physician, but those who are sick. I came not to call the righteous, but sinners (Mark 2:17)." Jesus is friend with sinners, *the poor*, whose conscience is afflicted for sin. The proud and the self-righteous see no necessity of Him. There is no forgiveness if there is no repentance. *Repent and be baptised every one of you in the name of Jesus Christ for the forgiveness of your sins* (Acts 2:38). The riches of God's kindness, forbearance and patience are meant to lead us to repentance (Romans 2:4). If you are thinking about how to obtain this forgiveness, it is to repent and put your trust in Christ as your Lord and Saviour. What is repentance? It is turning away from sins, your old life, and turning to Christ, your new life. Repentance starts by saying sorry, not a flippant one to get your way but a genuine one that involves hating what you have done and a desire of undoing it. Likewise, in Yuetching's forgiveness of Granddad, his remorse and his desire to make amends set in motion for it to happen.

That forgiveness is difficult is also because we continue to sustain the hurt and injury that the wrongdoing has inflicted us. Inevitably we are battered living in this sin-cursed world. But God is gracious and He heals His people. God has sent us Christ *to bind up the broken-hearted* (Isaiah 61:1); *The LORD is near to the broken-hearted and saves the crushed in spirit* (Psalm 34:18). There are many examples in the story that tells about healings. That great love of Yuetching's mother who died in order to save her defined who she was and provided the foundation of her self-respect even when the world was slighting her. This unchanging love was the power she drew to never give up. How much greater then is Christ's love for you when He left His eternal throne of ineffable light and glory and came to our world to die for you in order to execute the salvation plan for you? As mind-boggling as it may be, this love of Christ tells us that we are precious in God's sight for we are redeemed at a high price. Not only that, Christ pursues you – He seeks out His own who are lost and not the other way round, and He is persistent. This is mirrored in Chisau seeking out Yuetching at the beginning and how he never gave up looking for her even when she kept running away because to him, she was like a lost sheep without a shepherd. As Jesus waited for the Samaritan woman by the well in John 4, Chisau waited for Yuetching by the columbarium. Yes, this is how Christ has loved us, and we should be very assured in His love and care.

Love can be a very destructive force as seen in Sinyin while love can also heal as in Chisau's and Samyin's love for Yuetching. What is the difference? Sinyin's love for Chisau was selfish – in her love for him, she was really loving only herself; her love looked inwards to herself. The boys' love for Yuetching was the opposite; it looked outwards to the object of their love and tried to nurture her to fulfil her potential, i.e. to become whom God has intended her to be. Their love worked to build her up, not pull her down; it's constructive, not destructive. They loved without demanding what Yuetching could do for them in return. But it did not mean that nothing came back to them in return because love necessarily and naturally prompts response, especially gratitude which can take many different outward expressions. This kind of love is not static but transforming. Samyin landed on this project of nurturing Yuetching because of his situation in life with the Lee's family, at a time when he was not looking for love. As he selflessly wanting the best for Yuetching, he unexpectedly learnt what love really was. Love should bring out the best of you, not the worst, and helps you know and find yourself. The three of them bear this positive influence on each other. Their love was not indulgent but wise and purposeful, mirroring Christ's love for us. Our profession of faith in Him is not the end but the beginning of Him lavishing His love on us. In His hands, we are lifelong projects to be beautified. Yes, having redeemed us, His love is purposeful in making us conform to His beauty standard – in Christian terminology, it is God's will that we are sanctified. Indeed, the Bible talks of Christ's followers (His church) as His bride and He our bridegroom. This is how the bridegroom loves His bride: *Christ loved the church and gave himself up for her, that he might sanctify her, having cleansed her by the washing of water with the word so that he might present the church to himself in splendour, without spot or wrinkle or any such thing, that she might be holy without blemish* (Ephesians 5:25-27). This is Christ's vision of beauty for His bride – *in splendour, without spot or wrinkle or any such thing, that she might be holy without blemish.* While His love is to overflow us with blessings, we need be willing to embrace them by going through the transformation, as Yuetching had promised Chisau, who called her teachable. To love and being loved makes us vulnerable and our independence often stands in the way. Chisau tried to unblock it by appealing to Yuetching to unlearn some of her independence. Our dependence on Christ is total and He is totally dependable. The story ends with the wedding, which is not because it is the typical ending of a fairytale or a romance. Rather it is a scene we see the bride (Yuetching) being presented at her best, having overcome the shadows of her past and blossomed into whom she could be under the nurturing care and love of Chisau. This foreshadows the marriage of Christ and His Church on the Last

Day. Love should not be smothering that drives you away; instead, love should be liberating that makes you want to stay – a homecoming feeling at long last that Yuetching shared at the end.

Love builds on the foundation of promises and commitment, which is to weather the storms. We see a lot of that going between Chisau and Yuetching, who kept repeating that promise is made to keep, not to break. This gives security and assurance especially to Yuetching. God in His grace enters into a covenant relationship with His people and binds Himself to us with all His promises. He is faithful in keeping the promises, which are all "yes" in Christ. He remains faithful even when we are faithless (2 Timothy 2:13). This kind of covenant-based love is very difficult for us to grasp in an age of whimsical love. However imperfect, I hope to capture a bit of that flavour in Chisau's resolve to wait for Yuetching until he was released from his promise by her. It may come across in your eyes as ludicrous (as expressed by Sinyin in the story) but yeah, this is how our long-suffering God has been waiting for you and me to turn back to Him. Not only that, He goes infinitely further than Chisau in that His covenant with us cannot be dissolved; under no circumstances can it ever become void; His love never fails. How He has loved us is absolutely scandalous, immeasurably more so than how Chisau had loved Yuetching especially relative to her lowly upbringing. This truth about Christ will take us a lifetime to contemplate.

Another powerful healing tool of God is the truth. Jesus declares, "*I am the way, and the truth, and the life* (John 14:6)." The truth sets us free from lies and deceptions that we have been led to believe. Truth gives us a solid ground to stand on and puts our footing on a spacious place. It does not lead us to the pit or mire where we have that sinking feeling and feel losing our footing or our grip of life (like in Sinyin's case to contrast Yuetching's). Truth at times is hard to face but in the long run, between a beautiful lie and an ugly truth, the latter will lead us to health while the former death. God's truth has one characteristic that it is internally coherent. In other words, if things do not add up, they are probably not the truth. In Yuetching's journey, there were numerous occasions where hard truth was comforting. Even the final blow turned out to be a blessing and bring healing that Yuetching was grateful for in hindsight. In Christ's healing process, mind as well as heart work together to make us well. Our mind is set to gain knowledge of the truth which our heart believes.

God heals us by His grace, loads of them, and we will notice more when we know Him better. We have to acknowledge that our God is Almighty and Sovereign over all. Chinese may call it *yuenfan* but for believers, we call it God's providence. You may think that the story has a few important coincidences, of which you may question the likelihoods. From our perspective, things may happen by chance but from God's perspective, nothing happens by chance. Things happen according to God's appointed time and His plan, and there are no coincidences. Moreover, He has the power to make amends in our life. I personally think that it was a very sweet thing that God did for Yuetching when she unexpectedly came into possession of the photo collection documenting her childhood which she did not know exist. Having the capacity to enjoy the good things in life is also a blessing that God has intended for us to be received with thanksgiving (1Timothy 4:3-4). Samyin was the person God used to unlock that gift in Yuetching to enjoy her lot in life. There are many more examples in the story which I will leave you to spot.

The only thing that is left for me to say is what to do next if you would like to find out more about Jesus Christ and the gospel.

1. Pray to God, acknowledge Him, repent of your sins and seek His forgiveness, ask Him for guidance; cry out to Him and He will deliver you.

2. Do you have a bible? If not, buy one or download one onto your phone. (The popular version is NIV while I personally use ESV.) Start reading the gospels – Matthew, Mark, Luke and John in the New Testament. There you will encounter Jesus.

3. Do you have a trusted Christian friend whom you can talk to? Call him or her.

4. If you want to explore more on your own first, reading is the best way. Go to, for example, www.10ofthose.com which is a good place to start as it stocks a wide range of Christian materials to help you explore the Christian faith.

5. Find a church, but not just any church. Choose wisely, a church that will tell you what God wants to say to you and

not what you want to hear about God. You want to go to a Christ-centred, Christ-exalting, bible-preaching church, believing in salvation by Christ *alone*, through faith *alone* by grace *alone*, glory to God *alone* and in the authority of the Scriptures *alone*.

That you have read the book this far and the way it has impacted you is no coincidence but God's providence. He has called you, so what is your response? Are you going to run away from Him or are you going to take courage so that you may be healed and be restored to Him? A modern-day Cinderella is not a make-belief but real for any penitent sinners in Christ's love. It sounds too good to be true, because it is and sin is insanity if you come to see it. It would have been like Yuetching never responding to the call of love and in so doing she would have condemned herself to a life of brokenness, bitterness, loneliness and emptiness. Is this not insanity?

As a society, we are increasingly sceptical about happy endings. Feel-good movies have given way to sad endings. Have we become cynical? Have we collectively lost hope and believe that life can be perfect no more?

We are not perfect, and our life is not perfect, by no means, but His way and His purpose are unassailably perfect for all those who put their trust in Him as their Lord and personal Saviour. This was the faith of Yuetching: even when life crumbled, God held her in His hand; she feared not, not because life was plain sailing, but because God was always there to catch her when she fell and brought her back up again. *The steps of a man are established by the LORD, when he delights in his way; though he fall, he shall not be cast headlong, for the LORD upholds his hand* (Psalm 37:23-24). Underpinning the resilience of a tumbler was the strength she drew from the fountain of life.

Therefore life is a celebration, not about ourselves but about Him in the perfect work that He has done and is doing in us. In this context our "secrets" come to light and we are liberated from them, just like what Yuetching experienced at the end.

May this work be used by our Almighty God to bring many to Christ, to encourage fellow believers through their hardships and to sing praise to His wonderful name. Amen.

July 2020

Printed in Poland
by Amazon Fulfillment
Poland Sp. z o.o., Wrocław

62053240R00244